REVELATIONS
❦ OF THE ❦
AQUARIAN
AGE

"... a cosmic journey and the story of the hidden history of humanity whose wisdom secrets have been repressed by the patriarchy to keep humanity from realizing its spiritual potential. Barbara Hand Clow opens the door to understanding the importance of the Divine Feminine to heal our world and why the wisdom once taught by Jesus and Mary Magdalene, which was repressed by the Church for over 2000 years, is so crucial to the time we are living in now."

TRICIA MCCANNON AUTHOR OF
RETURN OF THE DIVINE SOPHIA AND
*JESUS: THE EXPLOSIVE STORY OF THE 30 LOST YEARS
AND THE ANCIENT MYSTERY RELIGIONS*

"A novel bound to enthrall those who were captivated by *The Da Vinci Code*. Well written and full of mystery."

GRAHAM PHILLIPS, AUTHOR OF *THE CHALICE OF MAGDALENE*

"An extraordinary new offering from one of the world's top visionary writers. *Revelations of the Aquarian Age* is a beautiful blend of wisdom and drama played out by a compelling cast of characters. A must-have for anyone seeking answers to the most profound sacred mysteries regarding humanity's divine cosmic origins."

ANDREW COLLINS, AUTHOR OF
GÖBEKLI TEPE: GENESIS OF THE GODS AND *THE CYGNUS KEY*

"*Revelations of the Aquarian Age* is a roller coaster of mystical downloads cleverly wrapped up as a well-researched work of fiction. I absolutely love the author's methodology of getting these ripe jewels into as many hands as is worldly possible. Blessings upon you, Barbara Hand Clow."

ANAIYA SOPHIA, AUTHOR OF *SACRED SEXUAL UNION*

"Barbara Hand Clow is a modern-day shamanic storyteller. The energy layered within her fictional work is all-seeing. She is indeed one of those very rare individuals with the ability to enlighten those who seek an alternative answer to the evil that currently envelops our world. *Revelations of the Aquarian Age* gives the reader the eyes to see what is hidden in plain sight. Her research, historical insight, multidimensional layering of detail and character development takes my breath away. Above all else, her novel's underlying message—that universal love and compassion will triumph over evil—is a celebration of the human spirit."

WILLIAM F. MANN, AUTHOR OF
*TEMPLAR SANCTUARIES OF NORTH AMERICA:
SACRED BLOODLINES AND SECRET TREASURES*

"*Revelations of the Aquarian Age* is a novel brimming with spiritual insights and 'heretical' lore, whose plot weaves around a modern alchemical painting of Jesus and the Magdalene. The author deftly uses the surfacing of secrets guarded by two ancient Italian families—the Medicis and Pierleonis—to stage what is in effect a plausible scenario for the *real* start of the Age of Aquarius: Christ's Second Coming."

TUVIA FOGEL, AUTHOR OF *THE JERUSALEM PARCHMENT*

"This book takes the reader into an unseen world of intrigue, mystery, and other dimensions. Recent historical discoveries exposing the motives behind the manipulation of facts by organized religion are brought to light as the world moves into the Aquarian Age. I'm looking forward to reading the next one! Another must-read by this enormously gifted author."

SYLVIA CLAIRE, CHt, LBLt, CERTIFIED PRACTITIONER
OF LIFE BETWEEN LIVES THERAPY®

REVELATIONS

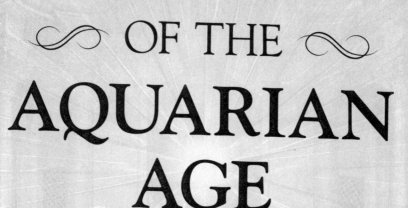

~ OF THE ~

AQUARIAN
AGE

BARBARA HAND CLOW

CANDACE
8-7-2019
9-23-2019

Bear & Company
Rochester, Vermont • Toronto, Canada

Bear & Company
One Park Street
Rochester, Vermont 05767
www.BearandCompanyBooks.com

Text stock is SFI certified

Bear & Company is a division of Inner Traditions International

Library of Congress Cataloging-in-Publication Data
Names: Clow, Barbara Hand, 1943– author.
Title: Revelations of the Aquarian age / Barbara Hand Clow.
Description: Rochester, Vermont : Bear & Company, [2018]
Identifiers: LCCN 2017013250 (print) | LCCN 2017018391 (e-book) |
    ISBN 9781591432951 (paperback) | ISBN 9781591432968 (e-book)
Subjects: | BISAC: FICTION / Occult & Supernatural. | FICTION / Romance /
    Paranormal. | FICTION / Visionary & Metaphysical.
Classification: LCC PS3603.L689 R47 2018 (print) | LCC PS3603.L689 (e-book) |
    DDC 813/.6—dc23
LC record available at https://lccn.loc.gov/2017013250

Printed and bound in the United States by Lake Book Manufacturing, Inc.
The text stock is SFI certified. The Sustainable Forestry Initiative® program
promotes sustainable forest management.

10   9   8   7   6   5   4   3   2   1

Text design by Priscilla H. Baker and layout by Virginia Scott Bowman
This book was typeset in Garamond Premier Pro with Goudy Oldstyle used as the
display typeface
Artwork by Liz Clow

To send correspondence to the author of this book, mail a first-class letter to the
author c/o Inner Traditions • Bear & Company, One Park Street, Rochester, VT
05767, and we will forward the communication, or contact the author directly at
www.handclow2012.com.

For Sir George Trevelyan and Toby and Teri Weiss

This book exists because of a 1993 encounter I enjoyed with Sir George Trevelyan in Old Sarum Circle near Salisbury, England, when I was there as a teacher for Toby and Teri Weiss's Power Places Tours. Sir George, then in his eighties, strode across the circle to speak to me. The fabled Grandfather of the New Age took my hands, looked deeply into my eyes, and said kindly, "You, Barbara, with many others, will carry the mantle after me. I see you standing tall in your power, witnessing the arrival of the Aquarian Age." I was stunned and never forgot the moment; this book is my response. Sir George, you are right. We are spiritual beings, Earth *is* the training ground for souls, and now we are ready.

I am archaic woman encoded with planetary intelligence traveling out into the stars to gather my knowledge of the universe. I return from cosmic realms in the morning and weave the stories of all time in my mind. All these levels are in my body, and I feel these levels in everyone I touch. I am the goddess holding the hearts of the suffering people. I am joy.

CLAUDIA TAGLIATTI

Contents

PART TWO
The Lost Gospel

PART THREE
Platonic Solids

PART ONE

Weddings

1

A Wedding in a Castle

"I can't believe the day has finally come, Pietro. It is almost time to go down, but my heart burns with uncertainty."

"Matilda, you've waited so long for this day. Are you unsure about Jennifer?"

Matilda and Pietro Pierleoni were in their bedroom alcove looking out the window. They'd paused for a moment after dressing for the wedding of their only son, Armando, at their ancestral castle in Tuscany. Gentle breezes flowing through the open windows meant it would be a perfect spring day. Early morning showers had freshened the olive trees; the air was moist and aromatic and water droplets on the medium green leaves sparkled in the sun. The distant sounds of guests arriving below for the wedding drifted up through the windows.

"It's not that; she is the perfect wife for Armando. But, I wonder whether he will be the husband she desires. I do hate to say this now, but you asked." She studied his concerned gray eyes, looking for reassurance.

"Well, my darling, every marriage is a journey into the unknown. We usually do it because we are blinded by desire or want children. Armando is a very successful painter at age forty-two; he's ready to marry. He loves creating, and he will devote himself to her because he is ardent. Come, we must go down now to greet our guests."

They walked thoughtfully down the long hallway, slowing momentarily by the entrance into the empty family chapel. They stepped side by side down wide stone stairs into a large vaulted great room.

When they reached the bottom of the stairs, a high-pitched bell clanged three times—time for the ushers to pull open the heavy dark oak doors to the entrance corridor. The guests began walking up the steps to the entrance to greet Pietro and Matilda. Lorenzo Giannini, their son's Jungian analyst, was among the guests. He was very excited about seeing the count and countess in a castle that went back before the Renaissance. As the crowd came forward one by one, the regal couple received them at the bottom of the wide stone stairs, which rose grandly behind them like a swan taking flight. Matilda had come down these stairs forty-seven years ago as a bride; soon her son's bride would do the same. Matilda was elegant in a beige brocade suit laced with golden threads, bordered in azure that brought out her clear blue eyes. Anticipation flushed her glowing skin brightened by sunlight streaming down from high windows onto the stone floor in front of the staircase.

The first guest to approach was Sarah Appel, a radiant young woman in a robin's-egg blue silk tunic that pulled across her breasts because she was carrying her eight-month-old daughter, Teresa. The baby, mystified by all the excitement, was looking around for somebody to smile at when she spotted Matilda's teary, shining eyes. She flapped tiny hands, looked Matilda straight in the eye, and smiled with glee. Matilda reached for a chubby hand exclaiming joyfully at the sight of the rosy little girl, "Oh, you brought Teresa! She is more adorable than ever." Meanwhile, Sarah's husband, Simon Appel, was in the cloakroom under the stairs prepping to be Armando's best man.

After squeezing Pietro's hand and whispering in his ear, Sarah went to sit down with her baby. Claudia Tagliatti, a tall and extremely thin woman, grandly swept up next wearing a clingy, loose-weave peach dress by Oscar de la Renta that revealed strong upper arms above long ivory gloves. Her finely sculpted neck bones also were visible as she paused in front of Matilda. She arched her chin and tipped her wide-brimmed ivory hat to peer out with intense brown eyes. In a dramatic low voice she said, "Ah, what a day for a wedding. I am sure you are so happy?"

Matilda grasped her hand, pressed it warmly replying, "Yes, and I'm happy that you and Armando are friends again. You look lovely, my dear, just lovely."

Claudia had been Armando's lover for a long time many years ago. Now she was forty-two and the owner of a fashion boutique in Rome. "Thank you. I'm sure you cannot wait for his children, finally."

Pietro, a short man with a purposeful demeanor belying an elfin twinkle in his eyes, stepped out to embrace Claudia. "My dear, you are beautiful today!"

She laughed from deep in her throat. "Ah, Pietro, what a day for you! My heartfelt congratulations!"

Next William and Mary Adamson came, Sarah's parents from Boston and old and dear friends of the family. William had been here when Matilda made her entrance as the bride.

Moments passed, and then Lorenzo Giannini gingerly approached. Pietro cast an astute glance at the dapper and intelligent-looking small man who bowed grandly saying in a jocular, confident voice, "Hello! I am Lorenzo Giannini! Finally, Count Pierleoni, we meet after I've known your son for so long. I'm honored to be here today. And Countess Matilda, a joy to see you again. Your serene and wise blue eyes were often in my mind's eye when I counseled Armando. It is so lovely to see you."

"I'm so happy to have a moment with you before the wedding to tell you I believe you saved my son. You were so remarkably patient with him for ten long years, and now he is marrying a lovely woman. We can never thank you enough for what you have done for Armando! Welcome to our family and our home."

Lorenzo was very touched and somewhat surprised by this intimate and unexpectedly warm welcome. He rarely knew what his clients' relations actually thought about him. He smiled warmly and released their hands to walk to the other side of the great hall where there were approximately forty chairs in four rows backed into the tower, all bathed in sunlight. The large white satin bow tied to the end chair in the front row indicated it was reserved for family, so he went to the next row to sit next to a long-legged woman in a clingy peach dress. *Is this her?* The stylish woman arched her back and turned to him as she said in an intimate low voice, "Dr. Giannini, I am Claudia Tagliatti!" She brushed his left knee with a slim hand in a white glove.

The edge of her wide-brimmed hat lightly pressed against his ear lobe, which irritated him. *Maybe she bothers me because I know the intimate details of her life with Armando.* He drew away slightly to whisper, "Lovely to meet you, Claudia. I must confess I feel I already know you." Then he pushed back observing the family members in the front row.

Claudia straightened her back to pull her hat away from the edge of his face and whispered, "Since you knew Armando for so many years, I do hope today we can have a few minutes together alone?"

The request made him nervous. As an analyst deeply entrenched in Roman society, he avoided contact with people who intimately knew his clients. But in this case, Armando's long treatment was complete. He only came back for an occasional tune-up to help him adjust to big events in life. Her request confused him because in fact he *did* know her rather too well, yet only from Armando's point of view. Regardless, in spite of all he knew about her torturous, long relationship with Armando, he was extremely drawn to her. *She is more of a woman than I thought she would be.* Still observing the people in the front row, he whispered back, "Yes, I would love to have a few moments with you today."

All attention was taken by the sound of music coming from a large hallway to the right of the staircase. A boisterous group of young musicians dressed as medieval court jesters swept into the great hall playing a lively cantata by Handel. Jingling red-and-black bells dangling from floppy hats created an air of merriment as the last of the guests quickly settled. The music stopped and all eyes moved to the top of the wide stone stairs. An old carved door creaked slowly open. David Appel joined his daughter and placed her white-gloved hand on his arm. He gripped Jennifer's arm firmly because she was shaking. They descended in rhythm to a Tuscan madrigal syncopated by insistent soft beats on a taut drum.

Armando stepped out from the room under the stairs with Simon trailing behind. They went to the side of the stairs to wait for the bride. Armando wore a dark green velvet suit lavishly embroidered with pompous heraldry and gilded rope trim. Foppish starched white ruffles burst out under his chin and edged the sleeves. Lorenzo was astonished! *This is a throwback to the eighteenth century! What is he doing? He looks extremely uncomfortable.*

Armando was outrageously handsome regardless of his silly attire. His thick black hair showcased a nervous yet reserved aristocratic face that gleamed in the sunlight shining down from the tower windows. He moved stiffly, his waist cinched by a wide leather belt that held a long sword adorned with the Pierleoni crest. He turned slowly and awkwardly to gaze up at Jennifer coming regally down the stairs. He stopped breathing. Matilda captured his nervous eyes and showered him with a joyful, approving smile. Armando smiled wanly back at his parents, bowed stiffly to them, and then they went to go sit in the front row. Lorenzo wondered—*Did Count Pietro wear that ridiculous sword on his wedding day?* However, it was fun to observe old customs that used to mean something. *After all, they are one of our most ancient Roman families.* Lorenzo was so entertained by the scene that he forgot about the lady sitting next to him who was glued to the scene with amazed eyes partially veiled by the rim of her huge hat.

Judge Giacomo Piccolomini, wearing a flamboyant medieval courtier's robe, strode like a fanning peacock across the stone floor to greet Armando as if this wedding were an affair of state. The father of the bride hid amusement as he gave Jennifer's hand to Armando. Armando bowed stiffly, looking David straight in the eye. Then David went to sit with his wife, Rose, who was also trying not to smirk at the unfolding scene. Lorenzo returned his attention to Armando standing with his bride as he shoved the top of the sword with his elbow to keep it from pressing his ribs. *He looks rigid. What a bizarre background he has! What century are we in?*

The judge slowly turned to face the guests. The acoustics in the hall were excellent, so they all could hear the judge speak solemnly about the joys of marriage and family. Lorenzo was touched by the meaningful and sincere vows between Armando and Jennifer. *They must have worked hard on this. She's an exotic, sensual bride and what a gown. Not many women could carry that off. Has Armando come this far because of me? They are real in the midst of this ridiculous Italian pomposity.* He heard a squeal that sounded like a parrot.

Baby Teresa had spotted her daddy up there and was waving her arms to be picked up. Simon turned his head slightly when he heard Teresa snuffle, then eek out a loud "Ahhhh!" Both parents knew a scream was coming next, so just before it was time to exchange the rings, Simon put his hand back behind his right leg and beckoned with his fingers. Sarah got up and smoothly passed Teresa to her daddy, who held her in his right arm while clutching Armando's ring in his left hand. Her eyes widened seeing bright golden ropes looped on Armando's shoulders. He smiled and chuckled as she reached for them, breaking his tight control.

The bride and groom exchanged rings, and Armando swept Jennifer into his arms, pulled back her veil, and kissed her wildly. The judge laughed. Then, to the tune of a pert and insistent Renaissance march, Jennifer and Armando filed out through the hall following behind the judge who carried a large book on an embroidered cloth elevated by both hands. Lorenzo thought the judge must have expected the silly pomposity. The guests came behind the wedding party and were drawn outside by gay madrigals and thumping drums. He barely noticed Claudia walking by his side because the wedding made him feel like he was lost in an old movie filmed in a foreign language with poorly translated subtitles. *I wonder if this says anything about what they will become? Whose dream are we in?*

The reception was set up all across the front lawn of the castle.

Claudia touched Lorenzo's arm and led him to a small table under an old olive tree at the edge of the action.

"Lorenzo, you may think you know everything about me, the most intimate details of my life, but you don't," Claudia remarked, removing her wide-brimmed hat while looking intently into his eyes. She startled him because, freed of the hat, her intense brown eyes cut into his mind. She was hawkish with black, perfectly cut hair that rippled and waved. She'd stopped smoking a year ago and longed for a cigarette. As the time lengthened past the last cigarette, her emotions were raw like the sharp edges of clamshells. By removing tobacco as the first step of self-reflection, she'd been forced to examine her biting sarcasm, witty cynicism, and overbearing intellectual superiority. One by one she was stripping away the aspects of herself she disliked the most, but now, sitting with Lorenzo, a powerful and brilliant man who certainly knew too much about her, she felt vulnerable, too bare. The need to defend herself took over. *Why did I ever think I wanted to talk with him?* Columns of waiters bringing out a Tuscan feast on large platters momentarily distracted them.

Lorenzo embraced her with kind amber eyes. "Claudia. Armando went on and on about you, but I wasn't listening to it. I don't remember what he said about you because I was busy observing him. If I know you at all, it is within a darkly obscured reflection in Armando's broken mirror. Yet, here you are with me on this beautiful, whimsical day in your lovely peach dress. So much time has gone by; surely, you are a completely different person?"

His well-formed mouth was remarkably sensitive and beckoned her, made her feel like touching his moist lower lip. She detected a range of ages in his personality—an eager young boy, an emotionally driven young man, a wise resigned elder. *He must have explored himself deeply during his own analysis.* "It's true; I *am* a completely different person. Actually, when Armando changed last year and expressed genuine concern for the people he'd hurt, including me, I was briefly attracted to him again. But he'd hurt me way too much; I couldn't risk it. Now he's doing exactly what he should—marrying a woman young enough to have his children. It would be a tragedy if this lineage ended." She paused . . . "Forgive me if I'm being intrusive. I heard you lost your wife last year after a long marriage. Do you feel terribly alone?"

Lorenzo perked up. He'd discovered, as most grieving people do, that talking about death makes people uncomfortable; it's taboo. The enforced silence while he was mourning made him feel bitter because he couldn't express his feelings. To talk about his loss seemed natural and normal to him, yet most people silenced him as quickly as possible. Lately, he had been feeling depressed and resented people for not reaching out to him; he felt isolated. So he searched for the right words to engage the topic. "I do feel terribly alone. I miss our simple routines— the sound of her footsteps in the house, traveling together, tinkering noises in the kitchen. We had a long marriage and raised two children, who are doing well. As an analyst, I assumed I knew what she felt and thought about. Then after she died, I found her journals in a little trunk, and I read all nine of them during the long, lonely evenings last winter. The truth is, after a thirty-five-year marriage, I didn't know her at all! I spent all my time on my clients." He stopped. While he spoke, a pale rose color brightened his pallid gray leathery skin. Claudia listened acutely noticing that when he spoke, there was a lost, hollow echo in his voice.

"Lorenzo, I think you are enduring very deep grief. Maybe you do not realize how deep it actually is?"

"Very well put, Claudia, and you're right. I'm grieving the marriage I never had although we were together so many years. She died of throat cancer when only sixty-five, a woman who seldom spoke about herself when she lived." His voice was strangled. "She talked about trivialities all the time, I tried to listen but I couldn't hear her. I was tone deaf to my own wife. It is so good to be able to say this to someone, since the analyst doesn't usually get to express himself. How did you come by such wisdom at your age; I believe I'm twenty-five years older than you?"

She nodded to acknowledge their relative ages and then said something that would catch any Jungian analyst's attention. "I'm psychic, Lorenzo. Your grief is displaced, not moving out of your body, as if you are in the shadow of death. You have two energy fields instead of one—an inner field riddled with dark and troubled emotions, an outer shell far away and almost detaching. Do you mind me saying this?" He indicated by his eyes that he didn't, so she continued. "I wonder *why* she left the journals, since with cancer she had time to dispose of them. What if she *wanted* you to see them? If so, it would be a gift from her to finally allow you to know her. I think if you look at it that way, your feelings might resolve."

He was charmed by her face, her exotic classic Roman beauty was like a jaguar ready to pounce from within the elegant flesh-colored dress. He shivered when she noticed he was studying her. *I can't believe I didn't think of that!* Finally, he replied. "And I'm supposed to be the one who is so insightful! Of *course* she must have wanted me to read them! She *did* want me to know her. No wonder I feel so alone . . . I miss her." He sipped some wine though he rarely drank, not wanting her to notice he was on the verge of crying, but of course she knew.

"Once I forgave Armando, a psychological transformation began that is still unfolding. I couldn't get anywhere with myself until we became friends again because I was so angry. You and I both know why he acted that way, but that didn't mean he had the right to take his pain out on me. We don't need to talk about that, but I do want to talk about what came next. After I truly forgave him two years ago, I quit cigarettes after smoking like a fiend for twenty years. I smoked and drank to blunt my pain, so once I quit, I had to face my suppressed emotions. This has been humiliating, an ugly experience, but I've been truthful with myself. Still, I am appalled by how alone I am, aloof and living in my head. As long as I could reach for a cigarette and think about ideas, I could avoid the truth about myself. Here I am, forty-two without a partner or a husband, but that's not why I'm lonely. I love living alone. I'm lonely because I see who I am; it's horrible to face one's truth."

"Fascinating. This insight is what I hope my clients will attain, and some do. We can't find happiness without facing ourselves first. You are on the verge of being a fulfilled woman."

Sarah was nearby talking in Italian to a few of the neighbors and glanced at her watch thinking Claudia and Lorenzo had been talking a long time. *What are they talking about?*

Claudia noticed Sarah, a very close friend, and was tempted to signal her over to their table, but she wanted to keep the conversation going. "I will tell you the truth. I wanted to be the bride we saw today. But his intensity and pain made me manic-depressive during my twenties. My parents hoped he'd marry me because he's rich. Actually, I'm amazed I escaped him with the pressure to stay together coming from many corners. But I did. In my thirties, I became strong and successful and spent my time making other women beautiful, enjoying lovers, cultivating new interests. But, I was hollow inside. Beauty distracted me while my addictions helped me live a complex lie. To answer you truthfully, I haven't thought about being happy or fulfilled in at least ten years."

Registering the sadness present with his own gaping emptiness challenging him, Lorenzo felt useless, unwanted, and unsure of himself. *How could I have thought everything was fine for thirty-five years? How could I have been with her all those years and not seen she was isolated and sad? My heart was reserved for my clients. Absorbing their pain left me with no feelings for the person who should have mattered the most. But, still, are women ever happy? They are so complex and needy.* "Claudia, you are finding yourself and many things will surprise you. I'd like to get to know you, really know you. If you want to know me, I'd love to be with you while you find yourself."

Claudia felt suspended in a dream, in another time. The depth of passion in his voice was meeting a newborn essence within her that instinctually reached for him. But, just as she was preparing to answer, Armando and Jennifer came to their table. She stood up with Lorenzo and lifted her wine glass to toast the newly married couple.

"Congratulations, years of happiness, and many children," Lorenzo said in a strong, clear voice while Claudia collected herself. Jennifer chatted with Claudia about her wedding gown while the older woman was wondering what life would be like for her. Marriage would probably heal him in some ways, but what would it be like living with Armando? *Does she know what she's getting herself into?*

The bride and groom coming to their table just after he'd asked Claudia for a relationship intrigued Lorenzo, a classic synchronicity. As soon as the couple floated off to the next table, they sat back down. He wondered if Claudia would respond or let it go. To his surprise, she picked up the thread at once.

"I would love to get to know you; however we might want to wait awhile. You need more time with your wife's journals. She will be free to leave this world once you understand them. You don't want her hanging around in your house, you know."

Lorenzo started laughing while slurping down wine to calm himself. He choked a bit and started a coughing fit mixed with laughter. "What an absolutely hysterical thing to say to an analyst! Do you realize how funny you are? It's even funnier that the bride and groom came over here just when I said I want to know you! What a madcap and lovely day this is. Whatever happens, you are my delightful companion today!"

Claudia laughed along with him, and they spent the rest of their time together at the wedding. During the beautiful May afternoon, olive trees and wildflowers absorbed their loneliness.

2

Jennifer and Armando

Jennifer was thirty-two when she met Armando in May 2013. The minute she laid eyes on him, she entertained fantasies of marrying him and having his children while living in a castle. Even though strongly attracted to him, she was cool and commanding, which drew him right into her grasping hands. However, while enjoying the whirlwind summer romance, she sensed there was something peculiar about Armando, a strange shadow. But she was irresistibly drawn to him as an intense, esoteric artist. Perhaps the shadow was merely his muse?

Whatever was going on with him, she wanted to have him, so she silenced him whenever he tried to reveal his past. She'd say things like, "Armando, what I feel is so precious I don't want to think about the past. Let's be in the moment. When you come home from your studio, I see many worlds in your eyes. You take me places I've never known."

Armando allowed her to prevail for the time being. One day they kissed and embraced passionately in his studio, and then later listened to Beethoven's String Quartet no. 15 while he mixed his paints. During the final movement, he stopped mixing and lost himself in her animated eyes. After the final grand stroke on the taut strings she said, "Only music expresses really intense feelings, not words." He had laughed and replied, "But what about my paintings?"

The next day he'd shown her his version of the Annunciation, an

13

exquisite gilded version of the Archangel Gabriel in ecstasy gazing at the Virgin Mary in midnight-blue robes. The frail Virgin standing tentatively in front of a stone tower in San Gimignano was delightfully young and innocent. A burning red sky raining down fire from the heavens was the backdrop for a modern city panorama of monotonous glass skyscrapers. The most powerful image, a fat twisted green serpent mysteriously curled up in a lower room of the tower, glared at the Virgin with sly yellow eyes as if her innocence had drawn him there from another dimension. Jennifer studied the painting while Armando sat drinking wine at a small round table. When she turned to look at him he said, "Tell me what you see in this painting . . . Words, words, I need words."

She sat down on the other chair. "At first, the fire and light in the upper world, a modern city, contrasted with medieval San Gimignano and overwhelmed me. In the middle world, time stops with Gabriel's sweet face enjoying the Virgin's wonder. Yet the serpent coiled in the lower realm of the tower makes me think of the tree of life emerging from serpentine forces. Once I grasped all three levels, then other aspects emerged: Gabriel has arrived from a very high dimension to gaze at the woman selected to birth the Messiah. As he arrives, the serpent in the depths of the tower coils while cosmic fire engulfs ugly new buildings—a modern Pentecost. I am in awe of you, Armando, I truly am."

"Ah, yes, well, but you do not know *me* yet. How are we going to know each other well enough to be married, if that's even what we want? This painting may be magnificent, but you won't marry my paintings. I want to tell you everything about my past; you *must* listen to me."

"Then I will have to tell you about my past, but I won't because it will come back to haunt me. I don't know who you were before, but I do know what I was, and you would not like it. We could lose this magic." *What if he knew what I did to another woman?*

Armando had no idea how he'd feel if he knew all about her. She seemed to be a woman without a past because she was so absolutely present when they were together. *Maybe she's right, maybe . . .* "Well then, my darling," he said getting up. "Perhaps you can explain to me why you won't have sex with me even though we are otherwise very intimate, even talking about marriage? Are you afraid to have sex with me because of something you sense about me? If that's the reason, you're probably right. Maybe you feel like *I* am that serpent?" he said in Italian twisting a lock of her hair around his index finger, which annoyed her.

"Not at all," was the honest if incomplete response from a sophisticated woman who'd had many lovers and watched the magic turn into boredom when too much was revealed. She'd found a man who was not boring, so she made calculated moves brilliantly designed to capture him before it was too late for her to have children. She held considerable control over him by keeping him at arm's length: he stayed in a nearby hotel when visiting her in Paris, and here in Italy she would not sleep with him in his parent's house before marriage. "I simply am not ready to have sex with you; I really don't know why. Perhaps romance matters more to me right now than sex. Getting to know our families and our day-by-day sharing are what matter to me," she went on. "My lovers were merely lovers, I never considered marrying any of them, but you may be my husband. With you, and I don't know why, I sense we should do things the old-fashioned way—have a real engagement. I don't want to have sex until I'm sure we'll marry. Can you handle that?"

Armando studied her with a painter's eye, imagining her as a previous lover who'd come back to him through time. Her beauty was very Persian—brown eyes with golden flecks that sometimes turned them amber. Innocence suffused her face like Gabriel's adoring face, but he knew she wasn't innocent; Gabriel probably wasn't either.

She pressed the issue, which he didn't like. "Can you wait?"

"I think so, but feel like we're going in reverse. Sex for me is intense, dark, conflicted, and violent. You don't want to hear about it, but I'm worried my past might bite back at me if we marry. Shouldn't we have sex, lots of it, to get to know each other? Make sure we both enjoy the experience? I mean, come on. This is the modern world, not medieval Tuscany."

"I can say the same thing about myself, but I won't talk about it. What's happening between us is different from before, possibly the very thing that makes me think I want to marry you. Like Gabriel in your painting, we can be in a sacred dimension, so why not? I've come to despise meaningless, amoral sex; I want a real courtship, an idea I never had until I met you. I can love you very deeply if you will grant me space. Once we are sure we'll marry—and we don't know that yet— then yes, we must come together to make sure that we are sexually compatible, the only good idea that came out of the sexual revolution."

"Hmmm . . ." Armando muttered while glancing at the serpent in the lower chamber. He knew she was playing him, which was making him angry yet stirring him. She knew she was risking the big test, the times when she'd pushed away men in the past. His mouth twisted slightly. He released the lock of hair while roughly pulling her close to kiss her deeply, grinding his pelvis into her wide hips. He was irritatingly needy; he couldn't handle being denied. Dark energy expanded in his chest.

She detected his hardness, strength, and passion, welcome because it matched her formidable masculinity. Overwhelming need coursing through her body stopped her breath. *Why not just surrender, why not? Then I'll know whether I like having sex with him.* Yet, there was a groaning, stretching energy in the room that distorted the air, something grasping for her. Kissing her roughly on the side of her neck, he moved down lower with a sucking force, her nipples ached. He arched his shoulders back to press his erection more fully into her pelvis. But, when she sought his eyes, she detected a green demon flashing in and out, with his face becoming flaccid and dissipated while he clutched her shoulders. "Armando, stop it right now in the name of God! Stop it! What is *wrong* with you?"

Blazing orange red light was edging into his dense body. He was exhausted, loosened his grip, and wanted to throw her on the floor like trash. "Bitch, who *are* you?" he snarled. He wanted to hit her; instead he clenched his fists.

She growled back in a firm voice, "Whatever happens, you are not going to be rough or violent with me, or do anything to me I don't want. I'm not a bitch. Don't call me one." She put her hand against his chest pushing him off to create distance. After a moment she commanded, "Sit with me to recover yourself." Like a guilty four-year-old boy, he sat down next to her.

Ten minutes passed while they sat. "That was close; you don't know how close. You're right; we need an agreement. You don't want to know what was going on inside me, but if we have an agreement, I think I can control myself. You're right; it's the only hope for us. I will agree to not have sex until we decide to marry. When we commit, I will need to have you before marriage."

The summer passed quickly with Armando sharing his art and family life with her intimately in Tuscany and Rome, taking a few trips to Paris where she worked. In the fall, things suddenly shifted when she said, "Now I trust you. I want you and I want your child. I know I can trust you to stay with me, I just know." They were dining in an ancient booth at a very intimate restaurant on the bank of the Seine across from Notre Dame Cathedral. She gazed through wavy glass at the hulking yet graceful flying buttresses barely visible in thick mist. Lines of light sparkled on the dark river. He studied her animated eyes wondering why he couldn't figure women out. *Oh well, all I have to do is figure this one out.* He hadn't noticed that she'd never said she loved him.

"Why the sudden shift?" He thought of the emerald engagement ring in the inner pocket of his dinner jacket that he'd been carrying around since arriving in Paris two days ago. *Has my time finally come?*

"I'm sure I can love you and make you happy, that's all. You'll be a wonderful father and our life together in Italy will be exquisite. I'm ready. Have *you* thought about it enough?"

As if a familiar page had just turned in the middle of a story that he'd read many years before, yes it was time for marriage. Actually, it had been easier getting to know her without having sex right away. He *did* know her well enough now, so he took her hands. "Jennifer, will you marry me next spring? And, will you be my lover tonight?" He reached inside his jacket to pull out the little black velvet box after he asked the question. The old Notre Dame bells echoing over the river clanged eleven times in the distance. She gasped at the large emerald and diamond ring. Offering it to Sarah and getting a different reaction a few years ago crossed his mind as Jennifer's eyes flashed with delight while she examined the exquisite family heirloom.

She hesitated. "Even if I take this ring, I will not be your lover tonight. You scared me last summer. Something was in you that I've never seen before in a man. I'm not afraid of you, but I can't have sex with you yet. I will think about marrying you next spring, but being with you tonight is impossible. I wish I knew why."

Armando slumped. *What can I say, what do I say? Can I tell her? Should I tell her?* He implored, "Without telling you about my past as you've requested, can I tell you something I've recently discovered during my therapy that has helped me see *why* I acted the way I did in the past. Can I just tell you that?" She nodded cautiously, dark eyes rapidly switching back and forth then penetrating his. They were on the edge of their seats. "I recalled being raped by a priest during my First Confession. Lorenzo helped me see that because I was so young, I was possessed by dark energy, subconscious demons. The vileness would jump out and make me abuse women, which almost happened to you when you said I couldn't have sex with you. But honestly, Jennifer, I think your strength blocks this force. You stopped me that day in my studio, and I've been feeling the thing loosening its grip. If we can love each other in an entirely new way, real committed love, then perhaps the demons will leave me forever."

Jennifer sat rigidly staring at the remains of her dinner in shock because she'd never heard of anything like that. She thought she'd seen and done everything with men, but had not encountered demonic forces. The fat on her last lamb chop was hardening, her spinach was limp, and when she took a sip of wine, it tasted sour. *But I think I love him.* "I have to talk to Sarah about this, since you asked for her hand first, but she married my brother. Can I go to see her when we get back to Rome? I think she can help me. You may be my husband soon, so we don't want to start out with dark things that we don't understand. Do you mind if I talk to Sarah? Meanwhile, I should not accept your ring."

"No, no, I don't mind at all," he said as he closed the lid and put the box back in his pocket. "Sarah is the kindest and most compassionate woman I have ever known. She'll help you; she'll help us. She really cares about both of us."

Jennifer visited Simon and Sarah in Rome early that September in the afternoon while Teresa napped. She thought she'd just talk to Sarah, but Simon asked to be included. When she told them she wanted to know exactly what they thought about Armando, they both said he'd faced his dark side and seemed to be transforming his abusive tendencies. They'd both thought all was well with the new couple during the summer. Simon said carefully, "Well, we thought you were having sex and everything was going well, but now that you say you haven't been and are concerned about him, well, maybe you should be. I think he's changed and Lorenzo will help if needed, but you should still be careful and trust your instincts. He's a deeply wounded and exceedingly complex and wonderful man. You're strong. Nobody ever said it's easy to live with an artist, you know all about it. If anybody can help him get beyond this, it's you. If you really love him, I think it's worth the risk to go on. But take your time."

"Spoken like a big brother. Thanks. I *am* uneasy; I think I should be. He told me about the priest that raped him and said you two know about it. I wonder if people ever get beyond that kind of trauma?" She detected an alarmed, disturbed expression in Simon's eyes.

Sarah was remembering when Armando tried to rape her a few years ago. She shivered at the thought of how terrified she had been when she saw a horrible, voracious, and angry dark force in him. Once she escaped, she thought she'd never go near him again, but finally years of therapy had helped him. By remembering his own rape, he could feel the pain he'd been inflicting on women. He had apologized to them, even to Claudia, and now was processing his demonic aspects through art with astonishing results. Also, Sarah believed a great shift had occurred in many people when the Mayan Calendar ended on December 21, 2012—the very day of Armando's breakthrough session with Lorenzo Giannini. *His recovery could be permanent. He's a tortured soul, very much like the great Renaissance artists who grappled with dark forces. Jennifer may be the right woman because she understands artists. And, she's older and more experienced than I was.*

"I think you may want a chaste engagement. Before sexual liberation many people, especially Christians, waited before having sex because they believed marriage protects against demonic possession. Religions have complex rules about sex and marriage because they think demons have easy access to humans during sex. These days the rules have been thrown out, but now that I'm married, I think they were right in some ways because in the modern world many people act like they're possessed by dark energy. And, considering Armando's wonderful parents, he'll master himself in marriage. He *needs* a wife and children to be able to process dark energy in his art. Jennifer, do you love him, *really* love him?"

"I agree with you. Even though I was once a modern liberated woman, I've changed. I think people are way too cavalier about sex, certainly I was. People act like they're no more than walking genitals with closed minds and hearts when they have sex. Don't laugh at me, Simon. I mean it." Simon gave her a good-natured push as she continued. "Any sex I have from now on will be heart centered. But I can't imagine marrying him without knowing whether I like having sex with him. Know what I mean?" Sarah smiled and took Simon's hand while Jennifer went on. "Maybe we can find a way to be engaged and still deal with that need. I'll think about your ideas."

There was a long pause and then Sarah said, "You haven't answered my question; *do* you love Armando?"

There was an even longer pause while Jennifer scanned her mind and heart. *Maybe I can't feel love for him because the dark energy repels me. Maybe I am too allured by the aristocratic lifestyle. What can I say to her?* They watched her quizzically. She murmured, "I think so . . ."

"Jennifer," Simon demanded, "*Do* you love Armando?"

"Oh, of course I do. I didn't know how to answer because the question makes me feel like I'm saying I've fallen in love with the devil. This is going fast, but, yes, I love Armando, I do." Still, Sarah wondered about the emptiness she detected in Jennifer's heart.

A few weeks later, Jennifer joyfully accepted Armando's engagement ring while dining at the Hassler Hotel above the Spanish Steps. He took her up to a suite with a stunning view of the Trinita dei Monti Towers. With the lights sparkling in all directions, farther in the distance the snaking, black Tiber flowed around deep bends, which caught occasional light reflections in the waves. Beyond the ancient river, stars twinkled in the dark sky surrounding the Vatican dome. After gazing at the view, he moved behind her, both now in front of the wide window. He slipped her blouse off her right shoulder causing the bra strap to slip down to a trembling elbow as he cupped a perfectly shaped small breast. "From now on I will be more honest with you than I ever have been with anyone. Wisdom flowing into my mind feels like the spirit that guides me when I paint, telling me where to stroke and add color. This will be our *only* night together before our wedding. We will continue to be chaste as we have been, except for tonight. We will find ourselves as lovers or we will not, but I have no fear. Our hearts touch and . . . "

She turned around to gaze at his face while saying in a determined voice, "You touch me. Your masculine face, softened by your sensitive mouth and wise caring eyes, fills me with joy. Remember, Armando, I have a photographer's eye, you a painter's eye. I see true beauty in your face. I hope to gaze at you forever, like having a perfect sculpture by

Bernini in my home. We will find each other tonight, maybe tomorrow morning. We will get to know each other for many years." It was time.

They were both extremely experienced lovers, experts at heightening desire with fine technique. The first time together was a long night joining their bodies to prepare for the transformation—marriage. Like the flight paths of paired swans that fly thousands of miles following the magnetic lines of Earth and the constellations, they touched and felt a merging on many subtle levels. They were a perfectly matched pair.

At breakfast while sharing prosciutto, melon, and sourdough toast, they fell silent to contain their thoroughly unexpected discovery—they were the same animal having an instinctual joining that surpassed all previous loves. Later over espresso, he said, "I fall silent with you, something I'd always hoped for in a partner. Silence will be our source, our eternal pool of love. I think it is going to be very hard to abstain until we are married, at least it will be for me."

"Funny thing is, I think we just had our honeymoon!" she replied, smiling blissfully. *I think I do love him.*

He retorted quickly in a very happy voice, "Oh no, you don't know what's in store for you! We will enjoy our honeymoon in Majorca where our family has a small villa on a slope above the sea with a path down to a private cove where I used to go when I was a child. Our whole family shares it. We'll watch the sun go down below the sea every night. We'll be there for a few weeks after our wedding since the climate is exquisite in May and June. Our honeymoon will be when we will draw down our child from the stars."

3

Lorenzo's Apartment

After the Tuscan wedding, Lorenzo returned to his old building on the busy Via Nicola Fabrizi in Rome, a short distance from his office in the Trastevere. His large apartment, surrounded by walled gardens, occupied the first story, and he rented out the two upper floors. He turned the old key in a large iron lock, opened the door, and went into the dark foyer. He turned on a light, paused a moment to sniff the stale air, and passed into the library through an arched door to the right. He went quickly to his favorite chair just as the last pale light was dimming, countless books fading into gloom. The library was stuffy, so he opened a bay window that protruded into the garden. The low traffic hum reminded him he was not alone.

The third volume of his dead wife's journals was there on the table by his reading chair. He switched on an alabaster table lamp and opened the embossed leather journal to a random page. *Whichever page opens will have meaning . . .* The spine cracked, reminding him to be careful.

October 10, 1985: Being home all day with two small children is a free ticket to the insane asylum! He's gone all day listening to fascinating tales spun by important people; I'm home—the zookeeper. While Antonio has a temper tantrum because I can't understand what he's trying to say to me, the baby wails because she wants to be fed or have her diaper changed. Today on my walk I felt like letting the baby carriage fly down the hill into the Tiber. What kind of mother am I? If I told Lorenzo I'm tempted to murder the baby, he'd tell me all about Freud's death wish, but I'd still want to get rid of the baby. I can't get pregnant again; if I do, I will die. What if I was Catholic like everybody else around here? I'd have to! Oh God!

Lorenzo thought about her primal urges. In those days when he came home, he thought the children were adorable while he dallied with them and she made dinner. They shared a chaotic meal, he did the dishes while she read to them and put them to bed, and then he went to be in his library. Life seemed normal, but now he could see how stifled she was. He got up and placed the third journal on a side table to exchange it for the sixth one. In the sixth journal, the children were older, in school all day while she kept house.

April 9, 1996: I went to the Vatican Museum today and sat in the Sistine Chapel for a long time to study the art. Layers of heavy time overwhelmed me. These are not my stories because I'm Jewish, yet the themes are from the Old Testament. Why are Christians so obsessed with our stories?

He tried to remember whether she'd ever told him she'd gone to the Sistine Chapel. *Why didn't she? We could have gone there as a family.* The emptiness of time gone by that could never be brought back made him tired after driving up to Tuscany and back in one day. His head nodded, yet he sat back up trying to visualize her walking home from the Vatican. But he couldn't picture her face. He picked up his favorite photo of her to bring her back, but her image faded into the past as he gazed at it. *She once was alluring.* He jumped up suddenly because he heard something fall off a bookcase—thunk!—glass shattered. He rushed to the sound and looked down at the floor. A Fabergé egg with a small beveled window that had once displayed a tiny colorful merry-go-round made of spun glass lay smashed on the marble floor as if someone had pushed it off the shelf! The grandfather clock chimed twelve times in the foyer. He yelled, "Eleanora, did you knock that off? What do you *want?*"

He picked up the pieces and threw them into the wastebasket screaming, "I always hated that ugly egg that you thought was worth so much money." Drops of blood on his index finger smeared as he screamed, "So, just like Claudia said, you *do* want me to read these journals, don't you? Well, I have, and you want to know what? They bore me, *you* bored me for years!" He stopped for a moment to calm down. "What can I do about that now? You are the one who never talked and then just died. You could've done more with your life, but you just wanted to diddle all day. Even when the kids left, you didn't want to do anything. You want to know what, Eleanora? To hell with your journals!"

Now wide awake, he shuffled to the back to make tea. After returning, he piled the journals on the hearth and made a low fire. Then he took them, one by one, stripped out a few pages, and burned them thoughtfully. He dumped the gilded and embossed leather covers. The next morning he was up early to open all the windows. When the housekeeper came, he instructed her to clean out his wife's dresser. Then he went to his office and called Claudia. "Hello Claudia, this is Lorenzo. I would like to take you out to dinner tonight. Will you join me?"

Claudia was home relaxing and was very surprised he'd called so soon. "Well yes, I'd love to; however, can you come to my home first? I live at 14 Via degli Scipioni, a block away from the Ponte Nenni, so can you walk here? I want you to see my home." She visualized his clear sparkling eyes as she spoke. "Oh, avoid the Lungotevere Michelangelo because of the traffic."

"Yes, I'd love to visit your home. I'll make a reservation nearby, since I know your district. I got back here and my apartment made me lonely. Why should I be lonely?"

"Well, darling, I must admit I agree with you. Everything is a choice, isn't it? *Ciao,* see you around five o'clock?" She put the receiver down slowly noticing how happy she was he'd called so soon.

Lorenzo opened the window over the noisy square as he waited for his first client. Since his wife's death, work had been his salvation. At night he dreaded going back to the apartment, so taking Claudia to dinner would be wonderful. In the late afternoon, he started out on the long walk over the Ponte Sisto to the Via Giulia, then back over the Tiber on the Ponte Sant'Angelo. He bought some flowers from a vendor behind the Castel Sant'Angelo and then walked on small back-streets to the Via A. Farnese. He hadn't taken a long walk for a while, so it was invigorating and made him feel young. He came to the Via degli Scipioni and admired Claudia's impressive front entrance sporting classic stone pillars. She opened the door and smiled warmly when he handed her bright yellow irises.

She led him into a small, intimate study. "This is my favorite room. Sit down here, and I will bring you some port after I get a vase for these lovely blossoms. Feel free to peruse my books."

He felt very comfortable in the charming small room with floor-to-ceiling white bookcases set in walls papered in crimson brocade. She brought the flowers and a tray with a crystal decanter and two small glasses. He admired her long, loose beige slacks topped by a midnight-blue draped blouse that came down over her waist, a very stylish outfit enhanced by deep blue eye shadow. "This room is warm and intimate, yet light and airy. Being here makes me realize I must purge my apartment. The energy is so heavy there. I have to get my housekeeper to throw a lot of stuff out now!"

Claudia eyed him thoughtfully because he seemed to be displaced and not aware of her, although he seemed to be very comfortable in her favorite room. She poured two glasses of port and said, "Have you emptied closets, personal things, things of hers you might give away?"

"Oh no, I haven't done any of that, but I did get the housekeeper started on her clothes this morning. I came back after the wedding and realized I must make the apartment into *my* space."

Claudia's library

She examined him closely. "Of course you must. So, are her things in every room, are they all over the place?"

"She crammed the apartment from top to bottom. The library was my little island, but she crept around it during the day putting her little treasures all over my bookcases." This made Claudia feel creepy. "Last night at exactly midnight when I was reading her journals in my study, a Fabergé egg fell off a shelf and shattered on the floor. I think *she* pushed it off, since there was no way it could have fallen on its own. So, I made a fire and burned the journals page by page. *So there!* You say I should keep reading them, but I don't want to. I already read them once, enough!" He glared defiantly at her smart uptilted face with a shocked expression and ejaculated more loudly, "Eee-nough!"

Claudia was quite taken aback, suppressing laughter wanting to rise in her body. She placed her left hand with a large carnelian intaglio ring over her ruby-red mouth and rolled her eyes under dark fluttering eyelashes up to the ceiling. Then she exploded with laughter. Lorenzo looked horrified. But then he started sniggering and then whinnied like a horse. Claudia's eyes were watering as she struggled for words. "Oh, I'm so sorry, but I couldn't stop it. It isn't funny, please accept my apologies." But she was still giggling.

"Claudia, you are a blast of fresh air! How lucky was I to meet you at the wedding? Life is for the living, isn't it? I don't have to read that stuff again. I've turned it over in my mind for months. I don't want that crap all over the place. It depressed me for thirty-five years, I can't breathe in there. Are you good with junk and antiques? Some of the stuff is good. If I knew how to dispose of it, it would bring me some money to buy the things I'd like. Can you help me?"

"It is so funny that you ask that because I *love* to clean out places that people have lived in for years. I love processing the layers of time so much that I once thought about being an antique dealer. People's things tell their story, which fascinates me. It's the perfect time of year, the weather is warm and balmy; so it *would* be fun! Soon it will get oppressively hot. Yes, let's do it. Let's clean it out as soon as possible! Before we start, ask your children whether they want anything, especially your daughter."

Later, when they were dining, the same natural intimacy returned. He'd reserved a quiet booth in his favorite enoteca tucked in under a wine cellar below the street. Her midnight-blue silk blouse had a slight sheen in the low light.

"You have lovely eyes, Claudia. They tell me your story without knowing anything about you. You've told me you've been very unhappy for a long time, yet tonight I see delighted anticipation in your eyes."

"You will think I'm flirting, and I don't care if I am. I'm excited because I'm here with you. Have you noticed that the world has been getting very weird these last few years? A few years ago, back in 2012, people thought the old world was ending. I think this is turning out to be true because things felt so strange during 2013. Now it's 2014, and the fabric of society is unraveling; many people talk about the tenuousness and strangeness of our times." He acknowledged what she said by nodding, so she continued. "Then you appeared at that whimsical wedding and made me feel happy; that's what you see in my eyes."

"Well, good," he responded, leaning back when a large bowl of orzo and spaghetti with meat sauce appeared. "Let's just be happy together, no matter what goes on in the world."

The appointed day for the cleanout was a Saturday in early June. It was going to be hot so Lorenzo went to get Claudia early in a rented van. She'd made arrangements with antique dealers to sell the good things, and she'd listed the addresses of places where they could donate the rest. She greeted him in blue jeans and a sloppy red sweatshirt with her hair tied back in a bandanna. Lorenzo laughed at her so she replied, "I don't have clothes for things like this because I haven't done it for so long. Besides, you look pretty strange yourself!" Lorenzo was wearing khakis and a cotton T-shirt printed with a garish image of Mt. Vesuvius melting Pompeii. She turned him around to see the back, which read—*The Volcanoes, 2012.* "Aha! So, you were one of the ones who paid attention to the 2012 predictions!"

He held open the door into the foyer, and she looked around to get a sense of how to tackle the job. "May I walk through the rooms with you to get a feel for what's here?" He nodded, so she went through to survey a dining room crammed with an oversized mahogany table and chairs and a droll china cabinet. She glanced at the china and the gloomy landscapes on the walls and said, "This will sell to younger people who like dark stuff these days; the antique dealers will take it."

He replied, "Yes, younger people do have very dark taste these days, and remember, I never cared about what was here. My home was my office, so strip out whatever you like."

The feeling of the apartment was very heavy and made Claudia feel sad. *Is this a good idea? Oh well, he needs help.* She was tempted to suggest maybe it wasn't time but didn't. "Do your children want things? Did you ask them?"

"I did. My son works in Germany, has a tiny apartment, and doesn't want a thing except one of her rings as a keepsake. My daughter lives in Milan, and she took the few things she wanted in her car after the funeral. They were both thrilled to hear a 'friend' is helping me clean it out to make it the way I want it." He winked at her. "I hate this dining room and don't want anything in here. I'll get new furniture and dishes. It depresses me, always did."

Claudia looked around at the huge beams and worn brick floors, great fundamentals for a really interesting room. The three bedrooms would be easy because he wanted to keep the basic furniture and just change the coverings, so that's where they started. With dozens of good boxes to fill, they piled up clothes for donation and sorted out pictures, lamps, and figurines to be sold. Lorenzo was slightly embarrassed about going through his wife's old junk, so he lifted Claudia's spirits by telling funny jokes and silly stories about the stuff. His intelligent sense of humor was wry and on the edge of sarcasm. She could tell he wasn't attached to any of it, so she kept him from just throwing things in the boxes by reminding him somebody else might want it.

He bitched, "She just *had* to buy something every time we went anywhere, she shopped a lot in Rome, and people gave her gifts. What a load of crap, the way she amused herself."

"Lorenzo," Claudia said while inspecting a yellowed melamine Art Deco clock the color of a rotting banana peel, "do you remember getting these souvenirs when you traveled, like this model of the Acropolis? You went to Greece?"

"Yeah, sure, but who wants a plaster model of the Acropolis, a pot metal statue of Pegasus, or a wooden rendition of Dionysius dripping with green plastic grapes? Or how about this wood version of Horus and the brass pyramid? I have some genuine ancient objects in my office that I treasure; that's different. She said this stuff kept her company, so you can see why it all has to go, off to heaven or hell." He sniggered as she drew emphatic black eyebrows into two long straight lines below her sharp-edged bangs.

After a few hours, Claudia sent Lorenzo off with a list of addresses for donating the clothes and junky objects and getting rid of the moldy paperback novels. She wrapped the china and valuables for the antique dealers. Claudia was surprised he kept up with her. Most people would be downing cold beers by now. Finally, the back part of the apartment was bare and stuff was piled up on the back porch. Would there be a chair left to sit on? When he came back with the empty truck, they cleared the porch, packing the truck for the dealers and off he went again. After a sandwich, he took her into the library crammed with interesting antique chairs, tables, lamps, and books.

"This was my sanctuary. I like everything in here except for the little crappy things all over my bookshelves. She got angry when I tried to remove them but now we can do it."

Claudia was fascinated. His library was huge and obviously very well used, but she couldn't read the book titles blotted out by angels, animals, Middle Earth gnomes, miniature houses, crystals, carvings, little boxes, clocks, and framed photos. She asked, "Was there some kind of meaning behind placing these things here? It all feels very intentional."

"She was doing something with them. She constantly rearranged them during the day, and if I moved anything, she put it back. She got really upset when I asked her to get them out of here. She was using them to control me in some way. I read the journals hoping to figure out why she had to have these things in here, but she never mentioned them. It seemed to make her happy, so what the hell? It must've been some kind of magical process for her; once she told me it made her feel like she was part of my research. Who knows? As long as she wasn't sticking pins in things and burying them in the garden, why worry? Tee hee."

He looked up at Claudia's face, thoughtful with lips pulled thin as if she was trying not to smirk. "If it's okay with you, let's pile them into boxes for the dealers by wrapping them without really looking at them; they give me the creeps. Use bubble wrap for the fragile things. If that Fabergé egg were genuine, it would've been worth a lot. Why waste?"

"Okay," he said. "But, let's keep the photos."

In two hours there were twenty more boxes filled, only books and photos were left on the shelves. "Lorenzo, your library is too crammed with furniture. Since the apartment is stripped, let's take some things out of here and move them into the other rooms." While they were working, the housekeeper had cleaned the rooms in the back and washed the brick floor that now needed furnishing. "Your things are charming, let's use them."

"Fine with me. I like all these desks and tables. Let's move some!"

Soon the whole apartment was set up with little groups of chairs, tables, and lamps. Looking around the dining room, Claudia said, "A new table and chairs probably won't cost you anything if you use your trade-in money, and I bet you'll like this room. Look for a hearty country table and matching chairs. I haven't said anything about your apartment because this was a big job, but I like it. Was it built in the mid-eighteenth century? It's comfortable, elegant. The library is outstanding with charming views, and I don't feel like we're in the city here."

"This building is older than you think, especially the dining and kitchen area, probably medieval. I don't really know, since the first mention of it in the city records is during the Renaissance. It was once a tapestry factory with the family living in the upper floors. I love this building. It will be great to decorate it the way I want after so much help from you. Thank you, and now you get dinner. I'm famished."

4

Majorca Honeymoon

Simon and Sarah were up with the sunrise to steal a few moments alone before Teresa woke up. Their apartment near the Spanish Steps felt crowded once the baby arrived, but they loved it anyway. While living there alone, Simon had enjoyed an elegant dressing room with an abundance of drawers for shirts and socks, extra closets for suits and shoes. Now it was Teresa's room and closet, with little dresses, jumpsuits, and tiny shoes competing for space with Simon and Sarah's clothes. Teresa loved waking up every morning in a cozy space infused with her father's cologne and her mother's perfume.

They snuggled on the dark green velvet couch with their coffee. Lace curtains in the kitchen waved in the early morning breezes as the rising sun made mesmerizing light patterns on the wooden living room floor. "Simon, I'm so amazed by how you care for Teresa. You held her most of the time when she was an infant. If I hadn't nursed her, I wouldn't have held her enough. Now that she's almost ten months old, she reaches first for you, not me."

"Yeah, well, I go away more than you do, so when I'm home, I want to hold her."

Sarah, who used his office on the days he wasn't working, continued. "Yes, but your nurturance surprises me. I expected to carry much more of the burden like my own mother. You do so much that I've been able to continue my writing." He barely heard her soft contented voice because the hypnotic light patterns on the floor were making his mind drift off to something that happened a few days ago . . .

Sarah had been gone all day. After Simon and Teresa took a short walk to the store, he sat on the couch watching her pull herself up to stand using the low coffee table for support. He couldn't take his eyes off her for a second, since she could fall back and bang her head or smash her chin on the table's edge. Gripping hard with little, fat fingers and grimacing, she stuck up one knee, pushed herself to standing, and wobbled on the other leg. Then she stood there rigidly and shook. Like an adult seeking approval for something well done, she challenged him with triumphant gray-green eyes. Holding his gaze, she smacked the table with a fat hand and waited. She expected an answer! "What is it little one? What do you want to know?"

With both hands pressed firmly on the table, she shook her tiny shoulders again. Then she squawked and laughed at Simon like a saucy mynah bird. She was in control, so he waited. After smiling triumphantly again, she made her way along the table's edge by putting one hand over the other with her little feet stumbling behind, until she got to his knees. He lifted her into his arms, smelling her sweet aroma, like the skin of a ripe peach. Now he wouldn't have to watch her every move as she slumped on his chest, cheek snuggling into his neck. Vibrating bliss enveloped his whole body—he slipped out of time. Shimmering blue white light morphed the walls, the table transformed into waves. He shifted slightly to glimpse her face. Her somber, wise eyes pulled him down a long corridor of crackled mirrors that reflected the earlier phases of his own DNA. Her sleepy face exuded contentment as she listened to his heartbeat. *We were one.*

Sarah's sweet voice brought him back to the present. "Simon, you are so far away. Where do you go? Where are you now?"

He sought her searching green eyes, the beautiful eyes she'd given to Teresa. "Well, I'm not in the caves under the Vatican, if that's what you're wondering." Before Teresa's arrival, Simon and Sarah used psy-

chic archaeology to uncover hidden realities. This happened spontane-
ously after he gave her an engagement ring set with an ancient ruby
from his family that had opened her psychic abilities. But they stopped
it when she got pregnant. "Do you miss exploring psychic realms with
me and Claudia?"

"Oh yes, I do, but can't with a child in the house. I do use the ruby
crystal when I'm working in your office. Claudia, by the way, is suddenly
very busy. I think she's seeing somebody, but she won't tell me who; she
just smiles at me enigmatically. It must be Lorenzo Giannini, judging
by the time they spent together at Jennifer and Armando's wedding."

Simon got up to fetch a sweet roll warming in the oven. As he
walked away, she enjoyed the light flashing on his straight back and
well-formed buttocks. *Felt so great after having sex and eating that delicious pasta he made last night; I never thought I could be this happy.* She
heard a squawk coming from the dressing room, so she rushed to get
Teresa who was standing in her crib peering into their bedroom and
banging the rail for attention. Sarah brought her into the living room
to nurse.

Simon returned with the roll cut in pieces and a bowl of fruit. He
set them down on the coffee table, fixing his gaze on Teresa sucking
avidly, filling her belly with warm milk. Sarah was dreamy. "Does feeding her arouse you? Is it pleasurable?"

"Of course it is, silly. I don't know why any woman would miss this
experience. It slows me down, feels so good, but it is not exactly sexual.
My whole body is aroused with pleasure, not just my genitals, if that's
what you want to know." She paused to bite into the delicious sweet
cherry roll and mumbled, "Will you be gone all day?"

He nodded, wondering what she was really thinking. "Today I'll be
refreshing myself on the Middle Eastern sects disappearing amid the
conflicts in Syria and Iraq. The *Times* knows I'm well informed about
them, you know the Mandaeans, Copts, Yazidis, etcetera, so they want
me to update my background. This'll be good for my career, and I'm
curious myself. Pope Francis seems to be a very good pope, but good

news is rarely what the media looks for; I could run out of work. I should branch into this area because I have the background. However, it could mean I will have to go to the Middle East, even though I want to be right here all the time."

Teresa finished with a great big smack and Sarah handed her to Simon for burping. "Maybe you can work on it without traveling?" She dreaded the thought because of the danger. The rise of ISIS and their macabre behavior terrified her.

"Possible but not likely, the scene is changing fast and few have my background. They know we have a new baby, and they were considerate when I talked with them yesterday. I told them we're going to visit our families in the U.S. in July, and that I couldn't go on assignment until after that. They agreed, I think it's the best I can get." Teresa distracted him by pulling on his ear and patting his cheek hard. He smiled warmly to soften Sarah's panicked expression. "Sarah," he said as Teresa plunged her hand into his pocket for keys and squirmed. "We may be tested, you know. We have to trust. We always knew there might be separations."

Her mouth fluttered, her eyes watered, and her cheeks sagged. "Yes, but I never thought you'd face danger; did you? It is really scary there, very dangerous for a Jewish American reporter. It makes me think of Daniel Pearl."

"Yes, true, but that changed things," he replied thoughtfully. "The paper protects us. We have better security, and our dateline bureaus provide reliable agents who handle the contacts for interviews. Actually, I worry the most about the high-profile female journalists who are a red flag to many Muslims. They cover their hair, but can't cover their faces while on TV. I'm not high profile, so I'll be okay. I hate to leave you, but I'll be okay, I'm sure. Let's concentrate on July and family."

A few hours later, Sarah and Teresa were picnicking on the grass in a section of the Borghese Gardens behind the Villa Giulia. *How will I manage in Rome alone? What if something happens to Simon? How would I live?*

∞

The driver brought Jennifer and Armando from the airport in Palma and the caretaker couple escorted them to the front entrance of the simple house with plastered walls painted in strong colors—turquoise, yellow, and blue—set off by sheer curtains. The furniture was painted white, carefree. The bright colors and freshness enhanced the views of the sea through thick-ledged windows. They settled into a casual routine with the caretakers discreetly providing meals and cleaning. He spent his days writing in a journal and sketching cottages, gardens, stone walls, and his new wife. She read except for when they shared a fresh meal or walked or swam, an ideal honeymoon with no distractions.

They strode up a rocky pathway on the wild and windy northwest coast of Majorca and turned to view the crystal-clear turquoise water below. Long ago, a Pierleoni ancestor bought the fisherman's stone cottage surrounded by hectares of steep land above Formentor Beach. They sold off most of the land in the early twentieth century, and in 1929, it became the site for the first exclusive resort for wealthy Europeans. When in the mood they dined at the resort; on some days they hung out at nearby villages, havens for artists and seekers of silence. After climbing up the last steep stair, they entered their porch, shaded by luscious grapevines heavy with clumps of red grapes, the perfect place to gaze out at the mirrored sea. The original thick-walled core built by a local mason a few hundred years ago was cool and inviting. Large add-on porches captured strong Mediterranean breezes that were almost constant except in summer. The gardens were filled with pink azaleas and purple daisies amid low rock walls. Beyond the rock walls, a large orchard of orange and lemon trees gave way to tall pines and beyond that, craggy black basalt mountains.

"Beautiful lady. What will be your pleasure before lunch? Wine, grappa, gin and tonic? Or how about fruit juice?"

"Thank you, Armando," she said sneaking a peek at the black shiny hair above his navel. She admired his tanned muscular legs, the perfect proportions of his body, and slipped two fingers up his calf to the inner side of his knee. "How about fruit juice with a splash of gin?"

"No reason not to, my love," he said as he touched the firm underside of a perfect small breast very visible in the deep V-cut of a white bikini top. Boldly she ran her fingers higher up his inner thigh, but drew them back quickly when a caretaker arrived with plates.

Armando came out with the drinks. "Only two more weeks. I want to stay here forever, but my sister is coming after we leave. I thought we might be bored at times since I had no idea what it would be like to be here with my wife. I'm having a wonderful time." *Peaceful, even though passionate sex riles me up.* "I've been sketching you to paint you when we go back to Castel Vetulonia."

Jennifer listened while savoring fresh peach juice laced with gin and lime. *What will it be like to live with his parents?* "You were so wise to give us ample time alone. I'm very comfortable with you, which I needed before joining your family. Here we can do anything we want, we don't have to tamp the fire. Back in Rome and Tuscany, it will be different."

Before leaving for their honeymoon, they'd inspected the three rooms that would be waiting for them on the second floor near Matilda and Pietro's quarters. It would be very private, but she wondered about emotional freedom since his parents would be there as they grew and changed in their marriage. Now that they were intimate, she was discovering the deep pools of chaos that lurked in Armando's soul; she was shocked how much she wanted to understand him. She rarely asked direct questions because he went on guard and kept her at a distance by making sexual innuendoes when she got too close. He seemed to be in another world a lot.

Earlier that day when she took a long swim, diving deeper than ever before, she was seized by the desire to know all of him. The gin now slipped her focus slightly outside the solid world; she felt like she was a light beam penetrating his inner lattices. She wanted to shatter him into geometrical shapes, to examine all his facets and angles. Being with him on Majorca was an unexpected love potion that enchanted her while they spoke, ate, and made love. His perfect proportions and the marvelous color of his skin, eyes, and hair surely came directly from higher dimensional realms, like Michelangelo's marble statues of male bodies. He smelled delicious, like a god from a mythic age.

He deftly evaded her razor-sharp mind that could analyze him better than he knew himself—the thing most men fear about women. Going deeper, she was careful yet persistent since he didn't object as long as she didn't push too far too fast. She didn't know she was trying to penetrate her own shadow through him. Looking into his murky eyes, she licked the rim of her drink with a taut tongue and said thoughtfully, "If I'm going to find my true feminine essence as your lover, I need to understand you. What are you thinking right now?"

He'd been tapping his fingers on the edge of his chair staring brazenly at her soft inner thigh, a cue that it was safe to ask. "Ah, but," he replied in a smooth voice, Italian accent more pronounced than usual because he knew she loved it, "that is an impossible question because I don't know myself, probably never will. There is no hurry. Anyway, I penetrate you when I fuck you, the joy of being a man. You engulf me. You were born for this, and from your body will come our child." He stroked her deliciously accessible small belly above the tiny string bikini. As he diverted her focus with sexual innuendoes, he knew it annoyed her, but too much talk annoyed him, annoyed him a lot. Who was going to be victorious?

"So, you believe that strongly about the nature of being male or female? As you know, these days many people would not agree with you," she said flatly, staring at him with a firm expression.

"That may be so, and that is fine for them, but that is not who we are or ever will be. We are together because I'm a man and you are a woman. To be frank—though I hate being pinned down as you've noticed—if I didn't clearly understand my gender, I'd be crazy. I've had a hard enough time trying to figure out who I am, but at least I know that I'm a man. What are you really trying to say?" He was annoyed.

Jennifer only knew she wanted him to reveal himself more but he wouldn't. Her opportunities would be less frequent after their honeymoon. "What if I don't get pregnant? What if all you get is a relationship with me? Then would you reveal your mind?" Armando didn't know she was on birth control.

"What do you mean, *reveal my mind?*" he said visualizing her perfect long legs wrapped around his waist while fucking her, getting hard from the visual.

"I want to know what you think about in order to understand who you are. Perhaps I'm wrong, perhaps I can know just by being with you and seeing what you paint, but I sense there is a special being in you, a person nobody knows. I can see that you're not ready, so I'll wait. I'm so grateful for this time alone. Please promise you will bring me back here every year?"

"Of course we will, one of the benefits of being a Pierleoni. My parents get closer when they come here, my cousins say the same, as does my sister. As for you, I will find out more about you when I paint you." He looked up and was surprised to encounter a camera lens. She'd caught him in a mood she hadn't seen before; he felt invaded.

"Sorry. I'm your wife and we only have a little more time alone together. I worry about how it will be when we're back in the family."

Armando felt potent sexual energy flowing in his loins. He said in a concerned, warm voice, "You must trust me, trust us. I'm going to find you in many different ways as your resistance melts away. I'm going to paint you over and over again, and I am going to fuck you until you surrender. You'll find me through artistry and intimacy too."

After lunch they retired to their chamber with salty sea breezes wafting through shocking pink fabric that accentuated the flesh-colored plaster walls. The only decoration was a painting by Armando of a fat nude with a chartreuse drape over her pubis in the style of Matisse. Sheltered within a white mosquito-net bower, he made love to her so intensely she nearly shattered. He made her feel drunk by repeatedly touching every part of her body. Then he fell into a sound sleep while she lay beside him feeling hot energy warm her pelvis. She slipped out through the French doors to the terrace to stare at the sea until he awoke. For now, she had nothing more to say. But he was not going to escape her desire to get inside his skin.

Armando lay in deep sleep with his consciousness spinning in his pineal gland, the cave of all minds. He was in neck-deep water next to a rock ledge with his feet crabbing soft, pebbly sand. Right beyond the sand ledge, the sea floor plunged down into midnight-blue water where Jennifer was deep diving while he guarded her. She plunged down using flippers to propel deeper and deeper, bubbles swirling behind her body. It seemed an incredibly long time before she surfaced. The first time she went deep, he was frightened, but could still see the bubbles and the white flash of her body down through the aqua sea in the deep blue water. His dream was of a long time ago watching a mermaid dive into the sea.

Will she come back to me, swim to me and pull herself up on the rock to sun her fish body? Like a rare male Siren, I sing my evocative song to draw her near. Her hair is thick, curly, and rusty red, her breasts full, her back sinuous, yet her lower body is fish. How will I enter her? Sunning on the slippery rock, she glances at me sideways, cool water running out of her hair tickling her nipples. A large emerald on her left hand captures the rays of the sun, a green flash deep in my eye sockets. Looking into her eyes for the last time, I rise out of my body flying above the rocks and the sea. Captured on the rock within her fish body, she reaches for me with a desperate look as if she will die when I ascend beyond the rocks and the sea. As I fly away up to the sky, she is the tiny dark figure on the rock by the sea far away in the distance.

5

Jesus and Mary Magdalene

Jennifer and Armando had been excited yet apprehensive to return to their new home in the castle. They paused, holding hands, in the cavernous upper hall with elegant dark oak carved doors at each end—one to the parent's quarters, the other to their suite. The heavy door creaked shut and they passed through a small anteroom into an intimate parlor dominated by a tall red-granite fireplace. Jennifer stopped right there. Crystalline sparkles in the granite glistened in the morning light streaming through tall French doors warming the floors. Looking all around, she exclaimed breathlessly, "Armando, this is lovely. I had no idea we would be treated to such luxury. Matilda even re-covered some of the furniture; so thoughtful of her!"

Armando surveyed the transformed rooms he'd so long ago shared with Giaconda while growing up. Her commodious bedroom with painted beams laced with faded flowers on leafy vines was now their bedroom. His old room off to the right side of the parlor was Jennifer's studio with a large inviting worktable and a balcony facing east to capture the morning sun. Someday it might be a nursery for their children.

After a few weeks of settling in, Matilda invited her daughter-in-law to a private lunch, insisting she must feel free to decline if she was busy or not in the mood. Jennifer was delighted since she was alone much of each day. They enjoyed caprese salad with asparagus and cold tarragon chicken slices served with a fruity white wine. Matilda said in a happy lilting voice, "I hope you love your suite? Ours is almost the same except our bedroom is larger. Would you like to see ours? Anytime. Our suites have the only original doors in the castle. Does the bathroom please you? I couldn't resist using those wonderful Portuguese tiles, but do *you* like them? I had so much fun doing over the suite for the two of you. It made me feel like a bride again!"

"I love our suite," Jennifer replied sincerely. "I enjoy every moment there with Armando, yet I'm also very happy being alone during the day. I really like having my studio there; I love the morning light after Armando goes to his studio. At the end of the workday, we have sherry while reading and chatting in our parlor before dinner. My work is going well, I take marvelous walks, enjoy reading, and I love joining you and Pietro for breakfast and dinner. This is a whole new life for me. I'm adjusting very easily."

"Lovely to hear, since this *is* a whole new way of life for you, a life that works if one is self-reliant, which I see you are. You have to be because Armando is obsessed when he works." Peering out through her pretty moonlike face, Matilda studied Jennifer's dark intense eyes. Armando's chosen one intrigued her. He seemed to treasure his time with her, yet Matilda suspected he'd rather be in his studio even more. "I hope Armando is not working too much? He's facing such a challenge with the major show coming up in Florence this winter. He has attracted the notice of the most important curators . . . they say he is as talented as any Renaissance painter. Such attention brings intense pressure to perform with new paintings. When he read that article, did it make him tense?"

"I suppose so. To me, it felt rather odd because nobody has praised that painting style for so many years. I've noticed he's the most relaxed when he has accomplished enough work each day," Jennifer commented circumspectly. "Actually, I can't relax myself without accomplishing a certain amount every day, so I understand."

"My dear, you can tell me; we can be frank. Do you think he minds the visitors that join us for dinner? He enjoyed guests in the evening before you married, but maybe not so much now? After all, you've just returned from your honeymoon."

"How thoughtful of you to be concerned. I think he enjoys the distraction of dinner guests after working hard all day. We get in touch during our late afternoon walks, and we can always dine alone if we want to. Everything is perfect. The guests are charming, and they are stimulating for me after being alone all day. Living this way is warm, creative, and social. And I don't have to cook, which is a real plus for me!"

"I'm so happy to hear that, and I have to admit I don't like to cook either. I love the fresh, healthy cuisine our cook creates from our gardens. Your parents must visit soon. They are utterly charming and your father intrigues Pietro. Please tell them again we'd love to have them."

"I would love for my parents to come, Simon and Sarah too."

"I ask them to come whenever I can. I adore Sarah, always have, and of course I love to see that sweet baby."

When Jennifer got back to their parlor, Armando called. He wanted her to come to his studio because he'd just finished a painting. This reassured her because they had not been very connected for a few days—sexually in particular. He was struggling with a challenging painting, couldn't sleep, and last night he'd moved to the daybed in the parlor to toss and turn. She went up to the tower immediately, kissed him warmly, and waited for him to draw away the cover. *Will this painting help me understand why he draws away from me?*

Propped up on a low trunk, the large canvas was higher than Armando, who stared dramatically at his wife. "Are you ready?" She nodded. He pulled away the cloth with a snap to reveal a painting totally different from the three-tiered scenes with the everyday world sandwiched between lower and upper realms, the format he was now being recognized for. The six-foot-tall, four-foot-wide painting portrayed a tall and intense man with large sensitive hands reaching down for a sensual woman in a blue robe with voluminous red hair, groveling at his feet. Her right hand reached beseechingly for him as he indicated with his hands and concerned expression that she should rise. But something rooted her to the ground. Her face barely visible from the side expressed the desire to obey yet some great force was pushing her down. Behind them, the grooved and indented cliff rocks outlined faces watching them.

Jennifer's gut lurched; she gripped her belly. He didn't notice it because her expression—wonder—got his attention. "His face is so loving, his presence so powerful. I assume this is Jesus and Mary Magdalene?" He nodded. "He seems to entreat her to rise, yet she grovels at his feet. Why?"

"I don't know why. I've been seeing this scene day and night since we came back from Majorca, the reason I've been so distant from you. I had to paint them, but they upset me terribly as they materialized. I don't understand it, not at all. Unlike my recent work, this is the *only* thing I can paint right now. Last week I fought my muse to avoid starting it. The dealer wants another triptych, but nothing else would come so I stewed. I was afraid of losing my ability to paint; that'd be worse than anything. I am nothing if I can't paint. People are waiting for my new work at the Florence show, so I gave in, but I felt insane. Once I started, I couldn't stop. My only distraction has been my time with you and our dinner guests, which helps me forget my studio for a while. I'm obsessed and I don't know why. Do you have any idea?"

She looked at the painting again. The Magdalene reminded her of how she felt when they were in Majorca, especially when she tried to reach into his mind. He'd been pulling away from her a little more each day, the distance making her anxious. *This painting may be of us!* "Do you feel like Jesus is you and Mary is me?"

"It occurred to me, but doesn't make sense. This is not how I feel about you, yet why can't I paint anything else? My multilayered works seem to be eluding me because of this damned single image. Do you think this is any good?"

"It is very gripping and powerful, it will stun the critics. Scenes like this were common during the Renaissance, yet your version is contemporary because it is very psychological. People will experience the Real Presence when they see it, the thousands that will view it. You are not losing your touch, but what does it *mean* to you?"

"I simply have no idea, none. You'd be shocked if you knew how little I know why I paint things. Please, you can say anything; talk to me. Maybe I had to paint it to get beyond myself?"

Perplexed, Jennifer turned back to the canvas. Jesus was sucking energy into his body from the ground while commanding the surrounding elements as the sky expanded his aura. Mary's endearing reach for him was creating a magnetic circulation of light between their bodies. Yet, the clouds above boiled like fire stanched in water, pulling his body upward, away. He was ready to fly, but she would not release him. *She does mirror the desires I felt for him in Majorca.* "While wandering around the Uffizi, I'm always amazed by how often I see the Magdalene with Jesus. She *had* to have been his wife and disciple; certainly many Renaissance artists thought she was. Since I specialize in capturing images that reveal people's essence, I wonder why so many Renaissance painters portrayed such obvious intimacy between Jesus and the Magdalene. Now, why are *you* doing it? Who cares if they were married? Really. The critics praise you for painting biblical themes, a painting style that has been the kiss of death for modern painters. Now *this?* Now that we've married, perhaps you are obsessed with this theme? Mary grovels, yet he wants to fly. Day after day I wait for you to allow me into your soul . . . Maybe you are expressing your struggle with how to handle me? Maybe you are the vessel for this great archetype because I inspire the essential male/female dynamic within your heart? Perhaps, like the Magdalene, I am keeping you from something grand?" She stopped.

Her words weighed on Armando's heart and silenced him for a few long minutes. "When this came through me, I bled. Your thoughts challenge me. When my brush approached Mary, her desire to know

Jesus twisted my guts. His need to fly drove me crazy. Tell me, my love, as she reaches for him, why does he want to fly beyond Earth? Her desperation makes me feel sick because I feel like he wants freedom from every human grasping for him. She . . . we . . . we've all sought his light, especially Sarah. Even the rocks seem to show that the Magdalene is his last chance. I couldn't let you see this painting until I captured his light this morning, and I did. Can *you* see it?"

Jennifer contemplated the painting again looking for how Armando got Jesus to look like he was ready to fly. The light in his upper body intensified exponentially or was it iridescence? Unlike a typical halo, his light came from reflections of lightning flashing in the heavens, golden fingers reaching out of intense storm clouds, a final cataclysm. An awestruck voice squeaked out of her. "Yes, I see it and everyone else will too. Like Fra Angelico, you've caught the otherworldly light manifesting in him. This painting is a miracle."

He slumped down totally deflated. "For so many years I wondered what Michelangelo thought about while he was up on the scaffolds in the Sistine Chapel. I've wondered the same about Fra Angelico. I always thought they portrayed biblical themes for money until the biblical stream came roaring through me; I can't resist it. I belittled religious themes, yet now I *must* paint them. Now that I see his light, I want to explore what the other disciples and John the Baptist thought about Mary, about Jesus. But, this archetypal stream could carry me away in a flood that might ruin my sales and reputation. I fear what this could do to our lives, but I can't stop it. Like a drowning man swimming against a perilous undertow, I *have* to paint or I will lose my life. Yet, I love you and I want to provide a decent life for our child. Are you sure you can live with a madman?"

What did I think marriage would be like? Look at my parents, think of Jasmine. His dark eyes were begging her to save him from drowning. Hating his needy burden, again she looked away to the canvas. This time she detected sound in the images, otherworldly waving tones that confused her rational mind. Out of the sheen on the still-moist oil surface, a rainbow emanated, a fusion of sound and light, the energy she followed when she captured her best images in the camera lens. She looked at his desperate expression. "It's so simple. I'm happy here with you. Whatever you need to do will be fine. This painting is magnificent and will move many people. I will be with you no matter where this stream takes you."

Claudia rushed to Tuscany to see the painting of Jesus and Mary Magdalene because Armando hoped *she* could unravel the mystery. Jennifer said she didn't mind Claudia visiting his studio alone, but while they were there together in the morning, acidic jealousy ate her alive. She had a horrible time: She couldn't get any work done, didn't want to see anybody, and couldn't even read. She tried walking in the forest, but the trees transformed into black dogs. She kicked a tree hard and cracked her big toe. *Now I know . . . now I know what this murderous emotion feels like—jealousy. It's sickening. Now I know how Jasmine felt.* She tried to dispel the thought.

Armando stood up to draw away the cloth while Claudia sat at the table. After he pulled it, she became totally silent. Then she gasped and coughed. "Claudia, I sense you know something. What's going on with me?"

Her dark occluded eyes fixed on the painting like a laser beam. Her legs were crossed with the upper foot encased in a rose-colored espadrille pumping up and down, her mind was whirring like a hard disk. She sat quietly for an agonizingly long period then said crisply, "Why is there a large yellow queen bee on the rock behind the Magdalene's head?"

Armando was puzzled and turned around to look behind Mary's head. "I really don't know; it's just there."

"Hmmm," she murmured while calculating. "For me to discuss this, tell me what Jesus is feeling, what is Mary feeling?"

He paused and stammered, "Well, as Jennifer already said, he seems to be on the verge of ascending but she is pulling him down."

"Yes, but," she interjected, "what does he *feel?* Try to express it for me, come on."

Armando spaced out grasping for something . . . "I, ah, sense that he may have just been pulled out of the sky. She is simply there, he's trying to go back up but she holds him down."

"Okay. What if he is Lucifer the angel of light returning to Earth called in by Sophia the Gnostic wisdom goddess? Are you familiar with that story?"

"Not really. I'm no more interested in it now than I was when you and I were together. Besides, he's Jesus not Lucifer. But tell me the story, since you will anyway." He got up to stand by his painting.

"It is simple," she began. "Sophia wanted to create the world—Gaia—filled with creatures who would worship the creator of the universe. With great effort, she made our world out of particles of matter from the waves in the divine mind. All this was fine and beautiful, but she'd disobeyed cosmic law by creating the world without Lucifer, her lover. Reality fragmented and became multilayered because he was left in heaven while she was on Earth—Sophia split the universe! Some Gnostics believed Lucifer came to Earth as Jesus to find her again to reunite and redeem the world." She paused then continued, "The symbol for this Gnostic teaching is the queen bee, and you painted it on the rock right behind Mary Magdalene! I think you've painted the return of Christ to our troubled times, a compelling and exquisite idea. I feel his divine presence as she holds him down while he longs for the sky. Wait until Sarah sees this. Modern Gnostics say he will return as an avatar. Here is the name for your masterpiece, Armando, you have painted the *Avatar of the Age of Aquarius!*"

"Jennifer wondered whether Jesus is me and the Magdalene is her. Yet you see Lucifer and Sophia."

This disturbed Claudia. She still loved Armando in many deep ways but was thoroughly done with him. She bored her eyes into Armando's, which made him feel like he was the one stuck between heaven and earth standing by the side of his canvas. He came to sit down beside her as she said in a sarcastic voice, "If you *are* fusing with your wife, which I find hard to believe, then perhaps *she* opened the gate for this painting? What do you think, Armando?"

"You know what?" he said helplessly. "I know less than you do about what this painting means."

"This is your greatest painting so far, so perhaps you don't need to ask me these questions? Just let it flow! We must leave the bee for later. The databank on the bee and Mary Magdalene is huge, too much for today. I'd like to have lunch with Jennifer."

Jennifer felt a huge wave of relief walking down the creaky stairs from the hall to the dining room to join them; all she wanted was to see Armando's face. Moving swiftly along in a light green sundress, she rushed forward to extend a hand warmly to Claudia who took it smiling as if delighted to see her. "So wonderful to see you, the first time since your lovely wedding. You are a bucolic picture of country beauty."

Jennifer looked into Claudia's intelligent dark eyes and said evenly, "It's wonderful living here with Armando and his family. I had no idea whether I would like it or not; it's a joy."

"Yes, I can see that," Claudia replied slowly surveying the rustic room with an oak table set for three with stemmed glasses and Spode plate ware. "I'm sure it must be. Few American women would like this routine, but you got used to European ways living in Paris, didn't you? Come sit with me for a moment while Armando gets the kitchen moving and brings us a drink," Claudia said, gesturing to the settee as if she were the mistress of the household.

"I suppose living in Paris made me more comfortable, certainly living in Tuscany with Armando's parents is wonderful."

Gripping, acidic envy burned Claudia's solar plexus as she listened to Jennifer's youthful musical voice. Envy slammed her back ten years; she wanted a cigarette. Armando came back with a stiff scotch on the rocks for Claudia and a white wine for Jennifer. Then he went back to the kitchen for his own choice. He lingered to give them a few minutes alone.

"How is your photography coming along now that you are in the country? Surely it is daunting to live with such a great artist?" Claudia said in a curious voice struggling to sound sincere.

"Claudia," Jennifer replied, sounding very determined, "the painting you just saw is remarkable. Because he works so much, my own work is coming along beautifully. After summer, I'll be in Paris a few weeks to do a major shoot. Our work and life are very pleasant." As she spoke, Jennifer felt like her sentences were getting all jumbled up in the potent energy coming out of Claudia's stunning chest, such a sexy woman. *She had all of him, she could have him again, and she knows it.*

"What is it *really* like to live with his parents, the castle routine? What is it that you like about it? I frankly am surprised you do," Claudia said with very little sincerity left.

Jennifer closed up when Armando came back to the room with a scotch. He took Jennifer's hand turning to Claudia. "Thank you for coming to see the painting. As always, you've given me insights. Will you share your thoughts about the bee while we have lunch?" He turned back to Jennifer and said, "Claudia noticed I painted a bee behind the Magdalene. I was unconscious of it; never saw it. Did you notice it?"

"No," she replied dumbly as they sat down. "What significance could that have, a bee? I've heard you know a lot about symbols, Claudia."

"Oh, great significance darling, but that is too much for today. I'll share it, but I need to think about it more myself. I can give you both one aspect: the bee symbolism is related to Artemis, an ancient goddess. Artemis is up above the mosaic of Hermes Trismegistus in Siena Cathedral. Anyway, here's a toast to happy times together, now and in the future."

As they raised their glasses, Jennifer's throat closed as she struggled to keep up with the all-too-familiar banter that made her feel small, stupid, and rejected, painfully aware of her lackluster responses. Armando glanced over once in a while while Claudia went on talking in a throaty voice, entertaining him the way she used to years ago, flirting to make herself feel charming. Armando couldn't find a way to stop her since it was just the way she was, especially when she was nervous.

Jennifer politely tried to keep up hoping she didn't seem to be a boring American who didn't know what to say. Things got worse when Claudia slipped into Italian to explain a very subtle concept that Armando was struggling to understand. Armando changed right back to English and turned to Jennifer saying, "Excuse us, Jen. Claudia and I just couldn't figure that one out without using a few Italian words, words we don't have in English."

"It's all right," Jennifer said very quietly.

All three of them knew it was not all right, especially Jennifer who felt small as she struggled through the rest of the lunch. It was a great relief to wave goodbye to Claudia.

6

Holiday in the States

Simon, Sarah, and Teresa visited Sarah's parents at their summerhouse in July. When they arrived at the restored quarry house, Sarah's father, William, captured Teresa by sweeping her into his arms, putting her on his lap, then jiggling the toddler into the air. "I'm Grandpa and all babies love me!" Teresa watched him, about to cry, then she raised her arms high and laughed and laughed.

Sarah's mother, Mary, laughed too. "Sarah, she is *completely* different than you were at this age. You were always quiet and thoughtful like a monk. Teresa is so precocious."

"Mom," Sarah replied softly, "this is the happiest time of my life, being here with Simon while you enjoy Teresa. We are all so lucky, so lucky."

"Saar-rah," William broke in, "even though you are a busy mom, I hear you are finishing a book related to your graduate thesis. How'd you do that?"

"Simon and I share childcare, Daddy."

"That's a big change from my time," Mary noted. "Few parents did that back when you were little. Teresa seems calmer with Simon, if you don't mind me saying so. She certainly is pleased with her daddy."

"I don't mind; it's true. We even can eat out in restaurants with her because Simon keeps her attention so rapt on whatever he's doing."

Simon deflected the attention back to Sarah. "I'm proud of Sarah because her book is really coming along. That Ph.D. thesis had to be so academic, but her fiction really flows." Teresa stopped playing the moment she heard Simon's voice and crawled over to him. He pulled her up, kissing a fat warm cheek while she showered everyone in the room with an enigmatic, knowing expression. Spritz, the family golden retriever, splayed out on the cool stone floor, thumped his heavy tail. Teresa pointed at him and growled.

"Writing historical fiction is my passion," Sarah said looking at William. "My characters expose hidden facets of the ideals and environment of our ancestors."

"Well, what's it about?" William demanded. "What *are* you writing about?"

Sarah collapsed back in her chair reaching for a lemonade. "Oh, Daddy, I can't say much about it yet because I'm in the middle of it. My characters are seeking the real Jesus before his identity was buried in dogma. They think he will emerge again in our troubled world, the same stuff I've been obsessed with for years."

"Do you really think anybody is interested in that, except for Christian fundamentalists?" Mary wondered while glancing around the room perhaps in discomfort about the subject. "Seems to me, different centuries had unique images of Jesus based on what their current theologians said. Yet now people seek him their own way. Is that what you're doing in your book?"

"Kinda. Lost documents and archaeological discoveries have revealed much new information in the last few years. A new story of Jesus is emerging as a real man fully in touch with spiritual realms, a normal man, married and a father. This encourages each one of us to be spiritual."

William thought his favorite daughter was off on a weird tangent that wouldn't do anybody any good. "Well, I don't get it," he grumbled. "Seems like the people who are actually interested in Jesus—priests, theologians, and hyper-religious fanatics—aren't going to take your ideas seriously, and regular religious people won't be interested in this type of book." Spritz rolled over on his back and splayed his paws out. His flapped-back lips bared large pink gums and white teeth—a mad dog grin accompanied by rolling eyes. Teresa pointed at Spritz and giggled while William went on talking to his silent daughter. "I paid for your Ph.D. to help you get academic standing, and now you're writing a book that could wreck your credibility. Why would *anybody* think *you* have anything to say about Jesus?"

Teresa focused her determined green eyes on her mother's face, and then she glared at her grandpa's firetruck-red face. She shoved Simon's arm, frowned, and then started to whimper. Simon wanted to hear what Sarah would say back to her father, but he had to turn his attention to Teresa. "There, now, little one," he said, forcing her to look at his laughing smile. "Grandpa is just being grumpy, just like doggy does." Teresa stiffened and made a barking sound still glaring defiantly at her grandfather.

William snorted and laughed. "Looks like the younger generation already knows all about what's going on. Time for a gin and tonic?" Mary sat back in the rocking chair thinking with her hands crossed above her waist. *That little girl understands everything we feel; she's aware of everyone in this room.*

The heat of the day was building, so after her nap, Teresa's parents took her to swim in the quarry pond in front of the house. Edged with sculpted rock ledges, the old pit had filled up with spring water and become a deep clear pool a hundred years ago after the last removal of stone. Teresa sat in the cool water splashing joyfully with her hands on a wide shallow ledge with her legs and bottom submerged. Sarah sat right in front of her on a lower step with water up to her waist while Simon swam vigorously out into deeper water. All was silent except for an occasional owl hoot, a snapping branch, or a hawk's scream. Teresa watched him swim away as she held out her arms crying, "Da da, da duh!"

"He will be back soon, sweet one. Daddy is having fun and we are having fun! See my feet, Teri, look there; see the little green fish?"

Quarry pond

Teresa forgot about Daddy when she saw a green shape wriggling and twisting in the water. She smashed the water's surface to frighten it away and then adroitly cupped water in her hands and dripped it on Mommy's arm.

"It is delicious, Teri, and you can drink it." Sarah cupped water in her hand and held it up to her mouth. Teresa threw back her head and spat it out laughing as it dribbled down her tummy. Simon swam back nearby them to watch. Sarah was like a mermaid playing with a faun. Blue mist around their heads fanned out to form water beads on the nearby deep green ferns that glistened in the sun. *This is sylvan grace.*

A week later they were relaxing on the large porch at David and Rose's Shelter Island house by the sea. Simon was anxious to see how his parents would respond to Teresa as she grew. At first they were quite reticent with her, careful, as if they didn't want to invade her space. Rose sat in a canvas lounge chair enjoying the salty air, while Teresa held on to the table next to her staring into her other grandmother's dark brown eyes.

"What are you thinking about, Teresa?" Rose asked with a tight smile, lightly touching Teresa's chubby shoulder. "Do you know who I am? I am your da da's mama, just like Sarah is *your* mama." The toddler rolled her shoulders and then did something her family deemed amazing: she took three pinecones out of a bowl on the table while grinning at Rose triumphantly. She lined up the three pinecones while eyeing David who was intently watching her. She took one and clutched it to her chest, gave another to Rose, then leaned on the edge of the table and squawked, "Da Da!" as she pushed a pinecone at Simon.

Simon moved quickly to grab her because she was gripping her own pinecone so tightly that she was about to fall over while giving out the last one with her other hand. Simon took it and then grabbed her just in time as she squealed ecstatically, "Da Dah, Mamah." Glued to the whole scene, David exclaimed breathlessly, "She understood you, Rose! She not only understood you, she also found a way to show you she did! Simon, did you see that?"

"I did. She does a lot of things like that. When I get discouraged about the world, I stop thinking and look at the world through my growing daughter's eyes. If this little being can be this conscious, then no matter how bad things are, we have a future. Children show us what's coming next, our window to the future."

Hours went by until the time Simon was waiting for—a private visit with his father in his study after Rose and Sarah went upstairs after Teresa went to sleep. Simon and David sat down next to a stained-glass reading lamp.

"Simon," David began. "You have a lovely family. Teresa arrived so soon that I worried about whether you and Sarah could handle it. I'm surprised by how well you are doing. You care for your daughter tenderly. Watching you makes me feel like I missed so much by not being with you when you were little. I'm amazed by how confident she is. Do you think it's because you and Sarah haven't shut her down?"

His father's clear gray eyes and kind expression always made Simon think in entirely new ways, the reason he loved their time alone. "I think we understand how she feels and vice versa."

"Hmmm, well, Rose had a strong intuitive connection with you and Jennifer. What seems new to me is a father caring for his child as much as you are. Of course, from your point of view, this probably seems natural. But, Rose and I are detecting a completely new stage in human evolution. I'm serious about this. We have been noticing that many fathers are caring for their infants and toddlers, some even mothering more than the mothers."

A red, crescent moon shining in the large wavy glass window with a view out to the sea diverted Simon's attention. Like the Islamic symbol of the crescent moon and Venus, a bright planet was just below the bottom tip of the moon, probably Venus. He looked back to his father who was observing Simon framed by the lunar light. "Maybe old ways are coming back? Maybe men were this way with their children thousands of years ago, ways that are still common with some indigenous people today. Maybe you're just talking about Western culture? Or, maybe this is how parents are with their children when reality is shattering? Dad, things aren't looking good these days. I'm sure you follow what's going on with ISIS?" David nodded. "Well," Simon said tentatively not wanting to say what came next. "The *Times* will be sending me to Iraq and possibly Syria soon, as soon as next month."

David slumped back in his chair aghast and blurted out without thinking, "Simon, you're a new father; they can't do that, *you* can't do it. There's nothing in the world that would make it worth it. Why would they send you there, why you?" His father's cry of anguish and fear ripped into Simon's heart.

Simon pulled slightly forward on the leather seat. "You may recall I minored in Middle Eastern religious sects in college . . . and you know I was fascinated. Remember when I studied abroad in Syria and Iraq? I also spent a lot of time in Egypt and Lebanon interviewing some absolutely brilliant Copt and Druze spiritual leaders, men I will never forget. Their religions are the oldest in the world, and some like the Copts adopted Christianity very early. Now they are threatened with extinction in the Middle East, a great threat to the West. Bush lit the Middle Eastern time bomb when he invaded Iraq, lifted the lid on Pandora's box. And now we have radical Sunni factions, such as ISIS, stripping away the protections for the ancient religions."

David noticed his son's voice was panicky. The possibility that his adored son, a new father and husband, could be sent to the Middle East made his temples throb. He muttered in a desperate strangled voice, "No, Simon, no Simon, you can't do this."

Simon felt like his father was forbidding him, not acceptable at his age. There was a long pause then Simon said in a clear voice, "Do you remember when I was young, when you told me to follow my principles to keep the world safe? That narcissistic, sick fool, Bush, unleashed the demons from hell in the Middle East because he didn't know the difference between a Sunni and a Shi'ite. Hell, I think our State Department doesn't know the difference even now! These ancient spiritual traditions have worked for peace in the Middle East for two thousand years, longer even; for hundreds of years they've maintained balances amid ongoing Islamic sectarian tension. Unfortunately, Western powers aren't aware of what they destroy. The spiritual leaders I've met stirred my heart and soul; I can't ignore what is happening to them. As a journalist, I must give them a voice. I will be well protected, the paper is very careful about that. I've decided I have to go."

David was so upset he had no words for a moment. Furiously he lashed out, "You *can't* do that to Sarah. You can't ask her to be alone in Rome with a baby while you go there; you can't!"

Simon feared estrangement from his father. *Be honest with yourself, Simon. You didn't have the balls to tell William about it when you were there last week.* Simon had planned to get a few minutes alone with William. But he didn't want to spoil their visit, so it never happened. Now he could see he'd lacked the nerve to tell William. "Well, Dad," he said, "what do you expect me to do, give up my profession? Few have the background for these stories. My editor thinks U.S. policy could improve if the public realizes what's happening to these minority sects, especially the Christian ones. My editor also thinks the government has to face the fact that most of what the U.S. has done in the Middle East has caused great harm and gained little. If the public feels compassion for these suffering people, maybe people will demand changes in these suicidal policies. The Western invaders are mostly Christian, so maybe if they realize Christians are suffering, maybe they can abandon their blind desire to control the world. I *have* to offer my skills and knowledge in this battle between East and West." He lowered his voice while engaging his father's pained face. "I don't feel my wife and daughter will live in a safe world unless I help reveal the truth. As much as Sarah hates the idea, *she* supports me. So, if you can't support me in this difficult task, then where are we Dad?" Simon's high cheeks were falling, he felt like crying.

"Son, I don't want to make this even worse for you," David said in a sad and heavy voice while probing Simon's expression. For the first time in his life, David realized Simon's life could be taken, just like that, in a moment. "As we've aged, your mother and I have been hiding our heads in the sand. Back in 2001, we hoped the chaos in the world would stop escalating but it didn't; I guess we knew it wouldn't deep down. I didn't hide from the world at your age; I tried to make a difference. So, I'll do my part to support you, that is, your mother and I will. One or both of us will go to Italy to be with Sarah and Teresa when she needs help. You can count on our support for them." He turned to gaze out the sea window illuminated by the red moon shimmering behind Simon's head. The ruby reflection carved out Simon's ivory profile like a cameo, a pearled face framed by wild dark hair against silver glass.

Simon's voice caught in his throat. "You and maybe Mom would go all the way to Italy to make sure they're okay? I hadn't thought about that, that's not why I told you tonight. I had to tell you in person because I know how much you will worry. Bringing pain into your life, Mom's life, makes me feel terrible with you almost in your seventies; you deserve peace of mind, to enjoy your granddaughter. Nobody wants this assignment less than me, but I have the ideal background. When I accepted my Fulbright to study this years ago, I had no idea this would come. I used to think being a reporter would be a great adventure, not a ticket to hell. These gifts were given to me so that I can give back. You always taught me if I give from my heart and offer everything I have, I'd be safe and protected. If I go to the Middle East with courage in my heart, I'll be able to write stories that will make a difference."

At his age, David no longer believed what he'd once taught his son about courage. Glancing at Simon's profile glowing in front of the red glass, he wondered where his faith had gone. *Am I just a lazy coward living in luxury dulled by fear? Why didn't I scream and fight harder when Bush used 9/11 as a ploy to increase the military and create Homeland Security and the TSA? I knew all about the arms manufacturers—Bush/Cheney profiteers—yet I did nothing.* "Simon, I have to trust you. Like any parent, I ache for your family to be safe and happy. U.S. foreign policy is coming directly back on all of us now, and you believe you have to do something about it; I see that. Your mother and I will make sure your wife and our granddaughter are taken care of while you are away; yes, of course we will."

Simon felt better as he thought of his parents helping. "I'm sure Sarah would love to have you visit in Rome; Jennifer's in-laws say you're welcome anytime. Armando says they talk constantly about you coming to visit, and Sarah and Teresa could visit Tuscany with you. I would love Teresa to have more time with her Auntie Jennifer. When I think about it that way, it could be a blessing in disguise. Actually, Dad, I'm not afraid; if I were, I wouldn't go. But I've been really worried about leaving Sarah and Teresa. I'd also love to see Jen get more support right now. She says she gets it from Armando's parents, but as much as I enjoy him, Armando is self-centered. As the apocalypse unfolds, he's obsessively painting it, and I think she spends a lot of time alone."

David cheered up a bit when he thought of seeing his daughter. David had enjoyed a warm and silent communication with her as a child, but she changed as a teenager. She was catty and nasty with Rose and ignored her father, acting like he knew less than nothing. David and Rose endured this stereotypical adolescent behavior and stopped worrying about her when she became a successful photographer. They were aware she was having love affairs, the norm for a liberal Jewish girl. However, in her late twenties she had a very long affair with a man they never met, so they suspected he was married. But what could they do with the affair going on in Paris? Then everything changed last year when she met Armando. As David thought about it, it *was* time to renew his relationship with his daughter. "Well," David said gravely, "that crazy Pierleoni castle is like a dormitory, so I know there will be room for us all to visit. They're charming and we love Italy. Meanwhile, keep me updated. You know you have someone to talk to who can understand you, don't you?"

"Yes, I do, and I will. We *will* be able to handle this with your support. The worst part for me is the separation from Teresa because I'll never get these early years back. In light of that, I made a pretty decent deal with the *Times*. I told them I would take this assignment for at least a year if they would allow me to go home for two weeks every two months, and they agreed. They'll cover all my calls and travel home. This'll work out because I can take on each six-week stint in a different location and work very hard in that area before anybody recognizes me. That's safer, a good arrangement."

After everyone was tucked in for the night, David lay awake seized with paralytic fear and horror while he listened to Rose's soft breath. His stomach churned, his head filled with pressure, and his eyes burned even though they were shut. Just before the sun rose, a flood of anger coursed through his wrung-out nerves. As he drifted off to sleep in the early morning light, he cursed in a disgusted whisper, "You bastard, George Bush. May all the death and mayhem you've caused come back directly to you. May the pain festering in your stupid, sick mind stay with you and not affect anybody else. Try asking your God to heal *you* instead of attacking the East in God's name."

7

The Green Zone

Simon flew to Baghdad late in the day on September 8, 2014, staring forlornly out the window. The rising orange red moon reminded him of the dangers he'd soon be facing. In early August, ISIS invaded Yazidi villages south of Mt. Sinjar and captured the women for their sexual slavery system. The international community desperately sought ways to rescue the captured Yazidis. On September 2, ISIS released a video of Steven Sotloff, an Israeli citizen and American reporter, being beheaded in an unknown location, probably Syria. The day after Sotloff's beheading, President Obama deployed 350 more American troops to Baghdad to protect U.S. diplomatic facilities. Originally Simon was to go to Damascus to meet with Druze elders, but those plans changed in light of these recent events. Instead, he would meet with Mandaean elders at the al Rashid Hotel in the Green Zone. Simon thought of fire, blood, and human madness as he gazed at the moon bulging on the distant horizon.

He pulled down the window shade to watch a video of Teresa's first birthday party. Her birthday was coming up on September 23, but they celebrated it a few weeks early because he was leaving. The first shot was of three babies and their parents jamming the parlor. He chuckled to himself as he thought about Sarah. She'd insisted on honoring an old Irish custom used to celebrate the baby's survival of its first year: Irish parents baked a cake, placed it in the middle of a room on the floor, and then put the birthday baby down a few feet away. *Why would anybody bash their kid with sugar shock on their first birthday? Considering where I'm going tonight, maybe Sarah needed that old superstition.*

The birthday party was a riot. After Teresa blew out a single candle, Sarah put her down six feet from a carrot cake slathered with orange-flavored, butter-and-sugar frosting. Teresa stared quizzically at the inviting cake, and then she scuttled for it sideways on her butt like a speedy crab. The other babies squealed and squirmed in their parent's arms while Teresa took the first turn. She made it to the cake and raised her shaking hands and screamed. Then she mushed her hands into the sticky, yummy frosting, pulling them out to lick her fingers, squealing while smushing the gooey frosting all over her face! Peering through gooey cheeks and eyebrows, Teresa howled triumphantly. All three babies shoved away from their parents and crawled over to smash their hands into the cake to grab hunks to stuff in their faces and squish on Teresa. So it went, a very messy un-Jewish feast, the Irish way to show gratitude for a child's first healthy year of life.

Simon choked up thinking about when they said goodbye as a cab pulled up. Teresa had been extremely quiet and clingy the day before. Sarah took her out for a walk so she wouldn't see Simon pack. Sarah thought she'd be able to make her feel secure, but they both knew their little one would be terribly lonely without him. *Why should any baby have to endure separation? Will Sarah be able to handle it? Should I have taken this assignment?*

Later, he opened the shade again. The limpid opal moon had risen high above the thick red atmosphere. As they flew over Greece, he promised himself he'd take Sarah and Teresa to Athens someday to see the Acropolis. An image of Sotloff on his knees in an orange jumpsuit flashed through his mind; a skinny knife held in a menacing gloved hand close to his neck. *What was going through his mind at that moment, the poor bastard?* Sotloff's death must not be in vain; he risked his life so that Americans could learn more about Syria, exactly

Simon's intention. Simon nodded off thinking he knew a few people who wouldn't take the trouble to learn anything about Syria, namely the old fools who started the war in Iraq in the first place.

David made arrangements to visit Sarah and Teresa in Rome and travel with them to the Pierleonis' Tuscan home at the end of September.

David spent a few days with them in Rome, and then Matilda sent her driver to bring them to Tuscany. Passing through Rome's outer suburbs, Sarah relaxed for the first time since Simon left. She'd been afflicted with profound insecurity whenever she watched the news. The world really was going insane, a simplistic response to reality that she had managed to avoid until now. After Simon left, Teresa whimpered morosely a few nights, then she switched to laughing through tears while Sarah rocked her and told her stories.

"Well, Sarah, you seem to be doing well," David said thoughtfully. "Is that so?"

"Actually, it is quite awful," Sarah said searching David's clear gray eyes. "Teresa cried the first few days, now she is just sad. Maybe the next time he goes away she'll understand he's coming back; I hope so."

Wanting to switch to a happier track, David said, "What do you hear from Simon? How do you think he's doing?" David had heard from Simon a few times and knew he was suffering terribly without his family, not something he'd share with Sarah.

"When I talk with him," she replied more cheerfully, "he's excited about interviewing the Mandaean elders. He says they really appreciate him for telling their story, hoping his articles will influence U.S. policy makers and the public. He's often very lonely after a long day of work, but at least he feels safe in the Green Zone. He misses holding Teresa terribly. I tell him what she does each day, which seems to help."

"I'd love to know what he thinks about the Mandaeans," David replied. "I remember being curious about them when Iraq invaded Kuwait in 1990, the *Marsh Arabs,* right?"

"Yes, they were called the Marsh Arabs, people who lived for thousands of years in the southern Iraqi marshes, remnants of the people of ancient Babylon. They also fascinate me. John the Baptist was their great prophet, not Jesus. They are remnants of early Christianity, followers of Mani, a major interest of mine. Even though this assignment is hard for all of us, Simon and I share deep interests, which helps me cope."

"I know that," David responded warmly. "And I absolutely agree, it's important to report on these ancient religions. If they are forgotten in the middle of this mayhem and chaos, it would be a great tragedy."

Patting David's hand, Sarah sighed and began again. "The reason I can tolerate Simon being away and in danger is because we are all experiencing radical global transformation, a change of ages or eras. As this transition builds, nothing makes sense. We need to know what we were before to determine our future. If we lose our ancient heritage, we're lost."

Sarah felt encouraged and warmed when discussing what she cared about most. David was smart, elegant, and compassionate like Simon, making it easy to muse out loud with him. "David, are you aware I wrote my Ph.D. thesis on Marcion of Sinope, the first Christian heretic?" David nodded. "Marcion thought Christianity should be a totally new religion because the Jewish God, Yahweh, was the god of law while Jesus was a god of love. Judaism was the old religion, so using their scriptures tainted Christianity as a new religion. Simon has pinpointed major affinities between the Mandaeans and the Marcionites. He says interviewing Mandaean elders was like talking with Marcion two thousand years ago!"

David was drawn into the passion and theorizing. "How fascinating. What are the similarities?" *No wonder Simon fell in love with her . . .*

"The Mandaeans revere some of the prophets in the Hebrew Bible, but not Abraham because they thought he was immoral. Marcion also scorned Abraham, noting that he tried to kill his son, slept with his maid, and allowed the pharaoh to sleep with his wife." Sarah shook her head describing Abraham's sexual behavior. "The Mandaeans, a religion much older than Judaism, had the same opinion of Abraham. Since they existed at least four thousand years ago, they would have been in the Middle East when Abraham first showed up. We sure can see why Marcion wanted Christianity to start with a clean slate."

"Well, you know, Sarah, some people might say you are wallowing around in a lot of old stuff that doesn't matter anymore, but not me. We need to understand the past if anything is ever going to really change for the better. If Christianity is driven totally out of the Middle East, there will be major political and social implications, things Simon wants to write about. I'm proud of him for wanting to report on this. As for me, it's time for my nap."

Sarah settled into her room and went over to the narrow turret window to view Tuscan fields bathed in otherworldly golden light. Her heart quickened when she heard Teresa squealing at Matilda far below in the vineyard. She looked back into the room at the crib next to her bed wondering whether Armando once lay in it shrouded in hand-embroidered Tuscan lace. Pink, yellow, and periwinkle blue wildflowers had been lovingly arranged in the same vase that once held roses from Armando when he asked her forgiveness. The flowers made her ache for Simon. *He'd love to be here tonight.* As she went to the bedside table to pick up a novel, a light tap on the door had her turning around again.

It was Jennifer. "Hi, Sarah, am I bothering you? Please say so if I am." Sarah smiled warmly and held out a hand to lead her in, but she stayed by the door. "Come with me to see our apartments. I love it here; I want you to see how perfect this is for me so you can tell Simon all about it. I'm so happy, so happy I married Armando."

Sarah followed her out the double doors. They walked quietly down the long hall past the chapel to the other end where there was a thick chestnut door that she'd always wanted to open. Jennifer squeaked the old door aside and led them silently past the carved Renaissance door of the Pierleoni suite. They went to the opposite end of the large hall to an equally special door. "This is where we live! Isn't it amazing?"

The arrangements intrigued Sarah, since this was how she might be living if things had worked out differently. Of course, now all she cared about was whether Jennifer was happy. *Could any woman be happy with Armando?* Jennifer led her through a small entry into the rooms while chatting enthusiastically, and then they nestled into two comfortable chairs in front of the fireplace in a commodious parlor. "Matilda reupholstered these chairs for us. I love her taste, yet how could she have known me so well? Maybe it is because I like what Armando likes? I have been completely comfortable since we came back from Majorca. I'm a hardworking loner, so I don't miss people. This is like living in a dream, a fantasy becoming more real every day. Even though this family is very aristocratic, they aren't snobbish or aloof. They gracefully live with what has been theirs for hundreds of years and love sharing it."

"I'm so happy this feels right for you, especially happy you feel at home here so that you'll feel comfortable when Armando's away. This space is perfect for you, so elegant and authentic, yet also so cozy. Imagine if this wonderful fireplace could speak." Together they scanned enameled carvings of vines and plentiful grapes on side panels cut into the granite, and on the center below the mantle, a bucolic scene of a Tuscan cottage with a family, animals, and gardens. "I especially love your studio," she prattled on while she studied Jennifer's face, seeking the comfort of Simon's features in his sister. *Jen is a mystery woman, a romantic creature from the past who found her place in the present. She's so much more Semitic looking than Simon who resembles his father in body type and facial expressions. Eventually, Jennifer will look like Rose.*

"Oh Sarah, what a lovely contrast this is to the modern world. This is the first time I've felt secure and happy since I left my childhood home to go to Paris. But how are you doing being away from your own country and caring for a baby while Simon is far away? This must be terrible for you; I can't imagine it, really. I know you're strong, but are you doing okay?"

Sarah felt the ache in her heart sink in deeper. "I love him because he's doing what he needs to do, but it's not easy." Her heartache tended to ease when she focused on her work and caring for Teresa, yet for her health, she took note of the ache.

"I know what you mean. He's my only brother and I'm proud of him, but I'm terrified when I think about him over there, so I just don't. Oh, I'm sorry. That probably isn't helpful to hear. I know him, and know he has to do it. He never could ignore his responsibilities."

Sarah appreciated the love and support from Jennifer, despite her fears. Seeing this contrast with her own family's reaction led her to blurt out a thought she didn't know she harbored. "Jennifer, my father doesn't understand at all. He is in Opus Dei, a Catholic power group, and you know what? He's probably never thought about all the Christians in the Middle East! He probably doesn't even understand why they matter so much to Simon and me!"

"I know you and Simon have always been passionate about these ideas, but what is it specifically about some old Christian strains and ancient Middle Eastern religions that makes this so important to you?"

It was a relief to share more of this passion with her sister-in-law, so she went right to the heart of the matter. "Well, have you heard of the three Fatima Prophecies?" Jennifer responded with a blank stare. "In 1917, three young Portuguese girls were visited by an apparition of the Virgin Mary six different times on a hillside. She gave them three prophecies, which the oldest girl wrote down. The first two prophecies were accurate descriptions of the first and second world wars, things the girls could not possibly have dreamed up. Under pressure, Pope John Paul II opened the third one in 2000. Many people think he kept part of it secret because Cardinal Josef Ratzinger, who later became Pope Benedict, had said earlier that the third prophecy refers to dangers that threaten the Faith. The rumor is the prophecy says the faithful will leave the Church, an apostasy, and then Christianity will fall to Islam. If this is true, you can see why Simon is concerned about ancient

Christian strains being driven out of the Middle East by ISIS, a modern Exodus."

Jennifer was getting more than she'd bargained for. Her dark brown eyes opened wide as she tapped her chair arm with an index finger. Then she spoke so softly that Sarah strained to hear her cracking voice. "This is much worse than I thought. It *is* really dangerous for Simon to be there, isn't it? *You* care enough about these weird prophecies to support his choice to go there? Forgive me, I have to ask."

Sarah drew in a sharp breath staring into Jennifer's nervous eyes. "We all are suffering in these times and the worst is yet to come. You must be aware that Simon, Armando, Claudia, and I have spent much time discussing these issues? I'd love to have you join our little group because there is so much more behind why we feel as we do, good reasons for why Simon has taken such a difficult assignment. You understand Armando's paintings, his version of the apocalypse, so you'll relate to what we talk about. If the apocalypse has actually begun, then nobody escapes without pain. We all will get sucked into it, the *whirlwind*. This isn't something I would have said until after 2012, the crazy end date of the Mayan Calendar." Jennifer's face was blank. "This is a huge topic and it's lunch time. Come to our group discussions to talk about what's going on. Simon can't join us when he's gone, so you can stand in! Next time we get together with Claudia, will you join us?"

Jennifer felt a knot in her solar plexus thinking about meeting with Claudia and the group, but she had to get beyond petty jealousy. The only way to deal with Claudia was to get to know her better as soon as possible. The worst choice would be to have Armando meet with the group without her.

8

A Private Conversation

Pietro was upstairs in the Tuscan genealogy room sitting in a dark green leather chair. Unlike the large library in Rome with thousands of books that were the heart of the house, this room on the second floor was rarely used and mostly contained information about local Siena history and the Pierleoni family. Although hot during the day, at night cool breezes from a nearby ravine wafted pungent cedar aromas mixed with pine through the windows. The thick door creaked open.

"Good evening, Pietro," David said warmly as he looked curiously around at glassed cabinets and old trunks painted with fading symbols. Huge dark beams supported a faded painted ceiling with more arcane symbols. "What a charming room, very medieval. Was this a library?"

"Yes. When our family started to come here less in the winter, my great-grandfather moved the old books to our library in Rome where the temperature and humidity are more controlled. We think it was decorated in the 1400s since many of the symbols are medieval. Please take a seat," he said, indicating a faded purple velvet chair that looked very comfortable. As David settled in he continued, "I thought you might like a chance to talk about everything going on right now. I'm sure you are worried about Simon, but none of us want to talk about it too much around Sarah who is already so aware of the dangers. But we both know the news is not good. The U.S. is getting sucked back in with airstrikes in Syria and Obama announcing he intends to root out the terrorists. I know he's tried to get American troops out of Afghanistan and Iraq, but these internecine wars don't stop because the grievances go back centuries."

"You're a father, you understand how stressful Simon's work is for all of us."

"I believe I do," Pietro replied circumspectly. "I've never feared for Armando's life, and I hope I never will because he is my future, the continuation of my line and time itself. If I lost him, that part of me would be amputated. Simon is delving into disturbing and contentious Middle Eastern issues that go back millennia; the danger is real."

"It certainly is," replied David, both men thinking of all that had been happening in the region of late. Over the summer ISIS pushed out the Yazidis and other ancient Christian sects that had been in Iraq and Syria for many thousands of years. Some Yazidis escaped capture and fled to Kurdistan where the Kurdish president Barzani gave them refuge, some fled to the U.S. and Europe. The Yazidis used to have some protection through the Christian groups that stabilized the region, but Bush blew the lid off the ugly Islamic sectarian conflict when he invaded Iraq in 2003. This intensified tension for the Christians who were providing educational services, food, and health services in the region, and now that they were leaving. The fabric of society in Iraq and Syria was shredding.

Breaking them out of their reverie Pietro said, "I want to help in any way I can. Please tell me more about Simon's assignment."

"Simon went there to meet Christian leaders, to tell their story. Americans don't seem to realize many of these sects are Christian. The U.S. media refers to Yazidis as devil worshippers, which is demeaning and untrue, a distortion of one of the oldest religious groups in the world. Horrible cruelties are being inflicted on them that are barely noticed in the U.S., barbaric abuses that turn my stomach. Simon is focusing on the ancient religions that adopted early Christian practices, such as the Assyrians, Chaldeans, and Mandeans, to help Americans see that a Christian exodus is unfolding. I admire Simon for exposing this tragedy. But that doesn't reduce our family stress, especially Sarah's."

Pietro took note of David's determined, ironic smile, a purposeful man with an excellent mind. His intaglio ring set in fine gold caught Pietro's eye. "David, your ring has a beautiful carving. Is it meaningful?" A scaly snake biting its own tail was carved around the carnelian gem, the *oroboros*—the eternal symbol for the continuity of life and ever-renewing cycles of time. David drew his hand slightly back and said nothing. After a long and uncomfortable silence David said, "Well, yes, it's meaningful to me because it was my father's ring."

Pietro knew he'd stepped over a line, but he decided to reach out once more because the situation was dire. He wanted David to open up and share in order to know how best to support the family, yet he hated being intrusive. "David, if you will, please glance up at the ceiling to see our family crest."

David leaned back in the old velvet chair to look up and was very surprised to see a faded family crest with a flying swan on the top of an encircled lime green serpent biting its tail, the oroboros! His eyes came back down to Pietro's playful gray eyes. "Well, ahem, you got me. But before we talk about symbols, may I ask you something?"

"Of course."

"How do you feel about what Simon is doing? You and Matilda adore Sarah. You once hoped she would marry Armando, as I understand things?" Pietro nodded gravely. "Now you are enjoying our sweet baby girl. I want to know: Do you feel Simon is being fair with his family?"

Pietro was surprised by being directly brought into family affairs. *Oh well, I started the whole thing by asking him to join me here and then pointing out our crest on the ceiling. Why is he so closed?* Pietro turned his eyes to the leaded casement window as he paused momentarily. David, exceedingly on edge, waited.

"All right, I will be frank. I admire Simon for what he has chosen to do at this time; I would have done the same years ago. Part of why I asked you to see me tonight is because I can help your family. Sarah will always be a daughter to us, the Italian way—once you are one of us, you never get away. You won't either. Your son is Armando's closest male friend and your daughter his wife, so I would do anything for Simon. But my hands, well, are tied until I know more, especially from you. I asked you about your ring because I may know what it means; possibly you don't? If you will be forthcoming with me, you'd be surprised by what I can do."

David felt a low-grade terror rising in his chest. His father had been in Italy during the second world war and bought the ring in an antique store in Rome. His father never took it off when David was growing up in Manhattan's East Side. He gave it to David just before he died saying it was from a European secret society, The Brotherhood of the Serpent. On his deathbed he made David promise to never tell the secret. David wanted to give it to Simon to wear in the Middle East to protect him, but thought it might do just the opposite. "Let's talk more about Simon," David said in a slightly demanding way while putting his right hand on his leg unmasking the intaglio from Pietro's eyes.

"I can ask certain people in Rome to discuss Simon's situation with the highest officials in the U.S. Embassy. Simon could be as safe there as he would be at home. All you have to do is ask."

David's mind whirred. Feeling at a loss was very unusual, so he gave in as he read Pietro's kind eyes. Something moved deeply in the place in David's heart where he was utterly terrified about Simon's safety. He felt helpless. Never in his life, not even when he watched his father reduced to a skeleton from prostate cancer, had he felt so impotent. He didn't know what to do with the emotion. Pietro held his gaze to show sincerity. David was not good at accepting kindness or help because he'd spent his whole life giving it to others. Suddenly David snapped, "What is this, Pietro, a Faustian pact?"

Pietro gasped audibly. *He must have really suffered. Why can't he just let me in, let me in to help him at such a difficult time?* He clasped his hands nervously intertwining his fingers over his belly. "David, you *must* know that during the Inquisition in Italy many Jews were forced to convert to Catholicism? My ancestors converted to save their lives, so you and I share the same faith. Now this hideous pain is coming back because when ISIS takes over a Christian village, they persecute people hideously, just as we were once persecuted. This dredges up ugly memories. ISIS beheads those who don't align with their 'values,' especially journalists. And beyond that, your son is part of my extended family. This is not a Faustian pact; I simply want to help."

David was softening because he could see that Pietro would do anything for Simon, things he could not do himself. Being a Jew in America had meant being clannish, few people outside their close circle knew David well. He *had* to accept Pietro's help, but it was difficult for a man who unconsciously isolated himself from people who reached out to him; the inner dam burst. He replied very gravely, "Pietro, please excuse my coldness. Few have tried or been able to do anything for me. I've led a charmed life, had all the money, all the family support, so as an adult I did everything for everybody else. Your kindness overwhelms me, but it also demeans me, I am on guard. Again, please forgive me."

"I'm not going to let you get away with that," Pietro replied quietly. "My kindness does not reduce you in any way, it is only meant for your son." There was a long pause while they both listened to the clock ticking loudly. It reverberated in David's head as he wondered whether the maids wound it up every day.

"Pietro, I must share something with you that is very hard for me to speak about. Since you are so willing to protect Simon, I feel released from my father's dying demand. I will tell you about this ring, my father's last words." David felt like he was only ten years old, just before he developed his adult will.

"You do not have to do anything for me to help Simon," Pietro said warmly. "I could have just done it without telling you, and maybe I should have. But, suddenly you came to visit us here, which made me feel like I should do it with your permission. I'm going to do it right away, tomorrow. The Vatican is where I go for something like this because of their international immunity, a very powerful protection system."

David glanced up at the green serpent in the Pierleoni crest. "No, I know I should tell you. Things change with time, so what my father believed back in the 1950s probably isn't the point now. My father told me this ring signifies The Brotherhood of the Serpent. Does that mean anything to you?"

Pietro crossed his legs putting his hands on his knee, tilting slightly back. "It does not. I've been told the oroboros on the ceiling is the union between earth and sky, the union of chthonian and celestial principles, in our case the serpent and the swan. I've never heard of this 'Brotherhood' as you put it, but I suppose it makes sense there is a secret order of the snake. Come to think of it, I've heard things like that. I may be blind to it because I've always been much more interested in the celestial aspect of our crest—the swan in flight over the snake.

"I've been studying our swan's symbolism because I'll be sharing our family's history with Armando soon. I can't assume I'll be around forever. It goes back thousands of years and is a very complex and fascinating tale, but there is no time for that tonight. You've shared a secret that is very deep for you, so I hope to share some things with you that you can't get anywhere else, things you may be looking for. You and I must take time together because neither one of us can talk this way with most other people. It's our ages, you know, as well as our moldy class background and arcane initiations. I'm happy you'll accept my assistance, and rest assured, Simon will be safe. Although I do believe what will protect him the most is your belief that he is safe; remember that. These things don't work without trust. Simon also must *believe* he is safe."

Pietro had to take a deep breath sensing intelligence beyond comprehension in David's face. *Is this man a magus?* David placed his hand on Pietro's forearm triggering an electric shock that went from his arm to his brain. "This may surprise you, Pietro. Telling you what my father said to me has unburdened me. I don't know what The Brotherhood of the Serpent is, actually never really *wanted* to know. Now I realize as I sit in your library with the outrageous green serpent on your ceiling, I think my *father* laid a Faustian pact on me, not *you!* By imposing that ring on me when I was ten years old and then dying a few hours later, he made me feel like *I* was part of the Brotherhood! I didn't choose it then, don't now. Sometimes it has felt like a weird time lock in another dimension. By telling you and breaking the secret, I'm free. Thank you for my release as well as for guarding Simon, which I'm sure he can use."

Matilda came downstairs the next morning and walked through the kitchen into the sunny breakfast room. Stopping by the edge of the door, she listened to Sarah telling a story in a singsong voice to Teresa perched in a highchair:

"Long, long ago, three Wise Men came from the East, the mysterious land of magical birds in green trees. The Three Wise Men were astrologers, teachers who follow the stars.

"A baby was born, just like you, Teresa, a very special baby." Teresa chortled.

"The baby filled the sky with so much light that the astrologers followed this light right to a cave illuminated by the planet Venus.

"Light from the cave streamed out into the world creating a new universe of fishes, animals, and trees.

"And, the Sun streamed into this lovely world, light from the Divine.

"You are light, Teresa, I am light, and hey, here comes Matilda, and she too is light!"

Matilda came in and gave Teresa a kiss. When she saw Matilda, she pounded on the highchair tray and squawked. "I'll get her some berries and peaches from the kitchen. Why are you telling her this story? It's not Christmas."

"I've written a little book for her and illustrated it to help her understand where her daddy is. The Three Wise Men can come any-time, not just Christmas. Actually, that's the point of the story."

Next Jennifer strolled in draped in a soft robe looking sleepy and went to pour a cup of coffee. "Armando just amazes me. He got up at five this morning and went to his studio. I don't know how he does it."

"Oh, as you know, he loves to work," Matilda murmured. "It means he's happy."

Jennifer sucked down a jolt of caffeine. "I hope you don't mind me coming down in my robe? I'll be getting dressed for breakfast, but I was too lazy to make coffee upstairs, so I came down to get some. Nobody is usually here this early."

"Wait until you have a baby," Sarah said with a touch of irony in her voice while looking at Jennifer who was very pretty without makeup. She looked like she'd had a long night of sex; Matilda was thinking the same thing.

"I can't wait. So I'll take my coffee and go wake up. See you at breakfast." Jennifer made her way back to her suite and softly closed the door. She walked into the parlor filled with sweet aromas from the olive trees, sat down in her favorite chair, and crossed her legs languorously.

Where did I go? He made me come again and again. I hope nobody heard me scream. The energy moving through my body was like an earthquake, never thought I'd feel anything like that. He told me he loved me over and over, kissed my feet calling me a goddess. He worships me and pulls me out of myself; I don't know where I go. I felt like I was sailing out the window and traveling up to a star. Where? Sirius? Once I got there, the council was waiting for me, the beings I met when I was a child. Armando, how did you take me there?

Armando was in his studio poised adroitly with a brush tipped in red paint. Fire released by rapturous sex was coursing through his body. She'd finally surrendered. He couldn't believe the force of the shaking release in her body. He could have gone on for hours but finally she was exhausted. He didn't come because he wanted to paint, and now sublime Eros shivered in his arms and hands. He painted and painted while getting a new insight: *My God, I'm going to be faithful to her like my father is to my mother. She's my partner. I don't want anybody else; I only want her. Jennifer, you've freed me! I'm free to create and free to be. I love my wife; I want her pregnant. Tonight, when I have her again, I'll make sure I come; it is time.*

9

A May–December Love Affair

During the summer of 2014, the easy closeness Claudia and Lorenzo found at the wedding deepened. Claudia wondered whether he was a brother or sister from a past life. Lorenzo let that idea pass, since he wanted to have sex with her. They were intellectual equals, just what she most wanted and perfect for Lorenzo after living so long with a bored wife. Lorenzo's library had archaeological and anthropological books she'd always wanted to read, so in the evening she read them in the alcove while gazing into the garden. He'd be in the back area researching the archetypal and historical fields his clients wandered into. His clients tended to be artistic, neurotic, very imaginative, and sensual, and as they explored the deepest recesses of their complex minds, doorways opened in Lorenzo's consciousness. He saw what they were seeing as if he was in their movie. Occasionally he emerged from the back with tea to share stories with her, since she was fascinated by the intricate landscape of the human psyche.

In wild and delightful contrast to his world, Claudia ran a high fashion boutique all day. She amused him with hilarious stories about rich Roman women and their insane affairs. She was a great mimic after a few glasses of wine, and often he thought his ribs would break from laughing at these unfamiliar aspects of Roman life. He'd not paid attention to the world of fashion, yet now Claudia's dramatic beauty intrigued him. She was in the material world, he more in the psychic, yet what really was the difference? Meanwhile, he was as horny as a twenty-year-old while aloof Claudia teased him. Very aware of her convoluted sexual history, he waited patiently. They both knew the time would come, so they just had fun all summer. Perhaps a shift would come in the fall, perhaps not.

They rarely saw other friends, not even Sarah. Claudia called once in early October after Simon had gone back to the Middle East. They chatted and teased about the instant attraction to Lorenzo, then promised to visit, but both women were very busy.

Actually, Lorenzo had been up to something odd the last few weeks—shopping for all kinds of things, not being available until late. Then one Saturday morning he called declaring it was time for something fun. He instructed her to come over midafternoon, no need to dress up. Claudia knocked on the door at 3 p.m., tingling with curious anticipation.

Lorenzo opened the door and swept her inside. It had been hot all day, so she was wearing a light-weave cotton jumpsuit that plunged in the back. Lorenzo was certainly acting strangely: she could swear he was leering at her. He took her left hand, spun her around, and then moved back slightly to take in the full view. "You are especially ravishing today! I can't keep my hands off you." He'd kissed her before, passionately, so she didn't resist when he pulled her adeptly into his chest barely covered by a white linen shirt. He wrapped his arms around her and began to explore her open back making her shiver deliciously. His cologne was pungent when he nuzzled into her neck, almost too sensual. "Wait till you see what I have to show you." He kissed her neck up to her right ear and then moved his open mouth back down to her collarbone causing another shiver.

"Lorenzo, what has gotten into you today?" she said pulling away, running her fingers through her hair.

"Come, Claudia, come with me." Mystified, she took his hand as he led her back through the dining room to the bedroom he'd once shared with his wife. She hadn't seen the room since they'd cleaned it out together, locked the door, and he moved into his son's monkish room. She thought he might be having some painting done, but when she asked, he wouldn't tell her. He opened the door and led her in. The once adequate room was now large! He'd knocked out the back wall to the garden and extended the room by putting in French doors out to a terrace. Filmy sheers obscuring glimpses of gardens and high walls beyond waved in the breeze. He'd found a large carved bed from Morocco and dressed it with ethnic fabric and voluminous pillows. An inviting cozy area with a gas fireplace had two cushy chairs, a coffee table, and a marble Aphrodite. He'd even broken into his daughter's room for walk-in closets and expanded the bathroom; a luxurious tub sunk deep into white marble beckoned.

"Fit for the Mata Hari, don't you think? I did it with the antique dealer who took the old dining room crap out of here; never had so much fun in my life!" Lorenzo's eyes sparkled with childlike joy watching her pleased expression. He drew her close again and reached around her back and said in a compelling, sweet voice, "Will you?"

His delicate hands roamed her back as a strap fell off her shoulder. She watched his eager eyes as her top slipped down slowly over a perfectly shaped, substantial breast. "Yes, yes, I will," she whispered.

It was easy to join their bodies because they already knew each other in so many other ways, no hesitation, no self-consciousness, and no reserve. They found a whole new way to talk to each other during that humid October afternoon. It had been a long time since either had a lover, and neither of them had found the right person until this moment. Libras always seek the perfect partner but rarely find one, so this mutual harmony felt destined. She murmured, "You play my body like a fine musical instrument."

"Yes, exactly what I was doing, since that is what you are."

∽

He'd prepared artichoke lasagna in advance. They started with a delicious Puntarelle salad, slightly bitter and crisp with a hearty red wine. "This is perfect, just the thing to share after becoming lovers. It was so easy, as if we'd always been together; I feel cherished."

"You are my dear, and we were wise to take our time. I needed to be completely free of Eleanora to share love with you. I will say a few things that will go forever in to the past: I would not have married her if she hadn't gotten pregnant, but I *want* to marry you. I'm too old for you but I don't care. I love you, so I don't care. You are exquisite. My clients all wonder why I've lightened up so much; it shows in everything I do. You bless me, Claudia; I haven't lived until now. We will share a thousand lifetimes. I've always had a vision of you, and when I saw you in that wacky peach dress, I knew it was you! You knocked me over at that wedding; I'm only standing back up today."

A few days later, Claudia was reading a book on super-string theory and the end of time. The phone rang. Armando asked her to come over to join Sarah who was arriving that night, it was time for their discussion group.

Armando and Jennifer greeted Sarah when she came into the library where a small fire had taken the dampness away and was reflecting golden light on the books. "So good to see you! Simon loves this room. He'd be so happy if he could join us tonight."

Jennifer took Sarah's hand and studied her face, lovely as always, yet now more thoughtful. *I'd love to photograph her again.* "You look well, Sarah; thank you for coming."

Claudia arrived and Jennifer took her hand, absolutely determined not to be jealous, but Claudia's hand was limpid, making Jennifer's belly clutch. "You look exquisite, Claudia. Thank you for coming." Claudia was dressed in a black satin jumpsuit with a plunging neckline set off by a large silver and bone pendant resting heavily on her taut and muscular chest.

Claudia's gaze swept the room while she held Jennifer's clammy hand. The regal library with the family lineages of Italian nobility gracing the walls always impressed Claudia. *Hmmm . . . bloodlines . . .* her eyes returned to Jennifer as she said, "I love this room because here I would never run out of things to read. My boutique bores me to death. So do you love living here?" She wondered why Jennifer was so nervous. *What's she afraid of? I suppose it's challenging to deal with your new husband's old lover, but please get over it.*

Armando was watching closely: Claudia was dressed to kill as usual and Jennifer looked crushed. "Come here, Jen," he called warmly. "Sit with me on the loveseat. Sarah, that chair is for you, and Claudia, that one for you." He placed Claudia as far away from Jennifer as possible, not realizing it meant Claudia couldn't avoid bumping his ankle. They all sat down as directed, yet even as they started talking his mind was trying to wander off—back to his painting, back to the worry about the reception it would receive at the upcoming art exhibit.

"Jen," Sarah began, "to catch you up, you need to know about the end of the Mayan Calendar."

"Yes. Simon ranted about it a few years ago calling it New Age nonsense, so when it was in the media during 2012, I blew it off. But, my father, who is nobody's fool, was interested. So, what's the big deal about the Mayan Calendar?"

Sarah gestured over to Claudia and as Jennifer's gaze followed Sarah's finger, the motion of crossed legs placed Claudia's sexy ankle very close to Armando's linen pants. Claudia arched her back like a big cat and peered at Jennifer. "I'll summarize it briefly, it is complex so stop me if you have questions. A Swedish biologist and Maya researcher, Carl Johan Calleman, analyzed a calendar found in Coba, a Maya site in Mexico. It goes back *billions* of years, and in it he discovered nine cycles of evolutionary acceleration that all functioned simultaneously once they got started. Supposedly these cycles all culminated on October 28, 2011, and then transformed into frequency waves."

"But, I thought the big date was 2012?" Jennifer broke in.

"Yes, that's right. December 21, 2012, is the date most often mentioned. But, the calendar that date is based on is merely the Sixth Wave in Calleman's system, the development of patriarchal civilization over five thousand years. People got into fights over the right end date, and during 2012 their squabbling drew attention away from people who think this *was* a significant moment in time, such as we do. Anyway, reality radically shifted in 2011/2012, and the *meaning* of this shift is what concerns us."

Jennifer was confused, and she felt like Claudia was talking down to her. Still, she engaged with courage. "Okay, maybe something changed then? After all, the world is spinning out of control in the Middle East, and I'm not happy my brother is there. Sorry, Sarah, I don't mean to say it so harshly."

The conversation gravitated to Sarah while Claudia's sexy foot brushing Armando's calf had Jennifer's attention. *Why does she act like that? Makes me feel crazy!*

Armando pushed back in his seat to listen to Sarah. "It's okay, Jen, I have to live with it. Remember when I mentioned the Fatima Prophecies to you in Tuscany? Well, Simon is in the Middle East exactly when the Third Prophecy may be coming true! Islam is becoming very powerful. So, connecting the Maya date, perhaps we are in a time of revelation. We must strengthen our minds to avoid being sucked into the *whirlwind* that always comes at the end of an age, in this case the end of Pisces. During these last two thousand years, the religions of Abraham have spread all over the world. Factoring in the 2012 ending as the completion of five thousand years of patriarchy, we need to reach back into Earth's religious roots, the mother goddess."

"Certainly," Claudia chimed in. "We must recover the goddess in these troubled times, don't *you* agree Armando?"

Jennifer, who was feeling crazy, made a huge effort to control her facial expression. *Why does she always have to ask him? Bitch!* Armando felt her rising heat when her arm rubbed his while he thought about what to say. "Well, to tell you the truth, I don't know, since I am totally obsessed with the religious themes from Abraham."

"Armando," Sarah broke in. "I think you need to be careful about obsessions when madness flourishes in the world. Abraham arrived in the previous age change—four thousand years ago when the Age of Taurus ended and the Age of Aries began, the age of organized warfare. I don't admire Abraham, and neither did many people back then. The Bible characterizes him as a user of women who was willing to sacrifice his own son. He is the great patriarch whose God has ignited religious wars all over the known world. I love your paintings, but these juicy archetypes might make you go crazy."

Armando listened attentively, as did Jennifer, who also had covert attention on Claudia's every move. *Here I sit with the two women Armando loved, my brother's wife and Armando's old lover. Why am I so jealous of Claudia when Sarah is the one he wanted to marry? What's wrong with me? I'm the one who is crazy.*

"But, Sarah," Armando replied. "I have to take what my muse sends me; if I get rational, I can't paint. If you keep going at me, little miss smart theologian, I'll get *more* obsessed with Abraham. I'll have all three major religions after my royal ass, just like they'll be after yours! Abraham did everything bad he could think of back then, but in our time the Catholics have come up with something even worse—pederasty!"

This statement coming from Armando created a break in the conversation giving Jennifer a chance to go to the powder room to collect herself. Sitting on the toilet staring at black-and-white tiles on the floor, she fumed. *Pull yourself together! Armando is going to know you're jealous.*

After the discussion meeting broke up, Armando took her back to the library for a cognac. "Jen, you can be honest with me. I think you're jealous of Claudia! I noticed it up in Tuscany, and I could feel it again tonight. What's the matter? There's no reason to be jealous of anybody," he said kindly.

"I've never felt this way before. I can't stop it; it's horrible. When she brushed your ankle with that sexy shoe, I almost died. I wanted to claw her to pieces."

"When she brushed my pants with her shoe, I was very annoyed," he replied in a matter-of-fact tone. "You should know that. What's the matter with you?" Suddenly he was irritated.

Hearing that tone just made it worse, since Claudia was the problem, not her. Bitch! Cunt! "Maybe if you tell me more about your love affair with her, it will help. When was it? Did you love her deeply? How long did it last?"

"But, Jennifer," he said, "I wanted to tell you about my past before I married you and you wouldn't let me. Now you're bringing it back to haunt me, and that is not fair! You said you didn't want me to tell you because then you'd have to tell me about yours, and you won't. Maybe you're jealous because of some weakness in *you* not me?" he said in a mocking tone. The chime in the grandfather clock rang midnight.

Rage boiled in her mind, acid burned her gut. *Who the fuck does he think he is? Fuck you, Armando!* "Okay, Armando," she snarled. "I'll stick to our deal; I *can* stuff it." She crossed her arms and glared at him.

Not liking what he saw, he studied her tortured and confused face. "Think of when we make love. Do you think a man who makes love like that to you wants other women? Grow up. I can't *stand* jealousy. It's spiteful and toxic, bitter, chaotic, and nasty. Envy doesn't serve you well, so *stop* it! You have everything to be happy about; you worry me," he said in a concerned voice stripped of reserve.

She knew he loved her and wouldn't very much longer if she couldn't control her irrational and insulting jealousy. *But, what did they do together? How did they make love? What did he feel when he gazed into those seductive brown eyes? Bitch!* She said in a squeaky voice, "How many *years* were you her lover?"

"Ten, but *damn* you, you're breaking your own rules. How many lovers did *you* have before we met? Were they all men or did you have a few women? Did you enjoy a *ménage a trois*? Did *you* seduce married men? You can't have it both ways!" He was angry and tense.

The rage burning in her mind turned her gut into acid. She struck out feebly and almost ripped his fine linen shirt with a high-pronged cocktail ring. White light blasted her mind in a furious explosion—rage. Her face contorted as he grabbed her wrists, holding them tightly, making her body twist. She felt like a little fool. "Stop it, you bastard! Just stop it!"

Armando glared at her enraged red face, and then he felt it, *the lizard!* His shoulder blades got hot and started extending out, his cock got instantly hard. His groin filled with fire as he exploded with power while twisting her arms backward. It hurt. "I'll show you what I can do with my cock when you act like a brat. Spread 'em baby, give it to me."

He seemed to expand and get taller when he wrenched her arms. She twisted herself loose, now afraid, which gave her strength. She rubbed her arms, which hurt terribly, and screamed, "No, Armando, no, not like that. We'll lose everything we've found. Stop, stop, *help* me!"

He heard it when she said she needed help. The only thing he could think of was Lorenzo as he released her arms and the lizard deflated. "Perhaps Lorenzo can help you with this jealousy if you'll go to him. You need to figure out what's wrong because you're acting crazy. And I'm not stable enough myself yet to be the one to help you. You're unhappy and triggering me. I'm sorry for my reaction. I've had to work way too hard to gain control of myself, and you're better than jealousy. You're not a fool, and we all need help sometimes. And who knows, you might already be pregnant. You need help."

She sat down in her chair and reached for the cognac. "Right; I don't know what's wrong with me. I hate jealousy but I can't control this right now. Claudia is your friend, Sarah's friend, and I want to get along with her. I know you don't want her, yet I wanted to kill her the minute I saw her. I wanted to dismember her like a harpy. I will get help. I still think I was right about the two of us keeping our past to ourselves. If you did tell me things, I'd probably be more jealous. I need professional help. But your behavior is unacceptable too. If you can't control your temper and emotions, I certainly wouldn't want you around a child, or myself for that matter."

He surveyed her distraught eyes as she rubbed her bright red wrists.

The lizard's hot passion terrified him, and he felt badly about hurting her. *Thank God I never told her what I did to Claudia. If she knew, she'd lose her mind, poor thing. Thank God she blocked me from sharing the truth last year. I don't know what's torturing her from her past, but Lorenzo can help. Thank God for Lorenzo, the man who keeps the secrets in Rome.*

10

Dinner in Rome

On a cool October morning, Lorenzo was in his office in the Trastevere thinking about Claudia while sitting at his large desk covered with an assortment of ancient sacred objects he used in his practice. *In five months I've gone deeper with Claudia than I did during my thirty-five years with Eleanora. Oh, how little I understood my clients' marriages and love affairs.*

He was passing his left hand slowly over the ancient objects on his desk to detect any magnetic attraction from the divine mind. *Who is Claudia?* He slipped out of linear space and time like quicksilver repelling glass. Passing his hand slowly over carved crystals and small ancient statuettes, he detected heat in his palm over a large turquoise scarab that had been found in the tomb of the famous Eighteenth Dynasty vizier, Rekhmire. He picked it up and cradled it in his left hand where it filled his palm as he ran his right index finger over hieroglyphs on the bottom—exotic symbols flashed in his brain. *Scarabs symbolize resurrection, attaining a whole new life after one has lived and then died. Yes, I was dead in my marriage. Now with Claudia, I am alive and connected. When I walk Rome's streets, I pass the living dead, yet a few are luminous and diaphanous, even transparent.*

Many years ago, Lorenzo analyzed Domenico Chigi, a brilliant Egyptologist at the Vatican Museum. The analysis had been profound and affected both of them. As a parting gift, Chigi gave him the valuable scarab saying, "This scarab is encoded with the star ascension codes that were still understood during the Eighteenth Dynasty. The pharaoh used it to traverse out to the Orion star system. Someday, you're going to ascend and this scarab will guide you." Lorenzo put the scarab back on its velvet pad, wondering what it revealed about Claudia. *Maybe I'm ascending with her?* The phone rang.

"Hello, Lorenzo, dear. I hope I'm not interrupting?" Claudia said sweetly. She rarely called; however today she knew he didn't have clients.

"Of course not. I was just thinking about you, and your phone call verifies the answer to my question. You and I knew each other during the Eighteenth Dynasty in Egypt, a time when many people could travel through all nine dimensions guided by the Heliopolitan mysteries. Right after that, the corridors to many worlds were severed."

"What a lovely thing to say on a chilly Sunday morning, but I'm calling about something mundane. Simon is back from Iraq and I wonder whether we might have them for dinner as our first guests? It's time for us to begin sharing our love. If we invite them for dinner, can we have them at your house, since you are more equipped for dining than I am? I want them to see your home."

"A wonderful idea! I'd love to have them if you will cook with me. Yes, let's invite them this weekend."

Sarah picked up the phone while having breakfast with Simon and Teresa and listened to Claudia's excited voice. She answered while Simon listened. "We'd love to have dinner with you. I thought so, something *is* going on."

"Yes, of course it is. We can't wait to see you both!"

Sarah put the phone down looking knowingly at Simon, who had heard everything. They laughed as they decided to leave their daughter in the care of the playgroup parents that owed them some childcare favors. This way they could be sure their toddler didn't tear their friend's home to pieces, a perfect adults' night out.

Simon and Sarah parked their small Fiat on the Via Nicola Fabrizi and walked down a stone pathway marked by the number nine. The fall evening was balmy and aromatic with eucalyptus spice from a nearby grove refreshing the dank odors of the Tiber. Simon gasped at Lorenzo's imposing entrance. "What a grand villa, just what I'd expect of the famous analyst. The gargoyles are fabulous. Ooooh!"

"Yes," Sarah replied. "The house must be at least a few hundred years old. Just think, we were there the day they met; Claudia was stunning that day."

Claudia opened the heavy door to lead them in. "It's three stories, and Lorenzo occupies the first floor and rents out the upper apartments. As far as we know, it was a commercial building in the late Middle Ages and was converted to a mansion in the eighteenth century. It suits Lorenzo because he loves Italian high style. He got it for an affordable price almost forty years ago when this side of the Trastevere was a slum. I love the way he designed his living space. The taxes are exorbitant, but the rent covers them. The bottom floor is very private because the grounds and gardens are reserved for us. Our favorite room is the library, which was once the main salon, so let's go there first." She led them to a sitting area with a fireplace and large window on one side, a bay-window alcove on the other, and the area beyond packed with stacks of bookcases. They craned their necks to view elaborately carved moldings that divided the high ceiling into geometrical frescoes of brightly colored mythological scenes.

Simon said, "I think I can make out the four seasons up there? This must have been a cardinal's house or the house of a wealthy merchant. What a great library for an analyst!"

Sarah surveyed the enchanting high ceiling, turning when Lorenzo walked in, anxious to have a look at him. She'd only met him briefly at the wedding, and he had looked like an old man, very distinguished, but still, old.

"Hello, Sarah," he said enjoying her excited face. "Isn't this room great?"

"Oh, yes, I'm so impressed," she responded while looking him over,

Lorenzo's library

the man who was now her dear friend's lover. He was ruggedly hand-some with a face animated by clear amber eyes with gray flecks and a friendly smile. He was fit, healthy, and very alert.

To Simon, Lorenzo looked twenty years younger than at the wed-ding. He was aware he'd lost his wife the year before, so maybe he'd gotten over it. Or maybe he was looking great because he was in love. Simon took his warm hand. "Hello, Lorenzo. It's so thoughtful of you to invite us. Your home is more marvelous than I could have imagined. You were so smart to buy it when you did. You can't touch a building like this in Rome these days."

"Right," Lorenzo replied smiling. "We raised our family here, which was ideal. It felt sinful to have it all to myself until Claudia came along. She's my frequent visitor and the house has welcomed her." He took Claudia's hand showering her with a glowing appreciative smile; obvi-ously he adored her. Claudia returned his gaze with total openness, an expression Sarah had never seen before. The clarity suffusing her face amazed Simon, who had never seen her glow with joy, certainly not when he dated her. In those days, when nobody was watching, her face, though beautiful, was apprehensive. "Yes," Lorenzo went on. "My life changed when I met Claudia. I live in a new world now, a world of joy and love. Just when I thought everything was all over, this beautiful lady came to me."

Sarah soaked in her friend's happiness. *After everything she's gone through, finally she has what she deserves, a brilliant partner.*

They sat down at a large planked table in a cavernous room with ancient dark beams and satiny white plaster walls, a regal and earthy space. Sarah asked, "Was this always a dining room?"

"Well, no," Lorenzo replied. "The original family, the di Benincasas, wove tapestries in this room. We made it into the dining room because I like the beams and the worn brick floor. This house was like a labyrinth, so it was fun to make it into apartments many years ago. I used the back storage area for the bedrooms, my kitchen is where they dyed thread, and my library was the sales room for their tapestries. The two upper floors each have four small, charming apartments, easy to manage because nobody ever moves out once they get one. The building goes back at least to the 1400s. We think the fancy library ceiling was plastered and painted in the 1800s when somebody had a lot of money."

The hosts brought out one steaming dish after another. Simon poured wine while Sarah sat peacefully as the table filled up with bowls of pasta, salads, bread, and a clay covered casserole with four steaming lobsters. They ate while chatting about the summer, and eventually they were ready for serious conversation as Sarah said, "Lorenzo, since you study archetypes and symbols, are you familiar with Plato's Great Ages?" Lorenzo nodded to indicate he knew about the 26,000-year cycle of precession with each Great Age around 2,160 years long, changing fields that inspire human cultures to develop its themes. Sarah continued, "Well, during the Age of Pisces these last two thousand years, humans contacted the divine through religion. Yet, as the Aquarian Age flows in now, somehow we will access divine consciousness on our own. What I wonder is, have you detected these ages in your client's minds? That is, do people have an inborn knowledge of the Great Ages, a cultural timeline?"

"Well," he responded thoughtfully, "what an intriguing question. Let me put it this way. When my clients go within, they discover rich and symbolic interconnected data. They actually do describe the symbols and archetypes of the Great Ages, come to think of it. For the last ten years or so, more and more clients have been describing the Waterbearer, the Aquarian symbol of a man tipping a jug of water and pouring it on the ecliptic, the apparent path of the sun through the stars. Your question fascinates me because when the Waterbearer shows up in a session, it tends to pour the water on the aspect of the client's life that is undeveloped. To offer a mundane example, recently a client saw himself pouring water over a startled golden retriever. It was so simple—he needed a dog! My clients know what they need because their psyche tells them. Yes, the great turning wheel of the ages—*Hamlet's Mill*—does seem to be an aspect of their minds. As for me, I'm *sick* of the Age of Pisces! Religious wars these days disgust me; ISIS is barbaric, and the Western Crusades are inane!"

"I agree with you. The battles over religions are dredging up all the worst Piscean elements," Claudia interjected thoughtfully. "Lorenzo, I've noticed that symbols can drive people mad. They find unusual things within and then begin to sing to odd tunes while the people around them begin to think they're nuts. And, if I didn't believe war will end eventually, I would go mad myself."

"True, my love, and the reason I'm in business. During times like these, people need to sort out their inner urgency to maintain their sanity. Analysis of our psyches seems to be a necessity when the Great Ages shift, exactly what Jung came to believe when he detected the early Aquarian vibrations coming in a hundred years ago. Such a genius he was! He could see that two thousand years ago, people *anticipated* the Age of Pisces because the Pythagorean and Greek Mystery schools were guiding people by the Great Ages. That's why people were waiting for a messiah, and some used mushrooms and hallucinatory drugs to probe their psyches for the signs of Pisces. Back then many people still accessed many dimensions, yet Jung could see that people in his times had lost this sense of the recurrent changing times; they were lost as people are now. These days people use drugs to get high but learn nothing from the experience, and very few explore themselves within or receive initiation from wisdom schools."

Sarah leaned forward betraying her excitement. "Yes! That's *exactly* why I'm delving into what was going on when the Age of Aries began to shift into Pisces around 200 BC, a time when many people could still feel the higher and lower dimensions penetrating their realm. They were obsessed with psychic boundaries and sought personal liberty by accessing other worlds. This rich cultural period ran the gamut of Greek and Roman licentiousness, Jewish righteousness, Stoic self-control, and potent alchemical experimentations like the Eleusinian Rites in Greece and the last vestiges of the initiation schools in Egypt. However, when the early Piscean vibrations flowed in, the powers-that-be manipulated people to control their access to higher and lower realms by herding them into religions devoid of the ancient wisdom. How do you handle their repression and the change of the ages in analysis?"

"Not easily, it's gotten worse with time, and I'm thrilled you are exploring the previous change of the ages. I'm having trouble keeping my own sanity during this shift, yet quantum physics guides me. As the Aquarian archetype intensifies, quantum principles are making sense to more and more people. Turning to science, the Age of Aquarius inspires us to seek our personal uniqueness in the cosmos again, very much like lone particles on a trajectory that are unaware of all the other particles. Regarding particle/wave duality, when my imagination ignites, it feels good to flip into a wave. These new perspectives boggle the logical mind—exactly what we need! Wave consciousness is working miracles for more and more people, yet we all struggle to understand the quantum world, even physicists do, because we have been mind-controlled by religions that constricted spirituality into a narrow channel for two thousand years. But now the proverbial Pandora's lid is lifting and we're flooding out of the channel."

Claudia broke in. "Quantum entanglement describes how couples join. Lorenzo and I bumped into each other at the wedding like two Leibniz monads rolling along solo. From that moment on, it was impossible to do anything but be together, simply impossible! I know the same thing happened to you two, yet now you are forced to be apart most of the time. How does that work for you? Does quantum physics have any comfort for you in your situation?"

"I'll take that one," said Simon in an articulate voice. "The model for what Sarah and I are experiencing *is* quantum entanglement. When I'm somewhere doing something, say having a meeting in two weeks with Copts in Upper Egypt, Sarah might be here in Rome investigating some obscure early Christian philosophy. We are in very close communication regarding where we are and when, and what we think about. This entangles and weaves our lives, gives us meaning. Like the two of you, we bumped into each other on a magical Roman day when nothing was expected; it just happened and everything changed. Real love *is* quantum entanglement—communication through light waves and many dimensions that create reality—and then we can find our other half. All we have to do is keep the fire burning, which we easily do because we are *not* merely separate particles. The quantum helps me make sense of the world, not easy in the Middle East. When Sarah and I are in wave form, not in separate particle form, we are one."

"And," Sarah added with determination, "there is more to it than that. In ancient Egypt, the great mystery was the triad—Father/Mother/Child—as the cultural ideal, for example, Osiris/Isis/Horus. I have it easier than Simon because I live with Teresa, the magical bridge between us as parents. Triads—links through the generations as we move through the Great Ages—pass wisdom down through time. *Our child opens the door to the coming age.* As the Aquarian Age arrives, parents and grandparents can see that each child is born with more knowledge than preceding people. When in the presence of our child, we flow in the waves of the new time. Simon flows with me, so even when he is away, he still is with Teresa in the now. When I'm with her, he is with us; she amazes us. We can see that evolution is proceeding on schedule even though the structures of the world are devolving at this time."

The cavernous room fell into a delicious pregnant silence. Sarah's angelic face radiating knowledge and love captivated Lorenzo. *My God, she is a saint. This is what painters try to capture when they paint the Madonna.* Claudia gazed into Sarah's green eyes, clear and peaceful as a high mountain spring. She recalled that day Sarah cradled her, held her like a mother, after she'd told the story of Armando's hideous abuse.

11

Jasmine

Jennifer's first appointment with Lorenzo was in early November. She explained there was no reason to feel jealous, yet she suffered irrational attacks and terrible anger whenever a certain lady was near her husband. "She was his lover for many years, it ended, but I go crazy when she's around. Once I married him, we were all supposed to be friends, but I want to *mutilate* her."

Lorenzo knew it must be Claudia as personal thoughts ran through his mind. *If it's Claudia, I'm not sure I can help. She's going to realize I'm in love with Claudia, and would that interfere? Yet, she may destroy her marriage without my help. What do I do?*

"Jennifer," he said in a kind and thoughtful voice, "I've been thinking while you've been describing your feelings. I've helped clients get beyond jealousy, a horrible emotion that can tear up your life. Armando loves you; it would be crazy to let this go on. But, there is something going on in my life that could be a problem . . . I may I know this woman. I need you to tell me her name to make sure."

"Her name is Claudia Tagliatti," Jennifer said in a hesitant suspicious voice. *Why does he need to know her name?*

"That is what I thought. Claudia and I have fallen in love, and we are very serious about each other. You may recall we met at your wedding?" Jennifer sat bolt upright. She didn't know what to say, so he continued. "This is not necessarily a problem, since often when one is plagued by jealousy, it is not actually caused by the person that makes them feel jealous. In this case, I really don't think so. But I may be too close to the situation. That is what you must decide."

"Dr. Giannini," Jennifer replied respectfully after a pause. "Claudia is not after Armando, and I am sure Armando is not attracted to her. Yet, still I am tortured. It's driving me mad! You probably are the *best* person for me because you know all about his past and know their love affair is long dead, so dead that now they are dear friends. I can easily see why you love her after seeing you together at my wedding; I wondered then. Your relationship with her doesn't matter. I realize it is really about me. These irrational feelings terrify me."

"All right, now that this tie is acknowledged, we can work together to release you from this obsession. The meaningful patterns just below the surface of your mind will amaze you. You are safe and private here, your time to consider things that disturb you just when you should be so happy. You have your whole life ahead of you—children, travel, being a Pierleoni. Please recline here so we can get started."

Jennifer lay back on the dark green analyst's couch listening to Lorenzo's compassionate voice gradually going deeper and then becoming hypnotic. "Now Jennifer, please call me Lorenzo because we are friends and I'm here to help you. I'd like you to tune in to a scene with Armando when you felt jealous of Claudia; please just say the first thing that comes into your mind. Doesn't matter what it is: a color, an animal, a person, anything. You may close your eyes if you like."

Jennifer closed her eyes when she felt the air in the room thicken. Street sounds and screaming seagulls drifted off and away . . . A raven gurgled deep in its throat, drifted away . . . She went back to the first time she felt jealous, the day they had lunch with Claudia in Tuscany after Claudia had been alone with Armando in his studio. She visualized Claudia's face in the dining room. "I hate her."

"Why?" Lorenzo asked in a curious voice.

"I hate her because she's beautiful," she said nastily.

Lorenzo reached for a clear tall quartz crystal that had a thin shank topped by a larger tip that looked like a crystal penis. It fit exactly into his left hand as he rubbed the shaft. "Is that all?"

"I hate her because she slept with him."

Lorenzo reached for a shorter crystal also shaped like a penis and gripped it in his right hand. There sat the famous Lorenzo Giannini with a crystal penis in each hand with his thumbs rubbing the heads, a reason to sit invisibly behind his clients. "Jennifer, I sense you know something more about why you feel this way. What is it?" His voice was silvery and dripping with curiosity.

A sickeningly sweet aroma pervaded the room that made Jennifer spacey. Lorenzo's crystals became heavy; he waited. "Jasmine," she choked. "I smell jasmine. I *hate* Jasmine."

"But, jasmine is a lovely tree with an exquisite aroma. *Why* do you hate jasmine, Jennifer?"

"I can't talk about *her*." Jennifer replied loudly. The crystal in his left hand made a snapping sound as he gripped it unconsciously.

"Her?"

"Yes, *her*, her name is Jasmine, my ex-lover's wife. She had it all: his children, his home, and his life. He wanted *me* not her, but she would not let him go. I was his lover for three fucking years! He loved to fuck *me*, not her. I wanted to murder her—even thought about it. Eventually he dumped me and stayed with her."

Lorenzo gripped the crystal in his right hand more firmly. "Was Jasmine jealous of you?"

"Of course she was and she should have been since I was fucking her husband, fucking his brains out all the time, everywhere, on the floor, on the desk, on the porch, in the car. He couldn't stop himself."

"These days many people think they can just do what they want. Do you believe that now that *you* are married?" He paused, no answer, so he said firmly, "Did you think you could just have him if you wanted him regardless of his family? Was *Jasmine* jealous, tortured, and miserable?"

Jennifer was softly weeping. "Of course I made her miserable and tortured her, and you know what? Until I felt this way myself, felt what she must have felt, I never thought about her. All I thought about was getting him, no matter who was in the way. When I seduced him the first time after photographing and touching him all day, he didn't want to do it but he couldn't stop himself. I entrapped him in my tangled sticky web. I blew up his photos and put them all over my apartment, feeding my obsession. He couldn't keep away from me. His house was chaos with three little kids. The only good sex he got was with me because she was exhausted. Now I see what I did to her. I tried to steal something that belonged to her, and I was wrong. Now that I have a husband I love, Jasmine is coming back to haunt me. I deserve it."

Later, Lorenzo sat facing her going over his notes. "By being able to feel Jasmine's pain, you will get beyond this jealousy. We need to stop now because of time. We made great progress today. You have a lot to think about, so I suggest we meet in a few weeks. Please go sit on the stone bench in the garden by the side of my parking place for a little while before you drive or walk home. Call me when you are ready to go more deeply into jealousy."

A strong Mediterranean storm lashing Rome frothed up whitecaps on the Tiber. Sarah was alone in her parlor staring at the gas flames of her fireplace. The wind made the copper gutters creak loudly and flapped the asphalt shingles on the building next door. *Climate change is getting intense.* Her parents called earlier because they couldn't get out the door due to record-breaking snowstorms that had clogged the streets of Boston. Simon was supposed to be in Upper Egypt, but he'd been sent back to Iraq to investigate the rape and sexual slavery system that ISIS was inflicting on the Yazidis. Sarah kept herself calm by meditating and praying, but she was worried because she felt like he was trapped in a nightmare. *Why?* A gust of wind slammed the kitchen window—*bang!*—so she tiptoed back to Teresa's crib to see if she'd been awakened. The toddler was sleeping soundly after a fussy afternoon asking for daddy to come home.

Jennifer had stopped by and the visit left Sarah feeling unsettled. They talked about the storms pounding the Eastern U.S., and their parents. Jennifer muttered ruefully, "My father thinks the main ocean current that keeps the eastern U.S. and northern Europe warm in the winter may be slowing. If it is, the powers that be will hide the truth as long as possible so that they can figure out where to move and what to do with their assets. This cold spell is freaky. My mother hates it, and my father is really worried."

"My mother absolutely hates the cold, too, yet this snowstorm is worse. She can't use her car and the sidewalks are treacherous." For Sarah, the weather was the least of her problems. Teresa had been very upset when Simon departed the second time. She constantly soothed her, but both of them were insecure without him.

"I've come to share something with you. I'm seeing Lorenzo Giannini for counseling, and he's wonderful."

"What for?" Sarah sounded surprised. "Aren't things going well with Armando? I thought they were when we were all together in Tuscany."

"Yes, things are going well for the most part. But I'm tortured by jealousy, a caustic and destructive emotion. There is no reason to be jealous of him. So, I need to understand myself better."

"*Who* makes you jealous?" Sarah asked as Jennifer shifted uncomfortably on the couch.

"Well, that's why I came to see you. I'm insanely jealous of Claudia. I know she's your friend, but does it ever bother you that she is so beautiful and exotic?"

"She *is* beautiful and exotic, but so are *you,* Jen," Sarah replied firmly. "Claudia was dating Simon when I met him, so you'd think *I'd* be jealous! But I'm not, because she isn't the type to steal someone's husband. Claudia is honest, very aware of bad karma, and doesn't play nasty games. Since it's soon to be no secret, Claudia has fallen madly in love with Lorenzo! Simon and I had dinner with them a few weeks ago and I've never seen two people so in love."

"*Claudia* dated *Simon?* I never heard that," Jennifer said staring open mouthed at Sarah. "Did she date him a lot? She gets around!"

"I don't really know, and I didn't care because Simon introduced me to her very soon after our wedding, smart of him because she became my first friend in Rome. They saw each other for a year or two but not frequently I think. Simon loved spending time with her because she's so intelligent and charming. He still does."

"See, that's what's odd about Claudia and Armando—she's so much more intellectual than he is. I don't know much about their affair because we agreed to not talk about our past relationships before we married. But, you once knew Armando well, so can *you* figure out why they were together?"

This question bothered Sarah because Jennifer's tone was snide, and she was trying to pry even though she'd already said she and Armando had agreed not to talk about past affairs. Sarah said nonchalantly, "Oh, I suppose they were young, great-looking Romans who loved art. I suppose that's why they were together." Jennifer's needy and veiled eyes suggested something hidden. *Sometimes it's hard to believe Simon and Jen are from the same family; her boundaries are lousy.* "Well, Jen, why *are* you jealous of Claudia?"

"Lorenzo and I are digging into my past to find out. Well, I should go now. If Teresa wakes up and sees me, she'll think of Simon." Off she rushed.

The encounter put Sarah on edge. She wondered how much Jennifer knew about *her* relationship with Armando a few years ago. *Probably not much, since she says they didn't talk about the past, good thing.* Sarah got out a box of crystals, and as she lifted the lid, her ruby crystal ring started vibrating. *Yes, there's something I must know.* The gutter creaked again and the kitchen window rattled, but not as loudly. She took out a small crystal ball that was absolutely clear except for two dramatic planar fractures that she stared into. "What do I need to know?"

Her stomach tightened. *His* face floated in a plane, the bastard who raped her in a previous lifetime in Portugal. She wanted to look away but she'd asked the question. The ugly scene unfolded again: The duke taking her the night before her wedding because he had first rights. After she married, constantly he tried to catch her alone and she never felt safe again. She wanted to avert her eyes, but had to know. Then there it was, even though the rape was harsh and cruel, she responded to him when her soul took flight as he fucked away. After that, she felt nothing during sex with her husband, nothing for her whole life even though she loved him. *Oh my God. Think of the Yazidi women and girls. No wonder Simon cares about them so much.*

She put her hand on her heart, covered the ruby crystal with her other hand, and stared into the crystal ball again. There she was on a ragged bed in horrible pain from an infected womb after giving birth to a son. Her husband brought her the baby that sucked and fussed while her life ebbed away. She was dead when he took the baby away. *Oh my God, that baby has been born again as Teresa!* She pressed her hand on her heart putting her left hand on the crystal to cover his familiar little face. Then she put the crystal ball away and went to the couch to think about what she'd just seen. *That face of that man . . . who? That bastard was Armando's past life!* She sat up straight to absorb the realization. *If Armando had gotten me that day, he would have ruined me and I would feel nothing with Simon, nothing!* She already knew that her husband long ago in Portugal was Simon's previous lifetime. *It's amazing how entangled we are.*

Staring into the low gas flames, she wondered how she could help Teresa feel more secure. Since in a past life she grew up without a mother who died just when she was born, Teresa might be overly sensitive to abandonment. *I wonder if that's why she gets so upset when Simon leaves?* Seeing Teresa as a boy was very compelling. *Who really fathered him? I wonder if I knew back then?* Often royalty fathered the firstborn of pretty peasant women. In this life she was beyond Armando and experiencing sexual joy with Simon. *Well, then, since I'm alive and we have Teresa with us again, I am beyond who I was before. I can make her feel secure, and I will, right away. This is not the past. We are all back together again to evolve, especially Armando. No wonder I was able to forgive him and grow to love him.*

She sat down at the kitchen table to write. Recalling her conversations with Simon during the last two weeks when they talked about Yazidi spirituality, words for Teresa flowed while tears dampened her cheeks. The phone rang. He always called when it was morning in Iraq.

"Hello, Sarah, I had a good day. Amnesty International is really helping the Yazidis. They are over here interviewing escapees from warehouses and the sexual slavery auction marketplaces, and the truth about what they're doing is actually coming out, things that normally never see the light of day, incredible that such barbarity still goes on in the modern world. I miss you so terribly much, and I miss Teresa. I would give anything to be with you in the kitchen right now. Are you writing tonight?"

Sarah flushed with warmth hearing his soft, articulate, caring voice. "Sweetheart, I really am okay. Teresa's not doing as well as I'd like, so I'm writing a story for her about Yazidi beliefs. Since you left, I've been gathering information about them. They are utterly fascinating, one of the oldest and purest religions in the world. Have you heard about the Peacock Angel?"

"Sure. As usual, we're on the same track. Yazidi religion goes so far back that it makes me think their ancestors of some 11,000 years ago must be the ones who built Göbekli Tepe. Of course, this can't be proven, but the way they've saved their ancient traditions, such as that story of the Peacock Angel, makes me think this is possible, and they've protected their bloodline for 10,000 years. To this day, marriage outside their group is forbidden, and no one is ever allowed conversion into their religion. ISIS is trying to wipe out their genetic line by raping the women and girls with blonde hair and blue eyes, the reverse of Hitler, an insane attempt to adulterate Aryan genes instead of breeding them! They have survived many attempted genocides, and their suffering is incomprehensible. ISIS is trying to destroy the heart of their culture, their women. Unbelievable! Letting that painful subject go, I must say good night, my love. Give Teresa a kiss from me."

The next morning, Sarah pulled Teresa up on her lap to share her Yazidi creation story:

"Long ago, the Peacock Angel, a magical bird, flew off Earth with seven sacred angels. Peacock Angel was the most beautiful bird in the world with a great fan of rainbow-colored feathers tipped with large eyes, god's eyes. Peacock Angel spread out its great fan to show Adam, the first man, that the waters will always flow, the sun will always shine, and the moon will cast its long shadows reminding us of the phases of time. The Peacock Angel is the divine creator who radiates nature's essence, the force that creates life.

"Eventually tired of being on Earth and wanting to fly away, Peacock Angel summoned six beautiful angels—Mercury, Venus, Earth, Mars, Jupiter, and Saturn, the leader—to care for Adam. We come from Adam and the people of the Peacock Angel guided by these same angels. With Mercury came awareness; from Venus, love; and on Earth they made their home. With Mars they learned to struggle; with Jupiter to make their fortunes; and Saturn taught them agriculture. Whenever the ages change, Peacock Angel returns to make sure they remember how to live the good life.

"Greater than the beautiful Peacock Angel is the magnificent Divine Essence, pure light. When the ages shift, Divine Essence makes a Whirling Ceremony—dervishes turning round and round to germinate the new Tree of Life. Peacock Angel perches in the burgeoning great tree spreading out his long iridescent feathers tipped with all-seeing eyes to watch each person. Daddy is with the people of the Peacock Angel because they are very troubled. Evil men want to destroy their way of life, yet they are primal caretakers of Earth. Daddy calls Peacock Angel to spread his fan in the Tree of Life to gaze at his beautiful people, then he will come home to you."

Teresa's bright eyes glistened while listening to her mother's story. She laughed when Sarah drew a picture of the Peacock Angel fanning out his feathers tipped with many eyes. She slid off Sarah's lap to put the picture on her toy box and put a rubber elephant on top and patted it.

12

Deep Secrets

A fierce December storm rattled the French doors of Jennifer and Armando's room in Rome as she stood out on the balcony watching the Ilex trees sway. Strong winter winds from the Libyan Desert coming across the Mediterranean were bending the stately trees in the Borghese Gardens just beyond their high walls. Tree branches cracking every few minutes were like whips snapping in the raspy, purring wind that ground into the thick red sandstone exterior walls. She wrapped her sweater tighter as she thought about Tuscany, yet sirens on the street below reminded her she was in Rome. She heard Armando's voice calling from inside. She came inside to greet him hoping he'd have some free time, since his latest show was hanging in the gallery through Christmas. Cold rain pelted the shutters—clack, clack—as he set a fire. Color emerged in precious embroidered fabric lit up by the glowing, flickering flames.

He brought her a port in a delicate etched glass, handing it over to her as she snuggled in the large reading chair next to the growing fire. Then he sat down on an opposite bench. "Well, now that I have some time, I want to know about you and Lorenzo. You have been so patient, beautiful lady, yet I know how it is with Lorenzo. So, as you discover yourself, do you feel more secure?" He leaned in studying her face, dramatized by the amber flames.

She gazed back scrutinizing him as the port moistened her full ruby lips. Marriage had softened his catlike rapacious body making him look a little less hungry. *I wonder if I should just tell him?* "Lorenzo could pull the truth out of anybody, even me, all the things I'd just as soon forget. Yet, still I think we should be careful about revealing the past. I *am* finding some things in analysis that explain why I'm plagued with jealousy. It isn't about Claudia, not at all."

He stroked her arm turning her closer to make her swing her long legs over the arm of the chair. Gleaming paneled walls enhanced her glowing skin as he massaged her muscular upper thigh while enjoying the softness of her crushed velvet pants. "She can't be the cause, so I'm thrilled you are seeing Lorenzo, since she's my friend. We were never right for each other because we are too much alike, both too intense. You seem to be feeling more secure, which really supports me after spending the day going crazy. You relax me, and I seem to calm you. May I ask you one thing, and don't answer if you don't want to." She smiled in assent. "I've heard that when a woman is plagued with jealousy, sometimes it is because her father was unfaithful to her mother, something she discovered when she was growing up. Is *that* the problem?"

"Oh, no," she uttered with alarm. "My father has always been loyal to my mother. She never had reason to be jealous." Regardless, her eyes were murky because the question reminded her of the pain she'd inflicted on Jasmine.

He saw the conflicting thoughts and feelings in her panicky eyes and figured she was protecting her father. But he wasn't going to push it because he wasn't going to share more about himself. His thoughts drifted off to his latest work, a large canvas where the rape of the Sabines was emerging. "Well, I'm happy it's not David, since I've thought of him as a rare man of great integrity. My father is very taken with him and wants him to come to Rome for a week or so, which would be so great for Sarah."

"I would love to have my father come again," she said as the sight of Jasmine, a harried mother of small children trying to get through the day, flashed in her mind. *Perhaps I'll feel less guilty if I tell my father? I wonder whether I should just tell Armando the truth?* She glanced at him kneading her upper thigh, which felt demanding. "Lorenzo says we should keep our sessions private at this point, yet maybe it won't always be that way." She stroked the black hair on his arm, supple because he used all his arm muscles while painting.

"Meanwhile . . ." he pulled her close and breathed hungrily on her neck wanting to stop talking. "We have two hours before dinner, let's take advantage of it. I adore you, my dear wife."

Later they dined alone with Pietro and Matilda. Heavy dark beams lit by beeswax candles from Tuscany enhanced the medieval feeling of the room. "Matilda, you look especially lovely tonight; your color is so vital."

"Oh yes? Well, thank you, Jen," she replied showering them with a warm smile. "I braved the wind and went for a long walk in the Borghese Gardens. I should do it every day."

"I suppose you spent most of your day in the library, Dad?" Armando asked.

"Indeed. Today I reread Livy's version of the rape of the Sabines. For me now, as a result of the news on ISIS and the Yazidi women, I think Livy was trying to make our ancestors look good. I think he covered up the truth when he says they were not raped. The Romans abducted them to marry them when their king refused to let the Romans settle here. We are descended directly from that abduction or rape. We are a combination of the original Romans and the Sabines; violence and abuse boils in our blood."

Pietro prattled on searching for the most eloquent words, so he didn't notice that Armando was staring with his mouth hanging open. "*That* is what you were doing today?"

"Sure. Why is that so surprising?"

"Because I just started a large painting titled *Rape of the Sabine Women* yesterday! I'm struggling to depict their fear, agony, and horror, yet as I was painting, I felt their excitement as virgins."

"*Really?*" Pietro sputtered, putting his knife down as Matilda listened and Jennifer paled. With the blood drained out of her face, she looked ghostly.

Jennifer broke in. "What inspired you to paint *Rape of the Sabine Women?*"

"I'm not sure to be truthful. Visions of the scene were torturing me, and I couldn't stop myself. Painting the scene was very erotic."

Matilda had noticed a thick sexual fog around the couple all day.

Jennifer shot him a knowing look and said, "What an astonishing synchronicity!"

Pietro nodded his head in agreement. "Armando, you and I are due for a long talk in the library, don't you think?"

Jennifer was deep in thought. *It makes me nervous, him painting the rape of the Sabines. Why would that bother me?* She had no idea Armando might be processing his own issues about raping women, but she could feel it. Matilda cast a glance at Armando seeing he was pleased to be invited to talk by his father; she knew perfectly well why he was drawn to the rape of the Sabines.

The great pre-Christmas storm in Rome finally ended. Fallen trees and branches were picked up and power was restored.

Armando had kept his painting of Jesus and Mary Magdalene out of the latest show. As his eyes scanned the figure of Jesus beseeching Mary Magdalene to rise, they fixed on the fat yellow queen bee on the rock behind the Magdalene's head. *I don't remember putting it there. What does it mean? The only one who has any idea is Claudia.* He picked up the phone to call.

Claudia was relaxing in her apartment, wondering whether she should sell it and move in with Lorenzo, when the phone rang.

There was a long pause after his explanation and invitation. Then Claudia said, "After I saw the painting in Tuscany, I was so intrigued by the bee that I came home and reviewed my sources. A new book on the subject has come out, so I read it. But, darling, this issue is so complicated that you will not believe it. I can't explain it without being with you and the painting. I am free today."

Jennifer came to mind, but he let it go since she'd admitted Claudia was not the cause of her jealousy. Besides, Jen had an appointment with Lorenzo this afternoon and was going to look at antiques in the Trastevere afterward. *How perfect is that?* "Sure, come on over. Go through the gate, park behind the coach house, come up the path, and knock on my studio door. I'll be here."

Pulling open the heavy wooden door, Claudia came in wearing loose black pants and a red high-necked tunic. "How are things with Lorenzo? I'm happy for you. I can't imagine two people more suited to each other." He smiled warmly enjoying the thought of her happiness.

"Yes, who would have ever imagined? I've never felt so fulfilled and supported. He's such a great human being. After what you and I went through, who would have thought we'd both do so well? Sometimes things actually do turn out for the best."

He rested a hand on her shoulder, which reminded her of his incredibly sensitive fingers as they approached the painting propped up beside an old wooden table with a bottle of wine, a basket of French bread, and a plate of cheese with fresh fruit. "I put together a small lunch while you were on the way because it is so kind of you to come right over. Thank you, Claudia. I really appreciate it."

She took a chair and reached for some grapes. *Funny. Now we're just comfortable old friends.* "Armando, you will have to listen carefully to absorb some really complicated facts. The bee will not make any sense without understanding some deep secrets about Jesus and Mary Magdalene, things that will never be authenticated by conventional theologians."

"You mean the Dan Brown thing?" he broke in.

"No, darling, way beyond Dan Brown, but what do you think about his ideas in *The DaVinci Code?* Actually, that's a very good place to start." Claudia was surprised he'd even heard of Dan Brown. *Jennifer must be waking up his brain.*

"As we know, I don't read much. But Jen gave me a copy of *Angels and Demons,* and I couldn't put it down because I loved imagining the Vatican getting blown to smithereens. But, when all the talk went around about *The DaVinci Code,* I considered its main thesis, but didn't read it."

"So," Claudia broke in, "what *do* you think about a marriage of Jesus and Mary Magdalene?"

"To tell you the truth, I always thought they were a couple because she's always near Jesus with her red flowing hair. It's right in our faces all over Italy." It was a thrill to be able to converse this way after feeling so limited intellectually with her in the past.

"Great start. This might be easier than I thought it would be. So, why do you think the Church hierarchy goes to such extremes to cover up the truth?"

"Well, if Jesus *was* married to her, that would be the end of priestly celibacy. The Church wants to keep things the way they are and have sex in secret and live in luxury. It's easier to keep all the money if priests can't marry and pass their property to their children."

"You are absolutely right," Claudia responded sipping lightly on the wine. "Yet, the hierarchy's cover-up is somehow out of proportion, don't you think?"

"Well, yes. They are laughingstocks, but they still are at the center of world banking, so the chuckle is on us. Really, we are fools for putting up with them, especially my family!"

She said in a sensual, conspiratorial voice, "Well, darling, wait until you hear *what* they are covering up; it's all out now. A famous filmmaker, Simcha Jacobovici, teamed up with a highly respected biblical scholar, Barrie Wilson, to publish *The Lost Gospel,* a book that describes the hidden aspects of the relationship between Jesus and Mary Magdalene. Dogmatic theologians are trying to muffle them, but the public can read and Jacobovici is well known. A truly shocking story is leaking out that explains the fierce cover-up on the personal life of Jesus giving scholars like Sarah real data on early Christianity. Wilson is a highly acclaimed professor of religious studies in Toronto and can't just be dismissed.

"The 'lost gospel' is an ancient Syriac manuscript in the British Library that is almost two thousand years old. It was not properly translated, so Wilson and Jacobovici hired a team of experts to translate it into English. We're lucky it collected dust until more advanced tools were available because recent imaging technologies have authenticated the radical and shocking text. If it had been found earlier, it might have been destroyed like many other scrolls were before our modern times."

"Okay, but what does it have to do with the bee?"

"Jennifer *is* having a salubrious effect on you! You are listening to me and using your brain," she laughed as she cut off a thick slice of cheese.

"Now, Claudia, that's enough of that. Get *on* with the story!" He was happy his wife wasn't around because he was really enjoying private time with Claudia. He didn't realize Matilda had noticed Claudia's vintage Fiat parked by the side of the coach house.

"Okay. Mary Magdalene is associated with the queen bee in some early sources, and the bee is a major symbol in Renaissance art, some say to indicate sacred lineages. Even today royalty often have bee fabric and art in their palaces. There is a chair in your library upholstered with red fabric and golden bees. I was very surprised you didn't realize you'd put a golden bee in your painting because it suggests you have an archetypal memory of the bee connected to Mary Magdalene. It popped out from the depths of your rich subconscious mind and your bloodlines, the reason your art attracts notice. You know things that leak into your work. Ironically, only now is the meaning of this coded symbol coming to light, and I think you executed this painting exactly when *The Lost Gospel* was being translated!" She broke off a piece of French bread, slathered on some mustard, and put a thin slice of Edam cheese on top.

"Claudia, even though it is really fun enjoying wine and lunch with you, I'm impatient. What are you *talking* about?"

She swallowed some wine to wash down the snack as she got ready to launch. "It would take me hours to explain all the details, so you just have to trust me or go read *The Lost Gospel* yourself, but you won't. It is the story of Joseph the Just and Aseneth his wife, seemingly just a story from the Old Testament. But in actuality, Joseph and Aseneth are *surrogates* for Jesus and Mary Magdalene. This is an *encoded text,* a common technique used by early Christian writers to pass dangerous and treasured secrets along under the guise of something familiar. For example, they took stories in the Old Testament claiming they prefigured the coming of Jesus, even though they really did not."

Armando looked hopelessly confused. "Wait. Joseph is the guy with the coat of many colors in the Bible, and I've never heard of Aseneth. So, if this is Joseph from the Old Testament, he can't be Jesus."

"Just hang with me, Armando, have more wine. The manuscript comes out of a biblical tradition, Syriac typology, that goes back to the first and second centuries when some Jews were becoming Christians while others remained Jews. Judeo-Christians specialized in finding parallels between the Old and New Testament because they wanted to keep the old scriptures and add their new ones. They used Hebrew scripture as a pedigree for Christianity; register that! They used typology—finding parallels—as a way to prove Hebrew scripture anticipated Jesus to support their new religion, exactly as Sarah says, the reason she thinks Marcion is so important."

"Oh God, Claudia, *so what?*" he said in an exasperated voice.

"Sparing you the details, the authors established that this text— *Joseph and Aseneth*—is actually the story of Jesus's marriage to Mary Magdalene. You'd have to study the book to decide whether you agree or not. Regardless, finally we have the story of Jesus as a real man who loved a great woman that could rock the world."

"I don't think so. It's just another esoteric trail that will end up as another dead end. Nobody gives a damn about this garbage, never did, and when are you going to get tired of the latest mystery?" He was annoyed and getting a headache.

"Damn you, Armando! *You* are the one who painted this bee, not

me! Your fabulous rendition of Jesus is so filled with otherworldly
light that anybody can see he came down from cosmic realms. As she
reaches for him while trying to hold him down, he is barely in his
body. Damn it, Armando! You captured the real vision of Christ with
Mary Magdalene and her symbol, the golden bee. And, the goddess
that Mary Magdalene embodies is right there in Siena Cathedral, the
bee goddess, Artemis, hovering over Hermes Trismegistus by the front
door! If you would just use your brain, you might be able to tell your
father some things. Your ancestors probably protected this story! Your
father probably knows all about it!"

Feeling sullen and stupid he grumbled, "Well, what's the text about?
What's the story?"

Claudia ate a pear she'd sliced while watching him to see whether he
was going to revert to being an ass or not. "It's the story of Jesus meeting her as an angel/human from a very high dimension. It is extremely
erotic, and also very exciting, filled with plots to abduct Aseneth/
Magdalene and their two children after Jesus dies. A very beautiful
ritual is described that involves the two of them eating a sacred honeycomb on their wedding night, the *real* first communion. To sum things
up, *Joseph and Aseneth* is a theology of redemption by sacred sex. There's
a lot of evidence early Christians practiced this ceremony, for example,
the Gnostics. The fourth- and fifth-century Church councils arranged
by Constantine excoriated this story from history and replaced it with
the dry, Pauline, celibate Christ. The primal theology in *Joseph and
Aseneth* suggests that Jesus and Mary Magdalene taught that we *can*
redeem ourselves with sacred sex, which I believe; maybe you still do.
This may be the background source for the sex rituals you and I once
performed when we were young."

"What about the damned bee?" he practically screamed as her comment about their past sex rituals was sinking in.

"To know that, we must consider what Aseneth stood for. We know
from the ancient world that Aseneth is actually Artemis, the great goddess. As Joseph and Aseneth, Jesus and Mary Magdalene celebrated

communion by sharing a honeycomb, since by her marriage to Jesus, she becomes the Bride of God, the goddess Artemis, and honey is the food of the gods. The Jews who worshipped Yahweh tried to suppress her worship long before the arrival of Jesus, but the people would not give her up. When the Age of Pisces began, Jesus brought her back as his bride. Mary Magdalene means 'Mary of the tower,' and Artemis was the goddess of the tower, a tower on her head to protect her people against a judgmental god. Artemis is the queen bee, and priests are meant to serve her in the temple to fecundate her. Beekeeping in the ancient world was sacred, and the power place in ancient temples was the *omphalos,* a beehive, such as at Delphi. She is the great goddess and Mary Magdalene became her high priestess by marrying Jesus. Subconsciously, it's the force that once drew us together to balance Rome, even though we didn't know it then," she said, staring intensely into his murky black eyes.

Armando was stunned because this *did* explain things about his behavior with Claudia in the past, things he'd often wondered about. He paused and then said very sweetly, "You've really forgiven me, haven't you, Claudia? We were young, we didn't know what we were doing, yet as we get older we can see what might have been driving us."

"I have forgiven you and you no longer hurt me because Lorenzo has found the goddess in me, my healing. I hope you find the goddess in Jennifer. If you do, you will live in the land of milk and honey no matter what goes on in the world. I'm leaving, I have to make dinner."

A heavy drape in a window above the library parted slightly as Matilda watched Claudia get into the silver Fiat and drive away.

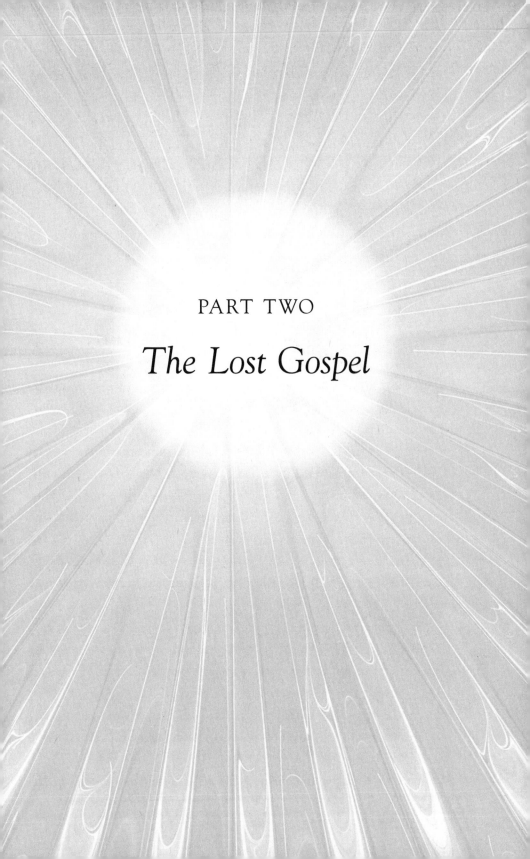

PART TWO

The Lost Gospel

13

Forgiveness

Shock waves rolled through the Western world when ISIS beheaded twenty-four blindfolded Coptic Christian men on a beach in Tripoli in February 2015. Simon was in Baghdad investigating the ISIS sexual slavery system, so David flew to Rome to support Sarah and Teresa. Pietro and Matilda had invited David and Rose to visit their apartment in Rome many times, yet this time Rose stayed home because she'd seen Teresa during the summer and had household remodeling to attend to. Pietro's driver, Guido, was waiting when David arrived late in the evening at Rome's airport amid intense security. Guido brought him directly to the house where Pietro was waiting.

"Hello, David, I hope your flight was tolerable? Was the security intense?" He led David into the library where a welcoming fire was burning.

"So thoughtful of you to stay up and wait for me, an unexpected kindness. Yes, security is very tight, but has to be in light of what's just happened. ISIS terrifies me and Sarah is very worried. Thanks for inviting me so that I can easily spend time with my girls and all of you. The fire is so cheerful. Rose sends her regards and hopes to come next time."

"You must be tired; would you like a scotch on the rocks, brandy?"

"I'd love a brandy."

"Jennifer is excited about your visit," Pietro said as he went to an old oak cabinet for a bottle of brandy and two glasses. "Armando paints all day and sometimes I think she's lonesome, but she walks a lot, visits churches and museums, and seems to be enjoying life. Of course, she's constantly taking pictures, yet I sense she is not inclined to continue in fashion and may become an art photographer. Actually, I think she simply enjoys being married right now!"

They sat down by the table with their brandy. Pietro wore an emerald green jacket with a white cross embroidered on the pocket that caught David's eye as he replied with a smile, "Not a bad life, I'd say. She lived in Paris for seven years, now she enjoys Rome, Tuscany, and Majorca. She can always take up her career again, but maybe she needs a break. I can't wait to find out what she's planning to do."

The brandy soothed Pietro's throat as he took note of David's worried brow in the firelight. His forehead was deeply lined and his mouth was tight. When they walked down the hallway, Pietro noticed he stooped slightly as if he was tired of life. Pietro said, "The trouble with what's going on now is these barbaric murders can't ever be taken back. ISIS is hardening the hearts of people all over the world. The clock can't be turned back to the Dark Ages, yet ISIS is determined to do exactly that. Many of the ISIS fighters were in Saddam Hussein's royal guard, thrown out on the street in 2003 by the Americans or tortured in the Abu Graib prison. They want revenge! The U.S. spawned the monster that is sweeping through Iraq and Syria."

"Yes," David said ruefully. "And my dear son is right in the middle of the whole mess, very painful for me, Pietro. Meanwhile, here in Rome you could be overrun by Libyan refugees trying to escape their horrible future."

"Yes, we are all very much afraid we will be overwhelmed by refugees because good people are being driven out from where they've lived for centuries. We can't just let them drown in the Mediterranean," Pietro said in a disgusted voice. "I admire Simon for what he's doing, people must have the truth about ISIS. But that's enough talk about something we can't do anything about. How's Simon?"

"As far as we know, he's well. He's strong and determined, very careful and well guarded. I don't allow myself to worry since you're doing what you can. Every night I visualize him being safe and comfortable before I go to sleep. Obama takes this threat very seriously, probably is doing more than we realize. However, he deals with the threat in the same old way—killing with drones, espionage, and bringing in more American soldiers and arms even though our planet cannot withstand more war. The terrorists are seizing U.S. arms and equipment and taking territory, and many Middle Eastern people wish the U.S. would just leave them alone."

"I agree David, but you've had a long flight and must be tired. I've been eager to talk with you ever since our last time in Tuscany, but I'm taxing you."

"I'm not tired yet, flew first class and slept most of the way. Actually, there is something I'd like to discuss with you, since we may have more in common than either one of us realizes. *How* were you able to offer Simon protection? What kind of group do you belong to? Normally I wouldn't ask such a question, but I feel the need. Who do you work with Pietro?"

Pietro stood up stiffly and walked over to the fire to get a poker to nudge a log. After moving it, the fire intensified revealing his grave expression. He put the poker down and returned to the table to pour a second ounce of brandy while David watched his severe expression. "Maybe it is time . . . I belong to a secret order that has been meeting in Malta for more than a thousand years dedicated to defusing internal Islamic divisiveness and East/West tension, among other things. Our role in the conflicts is to protect hospitals."

David was determined to go all the way in this conversation as he glanced a second time at the white cross on Pietro's breast pocket. "Thank you. I belong to a Mayan order that goes back at least fifteen hundred years to Teotihuacan in northern Mexico. Now that we're beyond the great transition date a few years ago, I feel free to talk. You are the first person I've told; even Simon doesn't know. We work with thirteen crystal skulls that are like radios; I have one of them. They resonate with the Earth's inner core, the dimension that guides us to transcend hatred and violence." He bored into Pietro's gray eyes to ferociously blast otherworldly light into his pineal gland.

David's extraordinary power sped up Pietro's brain moving him back in his chair as he took a long, deep breath. "All right, confidentially, we've influenced the Western world for better or worse for a long time; nobody really knows how far back we go. We have letters asking for help from the Eastern Patriarch in Constantinople when Attila the Hun overran the eastern boundaries of the Roman Empire in the fifth century. Very much like that terrifying period, the world is going out of control again, we don't know what to do about it. We usually can protect good men like Simon, yet even that might not be possible if this breakdown gets much worse. The West is disintegrating for exactly the reason you mentioned a moment ago—too much war, which threatens all life on Earth. *How* do you access Earth's inner core with those crystal skulls?" He poured David another brandy, noting his pupils had contracted to tiny black spots.

"We vibrate a point in the center of our crystal skulls that corresponds to the pineal gland in the human brain. For example, we linked all thirteen skulls in late 2011, the skulls synchronized and vibrated with the inner core at 40–60 Hertz, and the Earth released more information to us. Unlike your group, we do not manipulate global events, yet I've noticed that the intelligence we generate sometimes seems to alter reality. The advanced cosmic beings that guide our planet from the Mayan perspective—the *Nine Bolontiku*—receive information from the Earth's core through our skulls. Our group formed when the skulls were discovered in ancient caves under Teotihuacan, the sacred center where the first thirteen people received them and then passed them down through their families. There can't be more violence and war, Pietro. Earth can't take it. Do you understand?"

"I do. So what's it going to take to get the U.S. government to evacuate all its bases, disband its forces, and destroy its weapons? Islam will fight the West until that happens, most likely even past that. Global disarmament and agreements to never arm again are the only things that can end the death of our species."

David responded in a cynical voice, "The only way that will happen would be if the U.S. economy crashes, an outcome that I find hard to imagine. Certainly your elite group won't endure that."

"That may be, but there still are other possibilities. Dr. Johan Calleman, an avant-garde biologist, recently discovered some scientific proof for the things we are discussing. You say your group communicates with the *center* of Earth through the skulls, but our group attunes to the *boundary surface of the Earth's inner core,* which vibrates at 20–40 Hz. Underneath the Western and Eastern hemispheres, this boundary surface exhibits entirely different structures: the eastern edge of the boundary is liquid and melting, the western edge is crystalline. This profound discontinuity causes people living on the eastern side to think totally differently than those on the western side! This didn't really matter much until the West invaded the East during the Crusades. You have to realize that people in the East do not comprehend why they are being interfered with. They think the West is suicidal, homicidal, sick, and greedy, especially the U.S., and they are desperate because Western culture is making *their cultures* sick and greedy, undermining their religions. For them, ISIS is no worse than the Crusaders or the interrogators that recently tortured them in Iraqi prisons!

"Our habitat and precious resources will all be destroyed unless war is abolished, so we've informed our American members that wholesale U.S. disarmament is the only hope left for the human race. They can't imagine it because many of them have made fortunes off armaments for hundreds of years. David, do you believe Earth is alive and intelligent?"

"Yes, because that's what we get from our skulls. So, *how* do you attune to the boundary surface of the inner core? What information do you get? Our skulls contact the very center of Earth, and she tells us she cannot tolerate the death and maiming."

Pietro replied, "We raise our brain frequencies to 20–40 Hz in meditation, and the information we are receiving is disturbing: the great dissonance between the East and the West is intensifying tectonic, weather, and biological stress. We must each adopt natural ways of life or face death because Earth is flowing geomantic power to sacred sites on the surface to regenerate ecological zones for all living things. Those not in resonance with her won't be able to take it—they will sicken, particularly with cancer, or go mad by taking drugs to alleviate the pressure in their brains. Deep within, humans hear the Earth screaming."

"The information we get is very much in agreement. However, I think you know more than I do because your group works with Earth in a more political way than ours. Our links are psychic, a better word perhaps would be *shamanic*." Pietro looked up at David sharply when he said shamanic and nodded in assent. "So, Pietro, why does Earth specify U.S. disarmament? I mean, is there something unusual about the U.S.? Is America exceptional in some way, as Obama often has said? Rome and central Europe are located between the East and the West, so I can see why your group plays a chess game in Malta while the pope works from Rome. But why the U.S.?"

Pietro shifted in his chair. "Are you aware the Masons built Washington, D.C.?"

"Of course, everybody knows it," David said, watching Pietro's nervous eyes.

"How much do you know about it?"

This was a test David could easily pass. "You read in English, Pietro. Have you read David Ovason's *The Secret Architecture of the Nation's Capital* that argues Washington is still maintaining its original Masonic architectural plan?" Pietro smiled, confirming he'd read the book. "Good, then that makes this easier. You understand that every inch of D.C. is coded with astrological symbols, sacred architecture, and alignments of its roads to the equinoxes and solstices as well as to key stars. Somebody believed this plan would link D.C. with the cosmos, and each incoming president is informed about how this works after the election. Considering our discussion tonight, maybe they are contacting the inner Earth? But, that still doesn't answer my question about your work with the inner Earth. Why do you bring up D.C., of all things?" He noticed that Pietro was getting so excited he was having trouble sitting still. He got up to nudge the log again.

"Before you came, I had a long talk with Armando and shared what I'm about to tell you, the big secret that must be revealed, since to survive this perilous transition into Aquarius, all must be revealed. According to Calleman, the division line between East and West, the midline, is at 12 east longitude going through Tunisia, Rome, Berlin, and up through Scandinavia, basically where the East/West discontinuity exists. We are in Malta because it is close to this line, and many of us live in Rome or spend time here. The Rome vortex is marked by a huge pinecone sculpture in the Belvedere Courtyard in the Vatican, the symbol for the pineal gland. Stand next to it if you want to feel how Earth's power pervades the Vatican and Rome. So, here is the big secret: Washington, D.C., *is exactly 90 degrees west of Rome, making it the power center of the Western hemisphere.* The Masons chose this location for the capitol and aligned all the streets and monuments to access Earth/sky power—as above, so below. Ovason says the most powerful configuration is the triangular complex on Pennsylvania Avenue that mirrors the equilateral triangle in Virgo formed by Arcturus, Spica, and Regulus, the star that rules kings.

"Over time the U.S. abandoned its principles in order to sell armaments and torture. You once were growers of corn for the world; now you make weapons. The U.S. must disarm. If not, Earth changes, terrorism, violent weather, fires, and biological degradation will destroy your country. Unstable weather will cripple America if you continue to destroy Earth. The people you've armed are rising up, as are your own people."

David's solar plexus locked up as he listened to Pietro; he was finally getting some answers. "Thank you for this. America's Achilles heel is arrogance, and the power in Washington is weirdly arcane. American power is much deeper and subtler than I realized; I have a lot to think about. What I do know for sure is that this year is not going to be an easy one."

Pietro nodded in solemn agreement and put a hand on David's shoulder when they stood up to walk out of the library. The glowing embers would be rekindled early in the morning.

David got up late the next morning just in time for lunch with everyone. The first course, spaghetti Bolognese, was rich and grounding. "I'm jet-lagged and grateful for good Italian food. This is delicious! You haven't gained any weight, Jen. How do you do it?"

Jennifer was glowing with happiness. "I walk miles every day. If I didn't, I couldn't eat the delicious food dished up in this house. Here come the lamb chops. I'll walk them off this afternoon."

"Well, you look absolutely beautiful. Marriage agrees with you, don't *you* think, Matilda?"

"Yes. We've been watching her blossom. Even her Italian is coming along well, much more quickly than with most Americans," Matilda said, smiling approvingly.

After the long leisurely lunch, Armando went back to his studio, and David and Jennifer settled themselves in her parlor. She wanted to talk with him alone because Sarah and Teresa would be coming for dinner and staying in the house for a few days.

"I'm getting right to the point, since we don't have a lot of time. I'm very happy with Armando and love living in this house. However, some very heavy and deep things are coming up for me, maybe because I'm so happy. A few months ago, I was torn apart by uncontrollable jealousy, so I got some help."

David studied her face, which showed a few small lines wrinkling off her unfathomable eyes. *Maybe she didn't sleep well last night?* Nothing was said for a minute or two. "Why jealousy? Surely Armando is faithful?"

"Oh, it's not Armando, not at all, it's *me*. I've been seeing a Jungian analyst. Now I realize I shut you out of my life when I was in Paris in my twenties. That must've hurt you. I'm truly sorry." She looked into his thoughtful eyes giving him her hand, which he firmly grasped.

"Well, yes, that was hard for me, but I thought you needed space to find yourself."

Her mouth pulled back into a slight grimace as her eyes watered and her other hand flapped back aimlessly. He listened to the clock chiming in the hall. She pulled her legs up onto the cushy easy chair and slightly hung her head. She hugged her knees as she raised a face now streaked with tears. "This is so hard. I have to tell you something very unpleasant because I'll never be able to tell anyone else." She coughed while sweeping the tears off her cheeks. "Even though you raised me with sound principles, I had a long affair with a married man in Paris, a man with three children. I almost destroyed his wife, but she outlasted me. He broke up with me, told his wife the truth, and they went into therapy to save their marriage. I was bitter until I found Armando. He doesn't know about the affair, I won't tell him; this guilt is mine. Meanwhile, I'm tortured with jealousy over an old lover of Armando's, a woman who is his good friend. So I am in therapy."

David was churning inside. Her eyes pleaded, but he was disgusted. *How could she do that after the way we raised her?* "Jennifer, you know how I hate to hear this. Have you done anything to approach his wife to apologize?"

"I've thought about that, but I think it would hurt her even more. She never met me, which I think is best. Hopefully they have gotten beyond it. It was my fault: I seduced him. Once I got him, like a spider I ensnared him in my web, torturing him with hot sex. I drove him crazy and almost destroyed him, proud of my power over him. Now I fear some woman will do it to me."

"You have to be very careful about this. The thoughts and feelings you're having *could* trigger things in Armando. I have to say I hope now you see why it's so important to be faithful."

She felt very uncomfortable, judged just when she needed kindness and support, so she stopped talking. David waited but knew she wouldn't say more. She was always like that when she felt judged by him. "Jen, have you forgiven yourself? No matter what you did, it can always be forgiven. You *can* forgive yourself and let it go."

A small squeaky voice came out as she stared into his contracted hard eyes, "But can *you* forgive me?"

David was torn. Was she asking for help with something she couldn't forgive in herself? Would forgiving her weaken the sanctity of their family? *Will Rose forgive her if I can't?* "Do you feel the pain this man's wife endured? Do you realize their family could have been destroyed? She could have even killed herself because of you."

The searing pain in her heart was frightening. *The truth is, I couldn't go to him when I needed him, and I didn't. That's for sure, considering how he is treating me today.* He felt her withdrawal and pain. "I can't judge you. You were brave to tell me the truth, but I must be absolutely honest. You have not forgiven yourself, so it's not about me. I wish you'd told Armando before you married him. Why didn't you?"

She arched back in her chair and stretched out her legs, staring helplessly into his icy eyes. "Maybe I'm just a predator. I tried to get a woman's husband, and then when I wanted to marry Armando, I didn't tell him the truth about myself even though he wanted to tell me about his past. Maybe I'm too obsessed with getting what I want no matter what."

David processed this new information, yet still he didn't know what to say. There was a long pause. *She should have been honest with Armando. But, that's the past, damn it; get past the past!* "Any one of us can change and become a person who wouldn't act the same way again. What does your therapist say or advise?"

She walked over to the mantle then turned to her father. "His name is Lorenzo. He says this is all about me. He wouldn't have advised me to tell you, much less tell Armando. He says I can face myself, all the truth about what I've done, and when I've done that, I can be free. Yet, now I've told you and burdened you. I'm sorry. You'd be happier if you didn't know."

David felt a flow in his heart as he remembered holding her and stroking her soft hair when she was small and feeling troubled about things in school. *I think I didn't feel she'd ever need me again. All I do is worry about Simon, yet she needs me too.* He stood up and walked to her by the fire to embrace her and stroke her long black hair. "Who am I to judge? I love you no matter what you've done. Love is greater than judgment, a trait that dominates us way too much as Jews. I can't judge you, I don't. I simply love you for who you are. I forgive you, sweetie, I forgive you."

He held her tightly while he felt the resistance and pain flow out of her body. It would all be gone in time, the forgotten memory of a big mistake. As he held her by the fire, the long process of forgiving herself finally began.

14

Man on the Hill

Sarah drove through the open gate of the Pierleoni garden. She parked close to the house and took Teresa out of her car seat. Teresa wanted to walk on the stone pathway to the front door, so Sarah held her small hand and guided her on the uneven surfaces. She seemed to be so small. Her eyes widened when she looked up at the massive wood door with menacing gargoyles on each side. "Grandpa, *here?*"

"Yes, little one, Grandpa visits this house." The door swung wide open and they stepped into the great hall. David rushed forward with arms out; Matilda, Jennifer, and Armando staying behind. Sarah moved to the side while David hugged Teresa. Then she stood aside smiling shyly, the perfect little princess.

Matilda exclaimed, "Welcome you two! We're so happy to see you. And *Teresa,* my, my, you look lovely."

Teresa smiled politely then screamed, "*Grandpa!*" and rushed to get back into David's arms. For just a moment, time stopped while they enjoyed the happiness on David's face as he hugged her once more.

Sarah held Teresa's hand as they all walked through the long hall of tapestries. The toddler peered up at them with attentive curiosity while David held her other hand pointing at flowering trees, mythical animals, and grand ladies and men riding horses. Following behind, Jennifer whispered to Armando. "Isn't she adorable in that smock

131

Hall of tapestries

and fancy black patent leather shoes? She seems so grown up, yet she's not two."

"She makes David so happy. I hope we will be able to do this for my parents, don't you?"

"Of course. I hope to be pregnant as soon as possible—the reason I don't want to resume my work in Paris. I want to be here all the time to start our family."

"You are making me very happy, sweet one."

David led Teresa behind the tall bookshelves to a plush velvet window seat where a golden tabby cat lay sleeping. When Teresa reached for him, he raised his head, glared at her, and switched his tail. "Best not to touch him too quickly, Dante doesn't like to be bothered. Would you like me to lift you up so you can sit next to him?"

Teresa eyed Dante warily then nodded slightly.

A maid in a black dress and white apron brought Teresa some fruit juice and asked David what he wanted. Dante got up and thumped down to the floor switching his fluffy tail. The other guests relaxed by the fire while David sat with Teresa, but soon she wanted to join the group. Her Auntie Jennifer stood with amber jewels glowing in the firelight. Teresa came near and stared at her with level eyes. "Hi, Auntie Jen!" Sarah had worked with her to say their names properly for days before David came to Rome.

Dinner was soon ready, early because Teresa would not last long in the highchair. Beeswax candles and deep red wine were enchanting, and Matilda was surprised by how neatly Teresa fed herself while her eyes eagerly followed the action.

Pietro was talking. "David, congratulations on such a lovely grandchild! Sarah, I can see you enjoy being a mother. Ironic, isn't it? The world is a mess, yet we have our private joys."

Matilda was on Teresa's other side and noticed the gleam in her eyes when a cherry tart came out. "Ah, Teresa, you like dessert? I do too, my favorite."

Matilda was very surprised when Teresa answered precisely, "Yes, I love dessert. And, I love your flower walls over there, Auntie Matilda." She pointed, almost spilling her milk. Matilda looked over at the dark oak panels painted with delicate blue flowers on vines.

Sarah caught Matilda's eye. "She loves art and painting already. Isn't that amazing?"

"That's great because I have some wonderful books of famous paintings for young people, the ones Armando loved when he was little."

Sarah was about to reply, but could see Teresa was getting restless after dessert. "Teresa, please say good night. I'm going to take you to play with the babysitter!" Teresa said good night to everybody, and Sarah returned when the main course was being served. Dinner was slow and pleasurable. It was a joy to be with David again.

Jennifer and Armando sat by the fire in the sitting room next to their bedroom listening to the clock in the hall strike twelve melodious chimes. There was a scratch at the door. She opened it and in marched Dante switching his furry tail. "Hello, Dante, what are you doing up here tonight? Did that little girl bother you?" Dante ignored Jennifer and jumped up on her chair. He glared when she removed him to sit back down with Armando. "Piggy cat. My dad and I got some time alone to talk today. He is always so reassuring, a great father."

Armando was eyeing her sleek curves under an ivory silk peignoir. "He loves being a grandfather, gives him hope for the future. Anything special you discussed?"

"I told him that we are very happy, but that I have been struggling with jealousy. The first thing he wanted to know is whether you were being faithful, and I emphasized it was about me." Silk tickled her nipples when she noticed he was taking sneaky peeks. *Come to think of it, what do I know about what he does?*

"I'd say it is a little soon to worry about that; we're still honeymooning. You are gorgeous and sensual. Your breasts drive me crazy. When you stood up to let Dante in, I lost myself in your sexy ass."

Deflecting the conversation to sexual innuendoes, is he hiding something? Actually, he seemed a bit distant lately, but that often happened when he was painting a lot. "Too soon to worry? Are you saying eventually I will have to worry?"

The conversation irritated him. It was time to take her to bed before they started this insane argument all over again. "Of *course* not, darling! You'll never have to worry. I love you. Though there is something I want to bring up. But first, anything else to say about your conversation with David?"

"No."

"Well, I know we agreed not to share our past, but I think we should be open about what we're doing now. Do you agree? If you return to your career, you'll be alone with men, photographing them in very intimate settings and maybe traveling for work." He didn't notice her eyes retreat. "Women flirt with me all the time during openings and I always tell you about it. Often you're there and can see." He noticed she was edgy. *What's she so nervous about?*

"That's a good idea," she said in a throaty voice. "Did something happen I should hear about? Did you *do* something?" she said in a mildly accusatory tone while watching his facial muscles.

"Well," he said rolling the *l*'s, "I didn't do anything, *wouldn't* do anything, but there is something you should know in case you hear about it and misinterpret it."

She was sure he was lying through his teeth. "What is it?"

"Well, I asked Claudia to come to my studio last Tuesday because I needed help with the bee symbol in my painting of Mary Magdalene, the bee that came up in conversation in Tuscany. I feel like you'd want to hear it from me."

Mad and chaotic dizziness overwhelmed her; she couldn't hear well, her vision blurred, and her throat closed. Armando seemed to fly away from her. She felt insane and wanted to get up and move, hit something, pull on something, but she stayed in the chair. Dante looked up with quizzical amber eyes and stretched out his front paws. Then he jumped sideways and rolled when a hot coal popped out of the fireplace. Armando got up and flipped the ember back into the fire. Jennifer wanted to scratch him because he'd brought jealousy back. She struggled for control. She had to defuse the tension by chitchatting, so she said, "So, then, what does she say about the bee? How *long* was she in your studio?"

Armando felt his penis stir because she'd leaned forward making her small breasts visible under the low neckline. He was sweating, felt dizzy in the back of his head, his skin felt scratchy and dry. *Oh, God damn! The lizard!* Barely audibly he croaked, "Down!" Her confused expression alarmed him. "Oh, the bee, well she was with me for a few hours because I made lunch since she was kind enough to come over. She loves Lorenzo, you know, really loves him."

Jennifer was feeling so crazy that her fingers itched to tear his eyes out. Her brain buzzed, chest was heaving, and she just wanted to scratch him or die right now. "Oh, so you talked about *love* with her, not the bee? Does she tell you how *Lorenzo* makes love to her?"

Armando was looking at a mad Jewish shrew; he hated her. How dare she ask him things like that! *Bitch!* The lizard was burning his groin and making his penis hard. He said in the sly voice she'd heard once before, "We don't need to talk about Lorenzo making love to Claudia, we need to make love ourselves, you bitch. Don't you know that's what keeps a man home? Come on you slut, come on and do it!" He went over and grabbed her left arm forcefully yanking her up. Dante jumped up with all four legs rigid and shot for the door with the hair raised on his back as Armando shoved her roughly toward the bed. He went to open the door for the cat, came back, and grabbed her arm again.

She was contemptuous, yet relieved to just move. Jealousy was the worst feeling she'd ever had and at least his behavior allowed her to be angry with him instead of feeling crazy. She pulled his gripping hand off her arm saying, "I am your wife, you can do what you want with me, but don't hurt me. Don't, Armando, or you will be sorry." She lay down on the bed and began pulling her peignoir up over her thighs staring at him with smoking eyes.

He gazed down at her sullen hungry eyes and gorgeous available body. He hadn't been so consumed by lust for a long time; the size and hardness of his cock was a thrill. Fire licked his thighs as his heart beat faster and faster. He said in a snarling tight voice, "Turn over!" She rolled over and he ripped up her peignoir to survey her gorgeous broad ass while his cock felt like it would burst. He slapped her cheeks hard, then harder. *She's going to get what she deserves.* He made sure she couldn't see his red burning eyes and slack mouth with spit in the corner.

"Let's be clear about one thing, Armando. If you try to fuck me up the ass, I will scream! My father will hear me."

That raised the fire even higher. *Do I care? Yes, and Lizard, you are not going to take me over again.* Roughly he rolled her back over and closed his eyes saying, "Spread 'em, bitch, wide!"

She examined his cock wondering if she could take it. She wasn't sure who he was when he taunted her, but she wanted him, so her fluids flowed and it didn't hurt. "Up yours with the goddamned bee; up yours!" he growled as he thrust in and out like a madman, and then he came with a scream that could be heard in the hall. She dropped back exhausted from the pain in her thighs and buttocks as he collapsed next to her and fell into a deep sleep. He was gray and deathly like a shroud in hell, which gave her the creeps. She lay there thinking she had to see Lorenzo. But, what if Claudia's visit to Armando's studio meant Lorenzo wouldn't see her anymore? Damned bitch! *Lorenzo has to help me; he has to. I'm ready for the insane asylum. But he needs help too. He acted like he was going to kill me. What's wrong with him? Maybe I should have let him tell me about his past.*

Armando crept out of bed and went to his studio around 4 a.m.

Lorenzo went right to his office to meet Jennifer in response to her call before breakfast saying Armando had done something frightening. He hoped Armando had not reverted to his old self once the honeymoon was over. Tuning in to his collection of objects, the two crystals with crowns that looked like penises called to him, so he put them on the table behind the couch. Jennifer almost fell through the door, her hair disheveled, face strained, and her eyes evasive. "Thank you for seeing me right away. My father's here from New York staying at our villa with Sarah. I'm very upset, *very* upset, which they'll notice if I can't get over this." Lorenzo asked her to recline and sat down behind her, saying softly it was fine.

"All right, Jennifer, slow down your breath, feel my support, and relax knowing that we can get to the bottom of anything that troubles you." His empathic voice was very hypnotic. "Tell me why you are so upset . . . What comes into your mind, *now*."

She felt her chest contract and squeeze her heart as she sobbed in a clutched voice that he could barely make sense of. "He, he, is even going to take you away. He practically wanted to rape me. I didn't mind having it rough, it was exciting, but he, he is going to take *you* away."

He said gently, "Does Armando want you to stop seeing me?" *It would be very bad if the lizard came back.*

"No, no," she squeaked. "He'll ruin my work with you because he is seeing Claudia!"

Lorenzo paused, confused. He reached for a lovely Victorian intaglio of the Virgin Mary with a carved white ivory face, her bodice and halo coated in 22 kt gold, all set in a circle of seed pearls in a square alabaster frame. He touched Mary's face as he said, "Claudia told me she went to Armando's studio to help him decode a symbol in one of his paintings. She isn't 'seeing' him, Jennifer; they are friends. *I* don't mind if she goes to his studio. There is no conflict within me."

Jennifer expelled the breath trapped in her chest that locked her diaphragm. "That is what I needed to hear. I can't live without you right now; we both know this is not about Claudia. Armando acted very strangely last night as if the devil was in our room. I smelled sulfur and the cat blasted out. He didn't hurt me or do anything I didn't agree to. But, he was like an animal. What's going on with him?"

This made Lorenzo very nervous. *Damn! The lizard may be back.* "Well, of course, I haven't seen him so I can't answer that. May I take you slightly deeper to access the pain you feel? Are you willing?" he asked very kindly.

"Oh, yes, I'll do anything to get rid of this feeling. My father and Sarah are in the house with little Teresa right now, and I have to pull myself together to entertain them. This is too destructive; it tortures me. I hate to think anyone else in the world feels like this."

Lorenzo took a crystal in each hand. "You are going deeper into yourself to the place that knows *why* you love Armando, why you chose him as your husband. Can you tell me?"

Electromagnetic energy flashed all over the inner surface of her skull, she almost lost consciousness. But she could still hear Lorenzo's alluring voice through a long metallic tunnel. "Tell me, Jennifer, tell me why you chose Armando Pierleoni."

She was lying at the bottom of a hill watching a man in a hooded black robe coming down to her. He was switching a horsewhip back and forth saying, "Want it bitch, *want* it?"

Lorenzo was having trouble figuring out what was going on, but could see the man in black as if he was watching a movie. He asked carefully, "What does he want?"

In a slurred, exhausted voice, she said, "He wants to whip me and then take me, but I don't want him because he has another woman, a wife. This is a long time ago, like a few hundred years ago. I work in his house, have no choice."

"Who *is* this man, Jennifer?"

She whispered in a hushed voice, "My father, Lorenzo, I would've thought it would be Armando!"

Lorenzo continued to hold the crystal penises while gazing at the Virgin Mary. "Knowing this is another lifetime, do you want to see what happens?"

She choked and coughed. "He slaps my face and hits my shoulder with the whip handle. 'Slut! I'll never touch you again. You are worse than a dog. I hate you.'"

"*Why* won't he touch you again?"

She choked again spitting, "I told his wife what he does to me. She has all the money from her father, so she kicked him out!"

"Why did you tell his wife?"

She was sobbing softly. "I thought he'd want *me* if she went away. How could I be so stupid? I wonder if some part of Armando hates me? Maybe I have some kind of control over him that he dislikes? Maybe I married him to control him. Maybe I'm having problems with jealousy because I want to control *him* too much."

"Jennifer," Lorenzo commanded, "have you forgiven yourself for what you did to Jasmine?"

"I have forgiven myself because my father has forgiven me. Maybe it was hard for him to forgive me because of what happened between us long ago? Maybe that's why he's so judgmental about marital fidelity."

A little while later they sat down together in the alcove to discuss the session. Lorenzo asked her to hold the ivory intaglio of the Virgin Mary. "Now that I've found Claudia, I understand fidelity, which most of us need for trust. As far as I can see, we can't cope with the intensity of sexual love unless we can trust our partner; there's no room for others. People who can't trust live shallow lives, blindly hurting a lot of people. I assure you that you and I can trust Claudia, so you don't ever have to worry about not being able to see me. Now what I have to say next must always be between us: Armando is a very complex and potentially very disturbed man. I'll never tell you about the things he has done. That's for him to do if he ever wants to. But based on what I know about him, you need me for a while longer.

"Your session today was very fruitful because you got in touch with your father/daughter complex. Nobody really knows whether what you experienced today is an actual past life, or whether your psyche created a drama to examine something you need to figure out now. But, by breaking into this primal complex, you can individuate, that is, truly know yourself. By penetrating aspects of this complex in a past life, you can free yourself from your father. Only then you will be free to explore Armando's rich emotional layers, your great work. Armando chose you and you accepted him, but you still need help with him because he is such a beautiful and wounded human being. The most important thing right now is that you trust me, and then you will be able to trust Claudia. As we tread down this path together, a journey of deep initiation and healing, you will know yourself, Jennifer, the central purpose of life."

She ambled slowly down the stone steps in Lorenzo's tower feeling peace and contentment. As she went out the door to get into her car, it occurred to her that this is how Sarah seems to feel all the time. *Maybe she knows herself?*

15

Demon and the Bitch

Jennifer was back soon after breakfast. She slipped inside the side door and crept up the back stairs listening to the delighted squeals in the kitchen. Teresa was singing and banging on a large pot accompanied by David and Sarah's explosive laughter. She sat down in the small parlor and waited while Armando showered. He walked into the room drying his hair with a towel. He looked at her sullenly and asked, "Where were *you?* I came back from my studio to talk to you and you weren't here. Where did you go?"

"I went to see Lorenzo because I was upset."

"So, did you tell him I raped you?" he growled.

"Of course not, since you didn't; you just got carried away. Actually you were quite impressive," she said teasing him with dark eyes. "I'm not sure who you were, but I think it was you." He tried to hide a triumphant smile, but it didn't work. Men are such suckers. "I went to him because you triggered my jealousy again. It tears me to pieces, so I needed him. Claudia had already told him she'd gone to your studio, and he wasn't the least bit concerned because he trusts her. I will learn to trust too; I will. I'm not going to spend my time watching you like a lovesick teenager. Your intensity last night did scare me."

Armando sat down on the bench in front of her staring at her feet. "I'm not totally in control of myself, like last night. Yet you stayed with

141

me when I needed to express myself. I am a tortured soul, the reason I tried to tell you more about myself before you married me. Maybe it would have been better, but now I don't think so. What did either one of us know about marriage until we met? We are really getting closer, you know. We're getting to know each other in the present, not wallowing in shadows of the past."

She was like a veiled statue in the chair aching to tell him about her guilt and confusion. *If I do it in the moment, not in the past, maybe I can tell him?* She paused too long . . . "Yes, I think you are right, and that's what Lorenzo believes. I can't *find* you in the past because we are here in the present moment. Yet, it always seems so much easier to talk about things we've done, mistakes we've made in the past, doesn't it?"

"Yes, and for two people with tortured pasts, we did take the right approach, but it's even more complex for me. I struggle for words . . . the way I was last night, the way I acted, was not really me. Sometimes an ugly force overwhelms me that makes me feel, ah, like a snake, no a lizard . . . It comes out when I paint, my muse, maybe it's my alter ego, the reason I need to be alone in my studio. You got in touch with it last night. Yet, before you feel afraid of me," he said watching her nervous eyes, "at this point, I know a lot about this force, call it evil or reptilian if you like, because Lorenzo helped me get in touch with it and gave me techniques for transforming it. It always comes out when I'm angry and sometimes when I have sex. You made me angry last night because you were suspicious, but still I should have been able to control myself better. I am not the least bit attracted to Claudia. I love talking about emotional and intellectual things with her. I love her mind and her heart, and so do many others. She is the essence of integrity, and no one should cast aspersions on her just because she's beautiful and loves being sexy. I'm thrilled she's found a man on her level, and she will never betray him; never. She adores Lorenzo."

"I know that and I knew it last night. But, unresolved things in my past keep turning me into a jealous bitch! So, my jealous bitch made you angry and then your demon came out and attacked back. I think we need to know the demon and the bitch. I need to trust you, so that I can trust myself . . . I'm totally committed to our marriage, yet I'm not sure I should get pregnant until we know these parts of ourselves better. I don't think it's going to take long, but I think we could fall into a weird emotional trap if we have a child too soon." She held his gaze with kind imploring eyes.

While he sat there staring, all the women he'd hurt rolled through his mind.

"Being with Sarah and Teresa is making me think about being a mother. Sarah was ready for a child because she knows herself, and I think Simon found himself when he met Sarah. Teresa is very secure even though she longs for her daddy and her mother is lonely. Simon and Sarah know themselves, the reason she is so remarkably well adjusted."

A strange peace slid into Armando's mind when he realized this was right. He hadn't spent much time around small children and Jennifer's words were making him think about what it would take for him to be a good father. "You're right, Jen. It isn't time yet, but I need a goal. Let's get to know the demon in bed, but not when I'm angry. Be a bitch once in a while if you feel like it. It won't kill me and the bitch might teach you a few things about yourself."

She smiled happily. "Well, that demon was quite impressive and I won't mind teasing it out again. I think it's time for me to genuinely befriend Claudia. I want to know her better."

Matilda arranged for Catarina, the cook's daughter, to take Teresa all morning to play and color in the art room. Sarah couldn't believe it, a morning all to herself! She almost didn't know what to do with it. She was tempted to go into the library, but then someone might find her there and want to talk, so she decided to explore the ancient Roman house. As she walked up the marble staircase to the upper rooms, skylights above the long upper hallway cast diffused light onto soft black-and-white checkered marble floors. Six doors were trimmed with thick woodwork and elaborate lintels. The oldest double doors at the ends opened into suites—one for Pietro and Matilda, the other for Armando and Jennifer. The thick wall by Pietro and Matilda's door had a large, deeply coved niche that contained a beautiful white marble bust of Plato.

Her room was small with a balcony to the east warmed by the late winter sun. She wrapped herself in a wool blanket and went out to sit in a spacious wicker chair. The air was deliciously moist and cool. Seagulls crying rapturously punctuated by a raven growling on the roof spun her into reverie. "Where are you now, Simon, where?"

Simon was in the temporary Amnesty International quarters interviewing a young woman who had been captured by ISIS in August 2014 and later escaped. The pain in Simon's voice as he talked with the girl through an interpreter pierced Sarah's heart. The girl said in a hesitant, shy voice, "The man who took me and raped me said I was the infidel. He said raping me was a holy act." She pleaded, "How could *that* be?"

Simon answered firmly, "Your religious leader Baba Sheikh welcomes all of you back regardless of what you were forced to do. Rape is never a holy act. That man lied and has no power over you. He never touched the real you, your soul and your spirit as a vessel of the sacred Yazidi people."

The pain in Simon's heart was palpable for Sarah, intense sadness within a great breathing organic labyrinth. She intensified her heart and visualized the Peacock Angel sending a powerful beam of light into his heart, which flowed into the heart of the young girl. "You believe that, sir?" she asked desperately. "You believe I am untouched?"

"Yes, and when you get through this, you will have your own family someday."

"But, they took away my brothers and our men and killed them in the fields. I will have no family because our men are dead." She spoke so quietly he could barely hear her.

Sarah intensified the energy in her heart to make a halo around the girl. Simon sat back and stared in wonder at the pulsating blue light. "Do you see the light around you? You are holy, a young woman of pure love. The divine surrounds you with light because you have so much goodness in your heart; you are holy."

The girl held out her hands and arms marveling at the light waving out from them. The female translator gasped at the girl's luminosity, for a moment Simon could almost see through her. "You are transparent with the Holy Spirit. You are light, you are beautiful, and you are stronger than all those evil men." His dark eyes flashing with sapphire light made her believe him.

"My spirit is here with me again," she said. "It happened to my body and my body got away. They told me they owned me, but nobody owns me; I am not their property. They cannot have us."

Sarah took a deep breath aware of sticky tears on her cheeks. She stopped touching the ruby to look at her watch. A curious raven landed on the balcony ledge then quickly flew off in a whoosh. Two hours had passed like five minutes! She still had time for herself. The phone rang.

"Hello, Sarah! I'm heading to Rome tonight to join you at the Pierleoni's," said her father excitedly. "Pietro called me last night and talked me into it. What's the point of staying away while a party is going on? I'm coming! Your mother is staying here because she has too many things to do. I can't wait to see you!"

William joined the group a day later, and for the first time in many years, the cavernous stone structure was filled. Simon was thrilled to hear they were all together, Teresa with both her grandfathers in the same house. Sarah had never been so happy to see her father.

The morning after his arrival, William was alone in the library when Armando walked into the room. "Hello, William. Are you enjoying yourself?"

William appraised Armando, still not trusting him since he'd pursued Sarah. They'd been polite during last night's dinner, but he didn't feel like being alone with this young man. "Yes, I love this room. I suppose you do too?"

"Yes, of course. May I please join you for a moment?"

William wasn't happy about this, but he wasn't going to be rude. "Yes, of course."

Armando sat down close to the fireplace opposite William. "I've come to clear the air. You didn't like me when I was interested in Sarah, and you were right. But, now that we are all family, I'd like to get to know you. Sarah helped me when I needed her. I don't think I'd be married if it weren't for her, so I hope you can accept me?" *I wonder whether he knows anything about the things I tried to do to Sarah.*

William's skin was crawling with the same old creepy feeling, yet Armando was no longer a threat to his daughter. He felt like reaching out to him since he was Pietro's son. He didn't know what to say, so the first thing he thought of came out of his mouth. "*How* did Sarah help you? *What* did she do?"

Armando hadn't expected a question back, so American. He'd merely come to make peace since they were in the same house and related by marriage. He thought William would just be jolly and share a drink. There was a long uncomfortable pause . . . "Well, I can be frank with you." His voice was so low that William struggled to hear, so he read his lips. "A priest abused me when I was young, during my First Confession, and then I became a monster. You were right about me when you first met me. I would have been no good for your daughter. But I'm different now, I've worked through what happened to me."

William was totally taken aback; his heart fluttered. "I didn't hear anything about that, son, don't know what to say. Does your wife know about it?"

"She does. Simon and Sarah knew, so Jennifer had to know before marrying me. Sarah was very kind to me at that time, very kind." He watched William closely because he seemed to be unusually nervous—his face bright red. "Ah, I'm making you nervous by bringing this subject up. Please forgive me, William," he said very softly and kindly. "I don't want to make you uncomfortable in our home."

William felt like he was suffocating, having a stroke or a heart attack. He pulled at his collar to unfasten the top button. He looked over at Armando who seemed to be fading away. He started sweating profusely. "Can you bring me a drink? Brandy, Scotch?"

"Of course," Armando said getting up quickly wondering why the Irish always sweat when they're uncomfortable. He brought brandy to the table with two glasses. "Are you all right?" William looked a bit better after a slug, so Armando continued. "I know it must seem terribly odd that I would speak about something like this, but I've learned from therapy that I do better when I talk about the things that disturb me. I don't know if my pain from this abuse will ever go away. After all, it was not my fault at age seven."

William was feeling an unfamiliar mix of curiosity, compassion, and confusion. "Well, son, how did you ever get over such a terrible thing? What galls me is you were having your First Confession! I wonder if any Catholics escaped the fuckers—I, uh, that is I mean since Simon writes about it I know the extent of this horror."

Armando was watching him closely, something more was going on. William was nervously avoiding eye contact while tapping his fingers on the palm of his right hand, all the while his outstretched foot was jerking. He was acting cornered, so maybe the antidote was to say more to push past a barrier. "I'm not really over it. I was one of the lucky ones because the priest got away with it once and then my parents had him sent away. I shudder when I think of what this has done to people who were repeatedly abused." He glanced at William's clouded eyes . . . *Ah! He is one of the damned.*

William clutched the arm of the chair with one hand and slurped down more brandy with the other. Armando held the bottom of the stem while refilling it in uncomfortable silence. Then Armando said thoughtfully, "William, I don't know how to say this exactly, but I feel like there is something you need to talk about. If you do, I'm a good ear after what I've gone through."

The fire in William's groin rushed into his solar plexus. If that hot fire made it to his heart, he felt like he might die. He was determined to stuff it, but the potent discomfort was too strong. *I don't want to die of a heart attack, my granddaughter.* So he slugged down more brandy then growled like an Irishman in the pub, "One of the damned suckers did it to me, too. You are the first person I've told. The bastard rammed me against the communion rail when I was only nine. Like you, he only got me once, but it changed me. The world was gray after that, gray like an eternal rainy day." Glancing at Armando's shocked eyes, he raised his glass. "Here's to you Armando, another member of the boy's club."

Armando went rigid. William had transformed into a boorish, red-faced, fat Irish slob with watery eyes, a runny nose, and shaky hands. Armando deftly took his glass, put it down, and put his hand lightly on William's arm. "It's all right, William. It's good you've told me because I understand. I don't know whether anybody understands this who hasn't gone through it. I lost my innocence that day . . . before that I was a really happy little boy. I didn't begin to feel decent again until I married, and now I am finding happiness again. I'm a tortured soul; always will be. That's why I paint. But I'm getting better, and you will too. I'm not one of the damned in hell; neither are you."

William shook out a large white handkerchief, dried his eyes, blew his nose, and stuffed it awkwardly into his right pocket. "Funny thing, I didn't like you when I met you, yet you've ended up being the person I could share this with. Mary doesn't know, never will. I never could talk about it with anybody, not even the kids, who know so much about these things. They'll never understand my shame, which makes me *feel* like one of the damned. I sensed something in you, an edgy pain you were covering up with your fancy aristocratic manners. We Irish cover it up in the pub." Then he switched to a more comfortable focus. "The question is, how did the Church get away with it for so many years? It still goes on."

Armando took a small sip of brandy and then said in a voice filled with knowing, "We are so much more cynical here in Italy than you are in America. Sexual abuse permeates our culture—Italian art stuffed with fat, sensual, nude cherubs, portrayals of hell filled with damned nude men, statues of just-raped women. Sexual abuse pervades our art, keeping the issue right in front of our faces on the walls of our churches, art that opens hell in our eyes, our minds obscured by the layers of ageless denial. But you Americans are not, so your country is where the truth is coming out. You probably admire Pope Francis, but we are cynical because we know he's there to attract American money."

"We pay less money all the time; certainly I do. When you realize how sick the hierarchy is, it gets harder and harder to pay. I've supported Opus Dei for years but not now, and they'll kick me out soon if I don't pay. I am grateful to you, young man, because I've resisted letting go of this last piece of my religion, the dirty dollars. Opus Dei has been my tie to my Irish past, my family's story. But I don't need it anymore; I certainly don't need the confessional! And, heh! Now that I'll be coming to Italy more often, I can get my Catholic fix by going to museums and the Vatican."

"I keep painting in the old style, inserting portals into the new world that is coming. Do you still go to church, William? We are old titled Italians and we don't go anymore, not even Matilda. How about you?"

"Well, yes, we have been, and I suppose Mary always will. I don't think I will after today, son. I think I will liberate myself the way Sarah did, which hasn't hurt her a whit. She's as saintly as ever, even more so. In fact, now that we've had this talk, maybe I'll start talking to her about her research and writing. Soon, we'll be able to read her novel and then we'll know what she thinks about. I think she's a heretic and I'll join her. Why in hell not?"

Armando looked William over carefully to make sure he was really okay, since a half hour ago he'd almost called the doctor. His skin was white and clear and his eyes were feisty. "William, here's what I'd like to say, since you've shared so much with me. I'm in the early stages of my marriage, learning how to love a woman. You understand, like my father understands, because you both love your wives. Needless to say, what happened to me when I was young makes this process more difficult. Jen has her own struggles, and I think my difficulties make it harder, but we're working on it and we are getting somewhere. The Church would only screw us up. That's why a priest didn't marry us; it must have shocked you. The Church is dying because it has nothing to offer families. I'm out, our whole family is out, and you may leave. Supposedly the Third Prophecy of Fatima says the Church will shrink back to nothing because of an apostasy, the wholesale abandonment by the faithful. Well, I am pulling the plug."

"How will people get along without something to believe in? Really, how will they?"

Armando peered into his small, needy blue eyes. "William, you haven't believed in it for a long time and you've gotten along just fine. Maybe being honest with yourself and cutting the ties will mean you can believe in something new? In my case, I have my art and loving Jennifer is my spiritual life. I've finished a painting of Jesus that I want to show you."

William was hanging on every word. "Funny thing is, you're right, and you know what I believe in? I believe in my granddaughter because she gives me hope for the future. She is a splendid little being who doesn't have to believe in anything; she just is. We can be like that too."

They rose up together and walked through the library to go to lunch.

16

Jesus and the Bee

Dinner was a splendid affair. Pietro sat at the head of the table, the consummate patriarch entertaining his special guests. Teresa joined them for the first course and then went off with her babysitter. Pietro lifted his wine glass for a toast, "To the Pierleoni, Appel, and Adamson families! Let us share food and great stories!"

David stood up with William as they clicked their glasses. "To Pietro and Matilda, our excellent and kind hosts. No matter how lost the world may be, we will enjoy life and great Italian food. Thank you for inviting us."

As Sarah watched them toast, she wondered why her father seemed to be so different. *What's with him? He is comfortable and isn't slyly eyeing Armando like a red fox.* "Armando," she whispered. "My father seems to be changed tonight. Do you know why? Of course, he loves being in Europe, but this is different."

Armando had been totally engrossed in Sarah's natural beauty. *I can't help it; it's my painter's eye. It's her energy. She is as beautiful as St. Teresa in Ecstasy by Bernini.* "Ah, umm, well, we did sort of make peace today," he said placing his napkin on his lap and delicately sneaking a glance at Jennifer who was talking excitedly to Pietro. He whispered back, "Your father never liked me you know, especially didn't want me to marry you." Jennifer looked over at Sarah and noticed how beautiful she was wondering why Armando was whispering to her as he said, "We decided to bury the hatchet today because there's no more wood to cut."

Jennifer's solar plexus tightened up so forcefully that her knees hit a table strut and rattled glasses. *What on earth is going on? Get a grip on yourself, Jen; you're at dinner!* Her ears rang and eyes watered, then her skin flushed hot, but Armando's fierce loving eyes showed her there was nothing to fear tonight. She relaxed.

At ten the next morning, William and Sarah went down the wide steps to Armando's studio door below the first floor of the house. They went inside and gazed at the sectioned, corbelled brick ceilings in the large underground grotto, like an ancient monk's dining hall. Light from the north streamed through tall ground-level casement windows. "Was this once a wine cellar?" asked Sarah.

"Ahh, Sarah, building styles still interest you," noted Armando. "Actually, it is more historically significant than that, built during the high Renaissance, the best period in Rome. Before that our family used this lower area to store grain, wine, and meat we brought down from Tuscany. We also had gardens here and stored vegetables in the winter. We fed the masses on several occasions during famines. Lorenzo Bernini lived nearby and used to buy our wine and prosciutto! We're lucky it wasn't torn down a long time ago because when our house was built over these cellars around 1550, it was constructed *over* this part of the old storage system with steps down into it. There is a spiral staircase out of the kitchen to this space, our larder. I love this room because it's always cool. It's like a monastery, could have been one, and probably goes back to 1200. Look at the stone floors, worn down by so many feet. Let's look at my painting of Jesus and Mary Magdalene."

Sarah was stunned. Her novel was about the Holy Bride, so his portrayal of Mary beseeching Jesus to stay with her in this dimension caused Sarah to vibrate with intense fire as her parasympathetic nervous system assumed the Magdalene's pose. She held her arm down to keep it from flying up, losing awareness of where she was as if she were ascending.

Armando observed a cocoon of light developing around Sarah flowing into other dimensions, like Teresa of Avila in the *Chiesa di Santa Maria della Vittoria* with the sun streaming through the ocular device above her head. William said in a cracking voice, "Quite something, Armando. Both Christ and Mary are very commanding. She seems to hold him there on the rocks as he rises. Is he ascending?"

"I'm not sure," Armando answered lost in Sarah's light. *I wonder if she could ever let me paint her again.* "I'm not sure whether this is after he came out of the tomb or before he was crucified. What do you think, Sarah?"

Thankfully, the question brought Sarah out of her reverie. She was uncomfortable being in a high state with anyone except Simon. All she could see, as she refocused to answer Armando's question, was the large golden bee on the rock behind Jesus. *What is that? Why is it there? Why can't I remember?* "Armando, I don't know what to say. I'm overwhelmed by your portrayal of Christ's light as Mary struggles to hold him in our world. I had no idea anyone in the modern era could paint something like this. But, *why* is that golden bee on the rock behind Jesus?"

"That's amazing, the very first thing Claudia said when she saw this painting months ago and then came to visit it again last week. Typical of her, she had a long explanation for what it means that I could barely comprehend, something about the relationship of Jesus and Mary, especially the sexual aspects, based on a recently translated ancient manuscript. Supposedly the queen bee is a symbol for a sacred lineage from Mary Magdalene, Jesus, and their children—a hidden bloodline."

"Uh, Armando," William said. "So, you painted that bee there to cue people into the whole story? How clever."

Both Sarah and Armando looked at William quizzically. "Dad, what do you mean by clever?"

"Well. They say that painters slip in symbols to convey big secrets for anybody who has the eyes to see them. Like you can show images of things that you can't say in words or somebody will kill you. You've heard about that?" he asked in a confused voice. "Heh, I'm over my head. So why *did* you put that bee there?"

"I've been tempted to paint it over. Things come through on the canvas and I don't know where they are from, I change them sometimes. Since this bee seems to mean things to people, I'll let it be. I haven't any idea why the bee is there or what it means. Claudia says the bee emerged from my archetypal level, knowledge that flows in my blood. As for me, I think I should just let my subconscious flow when I work. If I think about symbols too much, the muse will abandon me."

"I agree with you," William responded. "I don't give a rat's ass about symbols. They say the symbol for Christ is a fish—so what? This painting brings me closer to the light of Christ than anything I've ever seen. It belongs in a church where it can inspire people."

"Funny thing you say that because I didn't put it in the last show, which annoyed my agent. She said she could display it in a spiritual way, have a special carpet in front of it or something, but I resisted. I had a powerful dream about the painting on display in the Medici Chapel in Florence where it emitted a powerful florescent green light. While it was there in the chapel, all the bones in the reliquaries became luminescent, exploded, and then fell as glowing blue snow all over Florence. What a dream that was!"

Sarah eyed Armando strangely because she could see his vision in toto. "Hmmm . . . maybe that is *exactly* where it should go! I've felt like liberating the saints imprisoned in those reliquaries myself. You are related to the Medici by blood, so maybe Pietro could arrange it. People must see this painting! It could awaken the light of Christ in Florence. The Medici Foundation always needs restoration money because that chapel is so complex and always on the verge of collapse. Make it happen, Armando!"

David knocked on Jennifer's parlor door after watching Armando go to his studio with William and Sarah. As he walked in, Dante switched his tail and strutted by acting like George III of England. "Okay to let the cat out into the hall?"

"Yes, of course. He struts up here in the morning after Armando leaves, cases the suite, then waltzes out. Odd cat, he watches Armando a lot. He keeps me company sometimes for a few hours. Come sit down."

David sat down, looking around at a tall wall desk with ornately carved bookshelves and exquisite small Florentine tiles. "Lovely desk isn't it, Dad? It's been here forever and belongs in a museum; this whole house is a museum. Do you like it?"

"I love this house; it's deeply meaningful because they've raised their families here for centuries. With the world going the way it is, I'm basking in the joy of being in a home that feels ageless. It makes me feel like we will survive. There has to be a place for living like this, not just seeing a desk like that in a museum. How are you doing? You seem to be happy and content. I'm becoming very fond of Armando, such an exotic and impressive young man, certainly very unusual."

"There's more than meets the eye here, even between you and me. I want to share something with you that I relived in a session with Lorenzo Giannini." David looked at the floor to focus himself because he could feel she was disturbed about something as she launched into the description of what she had seen. After she finished, she cried softly while David held her gaze. He reached for her as she said in an anguished voice, "That man was *you* in a past life!" He already knew it because when she described the scene, he watched it like a long-forgotten movie. He pulled her into his arms. "I don't want to interfere with Lorenzo, but can you tell me what he said about it? I believe we often return in the same families to resolve problems we didn't solve in the past."

"Lorenzo said this session is critical because it got me in touch with my father/daughter complex, my doorway to individuation, my opportunity to truly know myself in this life. We haven't worked on it further. What do *you* know about the father/daughter complex?"

"I'm not knowledgeable about it, but as I understand it, it is Oedipal, whether that's Freud, Jung, or both. That is, a son loves his mother, the daughter loves her father, and the big crisis for the child is to separate. A parent must never invade their child, especially sexually, because incest is destructive for the child and warps the parent." He paused reflectively. "I've always loved you very dearly and tried to support your freedom, but I wasn't perfect, I'm not now. What do you think about this recall? What does it mean to you? How does it affect you?"

There was another long pause. "I'm not saying this to hurt you and I don't think it is your fault, but I think you missed being able to do something; I really don't know what. I think maybe I was trying to get back at you by having a serious affair with a married man that almost ruined us both. He was a good man, like you. I think having the affair was my way to get back at you!"

Even though David knew he should probably leave it to her therapist, he asked, *"Why* did you want to get back at me?"

Like Alice in Wonderland, she became very small, a miniature person standing by his tall leg. Barely audibly she choked, "Because you wanted my mother, not me."

He held her firmly saying in a warm voice, "If I had not wanted your mother, you wouldn't be here. But, maybe you don't really want to be here? What on earth would I do if you weren't here? What about Rose, what about Armando and your brother? You are the feminine light in our world, Jen, a place that would be very dark without you."

She felt herself getting larger and larger as if she'd eaten the magic potion that clarified her feelings about her father. She drew away looking at him in total wonder. It all hit her at once—she wouldn't be here, she wouldn't have a husband, she wouldn't have a brother or a niece. She stood farther back as waves of knowing were passing through her saying, "You've convinced me I deserve my husband! I've secretly felt like I was greedy and grasping to marry him, even though his family is so much more than their money and heritage. Matilda loves Armando and Pietro is such a fine and loving father—*that* is why I married Armando; that is what you brought me up for. Miraculously, *this* is my home and I will stay here. A huge guilt complex has been shadowing me! I probably

felt guilty about taking you away from your wife in that past life! Then
I did it to Jasmine. I've felt like I don't deserve you or my mother, cer-
tainly not a brother like Simon, and *certainly* not a man like Armando.
But . . . I do."

"Want some fatherly advice?" It was a hot question since she'd never
allowed him to advise her; she wouldn't listen, so she'd always behaved
well enough to keep him quiet. If she did something really bad, such as
the affair in Paris, she made sure he didn't hear about it. All this her
father knew very well.

"Okay, Dad, shoot! I'm ready."

They sat down opposite each other. Because she'd escaped his
shadow, David felt lighter and considered his words very carefully. "You
have married a great man, a man the world will lionize. This will take
him away from you at times. I'm not an analyst or a psychologist, but I
think you are preparing yourself for what Armando is going to become.
It's incredible that you've penetrated this recent past life and learned
so much about our relationship. I think you sense a great wave of suc-
cess is coming that could overwhelm Armando, the kind of fame that
can ruin a marriage. You are finding ways to know yourself so that you
can handle it. Wisely you are drawing yourself into the inner circle of
this family so that all of you can protect him together. That's what I
see about you living with a great artist who could open the hearts of
millions."

"It's so amazing that you say this because you are totally right. Ever
since I married him and came into the Pierleoni world, I've felt smaller
and smaller. I've even given up my own work to settle in, which has
not been easy. The duchess Kate must have felt like that when she married William. She seems to know her importance as a wife, mother, and
public figure, but it must have been hard for her to adopt that role.
According to modern culture, Kate and I are dinosaurs, but I don't
give a damn because I know there's more to life than being a liberated
woman.

"By sharing with you today, you took me past something Lorenzo would have processed with me; I get it, you know. I see why I did some things, and I still have other things to figure out. But I can and will. I just want to be happy as Armando's wife because I'm becoming a new person, really new, an experience that surprises me."

"Well, my dear daughter, that's quite an accomplishment in a world falling to pieces. You will reassume your own work when you're ready or do something entirely different. I admire you for paying attention to what really matters first, your self-discovery, marriage, adjusting to life in a new country, even learning Italian, no small feat!"

17

The Lost Gospel

Sarah had to send her novel to the publisher by the first of April, so she had not seen Claudia to talk about the bee. At last, she was knocking on Lorenzo's imposing front door. It swept open and in she rushed to hug Claudia.

"Sarah! It has been so long. I've missed you so much. My new life with Lorenzo is *so* engrossing, yet I've thought about you every day. It's been months since we had you for dinner. I'm so happy Simon is home and you can take a break. We have so much to talk about!" She stood back to look at Sarah who was wearing honey-colored suede boots, black tights, and a leather miniskirt overlapped by a beige tunic. "You'd never know you had a baby. Good for you!" They went into the library to sit down on the two leather chairs in the alcove with a view out to the garden where traffic rushing by was blocked by a high brick wall. The garden, visible through pink magnolia blossoms and old wavy glass, looked watery as if it was raining.

"I love the way the old glass veils your view of the garden; such a lovely view. Do you come to sit here often? We'd never know we are in Rome except for the traffic hum."

"It is my favorite place in the morning after Lorenzo walks to his office before I drive to work. The soft and steady buzz of the morning traffic reminds me the world still goes on. And by the way, I've been thinking about selling my old flat. I'm never there, yet I'm finding it hard to let it go. I don't know why, maybe because my father gave it to me after I broke up with Armando, the kindest thing he ever did for me. Every time I go to call a realtor, I can't do it."

"Have you thought about renting it? It's so charming, and if you got the right person, they would take care of it." A light went on in Sarah's head. *Should I ask about renting it? Our apartment is so small now with Teresa's toys all over the place. Surely in central Rome the rent would have to be too high.* Just as Sarah thought of it, Claudia had the same idea.

"I hadn't thought of renting it, but now that you mention it, yes. I suppose if I had just the right person it would be a good idea, since property values keep on climbing in Rome, especially in this district. Can *you* imagine renting it from me?"

"Yes! Let me pass it by Simon, and you'll have to give us an idea of what you'd need to charge. It would be just the right amount of space for the three of us, and when Simon is away, his father could stay with me, my parents too. We would take very good care of it, since Teresa is a very orderly baby. Just think how she would love your little patio garden! I'll get back to you as soon as possible if Simon likes the idea.

"But what I really came to talk about is Armando's painting of Jesus and Mary Magdalene, specifically about the queen bee. I went to see it with my father, and Armando said you told him about an ancient manuscript that discusses Mary Magdalene as the bee goddess, a priestess of Artemis? Were you referring to *The Lost Gospel* by Simcha Jacobovici and Barrie Wilson?" Claudia jerked her head up and nodded.

"Great! I've read it, and it really moved me. It's the big hot topic in early Christian scholarship these days, or at least should be. Orthodox theologians hope it will go away if they avoid saying anything about it, but their killing silences won't work because Barrie Wilson is such a highly esteemed Christian scholar. And, Simcha Jacobovici knows how to get attention."

"Of *course* you would have read it," Claudia broke in. "What do you think of it? I don't have your background in early Christianity, but

I thought it was very credible." Actually, she thought it was one of the most important books on early Christianity she'd ever read, certainly the first book in the field that ever excited her.

Sarah began thoughtfully. "Of course, it is *very* controversial, but as a scholar in the field, I think they've made a very strong case for general readers. We scholars could write a thousand pages to prove that it is an encoded text, but that's obvious and the implications are astounding. It means the significant teaching of Mary Magdalene and Jesus is that *marital sex is redemptive.* That's revolutionary, Claudia, an extremely healing message, an essential truth we need right now." She was about to say more, but Claudia was so excited she interrupted her by standing up to pace in front of the window.

"I agree! *Joseph and Aseneth* is evocative and deeply sensual. Now that I've read it, I can't erase the images of their love in my mind, and then I saw Armando's painting of Jesus and Mary. He doesn't know anything about symbols, but that bee came right from inside him, the symbol for the Magdalene as Artemis! Also, Armando spends a lot of time in Siena Cathedral where Mary Magdalene has been right in our faces for hundreds of years as Artemis the bee goddess. Siena Cathedral is one of the most alchemical churches in the world with the great heresy right above the front entrance, a great example of how the secret tradition was kept alive in medieval art.

"Then there are paintings all over Italy of Jesus with Mary sporting sensual red hair. For God's sake, what about all the sibyls in the Siena Cathedral mosaics offering women's wisdom day after day that mocks the hierarchy, a medieval joke that makes fun of the patriarchal fairy tale. The twisted posts holding up Bernini's altar in the Vatican crawl with bees, well, *why?*" Claudia got up again and went to look out the window. "God, I wish I could smoke just one cigarette!"

"You're right, Claudia, and here's the background: The early Church fathers were obsessed with Greek dualism and asceticism, so they recast the sensual Jesus as an unmarried, celibate eunuch. Outrageous, since even Peter was married. The truth is, these early heretics—*Docetists*—

Artemis in the Siena Cathedral

prevailed. They claimed Jesus only *appeared* to be human but was purely divine. But, the anti-sex dualists insisted that Jesus was also a real live man and also divine, so he *had* to have been celibate, not tainted by women. Time rolled along, people forgot the real story, and eventually the ascetics who hated women invented priestly celibacy, the cornerstone of the hierarchy. When Jesus and Mary were alive, the religion of the great goddess Artemis was sensual and deeply sexual. The people loved Artemis, and Mary Magdalene was her priestess. Now, consider the consequences of asceticism—the death of Earth. We *need* the goddess teachings about fertility and sensuality to recover our sanity and protect the Earth! That's why *The Lost Gospel* is so important, yet theologians will do everything they can to bury it."

Claudia came back to sit down and interrupted Sarah a third time as she was wound up like a tight violin string. "The timing of this translation is amazing in relation to Karen King's fragment that says Mary Magdalene was the wife and disciple of Jesus—*another* 2012 breakthrough. Assuming these 2012 breakthroughs mean we're getting somewhere, then this new translation and analysis of *Joseph and Aseneth* might bring the religion of the great goddess back. This must happen because the hierarchy's denial of healthy human sexuality threatens us with extinction. For example, the Church's prohibition against birth control has exacerbated the population crisis that is strangling nature. The search for the real Jesus is the perennial search for the ideal spiritual man, yet the lie about celibacy among sexually active priests belittles the sexual spirituality of the goddess!"

Listening to Claudia's ruminations made Sarah wonder whether *The Lost Gospel* reminded Claudia of the sacred sex she said she'd shared with Armando when they were young, a story that always had felt very odd to Sarah. "Speaking of the rituals of the great goddess, is that what you were doing with Armando many years ago? I have to admit that I've found divinity with my husband. An incredible light went through us when we were married, a light from a very high source that's been guiding our marriage ever since."

"I'll go even further than that," Claudia replied excitedly. "All these breakthroughs at the end of the Mayan Calendar reveal what was really happening between men and women when Jesus was on Earth when the Age of Pisces began. The transition out of Aries into Pisces called for human compassion, a force that could end Arian warfare. The angry judgmental God needed to go once Jesus, a god of love, incarnated to experience sacred sexuality. But Yahweh, a murderous, jealous god, prevailed over Jesus. *The Lost Gospel* portrays Jesus uniting with the goddess, the resolution for the cosmic separation of Sophia and Lucifer in the Gnostic creation story. *That* is why the Church crushed the Gnostics, don't you think?" Sarah nodded in agreement even though she wanted an answer to her question, so Claudia went on.

"The patriarchy completely distorted the image of Jesus as a sexual male who loved the goddess. They castrated Jesus and called Mary a whore and almost aborted the Age of Pisces. But now we can see that the Age of Pisces actually *began* with a sacred cosmic marriage, the ultimate secret tradition. We need this story now so that both sexes can emulate this ideal in marriage to create sexual harmony, to terminate warfare and the denigration of women. Sarah, I'm sorry for talking too much, but I can't stop myself now that I finally have found real love myself!" Sarah wondered whether she would answer her question about the rituals with Armando.

"As the Age of Aries was ending, being born a woman was worse than death, a time when men killed for sport, raped for fun, and ridiculed sacred sex. It *had* to change, maybe the reason Jesus incarnated to find Mary. The story of their love and marriage in *Joseph and Aseneth* is a story of redemption through love and compassion, the central theme of the Piscean Age, the reason Jesus came down from on high, a cosmic miracle. By 2012 millions could see that Jesus was a sensual, heterosexual man and also divine. To finally answer your question, Sarah, yes, the rituals I carried out long ago with Armando were the ceremonies of the great goddess. We've honored her in Rome generation after generation to keep us from drying up under the assault of the misogynist hierarchy."

Sarah walked to the window reflecting on the hierarchy's iron grip and turned around. "Geez, about time you answered my question! Pope Francis is so sweet and amiable, but the hierarchy will never adopt good models for families. By leading the Church in a stable and nonjudgmental way, perhaps Francis is holding the Church together while people fully integrate the sexual revolution, which is not going away. You and I haven't talked about Francis. Maybe he *is* the ideal pope for these times. He has expressed admiration for women. He's trying to clean up the Church's financial systems, something very needed as Roman Catholicism shrinks globally. Last week, when Simon got back right after ISIS blew up Nimrud, he said he thinks the West is collapsing as people escape the chaos in the East and flood Europe. What will happen to Rome if it gets that bad? You know the city, what do you think? I'm so worried! What a time to raise a child."

Claudia thought about Sarah's needs as she went from one topic to the next, normally not her style. "Lorenzo and I talk about this a lot, and in that sense, Lorenzo is our elder. He says this level of chaos and change has come to Rome before, yet we've endured. He takes the long view since he believes chaos always erupts when the ages shift. As for Pope Francis, sometimes I think much more is going on with him than we realize. I've heard he thinks Mary Magdalene was a saint. As a Jesuit, he knows Church politics and finance, and he *is* eliminating some corruption in the Curia. Everything is falling apart around him, yet he is serene. What can any one leader do? He may be a saint sent from high places to help right now.

"Lorenzo and I believe we are all here right now for a reason, and we know things are going to get much worse. Plagued by the breakdown of the Age of Pisces on all levels—religion, finance, morals, and health—we must carry forward. Living through this transition will be horrific, yet creative potential is wide open, as it was during the Renaissance. You and I have never known such personal joy! I'm uncomfortable with the high-tech aspects of the Age of Aquarius, yet I have to believe this will be positive for our species ultimately. But, artificial intelligence terrifies me. Back to *The Lost Gospel* for a moment, since we've always been very frank. What does the idea of Jesus and Mary having sacred sex, we could say tantric sex, do for you as a woman?"

Sarah quieted down and closed her eyes while touching the ruby crystal. Sinking back into a chair she replied, "The real story of Jesus and Mary gives me peace amid this overwhelming breakdown. Many people are remembering their story as Pisces passes away amid the emergence of the Tree of Life, the organic structure of creation that has roots in Earth that branch up to the sky. Christ and his bride draw our minds into the cosmos. In my novel, the marriage of Jesus and Mary is a metaphor for the great tree. In the Garden of Eden, or Nature, where Adam and Eve exist eternally, the serpent is kundalini energy that fuses men and women after they've ingested the apple, wisdom, gnosis. The shyly smiling face of Pope Francis shines in the Tree of Life. Sometimes when I'm with Simon and Teresa, we're enveloped in such profound oneness that we can see the future in Teresa's eyes. Watch the world through the eyes of children, the future. That is what Jesus said, and now we are ready to hear it."

Later that night, Claudia and Lorenzo were eating dinner while enjoying a beam of light coming through a high window that hadn't been illuminated since last October. "It always comes back on this day. Thank you for making dinner. Your ziti is delicious. How was your day?"

"Sarah came to visit. I've missed her so much. She is so vibrant. I can't wait to read her novel. It should be out in the fall or winter. We've both read *The Lost Gospel,* so that's what we talked about."

Lorenzo smiled. "Very interesting; one of my clients may have gotten in touch with the same archetype. She went back to a childhood time when she'd stepped on a bee's nest, got multiple stings, went into anaphylactic shock, and was treated. She's had mild nervous tics lately, probably the reason her free associations led her back to being stung. She thinks the pricks and electrical sensations she's been feeling are somatic memories of all the bee stings. Then, oddly, a presence came into the room that was eerie and commanding. As it came in, I could see a tall woman with a strong kind face, and a bunch of queen bee egg sacks were hanging all around her solar plexus. My client was slipping into reverie, so I had to stop looking at the vision, but it must have been Artemis. I saw her statue years ago at Ephesus and thought the pods on her chest were multiple breasts, but later read they were queen bee eggs. Then my client went on to say her homeopath told her that the bee stings are probably the reason she's been so healthy all her life! She thinks her health is back just by getting in touch with that incident again."

"Isn't it fascinating that both of us would pick up on this archetype right now?" Claudia noted. "I've always felt a great resonance with the Pleiades as many people have for thousands of years. Many of the great goddesses were from the Pleiades. Maybe Artemis is associated with the Pleiades? The health of bees on the planet is very threatened right now. Maybe people venerated Artemis because they knew that plants don't grow without bee pollination. In the medieval version of her in Siena Cathedral, the eggs go all the way down to her feet and look like squashes, a medieval cover-up. It *is* Artemis, since she has the tower as a crown, the magdala."

"Maybe that's true, it sounds like I'll also have to read *The Lost Gospel*. It might help me with this client, certainly we'll enjoy talking about it."

Sarah and Simon were finally alone after putting Teresa to bed. The evening aromas were intoxicating as he flopped down beside her on the couch. "I had so much fun with Teresa today. I took her to the Pantheon. We went into the middle of the cavernous room and sat down together. She climbed into my lap and tipped her head back to gaze at the ceiling. The high vault mesmerized her, she asked me if this was heaven."

"My goodness, what did you say to that?" Sarah laughed.

"I asked her to tell me what heaven is, and she said it was the sky. She was annoyed that I didn't know! So, I told her the vault of the Pantheon is like the sky. She said her friend's grandmother just went to heaven. Then she asked, 'Is Amelia's granny here in the Pantheon?'"

"That's hysterical. I'm amazed by what goes on in her mind."

Simon turned to her and kissed her while cupping her cheek. She closed her eyes seeing yellow-green fields of radiant organic light—the life-force she always saw when he was turned on. Her breasts rippled with waves of desire as he continued to kiss her along her throat. She unbuttoned her blouse and looked into his eyes through a spiral vortex into his mind. He put his hand on her neck and slowly moved it down as she closed her eyes while he nestled his face in her breasts. They made love slowly and gently while breezes waved the lace curtains in the kitchen. Green radiant light pulsed violently in her skull when he came.

18

Everything Going Faster

Time accelerated during July 2015. After years of negotiations, world leaders signed an agreement with Iran to curb nuclear weaponry that ended many years of American economic sanctions on Iran. For the moment, the sword of Damocles was back in its scabbard. Pope Francis announced the creation of a new Vatican tribunal to review bishops who'd been accused of covering up sexually abusive priests. The *New York Times Magazine* published a major article by Eliza Griswold on the enslavement and murder of Middle Eastern Christians that caused many readers to conclude Western interference in the Middle East had been destructive. Simon reported on the desperate conditions in the oldest Christian communities in Iraq, communities losing hope for their future because it was impossible to know which of their neighbors supported ISIS, waves of people pushed out of their ancestral homes. Then, very ominously, massive airstrikes in Syria directed by the U.S. triggered an exodus of desperate refugees through Greek islands. The whole Middle East was on the move, while people leaving Africa were coming across the Mediterranean and landing on the beaches of Italy, Greece, and Spain. These mass migrations held grave implications for Europe.

Simon was in Iraq while David was in Rome helping Sarah move into Claudia's home. He'd already planned to be in Rome in July to see Lorenzo because disturbing thoughts were plaguing him; the ground was quaking. His uneasiness had begun in the previous September after his first deep conversation with Pietro in Tuscany. He stabilized after that until his next conversation with Pietro, and also his discoveries about his daughter made him uneasy. *Is it because I'm worried about Simon? Or are Jennifer's pressing needs dredging up old memories that I can't suppress?* All he knew was he needed to get a grip on himself or he wasn't going to be any good to anybody. With Simon in Iraq, he had to keep his act together.

A few weeks before going to Rome in July, David was pacing back and forth in his Shelter Island study pondering the bizarre speedup of violence in the world. *Why am I so uneasy? Am I reacting to all the fear in the world? But I don't think so . . . A shadow stalks me, a memory predator from when I was around nine years old when my father told me I couldn't be an architect because I'd be going into the family business.* After he'd told Pietro about the last few hours of his father's life, the old predator had appeared from an unknown time, the one he was afraid was under his bed or in the closet in his childhood room. As he felt like he was losing his control, in the world around him every hour was crammed with two or three times as much activity as in the past; information technology was eating the old ways of life. People seized with monkey fever frantically digitalized their fingertips off and took constant photographs and sent them all over the place, a hot new connectedness—exponential time acceleration.

The crystal skull hidden away in his cupboard was his guide, so he got it out, cupped it in his hand, and tuned in to its center. It felt dead . . . like the shadow haunting him. *What are you trying to say? Why are you trying to reach me?* Whatever it was vibrated into nothingness and slipped into a lower dimension. A trapdoor opened and quickly shut. *But,* like a pebble falling into a pond sending ripples out through his cranium, the answer drifted in his brain. *You do know, David.* Breathing and sinking more deeply within, he knew exactly what to do, see Lorenzo Giannini as soon as possible. *He's the one who can help, but I still have more to do with the skull.*

At the end of the Mayan Calendar, he thought he'd put the skull away for good, but here he was holding it in his hands again, his mind drifting back to when he was twenty visiting Teotihuacan near Mexico City with a group of Maya elders meditating in the Temple of the Quetzal Butterfly—El Palacio del Quetzalpapalotl. They'd recognized his father's serpent ring; David was the one they'd been waiting for. They invited him into their sacred pipe ceremony amid acrid copal smoke wafting out of the central courtyard. Upon completion, they handed him the skull. He gracefully accepted it while they explained he'd hear from Quetzalcoatl, the Plumed Serpent.

He never saw the elders again and decided they'd manifested in the temple from another dimension when he'd walked in, like a fourth-dimensional movie becoming visible in a sun slice of misting copal. Regardless, being in this ceremony was the most multidimensional moment of his life. It gave him the ability to see the world through Mayan eyes, so he dedicated the skull to saving the Earth and brought it out when he was inspired or troubled. When he shared the story of his father's death and the serpent's ring with Pietro, he detected the elders in Pietro's eyes, a wake-up call. *Some people are just way beyond time and place.*

But what is this memory predator? What's trying to pierce my boundaries? His appointment with Lorenzo was in mid-July, so when Simon asked him to go to help Sarah move, he was intrigued because he'd be there at exactly the right time. *Who scripts my movie; will somebody just tell me that?* In deep thought he slowly wound up the tower stairs to Lorenzo's office. *I saw him at the wedding, but I don't remember what he looks like except that he was an old dapper guy.*

He opened the door, and there was Lorenzo. "Hello, David. I'm delighted you've come to see me!"

"Thank you, Dr. Giannini. I see constant improvement and budding happiness in my daughter so I thought you might be able to help me as well. Thank you so much for what you are doing for her."

"Please, call me Lorenzo! My work is very relaxed, and we'll never get anywhere without being friends. I'm not doing the work; it's all Jennifer. It will be the same for you. Come, let's go sit down."

They went into an inviting alcove brightened by large, wide-open casement windows with deep stone sills. The clamor from the square below—a crazy mixture of Yiddish, Italian, and French syncopated by barking dogs—filled the room. "The Trastevere never changes, still a medieval ghetto," Lorenzo murmured as he pulled in the casements. Luckily, fresh air flowed in through high windows on the back from a quiet inner courtyard. It was hot, any breeze brought relief. They sat down on two comfortable small leather chairs with a table between as David glanced back into the room noting the analyst's couch with a table at the end where he caught a glimpse of a large, intricately carved, crystal cylinder.

"Well, why have you come to see me today?" Lorenzo asked with curiosity and excitement.

"Good, let's get right into it and not waste time because I've come all the way to Rome just to see you. Your ability to help Jennifer access a significant past life has impressed me, I'm thrilled to see her exploring deep levels in her psyche. She has, well, always had some difficulty with subtle levels, but not with you. I believe in reincarnation, so we've discussed her recall, and I understand what it means to the two of us, but I'm not here about that."

Lorenzo was watching David very closely because as he sat opposite him, someone was behind him—a dense gray shroud holding its hands up behind his head. He'd never seen anything like it in all his years as an analyst, humming in some other dimension, buzzing at a high frequency. "Fine, David, since talking with you about her sessions wouldn't be possible anyway. So, what concerns you today?" As his voice probed, the shroud's hands twisted behind David's head, like a dancer pirouetting. The eyes of the shroud, strange and compelling ocular wormholes into another universe, went opaque and filled with white mist. *What's going on with this man? What's this quantum creep?* "David, ah, if you don't mind, I need to go to my other table to get a crystal that I will need while I work with you. Do you mind me using my favorite crystal so that I can see the subtle dimensions more easily?"

David laughed and assured him he didn't mind since he used crystals all the time himself. He was mumbling as Lorenzo got up saying, "If you only knew . . . " Lorenzo went to get the cylindrical carved piece with a sharp point, central shaft, and a wide carved end back to a point. It fit perfectly in Lorenzo's hand. David peered at it. "It has many sides, Lorenzo. How many?"

"Ah, eleven, the most mysterious number of all, the number beyond manifestation in this dimension. Before you came, I sensed I would need it to help me see what you see. Now that you are here, I'm sure that is true. Normally I use it for my personal work, rarely bring it out for anyone else, but it was calling for you. Marcel Vogel carved it many years ago as a tool for accessing eleven dimensions. I have to say, whatever is going on with you, it's very multilayered." Lorenzo held the crystal with both hands and the shroud turned into misty white light with blue edges; it lingered.

David sounded spacey. "I feel lighter. I felt lighter the moment you took the crystal in your hand."

Tuning in to David's troubled gaze, he said, "Before I ask you to recline on my couch, is there anything else you can say about why you are here?"

"I feel like I'm being followed; I'm not solo. At first I thought I was in danger, but that's not it. Something or someone is trying to get through to me. Something is trying to reach me, it's robbing me of my peace."

Lorenzo locked his eyes into David's while keenly watching the form with his peripheral sight. The shadow behind David transfigured into a perfect dodecahedral sphere with the front pentagram as a window behind David's head. Like soccer balls, the bottom edges of the other pentagrams pulled all together making it spherical. The convergence lines sent out wavy sheets of light that resembled the aurora borealis. The platonic solid was so entrancing and elegant that Lorenzo almost forgot where he was as his fingers kept lightly caressing the long narrow sides of the crystal cylinder. David's eyes were closed, so he pointed the cylinder's sharp long tip into the center of the pentagram behind David's head and said in a soft yet very authoritarian and silvery voice, "David, someone with truly extraordinary awareness wants to reach you."

David said whimsically while still fully awake, "I want to know what this is, I do."

"All right, David. I'm going to stand up and come over to you to take your hand to guide you over to the couch. Is that all right with you? Will you come with me?"

David was now nine years old, and Lorenzo was the person he'd waited for day after day; he'd finally come! Long ago he waited and he never came, so he forgot about him fifty years ago. A vibration in the center of his sternum emitted words that Lorenzo could hardly hear, not David's voice: "I'll come with you."

Lorenzo held the crystal cylinder in his left hand while leading David with his right hand over to the couch, leading him like a small child lost in a trance. He placed the crystal carefully on the table and settled David on the couch being careful to make sure his whole body was tucked inside its edges. Without these edges, he could feel like he was falling down into the Underworld, the precipice above hell. Settling down, David felt like he was in a sarcophagus, a humming field above his body weaving threads of light into his cells like a multifaceted, perfectly cut oval diamond. Lorenzo sat down quietly and aimed the cylinder's tip to the top of a pentagonal spherical light form above David. In all his years, he had never seen such an exquisite manifestation, yet he knew exactly what it meant: a past life ready to express its full genius through David was descending. *Who is that?* Lorenzo silently asked his guardian angel.

"Now David," Lorenzo said in an omniscient, musical, and convergent voice, "someone wants to know you, someone who is a fragment of you in the past. Will you allow this being to come here?"

David squirmed around, but stayed within the edges. Wracked with pain, a weak, lonely voice squeaked out, "I'm cold, my bones ache. I'm trapped in my body like the devil in hell or Christ in the lower realms freeing our souls. I'm paralyzed, sick, abandoned; I am in hell. I lie in the streets like a dying dog."

Lorenzo's eyes moved rapidly side to side observing a bedraggled, freezing, skin-and-bones, nearly dead man, lying in a gutter on the edge of a busy street, his pants held up with safety pins fastened to his shirt. A street car flew by, whoosh! Above this dying form, the dodecahedral crystal pulsated and hummed, sending powerful rays of light to each person rushing by the crumpled moaning man. A man in an elegant topcoat felt a sharp pain in his skull and noticed a body in the gutter, walked over to look, and was astonished! *I know him, oh my God!* He turned back to hail a cab, gave the driver a large bill, and then lifted the almost weightless body into the back seat. He covered him with a jacket and reverently held his head. They rushed to the hospital with the diamond form following along, yet eventually it went away. After a few days in the hospital, the poor man died.

Lorenzo said very kindly, "You have died; tell me what is going on."

David was lying there soaked in sadness and pain from the cold dampness, dirty street, and throbbing, brittle, arthritic limbs. As he lay on Lorenzo's couch, David was blissful because he'd never be cold, wet, or abandoned again. He thought of all the comforts in his life now. Looking down at the bandaged form in the hospital bed mysteriously surrounded by a group of very wealthy grieving men, he wondered, "Why do they care?"

Lorenzo broke in gently. "Who are you?"

"It is only I, Antoni Gaudí, 1926, I died in the street. I have not finished my work."

The crystal cylinder was getting heavy as Lorenzo held it to the center of his chest.

"It does not matter. I was in such terrible pain for so long that I couldn't keep going any longer. It is all right; I go to my maker in peace."

But he wasn't going to his maker, that Lorenzo knew. Something very strange was going on, so he followed his intuition. "Antoni, why do you want to merge with David Appel? Why have you returned to be with David?"

David shuddered on the couch, feeling like he was thousands of years old. He watched many lives in a long line drawing back in a great stream into the mist. He could go right back through them all, right now here on this couch, a rocket ship through time. The exquisite geometrical light around his body informed him that this visitor, Antoni Gaudí, had more knowledge than all the wisdom he'd ever attained. A high-pitched, tight voice squeezed through his larynx translated by his third eye from an odd foreign language, Catalan. "I . . . I . . . I have to go there. I, that is, David *must* go to La Sagrada Família. I have to see if they are doing it right. I . . . I have to go back to my house. David, you Appel, you have to go there with me. That is why I follow you. The Age of Aquarius is rushing in, the light I saw during my life that nobody else could see. I see it in realms you can't see yet. I have to go see my helicoidal nodes, my towers and glass, to see if they are intersecting and spinning with the light as I planned. If something isn't right, I can fix it up here, but I can't see it in your dimension. You have to see with me, soon! You, Appel, you must bring Sarah, your daughter-in-law, with you."

"David," Lorenzo broke in firmly, "is this all right with you? Do you want to listen to him? This is the past, yes, your past, but still it is the past. You don't have to do anything it asks. Do you want it to go away? I can make him go away, forever, and we can talk about what came in. What do you want me to do, David? I am at your command."

In response, David zoomed right into the wracked body lying in the hospital to merge with the last vestiges of Antoni Gaudí's breath as he passed on. His solar plexus lurched because it was like being with his father when he died. But this man wasn't his father; this was himself in the life just before this one. It wanted something from him, wanted him to do something. It felt like he needed to create something new, and all he had to do for this man was just keep going, so he trusted the possibility. "You want me to go to Barcelona, do you? You want me to go to La Sagrada Familia with you? You want me to see for myself and with you, to share that fulfillment with you. You want me to go to your home? I will. Yes, I will, and I will see if Sarah will come."

Lorenzo was tapping his fingers on his knee after putting the crystal cylinder back on the table. "David, with your permission, may I enter into this? It's a bit odd to have one's previous life come around to ask you to do something for it in the current moment. Since I've never experienced that or heard of it, may I ask a favor of Antoni? Just so we can be sure you will be fine in this lifetime? This life is the one that matters."

"Sure, why not?" David replied. "I'm not afraid of who I once was and how I died."

"Yes, but you must be very sure you know where your current time node is located. If you don't, you may go insane; it happens to people every day, whacked right out of reality and can't get back. I'm not operating a time machine; this tower is not Dr. Who's telephone booth. You could get stuck somewhere. Also, we don't do Faustian pacts here either."

"Ask your favor of him, he will answer," David replied in a level voice.

There was a long pause. "Hello, Antoni," Lorenzo said in a light and friendly voice. "If David takes you to La Sagrada Familia and the home you love, will you let him go after that? Will you please promise me you'll release yourself out of time if David does that for you?"

The tight high voice came back through again. "Many of us are coming back now with the Age of Aquarius. All I want to do is be in my created space to integrate it with these powerful vibrations. When I designed it, I didn't know what I know now in the ninth dimension. That is all, and I will let him go. David will receive the full gift of my spirit body, my universal cosmic soul. That is all."

"All right, David. It's time to come back into this room. I'm going to count from eleven back to three to bring you back, and then we will add two and one."

Ten minutes later they were sitting in the leather chairs in the alcove. David was calm and invigorated. "David, this is virgin territory for me. What did you feel and experience?"

"I love Gaudí's work, always have. He's one of the great nineteenth-century geniuses. I've taken the family to Barcelona to see his work; Simon loves it. This encounter might be an ego boost for some people, but it isn't for me. Feeling his energy body—whew!—will change me forever. His energy body is immense and exquisitely geometrical. It was like being a flower stamen as its petals unfold, or like being in the heart of an astonishing geometrical creation when it forms. Expressed more exactly, science thinks that large crystals grow over a few billion years. Melding with Gaudí's form was like being a crystal seed experiencing all its growth in one hour. I'll never be the same again, and you bet I'm going to Barcelona as soon as I can. I want to experience the vibrations of Aquarius intersecting with La Sagrada Familia through its creator, Antoni Gaudí, when he apprehends its correct completion. My god, what an opportunity! What an amazing experience that will be!"

19

The Story of Time

Tuscany was hot and sweltering in July. Pietro asked Armando to come talk with him late in the evening after the breezes coming up from the ravine had refreshed the genealogy room. Armando thought about his father as he walked up the wide stone stairs. *Maybe our family has protected the real story of Jesus and Mary Magdalene? Perhaps my own father has some of the missing pieces.*

The heavy old door opened slowly making the hinges squeak as the bottom of the door scraped the old red tiles. Pietro stood in the alcove enthralled by the aromatic Tuscan evening. The sawing spiny legs of cicadas and crickets were playing a symphony to the stars rising above the distant mountainous horizon. Matilda and Jennifer were below in the living room enjoying time together.

Sitting down in a cushy velvet chair, Pietro smiled at his son. "Welcome to this room, our place to contemplate our family's role in Italy. We've barely touched the surface, it is time to go deeper, and I must admit I think we need to speed up. Even though you are not the kind of man who absorbs facts easily, images from far back in time flow through your hands. You are ready to remember things that most people have forgotten, your lineage, the Pierleoni story from the ancient days. Remember, we helped design Siena Cathedral. The story we've been told about the human race on Earth is false and is used by the elite to retain power. But, now the true story of Earth is breaking through.

"The story of human life in Italy for the last 50,000 years is recorded in Siena Cathedral. The floor mosaics portray renowned sibyls who still speak, Hermes who knows all, and the story of Jesus and the goddess there by the sides of the Last Supper window surrounded by the goddess, Artemis. The records of the sibyls, the alchemy of the magus, and the sacred marriage will be revealed. We are the guardians of this knowledge. We were nearly exterminated a thousand years ago when the Church tried to eliminate anybody who knew the truth. Yet, the Church realized essential knowledge had to be stored somewhere, so they patronized artists to veil it, portray it in real stories encoded in art all over Italy. Siena Cathedral holds the keys to the most ancient wisdom, Paleolithic astronomical alignments to the swan constellation, Cygnus."

Armando looked up at the family crest on the ceiling, a swan in flight above the snake in a circle swallowing its tail. "Father, I've always wondered about that swan above the snake. Does it symbolize flight and migration? Often I dream I'm a swan in flight."

"Hmmm . . . Magnetic crystals in the brains of swans orient their flight to the constellations marking the precession of the equinoxes by their migratory flight. Your innate awareness of these flight paths means you were born with this knowledge. Of course, all potent symbols have a surface meaning; then underneath there are more layers, keys to evolutionary records. Right now, our planet is on the edge of destruction, everybody knows it. Esoteric secrets must come to light now because power mongers are grabbing everything left on Earth, since they think they can exhaust our planet and then fly to Mars. They think money will save them, but we can't eat money! The only thing that can save Earth is remembering our true heritage, which always emerges for a while during the changes of the ages, transition times when advanced individuals can transfigure, become their greater selves while alive. Every woman is a goddess, every man a magus, both long for wholeness in sacred marriage.

"Right now we are an insane species because our story of the past has been distorted for 12,000 years. So listen to me very carefully, Armando . . . Our family crest reveals the circle of Earth time, the story of the last 17,000 years." Pietro pointed up to the crest. "The circular snake is a symbol for the cycle of the Great Ages, the 26,000-year-long precession cycle, Earth's cosmic orientation. The astronomy is very complex, and the astronomers have it all wrong because this cycle was called The Great Year of the Pleiades. But, all that matters now is attunement to the passage into Aquarius. During the vortex for this shift—1998 through 2020—we are integrating the early Aquarian field ruled by the planet, Uranus. Many are going crazy because they can't integrate the Uranian transformations. Conversely, many are making huge breakthroughs such as you have with your painting of Jesus and Mary. When I saw it, I knew you were ready for Swan Wisdom."

"May I break in?" Pietro's affirming nod was a relief because Armando thought it must be hard for his father to put this complex story together for him. "Please help me orient. My painting expresses something that happened two thousand years ago, yet you are talking about a much greater span of time. Why is *my* painting part of the story?"

"I can only say a few things about that because the main information that I must pass to you is so complex and mindboggling. Jesus came to deposit new consciousness that would mature all the way through Pisces for two thousand years. You have portrayed what he came to reveal, and your painting opens this awareness to others. The deepest elements of his teachings are finally available because we have gone through the sexual revolution after escaping Victorian repression. The Aquarian fields are helping people access cosmic energy, especially sexually as love discovered person by person; we are on a new level. That is the long story that we are living out, as you are with Jennifer. Now I need to tell you the story of time for the activation through 2020, only a few years from now."

Armando relaxed back in his chair to take in a pile of complex information that would pack his brain. *I have to understand this, or I can't make the right decision about revealing my painting to the world.* "Okay, I'll do my best to understand."

"In our crest the swan is taking off in flight above that section of the circle that marks a specific time—the Age of Libra around 17,000 years ago to 15,000 years ago—a time when we were enlightened. Our mentality began to decay around 15,000 years ago, and then we were traumatized by a series of cataclysms that were the most extreme around 13,000 to 11,500 years ago. During the last fifty years, science has found the evidence for this catastrophic phase—the Younger Dryas, the Gothenburg Flip—global remnants of cosmic catastrophes when our planet suffered extreme climatic oscillation characterized by rapid cooling, warming, and rising seas. We are experiencing similar climate stress again and remembering what happened long ago. Around 11,500 years ago, something bombarded our solar system and the Earth was nearly destroyed, a time when another planet—Maldek—*was* destroyed, and its orbit is filled with remnants, the asteroid belt." Pietro was seeking the right words but stopped talking when he noticed Armando's face.

Armando had an expression that Pietro had never seen before, as if he'd been bashed on the head. His eyes were wide and he was breathing heavily. "Excuse me, but for some reason this information is too much for me. Facts make my brain go blank, but what you are telling me is piercing a primal part of me, a place that knows this is true and knows I *have* to remember it. I'm having rapid flashes of inner light in the back of my skull right above the top of my spine. Isn't that strange? Why would I respond *there?*"

"That response is very revealing. It's what happens when people access repressed traumatic memory, like recalling early childhood abuse as you have. That part of your brain is your *reptilian brain,* your memory bank of past trauma. At this point in time, Aquarian rays are penetrating that part of the brain in everyone, so difficult for all of us. In popular culture, these cataclysms are called the Fall of Atlantis. However, due to the trauma repression, any scientist, historian, or archaeologist who mentions Atlantis is deemed an idiot even though most people resonate with the story of Atlantis—the Fall—because it actually happened! During the last fifty years, science has found evidence for these cataclysms, and their data exactly parallels the story of Atlantis. Many educated people now realize Earth's history before 12,000 years ago *is* the story of Atlantis. Ancient legends are repositories of repressed human memory that is denied because of the horror attached to them. After all, if it could happen long ago, why not again? Also, the story of Atlantis has been obfuscated. For example, many people say Atlantis was an advanced technological or extraterrestrial civilization, but there's no evidence to support that. In fact, it is an elite diversion concocted to make people think our ancestors *caused* the cataclysms. This makes people feel guilty, they can't think clearly, so they don't see that we *are* the ones threatening our planet, now. Do you follow me?"

Armando was breathing heavily and trying to calm down. "Just go slowly, father. I don't understand a lot of what you are saying. You told me these stories when I was a little boy. I've tried to grasp these ideas for years, but my brain fogs. Now I *feel* how important they are; I need to know this."

"Okay, son, I'll explain it as best I can, and do ask me questions. I *did* tell you the story of Atlantis when you were little, but after you were abused, you were afraid, so I stopped. As I've said, many people realize we experienced terrible cataclysms around 13,000 to 11,500 years ago because many popular books have been written about it and the evidence is accumulating globally. Our species is in the midst of a *mass trauma awakening,* a very exciting moment. But, when our species went through the difficult recovery phase until around 6,000 years ago, when civilization appeared, we struggled just to survive. The point is, we not only went through horrible cataclysms, we also lived through a long traumatic survival phase, and now our species threatens Earth.

"Pierleoni records go back to the Etruscans, who still retained the memory of their homeland on the Black Sea that flooded 7,600 years ago, and these ancestors retained stories going back many more thousands of years. We've kept these stories waiting for the time to release them. Our family crest reminds us we were once enlightened, the thing we need to recall to make the transition into the Aquarian Age. Millions need this story so that we can heal our trauma to get our sanity back, as you did by working with Lorenzo. Will our species destroy Earth? We will be in contact with the universe during Aquarius, but we can't get there without healing our trauma first; we can't pollute the cosmos with human violence.

"Experts, such as the British researcher Andrew Collins, have discovered astronomical orientations that match our Pierleoni records—the pathway of the swan to the stars that opens the skies, the star Deneb in the Swan constellation. This is a big deal because awakenings happen when science detects things."

"Father, I feel stuck in the survival period you've alluded to. I suppose it's because we don't know much about that time? I mean, everything was destroyed as you say, and people came crawling back. I can imagine destruction, since they do that scenario all the time in disaster movies. But after that, you say things were a mess and we don't know much about that time? Is that what you mean?"

"Indeed, we *don't* know much about the survival period because we repress the really horrible memories—people eating other people just to survive and women systematically raped just to get children to carry on lineages, like the Fallen Angels in the Bible. But, critical information about that period is emerging with the discovery and excavation of Göbekli Tepe in Turkey, scientifically dated to right *after* the big cataclysm! Göbekli Tepe's discovery has pulled the human timeline further back to the survival period; the site makes sense out of other strange sites and artifacts scientists have puzzled over. Now Armando, what we are talking about tonight could fill twenty volumes if we filled in the details, so I'm going back only to our ancient records. But first I'd like to further elucidate the technological story of Atlantis because that false interpretation has diverted many intelligent people, a confusion that you may have yourself. I want to clear it away before completing the true story."

"Okay," Armando said getting up for a glass of water and one for his father. "Tell me the false story of Atlantis."

"Atlantean legends are ubiquitous. The earliest totally reliable source in the West is Plato's *Timaeus*. Plato was the first great historian because whenever he's been put to the test, he's accurate. Plato said Atlantis fell around 9500 BCE, the *exact* scientific date of the global cataclysm! That is really amazing, and even more amazing is that Plato described the culture of the last Atlanteans in detail in the *Timaeus*. He says they were weird and primitive, so unlike us that hardly anybody pays attention to what Plato says. He says they were a primal, bull-sacrificing, male-dominant group of powerful magicians, *not* technocrats running laboratories and blowing up the world with charged crystals. In other words, people have projected modern foibles and faults onto the Atlanteans, we can't relate to them, so the thread to the past was cut.

"Considering how Plato describes them, they were the last remnants of the Paleolithic cultures that survived the cataclysms, for example the Magdalenians, a Southern European people who were very deeply in touch with nature, magic, and the energy of their own bodies, great geomancers who understood Earth's power. Their Megalithic culture left behind many stone formations that mark places of planetary power, knowledge that goes back to Swan Wisdom. But, I'm loading too much on you."

"You are; I have a headache. But I have to say Mary Magdalene's last name is a probable link."

Pietro leaned back and took a long drink of water while counting the number of strikes in the hallway grandfather clock, twelve . . . *If Armando, of all people, can put this together, this would indicate human thought really is advancing, which I have observed since the 1970s.*

Armando wanted to summarize all Pietro had shared thus far after he refreshed their water.

"I think I can do it if I construct my own timeline by going back to the beginning indicated by our family crest," Armando began in a determined voice. "If I go back to 17,000 years ago and then come forward, I can make sense of what you say. So, Father, up there on our ceiling we have the snake circle that I always thought was a fat green python eating itself when I was a kid, but actually it is the 26,000-year star cycle. Our symbol, the swan, is taking off in flight 17,000 years ago. Then after 2,000 years, 15,000 years ago, human knowledge began to deteriorate. Two thousand more years passed, and around 13,000 years ago there was a series of terrible disasters that culminated 11,500 years ago, when we were nearly destroyed by something that blasted through the solar system, the Fall of Atlantis. After the Fall, our species went through a terrible survival period for around 5,000–6,000 years, and then cultures developed around the world that built pyramids and standing stones. We've had 5,000 years of the evolution of complex cities, and now everything is going faster and faster; we are on the verge of destroying the Earth because we are so damaged." Armando looked up to see a look of utter shock mixed with exhilaration on his father's face, as if he was going to cry and laugh at the same time!

"My God, Armando, I never thought you'd put it all together. You really are ready for the story of time. You will be able to convey it to your children. Bravo!"

"You can't imagine what this evening means to me, father. I have always wanted to have your respect, yet I never thought I would. I was so horribly perverted that I couldn't hear you." Armando's eyes glazed over with milky tears.

Pietro took Armando's hand, peering through the wet film into his dark brown eyes, depths of passion rarely found in any man's eyes. "You've gotten beyond it; I always hoped you would. I couldn't share our knowledge with you because knowledge is power; yet, not sharing would cut the ancestral cord. Before I finish with some thoughts about the long past, would you like me to share my feelings about what happened to you? Can you handle that? We haven't talked about it."

Pietro's suggestion pierced Armando's chest because he was still barely able to talk about it himself. Sharing it with William had been his only relief since he'd stopped seeing Lorenzo. *What does my father want to say?* "It's a good idea, I'll handle it as best I can. I had a talk about it with William a few months ago, and we've bonded since then. Slowly, I'm getting over it. Nobody knows what this pain and shame feels like unless it happened to them." Pietro wondered at this remark but decided to keep his focus on his son.

"Very well, Armando, good. Your grandfather passed me the records when I was seventeen because he knew he was soon going to die young. Knowing so much so soon has not been easy, yet it made me think deeply about all these phases of time. My great delight has been watching the alternative researchers find pieces of the story and put them together for the general public. But as we've discussed, those times were horrific. The question is, do those memories affect us now? What if these horrific experiences are stored in our DNA, in our racial memory, and in our past-life memories—traumas set to go off like bombs when Aquarius comes in?

"Atavism—sexual abuse, murder, and cannibalism—are reversions to the survival period. As we awaken, there is a huge increase in atavistic behavior, such as with ISIS, madmen murdering people in the streets, and pedophilia. As the Aquarian energies arrive, dark energy lurking deep in people's souls from the survival period triggers them, and antipsychotic drugs explode pockets of pain in people who then go mad. This is the critical nature of our wake-up process right now. War, abuse, and ecological destruction are exploding the repressed pain in our minds and bodies, the darkness obscuring our souls. We *have* to heal our inner darkness to attain the next stage of evolution—humans as peaceful beings—just as you have, Armando. This is why I admire you more than anyone I've ever known. You are a model for what we each must do now. I am very proud of you. I think your paintings are helping people handle the Aquarian dark night of the soul as the light permeates our cells. You have real courage, son."

Armando's tears flowed and his nose ran; his father's approval was what he needed the most. "You have just explained to me *why* this priestly abuse happened to me—atavism! Not having a reason for why he did that to me impaled me; the evil in Father Cesare's eyes paralyzed me. Claudia believes the Church is a delivery system for the dark forces, the reason she could forgive me. You will never know the things I did to her." He glanced up at his father but his haunted eyes were too much for Pietro, who looked away.

"Armando, I can't hear it; I'm sorry. It hurt me more than you will ever know. The lust for power sucked the dark forces into the Church when having too much power dredged up the deeply suppressed urges lurking in the survival memories. I see signs of it all over the place, the bizarre panicked looks in the eyes of world leaders on occasion, like when Tony Blair supported Bush's invasion of Iraq. Be that as it may, the Aquarian Age is to be egalitarian, so that we can find our way out of this conundrum by *sharing* power. Power in the hands of the few is atavistic; in the hands of many, ecstatic. What matters to me is *you* have done it, faced your darkness. You were filled with exquisite light as a child, and then you got slammed down. But you found your way back, and soon you will probably have your own children. If you do, then I will know we are going to survive. Swan Wisdom is very complex and requires astronomical information that requires going into the galaxy, so we must let the details wait for another night.

"Check out some of these ideas with your group of friends and by reading more. Let's get together when you have absorbed the cataclysmic story. Meanwhile, I want to ask a favor of you. A few Medici descendents who control the Medici chapels are my old friends, and I'd like them to see your painting. May I show it to them?"

"Absolutely, go ahead and ask them to come here because I brought it from Rome to have it with me this summer because it haunts me. Show it to them and let me know what they say. Jen and I want to go to Majorca for the last two weeks of July, so you will have the privacy to show it to them then."

20

Goddess Rituals

On a hot and humid late-July afternoon, the Tiber reeked of rotting fish, garbage, and gasoline carried by a south wind through the Trastevere. Claudia sniffed the air on the patio and decided to have dinner inside; tonight was to be special.

Lorenzo puttered around in the library thinking about David Appel's session while thumbing through Claudia's books. After a while, he went to the window to gaze at the steamy garden still feeling the potent otherworldly vibrations that had permeated his office during his session with David. *His session was very genuine because he accessed the personal side of Gaudí, not a swoon with the famous artistic persona.*

Mulling over what dimension Gaudí came from when he sat down to dine with Claudia, he barely heard her voice echoing in his mind while sucking a piquant fresh mussel. He took a big bite of delicious linguini, chased it with red wine, then sprinkled Parmesan cheese on another squishy mussel and forked it. *Ah, a clitoris in one delicious bite.* Pouring red table wine from Umbria for herself, she was studying his thoughtful and distracted face.

"You really have something on your mind tonight. Do you know what day this is? A year ago today was when we realized we were falling in love!"

"I think you are right," he replied turning his full attention on her.

"Yet, for me, it's as if you've always been with me. I can't imagine a day without your beautiful eyes."

"I was not always with you, yet I can't remember when you weren't here." She stared at him thinking he didn't really know very much about her at all. He didn't even seem to be much aware that she was having some difficulty adjusting to a new home.

"Well, now we are here together," he said while enjoying the look of moistness and high color in her face brought out by being in the hot kitchen. "You are making me so happy in my home. I don't want to make the mistake I made before, that is to miss knowing you deeply. My work does distract me, but that's no excuse, whether I have a lot on my mind or not. A few days ago, a new client accessed a formidable and moving past life in my office that I keep turning over in my mind. Having experiences like that with unusual clients is my joy; it amazes me to see where they go, but you are my love. Well, I should share more about my work. When a client accesses a powerful persona, I'm reminded of the unseen depths within each one of us, the deep archetypal realms that churn our bowels. Yet, most of us show a guarded mask to the world, especially when we are older. Eventually, we just die, our stories forever untold, really how sad. I heard a lot about you in your twenties from Armando. Nevertheless, I have no accurate sense of the young Claudia. Who were you, Claudia, in your twenties, when you had a long love affair with an intense and disturbed young man? Who was that Claudia? What did she feel?"

A wave of alarm coursed through her nervous system, a mild panic. However, when she looked at his empathic face, she knew he sincerely wanted to know her better. Regardless of what he wanted to know, that part of her life was in a box she'd covered with a black cloth and hid in the back of the closet with the mice and spiders. *Who was I? Is any of the young Claudia left? If not, where did she go?* "Well, ah," she stammered while forking a mussel that squirted juice on her hand. "Armando and I had an esoteric bond. We performed spiritual practices to influence reality. You are a Jungian analyst, so you probably can imagine what we did and why. In your language, we became archetypes—a man and woman parlaying roles back and forth in a long slow sexual dance. We, ah, well, Armando was the male deity and I was the goddess to neutralize the asceticism and misogyny that rots the Church."

"Claudia," he broke in. "I must make sure I understand you. Are you talking about having sacred sex to reach divine levels—*hieros gamos?*"

"Yes, and I'm thinking about what I really want to say to you about it, since it's hard to find the right words for something so experiential. You're not judgmental, and your education in these matters must be profound, since these experiences fascinated Carl Jung. Talking about it with you could be good, yet I do feel cynical and slightly embarrassed after all these years. How could I have believed we affected those desiccated old fools in the Vatican? Once I left Armando, I forgot about what we did. As I think about it now, we conjured forces that coursed intensely through us both as gods and goddesses. It was ecstatic and mind bending, might be one of the reasons Armando is such a great painter. Yet, it became increasingly disturbing to me when lower frequencies came in that were lustful and potentially possessive.

"I'm very strong and kept the darker forces at bay, but poor Armando got dragged down lower and lower; it was horrible watching him degenerate. Our day-to-day personal relationship did not grow or deepen while we experienced every form of sex ever dreamed of by the human race. But, sex became intense and addictive, and I began to feel crazy. I felt like I'd walked into the wrong room, the door locked behind me, and my soul threw the key into the Tiber. Armando was losing himself; possibly he was using the rituals to block his repressed memories? And it wasn't just us, Lorenzo. We were a group of initiates exploring these realities. There was always a priest or two, usually a Jesuit. I'm sure that seems unbelievable, but for us, nothing was worse than the Church getting more power, since papal infallibility terrified all of us. Once the Church pushed its agenda that far, they terminated their personal responsibility. They were acting like gods."

"Some clarity," Lorenzo broke in again. "You're saying that as the

Church became power mad, sexually abusive, greedy, and claimed total access to the divine, your group carried out sex rituals that were designed to break them down?"

"Exactly."

"Do you *now* feel you were breaking them down, even though you just said you feel cynical, foolish to think you could make a difference?"

"Maybe we did actually affect them because we were so creative, the fun part. We made great theater with costumes and great masks, that's what I liked. We role-played: for example, a sexy woman would seduce a pope or a cardinal played by Armando. We played games in the Doria Pamphili Casino, and then we went through the inner door into the tunnel to the cave. It was very stimulating, very hot, and I think maybe the person we were targeting *did* feel our projections. I have to admit I've often wondered whether that's what took down Ratzinger, since as far as I know the group still carries on."

"Cave? This took place in a cave? Where?" *She could be right about Ratzinger's abdication, an extremely peculiar event.*

"You've heard rumors about it I'm sure, rumors about the Black Mass in caves below the Vatican? They're true! We believed we were awakening the goddess."

"Well . . ." Lorenzo pondered as he ran various speculations about the rituals through his mind. "In ancient Greece and earlier, what you describe *was* religion—the ecstatic and orgiastic Mysteries of Dionysius—the reverse of how things are now. And, this practice can be detected way back in the mists of time. To hear it goes on now is not surprising, but I do wonder about its efficacy in modern times. That is, long ago when all the people believed in hieros gamos, they fertilized their fields with sexual intercourse and menstrual blood, sometimes even sacrificial blood. They believed this helped the plants grow; however, now, few people believe that. *Could* doing it really make a difference in a culture that does not support it?"

She broke in heatedly because the wine going to her head made her feel contentious. "You and I just had a great talk about *The Lost Gospel* that describes Jesus and Mary Magdalene using sacred sex to connect with the divine. We agree that Christianity buried their real story and denied it ever happened. Regardless, *The Lost Gospel* depicts Jesus coming to Earth to share sacred sex with his chosen bride, a priestess who anointed him. Well, our group may have been on to something. Anyway, that's what I was doing in my twenties, hah!"

"Based on my Jungian research, for many thousands of years people believed they *had* to enhance the life-force to support nature. There's evidence Neolithic people had sex timed with the cycles of Venus to have healthy children. They believed sacred sex was the way humans protect the planet. You really have to wonder about this because Christianity drove out these rituals over two thousand years ago and look at our species now! We are sick and overpopulated, confused about gender, and have lost sight of genetic rejuvenation—what it takes to birth and raise healthy children. Our species may be degenerating because we no longer engage in goddess rituals. Like the migrations of swans to their nests, once the memory traces are lost, they are gone.

"I will surprise you, my love, my Claudia. I think you and Armando and your friends *were* keeping something alive that we need to remember. Maybe you kept the Naples supervolcano dormant! Now that we've had a year of love, it is time for you and me to have sacred sex; that is, intentionally connect to divine levels when we have sex. Why not? Maybe Jesus *did* come to teach men and women to connect in this way. As we experience the last of Pisces, maybe millions of lovers as they said in the sixties need to 'make love, not war' to nurture the planet in a lively and erotic way."

"To be truthful," she smiled enigmatically, "I've already started consciously traveling out to the stars, higher realms, when we make love. I see blue light, golden light, and organic green light in my pineal gland. About six months ago when we first started having sex, I found myself in a temple standing in a row of beautiful goddesses. We were being led to a sanctuary where a baby was being born when I was climaxing with you. I believe I birthed a child in another dimension. Since then, sex has been sacred and I can travel anywhere in the universe. I don't need to go down into a damp cave under the Vatican when we can do it right in the temple you made for us. As we complete the Piscean Age, we must weave together a morphogenetic field of sacred sex; we must *be* nature and welcome new souls when we make love. You are my divine partner, my god in the flesh. When we make love, we spin Earth on its axis as it travels around the sun!"

While she talked, her lovely face and catlike body entranced him. He loved the way exuberance rippled across her face as he took her hand and stroked her long fingers. "It really is that simple, isn't it? Having had children, I can see that the kind of love we're talking about tonight doesn't happen much when couples are having and raising children; it happens when they are lovers. This is what happens when sex is simply love, the force that drives the universe. Ironically, the Church says that only *procreative sex* is sacred, yet it is the opposite. You've given me a feeling for who you were when you were young, an earnest woman dedicated to bringing love back. I see who you were then and now you are my goddess."

She laughed happily stroking his arm. "You're only partially right: I have a strong suspicion Sarah and Simon would fully understand what we're talking about. I just wish he were home more to be with her. Then my old apartment would sing!"

David took Sarah and Teresa to Tuscany immediately after his session with Lorenzo. Sarah needed to get out of the heat and relax, and Teresa wouldn't stop talking about Auntie Matilda's great big house and wanting to pick grapes there and eat them. David hoped for another conversation with Pietro. The refugee crisis was pressuring Italy and Europe and the rising chaos worried him. He'd begun to fear the future and needed the mature thoughts of an intelligent European. A few days off in Tuscany and some time with Pietro would be a welcome relief from the world's escalating turmoil.

When they arrived in the late afternoon, Teresa was crabby and fussy so Sarah took her up to their room for a nap. Then Sarah joined the discussion about the refugees.

David paced nervously back and forth while Pietro and Matilda listened. "They are flooding across the Mediterranean from Africa and landing on the beaches of Italy and Spain. Middle Eastern refugees are moving through Turkey, making it to Greece, then moving north to get to Germany and Sweden. How is the European Union going to hold together? I think this is the greatest crisis in Europe since WWII. How about you?"

Pietro responded. "It's much worse: A new element has been added to people's mobility, cell phones, so almost anything can happen. The European Union eliminated borders, so desperate people would rather die than stay where they are. Meanwhile, where is the United Nations?"

"They won't do much except have meeting after meeting, committee after committee, while Europe takes the brunt of it. Simon is coming back in early August, thank goodness for that."

"That's great news," said Matilda. "We've prepared a lovely dinner, a way to make our worries go away for just a little while. So come David, Sarah, let's enjoy a good meal. Anna Maria is up in the hall reading in case Teresa wakes up."

They enjoyed a wonderful dinner. Eventually Sarah settled in with Teresa who never did wake up, and Matilda went to her room to read. David and Pietro went up to the genealogy room where they would not be interrupted to talk more about Europe.

David sat down in his favorite chair and glanced up at the serpent on the ceiling. "Thank you for having us again. As men taking a serious look at the world, we must talk. You are a cherished friend and we have common interests as fathers. I have never been so worried about the future with Europe facing a crisis potentially as destructive as any crisis in thousands of years. How about you? How do you sleep at night these days?"

Pietro studied David's finely boned, aristocratic face. "Well, you know, David, we Europeans take the long view. We've lived through centuries of conflicts over territory, power mongers, and elite manipulation. Our blood-soaked land is locked into the flow back and forth of political maneuvering. Something bigger is always going on, but we can't see it yet. Are you aware that Islam almost took over the whole Mediterranean in the sixteenth century?" David nodded.

"The West found out then what it was like to be subjected to terror from the cruel and barbaric Ottoman Turks. Like ISIS today, they were inflamed with hatred of the West after being assaulted and brutalized during the Crusades. The battle with darkness began when the Ottoman Turks decided to slay the dragon—the West. Just like today, a monster was unleashed in those days, the worst element of the Piscean Age.

"There were battles all over Europe and the Mediterranean when the West and the East fought for control of the known world. But all that came of it five hundred years ago was exhaustion, economic malaise, political blindness, and hatred of each other. These conflicts were so intense and went on for so long that the worst tendencies in both religions prevailed—brutal killing for God.

"Significantly, these days the majority of the refugees are Muslim, the vast majority of the territories they are moving into are mostly Judeo-Christian, and the refugees have *lots* of children. Peace will come only if people of all faiths can live together, so the major religions must adopt peace. Maybe they will when enough people realize what's at stake—Earth."

David nodded his approval. "Perhaps people will be so sick of violence that they'll adopt peace as Aquarius comes in. Battles over God have dominated over four thousand years, and at this point many people despise war. I'd like to share something of interest with you tonight. Are you comfortable with the idea of past lives; that we keep coming back to complete our intentions in the world?"

"Of course. There's no other way to make sense of anything, especially the battles we're referring to. People just keep coming back to settle old scores."

"Good, because I've just had an extraordinary recall that is forcing me to reconsider everything I'm doing with my life. Have you ever recalled a past life of your own?"

"Oh, yes," Pietro said in a thoughtful, low voice. "Getting in touch with some of my past lives has helped me advance more easily in this lifetime. Many in my group in Malta have looked into their past lives. I was a pope a long time ago, which has made me sympathize with the power struggles popes have to deal with. Would you like to share what you've found?"

"I was hearing such great things about Lorenzo Giannini, so I decided to go see him. He's an astonishing analyst, no one in New York compares."

"I've never done a session with him, but that's what I hear from everybody, especially Armando. I credit him with saving Armando; I am indebted to him."

David looked at Pietro and smiled. "Lorenzo says the client does it all. Well, in a deep trance I found myself in a battered and broken body in a gutter in Barcelona around a hundred years ago. I can hardly express to you how it pained my heart to experience myself that way. But he, the one I was, only wanted to ascend, only wanted to leave his body and go to heaven. His faith in God was astounding; he was absolutely certain God was waiting for him. I think I went into his life because I lack faith. I have no faith, Pietro, none. I don't believe I'm going anywhere except under the sod."

Pietro was listening acutely because he could see David was having a spiritual crisis. He said softly, "Experiencing his faith, is that what makes you feel you lack faith?"

"I'll let that pass for the moment to tell you who this man was because I think what he *did* during his life was the source of his faith. His wasn't the faith one has as a Christian, Jew, or Muslim. His faith was as extensive as the universe. This man was the Barcelona architect Antoni Gaudí."

Pietro expressed surprise and curiosity. "That's compelling, David.

What a fascinating connection. How did that feel? Gaudí is one of the great artists of all time. Seeing his work put me in touch with the highest levels I've ever attained. The faith you felt in him is totally accurate because Gaudí was profoundly Catholic, the essence of Catalan spirituality that reaches back thousands of years into the Paleolithic."

"True. But during the short time I melded with him, his *creativity* is what put him in touch with God, not his Catholic practice, regardless of what *he* thought. It was as if he was profoundly Christian before Christianity existed, connected with the geometrical structures that made it possible for Christ to incarnate as Jesus. Gaudí's geometrical field *was* Christ. When I melded with Gaudí, Christ was back on the Earth. Can you imagine that? And I'm a Jew!"

Pietro could see a diamond crystal behind David that was oscillating so fast it was popping light out like a beehive of photons. "I don't know what you mean because I haven't felt anything like that. What does that mean to you, what does that *do* for you?"

"I have a different body, a body in another dimension. I've always been profoundly woven into this dimension, maybe too much so because I enjoy my pleasures so much. Gaudí seemed to be hardly here, more alive somewhere else, the place his art comes from."

"David, I wish I knew more about this. The only person who talks this way to me is Armando, who also seems to be in other worlds a lot. Like Gaudí, he brings things back from those worlds. Maybe that is what it means to be an artist. Does this inspire *you* to be an artist?"

"I don't think so, although this experience might help me understand my daughter and your son better. In the session, Gaudí wanted me to go to La Sagrada Familia in Barcelona. That's what he wants of me. He wants me to go there so that he can be there, which would make me his conduit, and I can't wait. Just feeling the way I felt in Lorenzo's office makes it worth it to go anywhere to feel his energy again. So, once Simon gets back, I'm going to take them all to Barcelona. Then I think I will understand myself better."

"How fascinating; what a great experience that will be. It's worth pursuing this to access something you'd otherwise not be in touch with. Speaking of getting in touch, Matilda is going to miss me and we both need some sleep. Thank you for sharing this, David."

"Thank you for listening, it helps me make sense of things. I'll tell you what happens. I'll write you if I don't see you."

PART THREE

Platonic Solids

21

Majorca Dreaming

During an early-August afternoon, Formentor Beach on Majorca was deserted except for Armando and Jennifer, who were allowed to enjoy the beach anytime because the family had sold their land to the hotel a hundred years ago. The beautiful intimate beach was reserved for the guests of the resort hotel next to their villa, yet they were napping during the hot time of the day. The cares of the modern world melted into the hot and pristine sand as the pure and clear water soothed their minds. They were sharing a picnic lunch under the coolness of a large pine tree growing on the edge of the hot sand. Armando studied her alluring profile as she stared dreamily across Pollenca Bay watching the ferry leave for Menorca.

"Armando, darling. I love everything we're doing—dinner at the Barcelo Hotel, exploring Alcudia and the Pollenca Port, and our time in the sun and sea. But I also love to visit old churches and archaeological sites. Do you like to do that? Is there something special like that within a short distance of our villa?"

"Ah, my pet, I have to be careful with you," he said as he slid his index finger into the top of her bikini to brush a pert hard nipple. She shivered and waited for his answer. "I made sure the Catholics didn't snag you by keeping the priest away from our wedding, but I also have to be careful about taking you to Catholic shrines. This island is

200

steeped in the old Catalan Catholic mysticism. The people to this day perform very intense rituals, for example reenacting Christ's crucifixion on Good Friday. They still believe in the old religion. Yes, there is a place nearby that moves me deeply. I've always thought I responded to it because it was a pagan sacred site long ago. If you go there with me, you must promise me you will not let the monks steal you away from me."

"I'd love to go there, please. Monks will never get me. But why does it move you so?" she murmured kissing him lightly on his dewy neck while stroking his shiny black chest hair. He put his hand behind her neck and pulled her in for a deep kiss making her body sway into his. "I haven't thought much about it; I just feel very quiet and devotional there. It's wonderful to meditate in the chapel where there is an exquisite Black Madonna found in a field hundreds of years ago by a young boy named Lluc—Majorcan for Luke. He was tending sheep and goats for his father when he noticed a strange light in tangled bushes. Half buried in the ground was an exquisitely carved small figurine of the Madonna and Jesus with black faces and hands. He took it to the priest at the nearby church, who put it into a special niche.

"Word flew all over Majorca about the find, but when pilgrims came to worship her after walking for days, the niche was empty! The boy rushed back to the meadow, found her again in the same place, and brought her back to the priest. He put her back in the niche, but the following day she was gone again, and this happened a few more times. So, finally the priest built a small chapel right on the spot where she was found, the chapel for La Moreneta, the little dark one. People have made pilgrimages to her chapel for eight hundred years from all over Majorca and beyond. Stories like this of the Black Madonna being found, moved, and disappearing to where she was originally found until a chapel is built on the spot are common all over southern France and Catalonia, signs of a genuine Black Madonna. There are ancient burial sites and caves around La Moreneta's chapel, a sacred site for thousands of years."

"I would love to go see her. When I was in Paris, I visited many

Black Madonnas and they fascinate me. I saw a beautiful one in Tarragona Cathedral near Barcelona. When can we go?"

"Tomorrow would be great. The Monestir de Nostra Senyora de Lluc is only about 20 miles from here, nothing, a pretty drive. The monks serve a great lunch, and we might be able to hear the choir practice. The number of pilgrims who came to see the Black Madonna grew and grew, so Augustinian monks built a hermitage around the original chapel a few decades later. Dedicated to Our Lady of Lluc, La Moreneta has remained in place at the heart of the hermitage emitting her power. *She* will grab you if you don't watch out!" As Armando said that, he remembered how much the Black Madonna moved Claudia many years ago.

"Oh, how wonderful. I can't wait to go. La Moreneta, how intriguing."

They pulled into the empty parking lot at 9 a.m. and left the car. Armando took her hand and smiled because he was happy to be returning to a special place with his bride. His face beamed with happiness, since just driving up the mountain to the monastery made him feel otherworldly. "I brought you early because the *Els Blauets*—the blue cassocks boys choir—will be practicing at 9:30. We will sneak into the Minor Basilica and listen to them as if we've come to pray. At noon, busloads of tourists will arrive from Palma de Majorca, but we will be hours ahead of them. The choir stops practicing as soon as the tourists show up."

The front entrance to the monastery was plain, yet when they went into the courtyard, a striking Baroque façade, the Minor Basilica, was in thrilling contrast to the simplicity of the hermitage, like an ornate antique in a plain stone room. Their eyes adjusted to the subtle golden light as they slipped quietly inside the church. The opulent interior stunned Jennifer. The walls and the area behind the altar were laden with beaten gold, the high dome painted with colorful saints framed in gold, looking down. *La Moreneta brought a lot of money to this hermitage, or is that Templar treasure on the walls?* The only source of light in the basilica was the sun beaming through a large circular opening in the top of the dome like the Pantheon in Rome. Dust motes sparkled like snowflakes in the wide beam of light, a pathway rising to heaven. Approximately forty cherubic boys in periwinkle blue cassocks filtered in slowly. Jennifer could hardly contain her joy as she congratulated herself for marrying Armando. The choirmaster tapped his wand, raised his arms spreading out his brown coarse robe, and snapped his neck—go! Luscious tones of the "Salve Regina" in perfectly toned high voices filled the basilica vibrating the thick red jasper columns of the nave. Her chest expanded so rapidly that she was afraid she would start sobbing.

Armando watched her discreetly from the side as she became radiant, her face absolutely still as her skull bones expanded with the otherworldly voices filling the golden beauty. *Yes, this is the golden world, the reason I love this place!*

They sat there in heaven for over an hour listening to the early medieval version of the "Salve Regina" followed by Pergolesi's "Stabat Mater." After the choirboys filed out, they crept discreetly into the La Moreneta Chapel with Armando holding her hand firmly. No one was inside, so they went to the first pew right in front of the Black Madonna. They sat for a moment and then Jennifer whispered, "She looks Flemish to me with her beautiful courtier's dress and broad face. But how could a Flemish Madonna end up in a field around here?"

"Yes, you are right, and since she has been here for eight hundred years, she is not a fake." Jennifer kneeled and looked up to see her better, while Armando sat behind enjoying his own private thoughts. *I remember Claudia's face when she first saw her. She was filled with adoration as light surrounded her head. I remember feeling rejected when she wouldn't talk about it. Obviously it was too sacred, possibly too feminine?*

Jennifer studied the small exquisite figure, the Madonna with a broad face with enigmatic eyes and a slight smile as if she knew a secret she would never tell. She simply gestured with her right hand,

La Moreneta

palm open and up, to the infant she cradled in her left arm. The child also had a Flemish face and gestured with his right hand, palm open and up, to an open book he held in front of his chest. These two open pages displayed the Alpha and Omega—the beginning and the end— as if her child's presence was eternal. White-faced cherubs embroidered in the cloth behind La Moreneta stared down at the mother and child. *She is the great mystery, the Black Madonna. Makes me wonder whether she is Mary Magdalene with her son, Judah?*

Chatty monks graciously served them a simple healthy lunch and water from a nearby natural spring. Jennifer was the first to speak. "When we explored Pollenca, I was fascinated by all the cultures there—Phoenicians, Romans, Vandals, Arabs, and Templars. I was most intrigued by the period when the Knights Templar took control and built their church, Nostra Senyora dels Angels, just *before* the date given for La Moreneta's chapel. This can't be just a coincidence since many Black Madonnas were found in places in Spain and France that were frequented by the Templars. The Templars could have lost her in the field, or maybe somebody stole her from Nostra Senyora dels Angels? Anyway, today has been wonderful, so beautiful. I am eternally grateful to you for bringing me here."

"This has been a lovely and special day that takes my mind off what's going on at home. My father is meeting with some distant Medici cousins as we speak, the ones who control the foundation that runs the Medici chapels in Florence. He actually thinks he can talk them into displaying my painting in one of the Medici chapels. I can't imagine it happening, but it's worth a try, especially since my father is so taken with the idea. As for my feelings, if the first public introduction is not smooth, the possibilities for this painting will be diminished."

"Would they allow new art in there? If they say no, do you have any other spaces that will draw the right people for the initial show?"

"Well, yes, think of the Michelangelo Sacristy where all the tourists go; there's no space in there. What's odd about my father's idea is that he wants the painting to be put right in the main chapel for a month or so. I can't imagine that happening, but nothing stops my father when he really wants something. He has some cards to play with the Medici, no doubt."

"Well I hope his meeting goes well. Watch out, Armando, *you* might return to the fold."

He laughed. "I don't think so. During the Renaissance, the Medici were either heretics or atheists, or both, just like our whole family."

As David strode up the tower to Lorenzo's office, Gaudí's high energy pulsed in his pineal gland. He walked into Lorenzo's office with a serious expression. "Hello, Lorenzo. It's good of you to see me again."

"So good to see you again, David," Lorenzo said taking his hand. I've thought so often about our first session. I'm really happy you've come again."

David glanced at the table behind the analyst couch and noticed the crystal cylinder was not there; in its place there was an 11-inch crystal obelisk. "Ah, I see you have another crystal, an obelisk. Did you tune in to me before I came today?"

"I usually tune in to clients before they come; in your case, I had to, since you accessed such a high and intense lifetime. I have to watch out for inflation—you becoming entranced with your past and avoiding your current problems. You plan to go to Barcelona to visit some of Gaudí's works as soon as possible, so you could airlift yourself right out of your normal life. Today, I think we should access the previous life of yours that most affected Gaudí in his lifetime. Are you willing?"

David had his hand on his chin and lowered it when Lorenzo finished. He was irritated because he didn't want to do what Lorenzo was suggesting, but Lorenzo steered the boat. David had hoped to go back to Gaudí's lifetime to experience him as a working artist. "I'll follow your advice, of course, but I didn't think that was what we'd do today. What if this were to be my last session?"

"You will decide whether you want to do more work. Is it a problem for you because of the distance?"

"No, I'll be visiting Sarah and my granddaughter three or four times this year. But regarding the direction we take, do you mind explaining a bit more about why you want to access a lifetime that heavily impacted Gaudí?" He closely watched Lorenzo's quizzical expression. There was a thoughtful pause . . .

"David. You're a very developed man, so to be absolutely frank, guidance told me to bring out the obelisk for both of us. Then as I sat with it yesterday, I had a strong feeling we can't get further into Gaudí without first picking up something in his background; that is all."

"Huh." David relaxed. "Maybe you're right, since Gaudí felt very repressed to me. Perhaps a shadow locked him up?"

"Precisely. Frequently we have those kinds of shadows, and penetrating them often lays bare the soul's choices. We're layered like onions. If you're comfortable about taking this approach, let's do it."

Still, David was slightly annoyed, but he figured Lorenzo knew a lot more than he did. He took a closer look at the clear obelisk laced with wonderful planes, occlusions, and wispy, lacy fields that resembled nebulae. "It's beautiful." Then he reclined on the couch.

"Now, breathing with me, allow yourself to let go and tell me what is so beautiful about the obelisk?"

"All the interior fields," he said feeling suddenly so drowsy he thought he'd fall asleep. He slurred, "Whole universes in crystalline fields, cosmic forms mysteriously transferred to Earth."

"Yes, that is so. Ah, your voice sounds different. Who is speaking please?" Lorenzo was astonished by how easily David went into trance.

A very low, ponderous, and pompous voice responded. "Well, *you* Lorenzo, you don't really know about these things. I figured things out first."

"Oh, well great, and where *are* you by the way?"

"I am in Palma, Majorca, and I figured it all out with my wheels. I can take all the ideas ever thought by humans since the beginning of time, arrange them and spin them, and then I know all things." David rattled on describing a very arcane alchemical system that Lorenzo couldn't follow so he broke in.

"Ahem, would you please share your name with us?"

David flexed his shoulders, stiffed out his legs, and said loudly, "Yes, Ramòn Llull."

"Oh?" Lorenzo responded in a voice dripping with curiosity while his mind was going a mile a minute because now he knew *why* he couldn't understand what David was talking about. Llull was an early medieval computational thinker who is thought of today as the first computer scientist. Lorenzo knew very little about him. "What is the purpose of these fascinating wheels? That is, what do you *do* with them?"

"I invented this system to convert the infidel—Muslims and Jews who didn't recognize the Messiah when he was here."

"Did it work? That is, *did* you convert them?" He was watching David very closely because his body was tightening, jerking, and coming close to convulsing.

"A few, but they killed me for it. They did! They killed me."

Lorenzo stroked the obelisk while staring at an intense geometrical form hovering above David, eerie, like a humming spaceship. "Would you like to tell me about that sad day? You don't have to if you don't want to." Geometrical light forms vibrated the forms and fissures in his obelisk threatening to shatter it, so he surrounded it with both hands as it got hot.

"It's bad, really bad because it didn't end there," David said writhing. "Angry Muslims are stoning me in the street in Tunisia . . . Rocks bruise my ribs, my back, my legs, and one hits me in the chest, then another one above my right eye as I fall. They left me laying there in the street like a pulpy bloody mess for the dogs, but I didn't die. A woman took me to her house. She washes me, anoints me, and oh . . . my . . . God . . . it's Rose, my wife now. I wanted to die, I really did, but her comfort was so divine that I lingered and lingered with her. I never felt such love, openhearted mother's love."

"When did you die?" Lorenzo asked gently.

"Later, a year later, but that was not the problem. When I died, Antoni Gaudí died in the streets in Barcelona. I died twice at the same time, so I don't know anything about Gaudí."

Lorenzo knitted his brow as he realized that for some odd reason, these two deaths were simultaneous in David's psyche, maybe because both traumas happened in the street, an ugly death for anybody. Yes, this could block David's access to Gaudí's whole lifetime. "Let us go to Gaudí as a young boy, maybe even a baby. Let us see how Gaudí felt after being stoned for proselytizing during his previous life as Ramòn Llull."

David jerked, then lay still and said nothing for many minutes. "I'm so heavy, Lorenzo. Can't you lighten me?"

"Just stay with the density and don't worry. This is how it feels when you access a blocked part of yourself; breathe and let I happen." There was a longer pause as David felt like he was turning to stone and felt terrified.

"Oh, how delightful," David suddenly said in a childlike, happy voice. "I'm by a stream in the gorge close to my home by the sea near Tarragona. I'm playing with my friends in the water on lovely smooth stones. I'm a totally happy young boy. The Church makes us all feel guilty, responsible, depressed, too fixed and determined, so we play in the streams and forest as much as we can. Llull shadowed me even when I was a boy because I'm not devout enough for him, don't pray enough, won't sacrifice enough for him. He blocks me because his mind is like an efficient machine—robotic. I escape him when I create, especially when I design things that are alive like nature. His brain is so logical, it constricts me. He thinks he knows so much, so I make beautiful things out of tiles, shells, trees, and bones. I banish him with beauty."

"Okay, David. Would you please ask Llull what he wants of Gaudí? If he will tell us?"

The low, heavy voice came back again. "You are the one, Gaudí, who converts people. I never could do it and died for trying. *You* are the one who is doing it. You came back and realized that beauty is what leads people to God, not logic. Logic only leads to traps, and they murdered me because they hated my traps."

"Ramòn Llull, when Gaudí died, did you finally die too?"

"Yes, but the part of me that would not die was my heart because it opened when that lovely woman cared for me, that woman, David's wife. Listen to me very carefully because this will be hard to understand: that woman's love was my source of love during my life as Gaudí. She was my muse, who poured love into me while I created. I had feelings of outrageous joy that were unknown to Ramòn Llull except during the last year of his life. And in this life, I have my love with Rose; I've never needed anything more."

A huge field of pink light surrounding David was moving Lorenzo into a trance. "It is time, David. We've found what we need to know. The life that shadowed Gaudí, Ramòn Llull, has released you. It is time to come back."

They were in the alcove again. David was thoughtful and nonverbal, so Lorenzo began. "That was lovely and also very interesting. We didn't really explore Llull much; we may not need to. While he was around, my brain felt like a computer clogged with spinning, complex programs. Maybe Llull developed a huge and integrated data bank, a cosmology that Gaudí expressed in his art. Do you resonate with that idea?"

"It's the wheels. I couldn't see what they were, but I could feel their simultaneous interactions. It was like having the Kabbalah spinning in my brain, which may be why I respond to the Kabbalah. As Gaudí, I could feel myself always trying to express those complex, interactive spinning fields. I could actually feel myself making those structures spin together into the design of a building, and then I cloaked them in beauty. Things had to flow, be round, and covered with gorgeous materials, just like the beautiful smooth quartz stones sparkling in my childhood river. The spinning wheels were contained by the beauty of the buildings and churches I designed, yes."

Lorenzo laughed heartily and said, "I *have* to mention something to you. Llull was born and died in Majorca in the fourteenth century just when the Palma Cathedral was being built. Then in the nineteenth century, Gaudí was brought there to completely redo its interior! How's that for a coincidence? I mean, David, Llull would have seen the early stages of the construction of that cathedral, probably at least the bones of it, and then he got to decorate it later in another lifetime as Gaudí!"

"That is something to think about, isn't it? Thank you, Lorenzo. Just imagine what Gaudí must have felt when he worked on it. I think we went about this in just the right way today, you were right. I'll come to see you after I've gone to Barcelona. Maybe I need to go to Majorca, too!"

22

Meeting the Medici

A white Rolls Royce Corniche carrying three passengers glided up the road to Castel Vetulonia. Pietro waited in Armando's studio while Guido showed the other driver where to park and then led the three to the tower door.

Matilda was on the balcony opposite the tower enjoying the morning sun. She had distant Medici relatives, so she wondered whether she'd recognize anybody amongst the people who worked for the mysterious Medici foundation that ran the Uffizi, Medici chapels, the Academy, Bargello, and other places created by the Medici. There was always so much gossip about the glamorous Medici lifestyle—houses, travel, fashion, and parties—yet few knew how they ran the foundation. Even Pietro knew very little, but that didn't matter when he put out the call for the members to come see Armando's painting. She heard feet shuffling along the stone pathway below, raised her bright blue eyes above the top of her book, and watched.

Guido was first in line with three people following behind—two men in business suits and an elegant, tall, willowy woman in fashionable attire. Matilda watched them closely when they turned sideways as Guido opened the door to the tower. She did not recognize anyone.

Pietro was waiting inside by the studio door listening to their soft voices as they came up the stairs on the north side of the ancient square tower. They made it to the top landing and came through the door. "Welcome, welcome. Giovanni. How great to see you here after so many years. Alessandro, you are looking so well, and lovely to see you again, Maria. You are exquisite as always. Here are three chairs for you. Sorry they are not very comfortable; this is Armando's country studio and he doesn't get many visitors here."

"Ah, Pietro, the pleasure is all ours," murmured Alessandro. "We have all been following Armando's work with such interest, especially his recent show in Rome. It is so kind of you to invite us to view a painting he kept out of the show. If I understand you correctly, he kept it out because it is very spiritual? But, well, it seems to me all his work is spiritual."

"Yes, but he had reasons, and you may decide millions must see this painting. I hardly need to remind you of our world situation that threatens art and beauty. ISIS removed its mask when they destroyed Palmyra, the most exquisite Roman site in Syria. If such a thing like that could happen, next some idiot will bomb the Uffizi! Your family has done more for the preservation of art than almost any family or dynasty in human history; now your contributions are more important than ever."

"I cried when I heard about Palmyra," said Maria quietly, "a beautiful place. Barbarity sweeps the world again, which sickens me. I thought the Crusades were over."

Pietro nodded respectfully. "To avoid wasting time because you are all very busy, please allow me say a few things about Armando's painting, and then we can view it. As I believe you know, our family descends from Fra Angelico, the reason my son is named Armando Angelico Pierleoni. Fra Angelico was a magnificent painter of ethereal light, so we were delighted when Armando showed such promise as an artist in his early twenties. He has developed his work diligently and expertly, is even admired outside Italy. Critics say he is a throwback to the great Renaissance painters, as if he is continuing their alchemical breakthrough."

"Yes, this is so true, Pietro," Giovanni interjected. "When I viewed his large triptych in his recent show, I wanted to buy it, but it was already sold. I'm sure my ancestor Cosimo III would have bought it because it depicts the three levels of our earthly existence—hell, purgatory, and heaven—in a modern context. We've heard rumors the Vatican got that painting through an anonymous buyer."

"Ah, unfortunately right," Pietro replied. "Armando retained the painting we will see today to make sure the Vatican *never* gets their hands on it, and now he is concerned about its public introduction. As you will see in a moment, Giovanni, it would have been a disaster if the Vatican got this one because it would disappear into a vault. The painting we are going to see today might shock you, so first I'd like to make a few fatherly comments. Of course, all this is in confidence, just as nobody will ever know you came here today." Pietro paused for a moment to cough. "Well, my son has been a tortured soul. No need to go into the details, since we all are tortured souls after what the Church has done to us for hundreds of years. The interesting thing about Armando, something I believe matters for this painting, is that he went to a new level when he married last year. Marriage has steadied him and intensified his sense of purpose. Once that happened, I began to notice he seemed to be out in other dimensions a lot, rather than just being located only in this solid one."

The three Medici involuntarily looked at each other simultaneously then resumed their attention on Pietro.

"Last fall I detected a halo around his head during the period when he was executing the painting you are about to see." Alessandro's Gucci loafer scraped the floor almost slipping. "Also at that time he seemed to be struggling with turbulent emotions, and then what came next is this painting." Pietro walked over to the painting, took off the cloth, and walked back over to stand beside the three of them to see how they would react.

A vacuum occupied the room as if the air had been sucked out of the tower. Maria held her breath with eyes wide; Giovanni was shaking slightly; and Alessandro seemed to be very upset, wringing his hands. All three were fixated on Jesus ascending into the ethereal realm through layers of divine light drawing him upward. Pietro watched Maria's eyes turn to Mary Magdalene. She twitched when her right hand rose up involuntarily to point at the bee. Alessandro and Giovanni's heads turned to Mary Magdalene, and then all four of them fell into deep silence. Pietro fell in so totally that Alessandro's voice startled him. He came forward to see their faces more closely, hoping they wouldn't mind. Alessandro's face was ecstatic, agonized, and wet with tears.

"My God, Pietro. I have waited for the Real Presence my whole life. The love she feels for him is ecstatic, fills my heart with joy. I am transparent, Christ is here with us, now."

"This is truly extraordinary," Maria remarked. "How did he get this, how did he do it, paint that active quantum flux above Jesus? What about that bee?"

"That's what amazes me the most, Maria," Pietro said as he served them amber grappa in small crystal glasses. "Armando does not lie to me; I would know it if he did. But until I could trust him, I didn't tell him the secrets. When I asked about that bee, he said he wasn't aware that he painted it there behind her head until a friend pointed it out! He wanted to paint it over, but she persuaded him not to touch it and told him all about a new book that explores the bee and Artemis."

"Yes, it is the signal," Giovanni broke in, a resigned tone in his voice. "We can be frank here, Pietro. We all know you are a key Templar researcher; you've kept your family secrets and passed them to your first son. That's why we were happy to come today, especially since you've never asked us before. But, the goddess Artemis and the bee, that's *our* family secret, and I believe not *yours*? Of course, if you say your branch has retained this knowledge, we will believe you. But I thought we each had separate strands through all the generations to avoid detection by the Inquisition. It was too dangerous for any one person to know too much, but that is changing. The three of us know what this painting means. Armando has depicted the tipping point between the dark and the light, just when we are nearly exhausted by the dark dominance, the world soaked in rampant evil."

Giovanni paused to look deeply into Alessandro's eyes, and then into Maria's to see whether they were in agreement or not, and went on. "This painting captures the Real Presence of Christ, a force that can unite Christians, Jews, and Muslims if enough people see it. This painting shows that Christ's light belongs to all the people on the planet because we can see his light when Mary is with him. So, to the matter at hand, what can we do for Armando to help bring this to many people?"

These three visitors were the key directors of the foundation, the Medici art collections. If you put the art all together, it is like a gigantic puzzle that reveals the pre-Flood magical arts. When the pieces are identified and assembled, the secrets will be known and the prophesized peace will come. They believed this convergence would occur in the Age of Aquarius, as did Pietro. The foundation had protected the fragments up to this point because the forces of darkness were obliterating precious knowledge, just like what happened to Palmyra. Furthermore, the Medici displayed their precious art to as many common people as possible over the years because comprehension by the people keeps ancient memory alive. Pietro stood by his son's painting while they studied it more. Then he said in a slow, measured voice, "What I'm about to ask of you is outrageous and may be impossible because of tourists in Michelangelo's sacristy. Yet, ironically, if tourists from all over the world could see the love between Christ and Mary, more will welcome the return of the Goddess and her consort.

"Tourists come from dawn to dusk to the Medici chapels to see the Michelangelo sculptures in the sacristy that portray the spiritual lives of the Medici. Meanwhile, the nearby Chapel of Princes is large, hardly anybody spends much time in there, its altar is never used for Mass. A few months ago, I had a vision of Armando's painting in front of the altar with guards blocking any photos. In fact, I think you'd need to take people's cameras right at the front entrance of the museum."

The shocked faces of the three Medici silenced Pietro, so he nervously refilled Giovanni's tiny glass.

"The reliquaries, Pietro. We can't do it because of the reliquary rooms on each side of the altar."

"I thought you might say that, but there also are reliquaries downstairs. Just think, they might all wake up, saint's bones rattling to celebrate the sacred love story! This sounds like a joke, but I don't see why you can't do it, that is just because of the reliquaries."

"Pietro, with all due respect, the three of us will have to meet alone to discuss your request. We may have to take it to more foundation members. We may have to ask you to bring the painting to a meeting to have more of them see it."

Pietro put his hand on his cheek. "I don't think Armando would do that. He acts like this painting is the Shroud of Turin. Maybe he could bring it to the chapel to set it up in front of the altar so that more of you can see it there. He probably could do that in the middle of the night."

Alessandro chuckled. "Pietro, are you trying to cause an earthquake or explode the Campi Flegrei supervolcano? Pompeii erupted at the beginning of the Age of Pisces, and everybody knows tectonic stress increases when an age is passing. Campi Flegrei *has* recently been active again. Just joking, but we could rile up earthly forces we must always respect. Let's not forget the Medici family crest originally had six red balls that signified slaying the dragon in Mugello where our family originated. As we understand it, our job is to subdue the dragon."

Pietro replied thoughtfully, "It *is* time to slay the real dragon, the Church. None of us will survive unless the real story about the marriage of Jesus and Mary is revealed at the dawning of Aquarius. You, of all people, know that."

They did know. They had been waiting patiently during the last five hundred years since the Renaissance. They'd taken many dangerous risks, such as displaying a multitude of paintings of Jesus with Mary Magdalene nearby in the Uffizi, as well as many other controversial works of art.

When they left, Matilda watched them come out of the tower, and this time she recognized one, her secret for the moment.

Armando and Jennifer were having lunch on the patio, the only cool area of the semitropical house. They were both very tan after going to the beach almost every day for a week. She was feeling flirtatious and he was excited because his father had called to tell him that the Medici committee was considering displaying his painting.

"These times are so weird," she said in a serious voice. "I avoid the news as much as I can, but I just can't get Palmyra out of my mind. The fires in California terrify me. I can see that people are afraid everything they have will burn up; imagine that. Do you think ISIS's ugly energy is fanning the flames? Sometimes I do, sounds crazy."

"My dear, I admit I do find myself thinking that way at times, but it makes me feel crazy so I try not to, especially here in Majorca. Palmyra's destruction breaks my heart. I have gone there twice to enjoy its rare serenity. The Romans chose the site because of its exquisite geomantic peace, its spiritual light. Nothing upsets me more than the destruction of beauty. Have you ever gone to Palmyra?"

"Once," she replied as her mind wandered back to her visit there with Jasmine's husband. They'd stolen three days just for themselves, and the sex was so outrageous that Jennifer thought he was ready to leave his wife and ask her to marry him. He'd faked a business trip to Jerusalem, but got nervous his wife would try to reach him on his cell phone because the baby was sick when he left. By the third day he was impotent after drinking too much. This was okay with her because she was exhausted, but he freaked out when it happened with her. He thought his wife was the problem because she was always tired. After they got back to Paris, he avoided Jennifer because he was afraid of getting caught. He broke up with her, telling her to never call him again, and she was devastated for months.

"Penny for your thoughts, beautiful one; you are a million miles away. Are you thinking about a trip of your own to Palmyra?"

She jerked, which really made Armando wonder. "Well I, ah, *was* thinking about when I was there." Her mind was running a mile a minute because she so much wanted to tell him. *Can I tell him? Do I dare? Will he hate me? Will he break up with me if he knows the truth?*

"Sweet one, you look like all the cares of the world are on your shoulders, yet here we are having a lovely lunch in Majorca. Is it the fires, the destruction of Palmyra, or possibly you are remembering going to Palmyra with a lover?"

She shook herself as if to get a hornet off her arm and turned to gaze into his eyes. Her smoky, soulful expression upset him. She seemed helpless as he gently stroked her arm wondering what to say next.

"Jen, isn't it time for you to just be honest? You can tell me anything about your past, since our agreements have been clear from the beginning. Literally anything you share is okay because we have not lied to each other; at least that I know of. Is there something you'd like to tell me?"

Her blood felt like magma rising in a volcano because watching the news of the fires and the bombings had roiled her up so much. Hot frustration burned through the anxiety that encased her heart. *Will Simon get out of the Middle East before they kill him? Are we all going to have to avoid crowds and limit travel? Will there be anything to live for much longer? It's too much for me; I can't hold back anymore . . .* "I was there with a lover for three days. I am not ashamed of that, but he was married and the father of three children. I almost ruined his life. I taunted him and seduced him; he couldn't resist me. Armando, I almost destroyed a family. That's what Lorenzo and I have been working on. My guilt made me jealous of Claudia, jealous of her because of what I'd done to another woman." She paused and cast sad eyes off to a lime green wall looking like she was sixty years old.

Armando bit into his ripe juicy peach. "*That's* what you've been worried about? Is that the worst thing you've ever done? What do you think happens in the life of a beautiful woman who doesn't marry until she is past thirty?"

She pushed away her plate with a half-eaten ham sandwich as deep grief closed her throat. "But, Armando, I almost ruined a family, a family with three children."

"Jen," he said, rising up from the table to go knead her shoulders. "As the old saying goes, it takes two to tango. He did it too, married guys do it all the time, and he's probably done it with somebody else since you. You were hot and horny, so was he. Maybe his marriage lasted because he let off some steam."

"That all sounds very easy, but I would die if I had a child and you did that to us. I did something to another woman that would kill me if it were reversed. That's breaking the golden rule—do unto others as you'd have them do unto you."

For him, this just was no big deal. "Look, I want to know why this bothers you so much? Jewish guilt?"

"My father was horrified when I told him. He forgave me, but it was really hard for him to do so. Maybe it *is* Jewish guilt."

"Was this guy French?" Armando wondered since she was in Paris. "If he was, European men do it all the time. If you wanted to make sure it wouldn't happen to you, you shouldn't have married a hot, sneaky Italian like me!"

Jen looked up to see his teasing smile and rolled her eyes. As he continued to knead her tight neck, she said, "It's such a relief to get this off my shoulders. It was a long time ago, and I can't even remember what he looked like. Thank you for being so understanding."

"I'll accept your gratitude on one condition. I still want to keep my side of things confidential. Sometimes being open means laying your own guilt on someone else, and I don't want to do that to you because mine is still too intense. Knowing things about my past might hinder your work on yourself, your work with Lorenzo, and what good would that do? Is that okay with you? I'm really happy that you've relieved yourself of this burden, and it sure doesn't bother me."

Armando walked around to take her hands and she rose from her chair into his open embrace. "Now I want to go to bed and reenact wild sex with your married lover. I love role playing; you have no idea how many men you actually have around here."

They went into the warm breezy bedroom. Armando was ready for some fun and Jennifer felt renewed. As she watched him walking around catlike, she realized she'd been holding back from him because she hadn't told him the truth about something that made her feel so guilty. Armando was wearing shorts and a linen shirt. He turned his back to her, took off his shirt, and then he turned around and said, "Here we go! I am him, whatever his name was; c'mon, baby, do it with me!"

She was wearing nothing except a tiny pink thong, an absolutely gorgeous sight in the eyes of her lover. She watched him with level eyes as his penis started rising. Her heart was light and happy, she felt free. When he came to her ready to make love, he thought about telling her about the Templar goddess rituals and the Black Madonna, since she'd responded so deeply to La Moreneta when they went to the hermitage. Maybe later because when he sunk his face into her crotch, he found the Black Madonna.

23

Barcelona Dreaming

Matilda and Pietro were in the library before dinner, enjoying being alone in the house one last day before Jennifer and Armando came back from Majorca. Subtle fall equinox light was shining into the rows of books lighting up the genealogies on the back wall. Matilda was engrossed in an ancient family tree made in Florence that delineated six generations of marriages between the Sforza, Chigi, Medici, and Pierleoni families. She was curious about this one because it went back to Matilda of Canossa. Many years ago, her mother had told her she was named after her, a very dramatic twelfth-century woman rumored to be the mistress of Pope Gregory VII, one of Pietro's illustrious ancestors. "Pietro, now that the three Medici have come to see you, I'm more curious about our family trees. I wonder why I was named after my ancestor Matilda of Canossa? I suppose I'll never know, but I've read she was a wild woman. Must have been if she was the mistress of a pope, your ancestor."

"Dear, when one goes back a thousand years and then comes forward in time, there are countless distant relatives around us if we've remained on our estates. My family believes Jesus was married to Mary Magdalene and founded a lineage that people have been tracing ever since. If true, then their sacred blood is diluted in the veins of millions today, especially in Italy. I use our genealogies to remember our stories.

221

I *am* related to Gregory VII, who was a wild pope, so you are *my* wild Matilda! If there *is* a bloodline from Jesus and Mary, since our blood is crystalline, perhaps the coming Age of Aquarius means we are royal people? I hope so, because as the Age of Pisces falls away, the chaos and meaninglessness of what people believe in saddens me so."

Pietro was pacing back and forth with an amber scotch in hand. "Matilda, we're in the middle of the worst humanitarian crisis in Europe since WWII. I thought Angela Merkel was insane in early July when she opened Germany's borders with very little notice and encouraged more refugees to come. And I was right, the flow became relentless, so she had to shut the borders back down. A million refugees are expected to make it to Germany this year! The European Union is trying to force other European Union countries to take them according to quotas, but the resistance is huge, especially in Eastern and Central Europe where former Communist countries have little sympathy for those fleeing tyranny. They're not all refugees either; some are people fleeing for a better chance in life. Surely some of them are radicals, even terrorists. This chaos is going to shred the European Union just when we need a united front."

"Yes," Matilda responded. "What amazes me is the way they communicate by means of cell phones to figure out what to do, where to go next. This is so much like the fifth century when the barbarians flooded the outer reaches of the Eastern Roman Empire and eventually made it all the way down into Italy, except now they do it online!"

"Yes," Pietro replied as Matilda sat down in a large leather chair and reached for a martini. "The smugglers lie to the desperate people, telling them jobs and benefits await them if they can just make it to Germany and then take their money. A few weeks ago, global media reported Germany was offering asylum to any Syrian, causing a flood out of Turkey through Greece, and now more are coming up right behind. This is unbelievable! As for Italy, migrants from Africa are making it across the Mediterranean and flooding into Rome; now add Syrians. Our antiquated bureaucracy can't handle it, so they get stuck in Rome, terrible for tourism. When we go back to Rome later this fall, remember that you must be much more cautious about where you walk because it's impossible to know who's around. I don't think you can walk alone in the Borghese Gardens anymore."

"I agree, and I won't be. What upsets me is that everything is going too fast; the pace of events is stressing my nerves. But can we let this unpleasant topic go for a moment?" She paused as Pietro nodded then shook his head as if to clear it. "Sarah called with interesting news. David is taking her with the baby to Barcelona. Simon is meeting them there because he has just finished an assignment in Iraq. She is so excited because they all love Barcelona."

"Have you thought of having Teresa up here while they go? Teresa adores you, and it's hard to travel with a child with things getting risky. I think you would enjoy it very much!"

"I did think of that, but I just can't imagine Sarah doing it. She's never left Teresa. But, she *is* used to me and loves this house, and of course I would love it. She just had her second birthday, so maybe it's possible."

Matilda called Sarah right after dinner and pleaded with her to let Teresa visit for a few days, using the excuse that her own granddaughters are older and don't visit much. Sarah was still undecided until Matilda mentioned Jen and Armando would be there to help. Then Sarah surprised her by laughing and saying that Teresa would miss her mom for about one minute once she saw the castle. Sarah was grateful and excited when they finalized the arrangements.

Sarah hopped out of a cab, in a robin's-egg blue jumpsuit, at the Placa St. Jaume and dragged a small rolling bag hurriedly to the nearby Neri Hotel. This was the sweetest dream of her life! Guests hanging out in the hotel library by the front entry hall looked up when a very good-looking dark-haired man in a khaki trench coat rushed through the lobby with his arms out wide to sweep a pretty young woman into his arms. Nobody even tried to stop staring. Sarah was crying and Simon screamed, "Oh my goddess!" David, who was standing by the lobby desk, found himself so overcome with joy that his knees almost gave out. Even the desk clerks stared at the happy young couple.

"Where is she?" Simon exclaimed pulling back to look at Sarah while holding her shoulders.

"Don't worry, at the last minute Matilda persuaded me to bring her up to Tuscany. When I dropped her off she was having so much fun that she dismissed me with a happy wave. Now you and I have some adult time. I don't know about you; I really need it."

"Oh damn, Sarah, how great! I have some serious things to share, so even though I can't wait to see her, this is perfect. How lovely, and you are beautiful, my dream come true."

As she reached up to wipe away her tears, she became aware of the other people in the lobby. David came over to embrace both of them. "Son, you will never know how I feel right now. You are safe, with your wife, and we are going to La Sagrada Familia tomorrow with the special early tickets that Pietro arranged. After what you've been through during the last six weeks, being there will take away the stress. We all need it."

They had a leisurely dinner of many courses. The other dinner guests tried to ignore them, but didn't succeed. *Who are they? The older man is obviously the younger man's father. Where did he find her? She's a world-class beauty.* Sarah was tingling with excitement as Simon ate her alive with his eyes all through the long dinner. David thought they were funny and persuaded them to skip dessert. He excused them to go up to their room and was extremely amused when every single head in the dining room turned in unison to watch them walk out. Their love, energy, and youth were palpable.

Simon shut the door and went to her as she drew the drapes. "You're an eyeful for a lonely and stressed-out man. You are as beautiful and desirable as ever, in fact more so because of the wisdom in your face. I've got some amazing things to tell you, but they'll have to wait, or I'm going to split my pants." They fell onto the large bed laughing and lost all control. She felt like she'd never been happier in her whole life as he stripped away her clothes and lost himself in her body. It was awesome to feel joyful again after so many long months.

Later, she stood out on the balcony feeling a soft breeze, wondering who'd been in this room hundreds of years ago, since the hotel had been the archbishop's palace in the seventeenth century. The balcony she stood on was only twelve feet from the opposite balcony and the narrow street two stories below thronged with late-night revelers spilling out of the Barri Gotic. It was great to enjoy the crazy street scene without feeling unsafe. He awakened and soon she felt a hand on her shoulder. "Come inside, darling. I have something to share with you that will make you very happy. For the first time in a year, I have great news."

He fished two brandies out of the wet bar and sat down with her in the sitting area. Soft breezes moved the drapes as laughter floated up from below. She studied his face, careworn but so beautiful to her, as she awaited his news.

"I'm coming home, Sarah! I don't have to go back in two weeks and maybe forever. The *Times* made the decision for me. I would have stayed with things, but they've given me a new assignment, maybe the best one of my career. I'll tell you all about that in a minute, but for now I want you to know that after these four days in Barcelona, I'm coming home and staying."

Sarah was in shock and mumbled, "What? How! Is this for real? I can't process it!"

He stood up and walked over to grip her shoulders. "It is true, darling. I'm coming home! We're going to enjoy Claudia's sweet apartment together."

She sobbed with relief. "I've had to harden myself so much day after day to take this and still be a good mother for Teresa. I can't believe this nightmare is ending!"

"It is, baby, and now I'll tell you what's next. At last we can be a team again, maybe even be psychic; I need the ruby to tell what's going on." He touched her ring as he organized his thoughts. "Are you too tired? Should I wait until tomorrow?"

"Are you kidding? I want to hear every word, every single one, *immediately!*"

"Be prepared to have your pretty brain blown. Do you remember our discussions about the ossuaries in Jerusalem, the ones I wrote about for the paper?"

"Of course. I loved those articles. As far as I'm concerned, if the truth ever gets out, it will collapse the Catholic Church."

"You're more right than you know. New information on the ossuaries is coming out. Since I've already written about them, the paper wants me to follow up and cover the latest findings. My research will probably dovetail with yours!"

Sarah thought back to past conversations about the Talpiot tomb, discovered in 1980, that contained ten ossuaries inscribed with the names of various members of Jesus's family, yet one ossuary disappeared right away. An antiquities dealer, Oded Golan, presented an ossuary in 2002 that was inscribed "James, son of Joseph, brother of Jesus," which was put on display in Ontario in 2003. Israeli authorities deemed it a forgery, seized it, and Golan had to fight in the courts about his ownership of the relic for eight years. They almost ruined him, and the complex legal battle over the ossuary drew attention away from the astonishing fact that the Jesus family tomb had actually been discovered.

A big bestseller about the Talpiot tomb—*The Jesus Family Tomb* by Simcha Jacobovici and Charles Pellegrino—was published in 2007, and James Cameron made a documentary about the tomb that attracted a lot of attention. Meanwhile, the court case dragged on and on, and the public forgot about the whole thing. Hardly anybody noticed that Oded Golan was finally acquitted March 4, 2012, and the ossuary was returned to him.

Simon continued, "Well, now that more attention is being paid to the Talpiot tomb, I'm back on the case. I'm thrilled because the public needs to wake up, and I can base in Rome. I don't really have much more to say about the Yazidis and sexual slavery. Frankly, it just saddens me, so I'm thrilled to be home!"

"I realize now," Sarah broke in, "the author who wrote *The Jesus Family Tomb* is the guy that wrote *The Lost Gospel,* Simcha Jacobovici, a controversial book about Jesus and Mary Magdalene that came out in late 2014! I didn't connect the dots until now. Claudia and I have been discussing *The Lost Gospel,* and even *Armando* has read it—imagine that! They funded a new translation of an early first-century document that is a truly authentic and heartwarming story. We've been discussing it because Armando finished a very important painting of Jesus and Mary that parallels the themes of *The Lost Gospel.* While you've been away, we've all been quite amazed by Armando's work."

"We'll be able to have roundtable discussions again, which I've missed so much. I can tell you about the ossuaries and other things, but I can see you're getting sleepy, darling. So, let's go to bed because we're going to La Sagrada Familia tomorrow early."

They arrived at La Sagrada Familia at exactly 8 a.m. amazed to see long lines going all the way around the church though the doors would not open until 9 a.m. David said, "I don't know how Pietro does these things, but looking at these throngs of people, I'm thrilled we can get in early." The museum guard examined the passes, frowned, and then called a supervisor on his cell phone. A man approached wearing a police uniform looking them up and down as if they were criminals. Sarah smiled demurely.

"Ah yes, David Appel; very good to meet you, sir. Normally this would not be possible, but you have connections. You will be alone in the church for an hour and then the people will begin to come in. Feel free to stay all day if you like. Please enjoy Gaudí's masterpiece. Oh, you can bypass the metal detectors because we haven't turned them on yet."

All three of them tingled when they came into the church. David felt a strange shift in his body as if something had slipped into him.

Sarah watched him openly. "You okay? You look . . . transparent. Like I can see through you."

"I think I need to be alone. Please go off with Simon and I'll be fine." He walked away and strode right into the center of the nave as if he was being pulled.

Sarah looked quizzically at Simon who shrugged his shoulders. "It's okay, Sarah. He's much more of a mystic than you realize; he keeps it under wraps. Let's go meditate and we'll find him later."

David was involuntarily drawn to the center of the nave where he stopped and stood with shoulders back, arms splayed out with hands facing forward. The energy coursing through his body would not allow any other stance. Tall columns colored in exquisite pastels rose up a few hundred feet from square bases, transforming into octagons, then into sixteen sides, and then into circles at the top—three-dimensional intersections of helicoidal columns, some turned clockwise, some counterclockwise. He barely saw the columns because his eyes were drawn to colorful mosaic medallions that shot out rays of light that beamed down into his body and rooted him. When the beams penetrated, his cells started spinning madly and made his body shake, but he held his ground there for almost a half hour.

The pentagonal light form floating above his body was absorbing the beams of light from the medallions. His body and mind flooded with the knowledge of all time—lives and history sweeping through his mind so rapidly that his brain was flashing like a multicolored kaleidoscope. *My God, what a genius: Gaudí.* He heard a commanding and confident voice:

Welcome, David. You've brought me here and I see all is well. Now I will rest, the greatest forces in the universe are completing my church. David, listen and never forget: Hearing is the sense of Faith and seeing is the sense of Glory, because Glory is the vision of God. Seeing is the sense of light, of space, of plasticity, vision is the immensity of space; it sees what there is and what there is not.

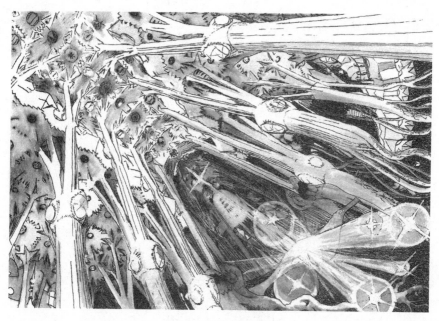

La Sagrada Familia

Gaudí flew up into the universe, welcomed by a choir of blue angels singing for his soul.

Simon and Sarah stood nearby watching David being obliterated within a column of light that came all the way down from a lens in the high ceiling. "Simon," she whispered, "have you ever seen him like this? He is completely diaphanous as if all the cells in his body are crystalline as that amazing light passes through him."

David took a deep breath and returned to his body. While walking back to his son and daughter-in-law, he decided not to tell them he was a fragment of Gaudí. He was free after feeling very constrained for most of his adult life, that's what mattered. The nave began to rustle with the muffled voices and stifled comments of awe coming from people who were streaming in. *If I die tomorrow, I will have lived this life to the fullest. I've released him, now I am free.*

24

Parallel Secrets

The Medici Foundation called to say they would display Armando's painting in the Chapel of Princes mid-October through Christmas. Later that evening, Pietro relaxed in the genealogy room with Alessandro. The only audible sound was brass rings scraping softly on iron bars hung with heavy burgundy drapes that periodically swayed in the night breezes. When Pietro came out of deep thought, Alessandro was staring at him, waiting.

"Well, Pietro, what an honor to be invited to this room, a historic moment. Our ancestors have not always gotten along with all the rivalry between Florence and Siena, yet for you and me that is the past. As we both know, it is time for you and me to talk. I propose we each ask one question to ascertain something we'd like to know. If either one of us does not want to answer, then another question will be asked, maybe even another. Your expression suggests you are willing, so I shall begin with the way we Medici share." Pietro nodded gravely.

"The family crest on your ceiling is the only one I have ever seen with the oroboros and a swan taking flight. Please, will you decode the Pierleoni crest for me?"

Pietro shifted nervously in his seat as he considered Alessandro's craggy face. The deep, long lines between his nose and cheeks made it look like a sword had sliced his face. His disproportionately tall forehead looming over impenetrable coal black eyes made him owlish, yet tonight, excited curiosity suffused his face while he patiently waited. "Alessandro, after all these years, you would ask the one question I can't answer. Lately, I have been teaching Armando about our crest, and I have not yet shared all the information. But, you do know what the oroboros means?"

Alessandro nodded. "Yes, yes, of course. It is the swan that draws my interest."

An old floorboard creaked out in the hall. Pietro rose up quickly and went to the door that was slightly open to pull the breeze through. He didn't see anyone. Matilda, with her heart thumping in her chest, had drawn quickly back and hugged the wall. He shut the door.

"Yes, the swan," Alessandro continued. "But of course, Armando must know first. So, assuming we are not being spied on, may I ask another question?" Pietro nodded wondering who'd been out in the hall. *Who wants to know what I am discussing with a Medici—Matilda?* "Pietro, do you know what the Knights Templar found in Jerusalem during the Crusades?"

Pietro pushed his chair slightly back scraping the tile, put his head down for a moment, then looked up. "Yes, I do know, and that is my answer. I will not say anything more."

Alessandro chuckled. "Ah, cousin Pietro, I do not think I shall let you off that easily. A yes or a no is not really sufficient, don't you think? Let me put it to you this way: we both know that it has to do with the ossuaries in Jesus's family tomb, and, anyway Pietro, we are not going to kill you. If we'd wanted to kill some of you a few hundred years ago, you wouldn't be here with me now, but here we are." Alessandro discreetly rested his right hand on his knee exposing a gold ring set with an oval lapis signet engraved with a serrated X-cross.

Pietro's heart began beating so fast when he spotted the symbol on Alessandro's ring that it scared him. *It's amazing how deeply ingrained this damned secrecy is.* He coughed. "Alessandro, my dear cousin, please be considerate. I'm sure you know much more about things than I do, so what's the point? We've had too much death over these things."

"Of course," he said looking compassionately into Pietro's eyes seeing that he was very distressed. "Pietro, I *can* divulge a few things on our side, then perhaps you will speak more freely. Let me put it this way: the reason we will show Armando's painting to the public as soon as possible is because the time is ripe. As Pope Francis said last September, the world is at war, a protracted WWIII, the game changer. I'm sure you know that the truths we hold so tightly are what the world needs to halt the destruction. There will be no winners if this goes on much longer; the barbarity is truly horrible."

Pietro controlled his breathing to relax his heart. "Alessandro, may I bring out our record crystal? Perhaps it will help us." Alessandro nodded, so Pietro went to a small corner cupboard, opened it with a large key, took out a very large clear crystal, and put it on the table between them. They both stared into it. "Do you believe the pope knows everything that we know?"

"Is that *your* question, Pietro? If so, it is fine, I will answer it. But it *will* be your question."

The many things Pietro would have loved to ask him ran through his mind, but this *was* his question because he'd always felt he could play the game better if he knew how much the Vatican actually knew because his order was so deeply involved with the Vatican. "*That* is my question."

"All right. As far as we know, and I believe we *do* know, the pope does not know half of what we know. If he did, you and I would not be sitting here tonight. But, my reply is a bit of a yes and a no, so first I would like to add some things hoping they will inspire you to fill in more information. Pietro, be assured of it. The Vatican would have controlled the world if they'd gotten the information about what we found, gathered, and dispersed during the Crusades. I'm beginning to think your family has been as good at protecting the secrets as ours has been. Since you can trust me now, I can tell you that I see you already know what the nine knights found. That way, we'll be on the same black-

and-white checkerboard. You can share with me because we will be displaying Armando's painting in front of the reliquaries." He stopped, swinging a foot all dressed out in thin, gray wool socks in an Armani slipper and straightened his fingers on his knee drawing attention to his ring again.

This last comment slammed into Pietro's body. Alessandro was hinting as heavily as he possibly could to draw something out of him. *What does he want?* Blood pulsed through his temples as he stared into his record crystal and saw an exquisite flying swan inside—*it is time.* "All right, since you have been so forthcoming, so will I be: the relics brought by the nine knights are in your reliquaries and in one of mine too. I will *not* say more."

"Ah, Pietro, to be sure, that's what I had to have," he whispered in a low voice. "Our reliquaries contain the bones of Jesus, his wife Mary, and his son. We have them because the Templars brought them back to us."

Pietro looked at Alessandro's craggy worn face trying to imagine the burdens he'd carried all these years. Generation after generation his family had protected the reliquaries by labeling them as popular saints, displaying them where all the people could see them. Pietro offered, "Well, you know, it is good we can share this because the secrets are leaking out all over the place now. For example, with modern research techniques, the investigators of the Talpiot tomb are getting very close to the truth. The authors of *The Jesus Family Tomb* have said that the three skulls in the isosceles-triangle formation were placed there long *after* the tomb was sealed two thousand years ago, since they were found in newer soil deposits on the floor of the tomb. As we all know, the skull and crossed bones are the main Templar symbol. They speculate that around one thousand years ago, so very close to the First Crusade, somebody conducted a ceremony in that tomb, which for the Templars would have been one of the most sacred places on Earth.

"Since *The Jesus Family Tomb* was published in 2007, scientific analysis has verified the first-century origin of the ossuaries; they *are* authentic. Going way back, logically, early Christians would have known about this tomb and kept it hidden, since the Roman Church was destroying any records of Jesus as a normal man with a family who died and was buried—most importantly, *not* resurrected. The Templars knew the location of the tomb and went there during the Crusades, one of the *purposes* of the Crusades. The things you and I have been afraid to share with each other are coming out in alternative research. Finally, the burden is off *our* shoulders with enough ground swell for the real truth to be shared with everyone!"

Alessandro broke in. "You are right, Pietro. I too have assiduously followed these brave researchers, such as the Canadian Templar William F. Mann who writes about Templar sites in America. What he reveals is such a shock to people who still believe Columbus discovered America in 1492, that they can't register it! I cried when I read his book, *Templar Meridians,* and he is bringing out another book next year that we must discuss once we've read it. We are hearing the real story of America, a revelation for the Age of Aquarius. As religious lies are being exposed at the end of the Age of Pisces, the story of the Jesus family lineage is the big revelation at the beginning of the Age of Aquarius!

"We Medici have saved this story with art, especially in Italy, for example, displaying Armando's wonderful painting. People need to wake up on so many levels. If I may ask, just between you and me as fathers who bear the burden of instructing our sons, why *haven't* you explained to Armando the full meaning of your family crest?"

Pietro coughed and sat back in his chair while staring into his crystal gazing at a ruby-red Knights Templar cross in the center. "Armando is not quite ready." Alessandro was on the edge of his seat staring at the Templar cross shimmering in the record crystal when Pietro surprised him. "My dear, dear Medici cousin, our Pierleoni family records go back *seventeen thousand* years ago and more to the Aurignacian period, the Paleolithic, when we were still enlightened, the time before the cataclysmic regression. The point is Armando is not ready to comprehend such ancient knowledge, so I haven't shared it with him. I will, within a few years for sure. He's not asking the right questions . . . yet."

Deep warmth and joy flooded Alessandro's heart, his pineal gland oscillated at a high vibration, and his eyes were misty. "My God, Pietro, we were sure that record was lost, and now you say your family has retained some pre-Flood knowledge? Incredible, this is true joy and happiness for me. As for us, we have been eagerly following the Göbekli Tepe excavations because the site links us to the deeper past 11,500 years ago. Its discovery has made me feel that we *will* recover the original information and remember that we are a grand species with cosmic freedom, what Cosimo III was looking for when he brought Marcilio Ficino to translate Hermes. Now I see that we will know, maybe while you and I are still alive. I am beginning to see why your family has always been the most guarded one with all your silly shadow games like the Siena contrade and the mad Palio races. I wait for the time when you will instruct me in your most ancient wisdom, a joy! As we move into Aquarius, we are to recover our multidimensional intelligence."

"You are more right than you realize, so I will share more. Spend time in Siena Cathedral and in the central plaza where we run the Palio. The ancient wisdom is encoded there and protected by our family going back to the Etruscans and before. For us, the thread disappears into the mists of time, but like Ariadne, we still hold on to the end of the thread."

"Thank you, Pietro, you are so kind. I look forward to spending time with you again as soon as possible." After taking his leave, he walked down to his driver waiting with the car.

Pietro was surprised to find Matilda still up waiting for him. He was very tired, but she wanted to talk. She offered him a brandy, which he declined. "I think you heard me in the hall outside the genealogy room? I backed down the stairs when you shut the door; it was me."

"Matilda, why on earth would you ever spy on me? There are no secrets between us." "Well, yes and no regarding secrets, I'm not stupid you know. I know you and Armando share all kinds of secrets. I am a member of this family, and I don't see why I'm always kept out."

"Matilda, our family has information that could be dangerous for all of us. For thousands of years, we have passed it from father to son."

"I know that, Pietro, and I haven't cared about it much, but now it bothers me. My concern began when I noticed Claudia coming to spend hours alone with Armando after he married Jennifer. When the Medici Foundation people came to see you in Armando's studio, I was not invited. It is rather hurtful; these actions reduce me. Surely you don't want to glorify the patriarchal tradition?" She stared defiantly into his cautious eyes.

"Dear one, please, I will have that brandy. I see what you mean from your point of view. Really, there are some things I must still hold in confidence, but there are other things I can share. Perhaps if I share more things with you, it will all come clear."

"Please yes, this is getting tiresome. I feel left out, demeaned as though I am being treated like a mere woman." She did look very hurt.

"Ironically, Matilda, much of what is at stake has to do with the most hallowed sense of what it means to be a woman. Just trust me that it's not because you are a woman that the passage system has been male to male; your concern is another sign of the big shift. It's no secret that Armando's painting is of Jesus and Mary Magdalene; you've seen it."

Matilda took a deep breath and put her hand on her heart. "Yes, and it has changed me. I've always wanted to know why the Church lies about the family of Jesus, making it look like he didn't have any siblings, yet there they are in the Bible. When I absorbed Armando's painting with its sanctity, grace, and heavenly expression, I finally understood: *Jesus was divine because he was married to her.* When the story gets out, the Church is doomed."

"How right you are. Going back to Pope Gregory VII and Matilda of Canossa, our families knew all about their sacred union. They were deeply bonded, probably the reason he was one of the great popes."

"So, it *is* true," she broke in. "They *were* joined—my ancestor and your ancestor—which means this affects our union. I've always felt our marriage is very sacred, Pietro." She peered deeply into his calm gray eyes detecting the joy she found there when she first encountered him—a spark from a higher realm that meant they would be together for the rest of their lives. "Be that as it may, I think this blood mixing has affected our children. Armando and Giaconda are fine, but our first two little ones couldn't survive and died young; I think it was the bloodline."

Pietro could not bear the thought of it. "For now, let me share with you what I can comfortably say, things that will interest you very much. The reason the Medici came to see Armando's painting is because I wanted to ask them to display it in the Chapel of Princes in front of the altar. I did ask them."

Matilda's eyes were like saucers and when she tried to speak, her voice wouldn't work. She squeaked, "And, have they agreed? Pietro, this is the most shocking thing I've heard in my life." She took his hand and held on to it for dear life.

"Yes, Matilda, they have."

"Does Armando want this to happen? Pietro, I don't know where to put this in my mind. This is too astonishing!"

"It is unprecedented, and even I don't know why this must happen. I saw a vision of it in my record crystal as I gazed into the future; I had to tell the Medici. This is the first time I've asked anything of them, the first time anyone in my family has asked anything of them in hundreds of years except for marriages. I told them about it so *they* could decide whether this should happen. My request must be part of their story, something they've been waiting for, since they've agreed. That was Alessandro you were spying on earlier, and we will be having more important talks after so much separation. The Church separated us, but that is over now. We are not afraid of the Vatican anymore."

"Is this what Armando wants too?"

"I can't answer that for sure, but I think he feels we must do it. Of course, I'm sure he's very honored. Keeping the painting out of the last show really angered his dealer. Then later we found out the

Vatican bought that wonderful triptych at the opening, and he really began to worry about his significant works. Showing his Jesus and Mary Magdalene painting in the Medici chapels means the Vatican can't hide it from the public. If they had gotten it, they would have hidden it in a vault, a painting that could collapse the hierarchy!"

"Isn't this dangerous? Won't they try to destroy it, even murder Armando? I'm frightened." Her small mouth fluttered.

"The Medici will assign special guards in the chapel day and night so that a fanatic can't slash it. As for Armando, I have special ways to protect people."

"How can you do things like that?"

"For years these things have gone on. Are you sure you really want to know?"

She stood there silently thinking about it. "A part of me doesn't want to know, but reality is changing now. I can't be a Pollyanna. I want the truth, Pietro."

"Okay. Let me put it this way. Within the Vatican, Italian, American, and European organizations, there are protection services. These inner circles know that the various old families know way too much about them, for example we know they stage mass trauma events, such as 9/11 in the U.S. So, we agree to not talk about certain things we know, and they protect us if we need it. I think it is best to leave it at that, don't you?"

"You could actually make sure our son and those we love are safe?"

"Yes, and when you think about the little girl you just enjoyed, there has to be fairness and compassion in this world. I work with my order, the Maltese Templar, to find ways to make the world safer for all people. For a thousand years we've done what we can, and soon things will be changing in really exciting ways. Each family guards certain secrets that we do not share with each other because it is too dangerous. We learned that lesson when Philip IV of France tortured Jacques de Molay in 1307. Actually, Matilda, I'm relieved we're having this talk because things will go so much faster when Armando's painting is seen by the masses. I will *need* to talk with you in the coming months." He smiled warmly and took both her hands.

"Pietro, this separation has not been good. We need to walk together in this world."

Pietro embraced Matilda for a long time. Then they went to bed and fell into a deep sleep.

25

Chapel of Princes

Something very unusual was going on in Florence during mid-October 2015. The Medici chapels were closed for a week, unprecedented, and the local citizens wondered what the Medici were up to this time. As usual, the Medici were doing as they pleased, but no one could recall a time when they just closed a museum on short notice. Everything was being rearranged upstairs in the Chapel of Princes, and a large sign placed by the entrance said absolutely no photos would be allowed during a special exhibition. Something was going on display that was changing all the rules, so smart locals bought up the tickets for the coming weeks because they sensed something unusual was about to happen.

The bells in the campanile next to the Duomo—Cattedrale di Santa Maria del Fiore—rang out twelve times sending sweet music throughout the Piazza de San Giovanni. Lovers kissed passionately when they heard the beautiful bells. Meanwhile a large black van pulled up behind the Medici chapels near the shuttered day market. Armando and Guido hopped out, waved to the guard by the back door, and within minutes, four guards came out to help them carry in the large shrouded painting. Guido stayed with the van while Armando trailed behind the guards. They brought the painting through the museum and up the wide stone stairs to the large and cavernous Chapel of Princes. When they entered the room, Armando peered into the dimly lit, large octagonal chapel capped by a dome rising a hundred feet above the floor. The tombs of six princes of the Medici royal line lined the walls, and four spotlights up in the dome aimed down at the ornate altar. When he looked at the altar bathed in excellent light at the opposite end, he remembered something . . . That altar was put there in 1939 for the visit of Hitler and Mussolini. He shuddered.

Two guards carried the painting over to the altar and placed it in front. *Gone!* Armando muttered. *That's the end of Hitler and Mussolini for a few months.* They set it up without removing the cover. The light coming from high in the dome really pleased him. *This will be magnificent!* The painting was raised a few feet, just the right height so that crowds of people could see it easily. They would not be allowed to stand in front of it with their tablets and iPads aimed at it instead of really looking at it. Each visitor would be given a beautiful card with a high-quality print of the painting to take home. He was pleased with the perfect symmetry of the arrangement; the altar was in exactly the right place. He said to the guards, "*Signore, per piacere.* May I spend an hour with the painting while you guard the entrances?"

When the last footsteps of the guards at the bottom of the stairs echoed through the empty museum, he pulled the cover. Then he walked around the large space a few times to admire the mosaics on the walls and the tombs made of jasper, porphyry, alabaster, lapis lazuli, coral, and mother-of-pearl. He lingered in front of a pompous statue of Ferdinando I dressed in an ermine cape and jewels and said to the lifelike statue, "I hope you will enjoy some action in here for a change." Then he sat down in a chair placed among others for the viewing of his painting. Jesus ascending as Mary reached for him looked like Jesus was about to fly up into the dome. Mary, with sensual long red hair and glowing white skin, was a strong woman amid the Medici family crests and ornate civic shields. *Yes, this is exactly the right place for people to see it.* The doors to the reliquary rooms were more noticeable now that the easel partially blocked the ornate altar; the painting became the altar. He returned his gaze to the canvas. *Ah, yes, the very first layer of swirling long strokes keeps Jesus moving, flying.* Then he saw it—the subtle luminescence around Jesus's head. *The titanium paint works in this light. The light must be exactly like this.*

His eyes were drawn to the side of the Magdalene's face. He felt her desire for Jesus in his own heart as his eyes followed her right arm to the hand reaching for him. She yearned for him, and the dome contained this feminine force as his heart expanded into its greater geometrical form. *I hear it! I do! The silvery sounds of a choir of angels singing to the light of Christ.* Then a great low voice coming through wind and water trickling over rocks boomed,

Armando, we begin.

A strange rattling sound in the reliquary rooms disturbed his ardor, a chill clenched the muscles in his legs. Then the odd sounds ceased. *I have to do it. I have to go back into those rooms to see if everything is all right in there.* He went behind the painting fastened with straps to the altar. *Somehow that's significant.* He walked through an arched door into the reliquary room on the right and peered through the protective glass at one gilded and bejeweled reliquary. Looking closely at the little quartz box in the center sealed with a glass top, there it was, a small white bone. *Yes, no doubt about it, that bone is glowing, very subtle but noticeable.* He went around the small room to check the rest of them and detected glowing light in the bones. *What's going on?*

Claudia and Lorenzo had arranged a special Saturday afternoon, warm with the French doors open to the garden, lacy sheers billowing out in the light breeze. Claudia was stretched out on the bed up against a large Moroccan pillow, nude except for a loose wrap. She was watching Lorenzo moving around the room, occasionally glancing at her lying like a lazy cat following him with dark eyes. He lit candles, gathered precious essential oils, and then he shut and locked the French doors and pulled the drapes. He took a fat joint and matches out of a carved wooden box, lit the joint and sucked on it, and then came slowly over to her as he took a deep drag and kissed her to pass marijuana smoke from his lungs into hers. She touched him delicately with her left hand as he touched her breast.

He rubbed massage oil onto her long enticing legs, her arms, then used patchouli to massage her abdomen, inner thighs, hips, breasts, and chest, and finally her pubis. Claudia was in an altered state that made her feel thick and watery as she filled with otherworldly light. When she closed her eyes, she could see organic green light that was alive like the bioluminescence of plants. Her head fell far back as she said thickly, "Lorenzo, I am so far away, I feel like I am in the stars."

"You are darling, that I can see, and as we touch, your skin is intoxicating, your nipples erotic." They lay together stroking and touching when a light appeared between them that started growing larger as if it was alive. They both began to vibrate, breathing softly to circulate the delicate pulsating field. She whispered, "I feel it, I feel the subtle presence of the Divine. As I feel it, I sense you feel it with me. Magnetic currents deep in our cells will flow when we orgasm; we are on the sacred edge, I feel it."

He entered her body, and when he entered, she expanded. He went deeper into her, and for an undetermined amount of time they were in such high consciousness that they couldn't detect the room—they were nothingness in the solid world. She swam in the shimmering light of other worlds as greenness filled her expanding spherical field.

Later wrapped in soft robes Lorenzo said, "I have tasted it again, the honey of heaven. If everything ended, everything went away, it wouldn't matter to me. All I would seek is you. I'm devoted to you, so in love with you that I am complete. I never imagined anything like this existed. With you, I am whole, more than I ever was before. You are transforming my work, with my sessions reaching an entirely new level. Recently, a client accessed a remarkable past life as well as the life previous to it that was blocking him. We accessed that earlier lifetime, and it merged into the more recent one; the fusion resolved a huge block in this current life. His consciousness flowed freely through both of those past lives and miraculously released my client. I knew how to help him break these ancient locks, yet I don't know how it will affect him. I hope I will see him again. I am amazed by how our love is empowering me."

"And I am becoming more psychic, Lorenzo, potently psychic the way Sarah is. I have always been profoundly intuitive as you know, but with this new ability, I x-ray reality. When I figure things out, I literally see things. That bee on the rocks in Armando's painting has been giving me visions, like the way I felt the other day when I was reading the new translation of *Joseph and Aseneth*. As she prepares for him before their bridal night, the text says she has 'the appearance of virtue and marvelous beauty of the gods.' I could see her like that when I read those words! I am becoming what I see as I see it, my elixir spreading all over the world."

"Darling, I think I understand you, things so difficult to express in words. I think we are given sight when we become whole and share the sensual way of being, the gift of love. You feed me, so I need no other food; Mary needed nothing more than a honeycomb. All that remains for me is my curiosity about my clients and my desire to help them break through their blocks. What a profound reality we inhabit when we go through the doorway to the Divine, our bodies."

"When I reread the story of Joseph and Aseneth, something awakened in me. When others read it, they will wake up. With you I was in another world, somewhere in the stars, yet I was totally here. We must be fully sensual while in this world—certainly sex is the best way—and then the doorways to other worlds fly open. You open the gates of heaven when you penetrate me."

Armando watched the towers of Siena in the distance as he drove back to the castle with Guido. "What was it like in there? Was everything okay, sir?"

"Yes, thank you, Guido, quite all right. They will guard it well and the people will enjoy it. It was hard to leave it, but the right thing to do. I trust the Medici; all will be well." After arriving at the castle around 2 a.m. Armando was very surprised to see that Jennifer had waited up for him.

"I must hear all about it. How does it look? How did you feel about leaving it there? I must know and then we can sleep."

Armando considered her earnest face, her lively curious dark eyes. She'd been reading and napping. Her blue silk robe slipped off her right leg as she crossed it over the left one. The robe, loose and partially open, exposed the swell of her small, perfect breasts. His breath caught in his throat when lizard-level lust seized him! He leveled his eyes, put down his brandy, and came over to massage her thigh aggressively. He buried his face in her breasts while grabbing her crotch as she arched back joyfully. "Let's go to bed right away," he said as they got up and walked into the bedroom. He had so much energy that he felt he could crush her. Laid back, she exposed herself fully to his gleaming eyes as his shoulders extended into magnificent wings. He undid his belt, took off his pants, and displayed a huge erection, a tremendous snake.

She was shocked but determined to take it as she responded to the potent sacred blood coursing through his body. She smiled. "Darling, it is tonight, I can feel it."

He came to her, penetrating her while he supported himself with his hands on the bed. He felt like he was twice his size and could hurt her. She stroked his arms and back saying, "There is no hurry darling, slow down, feel the energy all around us, we are inside a beautiful cocoon of blue light. Armando, be slow, I think our child is near; do not shock me."

He breathed deeply wanting the force to flow through his body, seeing the luminescence again, the subtle light of the reliquaries. *Did my painting bring this light?* She moved under him, guiding him, as she said, "I see it Armando; I see the light, our child's soul. Come to me, be with me, our child will come tonight."

He pulled his body up higher with his cock fully inside her body while he straightened his arms to see her better. She glowed like an angel painted by Giotto, the angel of the mother. He stared at her in wonder as if he was seeing her for the first time with her body firmly containing him. His orgasm wound up in his lower back like a snake released in his buttocks flexed against her thighs to heighten her ecstasy. As he moved her hips, her strong thighs gripped all his power. His cock burned with red-hot energy thrusting all the way up his spine and into his skull when he came. A high keening call came from her, like the cry of a peacock. Their mutual orgasm was so intense that they rolled quickly apart, spent. He murmured, "The painting is there, it is happy, I can sleep."

He fell into sleep immediately. She lay beside him feeling his precious sperm swimming around her illuminated egg. She felt a tiny prick; a strong and active sperm pierced the jelly surface encapsulating her egg. She lay on her back with eyes closed spreading out her arms and legs barely breathing, feeling the subtle presence quicken in her womb. As she felt it, light flooded the front part of her brain from the homunculus hovering above her head, a small little being; her child. She whispered, "Come, you are welcome. We have been waiting for you. Come, come now that we are ready for you."

They were up late the next morning and ate breakfast alone in the room behind the kitchen. He said, "I don't know how to say this exactly. Everything is going to change for us. The painting is going to create things we can't yet imagine; but I feel the shift now. It will help resolve some of the difficulties in the world, some of the stress here in Italy. As the people go in, you can go there to watch it happen. This will really be something, Jen, something very good."

"I know. I have a request, since we have a few days before the painting goes on display. I would like to have Simon and Sarah come up for the weekend with Teresa so that we can all talk. Matilda will be happy to watch Teresa. Yesterday, she told me she misses her already; she absolutely loved having her for a few days. It's been so long since we've all been together, yet so many things are going on. I'd like to know what they are thinking about, and I bet they'd like to go see the painting. Would you like that, darling?"

"Oh yes. Sarah calms me, and Simon's wisdom guides me. It will be hard for me to handle the public response to the painting, but not if I see Simon, my brother protector. I will be having a continual visceral response when the public sees the painting, since already I feel slightly nauseated. The fear that it will not be received well is hitting me hard. Sweet one, I don't want to make you feel jealous, but I think we should include Claudia. Would you mind if we also invite her?" He watched very closely and didn't detect any change in her eyes, so he went on. "I feel like I need her support right now, and after all, she invented our group discussions, our salon."

"Armando, five would be a perfect number, a pentagram. But, should we invite Lorenzo?"

"Hmmm . . . that is tricky. Of course we must, even though you are still seeing him. He might feel it would not be wise. Claudia will know what to do. Would you like me to call her to invite her, or would you like to?"

"I'll call Simon and Sarah, you call Claudia because you can probably work out inviting Lorenzo with her more easily."

"Good. I'm impressed. You really are beyond jealousy."

"Yes, and I'm happy."

"And, beautiful one," he smiled, "you think you might be pregnant? No wine for ten months!"

"I've already thought of it."

Simon and Sarah were thrilled to come up for the weekend. They'd been back in Rome for a month, and Simon had just finished a huge amount of research on the Jerusalem ossuaries. Sarah's novel, *Queen Bee and the Olive Branch,* was at the printer and she was very anxious to see the finished book. Little Teresa talked constantly about Matilda's big house, so she squealed when they told her about the visit. Claudia's response was intriguing.

"Armando, darling, I will ask him, but Jennifer is still his client.

He's really strict about such things, believes he's avoided a lot of trouble over the years. Some clients think he is a god who can save them; they project crazy emotions on him. I will call you back after I talk to him, but as for me, I will come. I've missed our time together, and we are so lucky to have Simon back. We must take advantage of the chance to pick his brain about the Middle East."

Claudia called Armando back a few hours later. Just as she thought, Lorenzo was happy to have her go but would not come himself. He had some deep research he'd been putting off, so a weekend alone would be excellent. All five of them were excited about getting together.

26

Tuscan Gathering

The aroma of olive and eucalyptus leaves drying on the ground was enticing on the chilly October night in Tuscany. The Pierleonis served Simon, Sarah, Teresa, and Claudia the last of the harvest—three different squashes, with homemade pasta and venison glazed with Matilda's famous brown sauce. Matilda raised her wine glass to look at everyone with her sparkling blue eyes. "It is such a joy to have you all here together! Pietro and I have watched your friendships deepen over the years, and now here we are sharing life together, including having a little one in our midst. Sarah, I'm enjoying Teresa so much. We loved having her while you were away. My growing family warms my soul!"

Simon stood up as all eyes turned to him. He was suntanned and thinner after being in Iraq, his face veiled and intense from seeing things most people can't imagine. "Matilda, Pietro, Jennifer, Armando, I'm delighted to be here!" Claudia was remembering him as a lover a few years ago—his youthfulness, attractiveness, and stunning genius, but then she recalled the recent afternoon with Lorenzo. *Yes, I've found my other half. He completes me and makes me more than I ever was. But I will not forget Simon; I'm glad I had him when I did.*

The five friends gathered in the library with a great fire burning low under a huge pine log that sucked the dampness and chill off the thick stone floors. They were in a circle of easy chairs with a large table in the middle.

"I'll start this," said Claudia eyeing Jennifer. "Armando, how do you feel about having your painting in the Chapel of Princes? I must admit I was shocked when I heard about it. How did that *ever* happen?"

Armando was watching both Claudia and Jennifer. Alarm bells went off because Claudia came in a tight black jumpsuit with a low neckline. Her ample chest was mostly covered by many strings of red amber beads, but the enticing cleavage could not be missed. Her straight bangs waved back and forth, emphasizing her extremely large, insightful chocolate eyes. Meanwhile, Jennifer gazed at her with a warm and open expression. "My father arranged it. We have good relations with our Medici cousins, yet their willingness to display it in the chapel is unprecedented. As for me, I must be sure the Vatican *never* gets that painting; I have reasons to be cautious. The Vatican sent an anonymous agent to my last show who snapped up the three-level triptych—*Gilded Sinners*. This really bothers me because nobody will ever see it again! Anyone who studies it closely can see twisted forms of priests abusing little children in the lower level, hell. Now it's probably in one of the Vatican bedrooms to turn on a cardinal."

Simon broke in. "*Why* would the Vatican want to get your latest painting? I haven't seen it yet, so this may be a stupid question, but why?"

Sarah and Claudia exchanged knowing looks as Armando answered. "The Vatican is afraid the flock will dump the Church when they realize Jesus was married. People who have seen the painting say they feel how much Jesus loved Mary Magdalene and his holiness came from being with her. This emotion flowed through me when I was learning how to love Jennifer." He smiled warmly at his wife. "People will demand to know why the Church portrays Jesus as a celibate eunuch. By the way, my father reserved tickets for all of us for Monday."

"Yes, the Church definitely wants to avoid those kinds of conclusions," Simon replied. "My article on new discoveries in the Jesus family tomb dovetails with this building revelation, a logical counterpart to your artistic approach, Armando. You all know a lot about the ossuaries, so tell me if I bore you and we can move on to something else." He took note of their eager eyes.

"It starts with the Jerusalem ossuaries—bone boxes used as a burial practice in Jerusalem until the Romans destroyed the Temple and ended it. It was a weird practice, for example the ossuaries in the tombs were all aligned to the Temple Mount."

"That's what first got *my* attention," Sarah broke in wondering about Claudia's fixed stare on Simon.

"In 1980," Simon went on, "during apartment construction in the Talpiot region of Jerusalem, a tomb was uncovered. It contained ten ossuaries, one of which immediately went missing. They were inscribed with the names of various members of the Jesus family, and one had an inscription that probably refers to Mary Magdalene. As usual, doctrinaire archaeologists debunked the find, but highly credible alternative researchers went crazy over the find. In 2002, an antiquities dealer stunned the world when he announced he had an ossuary that was inscribed 'James, son of Joseph, brother of Jesus.' There were front-page stories about it in the *Times, Washington Post, Herald Tribune,* and almost every other paper in the world.

"I wrote a long story about both finds for the *Times,* and I never stopped following the story because I believe it is critically important to Christians, Jews, and Muslims alike. The damned Israeli Antiquities Authority confiscated the James ossuary and put the dealer on trial for forgery for eight long years! Meanwhile, this ossuary probably did contain the bones of the brother of Jesus; it probably *is* the one that went missing in 1980. Way back then I smelled a rat, and now the rat is rotting."

Claudia broke in. "How does this relate to the shift Armando's painting might evoke?"

"For starters, the Vatican wants to suppress the ossuary finds at all costs just like they will want to prevent people from viewing Armando's painting. Think about it: What were the bones of Jesus doing in a tomb if he resurrected, the central belief of Christianity? And what were Mary Magdalene's bones doing there with the Jesus family?"

"Excuse me, Simon, since I've never heard about any of this," Jennifer chimed in. "You are saying that a tomb was found containing ten ossuaries that were inscribed with Jesus's family names plus Mary Magdalene, but one of the ten was stolen and may have turned up in 2002 inscribed as James, the brother of Jesus?"

"Exactly right, the basic story that's stirring up a hornet's nest. Sarah, do you remember when I told you about the ossuaries that Father Bagatti found? You may remember how mad I was at the Church for silencing him?" She nodded and smiled remembering how he used to rant about it. "The facts are, a Franciscan archaeologist, Father Bagatti, found an ossuary on the Mount of Olives that was inscribed with St. Peter's name correctly—*Simon Bar Jonah*. But, the Church has always claimed St. Peter is buried under the Vatican, the basis for the pope running the Church. The pope silenced Bagatti and stopped the news in its tracks!" Simon was practically shouting, which made Sarah giggle. "Bagatti also found the ossuaries of many early Christians including Mary, Martha, and Lazarus, but the remains were socked away in a nearby semiprivate museum. Then immediately the Vatican announced they'd found more evidence for St. Peter under the Bernini altar, just another damned lie."

Armando sighed. "Oh, well. So what about the new evidence you mentioned?"

"Sorry, it is rather technical. A researcher for the Israeli Geological Survey, Aryeh Shimron, analyzed soil samples from the Talpiot tomb, the nine ossuaries in the warehouse and the James ossuary. His analysis proves that the James ossuary *is* the missing tenth ossuary. Trust me, his findings are impeccable. This destroys the orthodox version of the Resurrection; it means Jesus was a normal human being."

Armando interrupted in a very quiet voice. "If this is true, then it validates my painting, doesn't it?"

"Yes, it *does!* And there is a whole lot more I can say about my research, but hey, I don't want to do all the talking."

Claudia joined in. "Might this have something to do with your phone call to me around three weeks ago?"

Sarah looked at Claudia with wide eyes, and then turned to Simon. "Does this have something to do with you being up all night lately? You've been down in Claudia's library reading almost every night. Are you *finding* things in her books?"

"Right, Sarah, it must be my library," Claudia broke in looking back at Simon. "If you recall, you called to ask me if I minded you reading my books, and of course I said it was fine. I have things in my library that go very deep into arcane ideas, and I've only taken some of my books to Lorenzo's. I took all my books about Mary Magdalene, the Grail, and Templar lore over there, so what *did* you find in my library?" She was unaware she was rapping her fingers sharply on the table.

Simon drew a deep breath and replied triumphantly, "You've missed some things, Claudia. You have a great section on alternative theories about the peopling of America—wonderful books about the Aurignacians, Magdalenians, Egyptians, Sumerians, Phoenicians, Vikings, Celts going across the sea to America—books that prove the Columbus 1492 story is horseshit. That's the point, isn't it?" he ranted. "All the damned lies. What *are* they covering up?" He paused because he knew Sarah was trying not to laugh at him, but went on anyway. "*Why* did the Church invent a celibate Jesus and viciously torture anybody who said he was married and had a family? *Why* do Catholics have to believe in Mary's perpetual virginity? *Why* do people in the U.S. insist Columbus discovered America when he so obviously did not? Europeans can't believe that Americans still fall for that bullshit! Anyway, I started compulsively reading your books late at night after doing research on the ossuaries all day, and I hit a gold mine."

"Simon," Claudia interrupted, "is this about William Mann, the guy who wrote the book about the Templar meridians?" Dante sauntered into the room grabbing her attention. He glowered at the group and then lay down in front of the fire swishing his tail.

"Yeah, Claudia, and more. How about your book by Pohl on the journey of Henry Sinclair to Nova Scotia in the late 1300s? Henry Sinclair, the Templar. Did you read that one?"

Claudia's mind was spinning while the three others were on the edges of their seats listening to the two of them banter. Jennifer understood everything they were saying and was fascinated and very pleased with herself for catching on so quickly. Sarah was glued because she'd been trying to figure out what Simon was doing late at night. Claudia finally answered, "Yes, Simon, I've read both of those books and certainly the Templars were involved in early explorations of America, but so what?"

"What you probably do *not* know being Italian is that Americans are taught in school that the early settlers of America were religious dissenters escaping the battles between the Protestants and Catholics. The real truth is, many of these people were escaping the *Inquisition*—here we go, back to the fucking Church again."

"Well, so *what?*" Claudia practically shouted, causing everyone to chuckle at the excitement and energy between Simon and Claudia.

"Claudia, you didn't read that book by William Mann carefully enough or you've forgotten things." Claudia crossed her arms and glared at Simon like a furious imperial eagle. "The Templars went across the sea to America because they wanted to find a place for the dissenters to live because the Inquisition wanted to exterminate them. So, think about it, all of you, because the light has finally switched on in my head, but I don't know what I'm going to do with the information because it is too arcane for the *Times*. The Templars were protecting *the* bloodline— the lineage of Jesus and Mary, the Holy Grail—in *America,* the story the Church never wants anyone to hear about."

Sarah dropped her glass of water on the floor and it shattered. Dante sprung up and streaked past to run out of the library scraping and scrambling across the stone floors. They all sat with their mouths wide open staring at Simon. Claudia looked at Sarah who was staring at her empty hand in disbelief and said, "Oh my God, I never connected the dots. Damn it, Simon, leave it to you to make the connections; I'm impressed as always. Does this have anything to do with your work for the *Times?*" Sarah carefully picked up pieces of glass while Armando sponged up the water, breathing a sigh of relief because she'd been wondering the same thing. She'd gotten used to being alone, and lately Simon acted like a madman. They were so lucky to have the apartment with the little library and gas fireplace for him to use late at night.

"Well, there are *more* dots to connect," he said in a determined voice. "Let's go back to the Talpiot tomb. Even though Israeli authorities, the Catholic Church, fundamentalist Christians, and Jews ignore these fantastic tomb discoveries, they are sacred to Christendom and should be protected and venerated. The Templars were obsessed with the Holy Family and made Crusades to take Jerusalem and rule it. Well, *why* would the Templars go to so much trouble to go down and take Jerusalem from the Saracens? Think about what a challenging and crazy idea *that* was! So, *why* would they do that? Running on logic, the early Christians would have known where that tomb was, and there is evidence for that. Wouldn't *that* be a good reason to take Jerusalem? Remember, bones were sacred, like the reliquaries in the Medici chapels, more valuable to some people than diamonds."

"Why didn't *I* think of that? This cover-up is so intense and insidious that it fogs my brain, you know? The constantly repeated fake story diminishes our intelligence, fogs our minds."

"Yes. My brain isn't scrambled because I'm coming at this through the limited window of the Talpiot tomb, the key that opens the lock, the key that everybody needs. And for your 2012 records, Claudia, the James ossuary was validated in *2012!* This is a vast topic, it's late, so I'm going to save a piece of this story for another meeting, soon I hope. But I want to add one little teaser because I think what we are talking about is part of the experience of seeing Armando's painting Monday, since the Medici arranged for this display and they are probably Templars.

Armando, I'm sure your father is a modern Templar or something close to it. The fundamental issue is, did the Templars visit the Talpiot tomb during the Crusades? There *is* evidence—the three skulls. Claudia, you read about in *The Jesus Family Tomb*. Do you remember the three skulls they found on the floor of the Talpiot Tomb?"

"Yes, I dimly remember that, and I will reread the book immediately. When I first read it, I couldn't hold it in my head, but now I'm registering it. Simon, I'm so happy you are home; we need you. We need each other as we put all this together because this awakening is so mentally taxing, emotionally intense, and maddening. It is best not to go any further with this right now until we've absorbed this part."

"Yes, Claudia," Armando responded. "I'm getting tired, and I can tell Jen is too, so let's call it a night. Okay with you all?"

Sarah nodded saying, "Yes, of course it is, but I won't sleep tonight. May Simon and I use the library for a little longer, since Teresa will be asleep in our room? As you will see in a few weeks, I went down this path in my novel but from a different perspective. Things are coming together in a magical way, but it is so mind-bending. Your painting will rock the world, Armando, so tomorrow we get to observe people responding to it. Remember, millions in the world are wrestling with the things we're talking about tonight and adopting a whole new view of the past. We know that because of all the popular books about Jesus and Mary Magdalene."

27

Two Messiahs

After making sure Teresa was soundly asleep, Simon and Sarah crept back down to the library to enjoy the last of the fire, rehash the evening's discussion, and have a few moments alone. He handed her a cup of tea as she shivered. "Even though I've read your novel in rough draft and loved it, I know you well enough to know you've already moved way beyond it in your current thinking. What have you been thinking about these days, Sarah? You are the resident expert on early Judeo-Christianity, and much of what we know comes from you. So as I piece things together, I'd love to hear anything more you have to say about the early Christians."

She warmed her hands around the cup while organizing her thoughts. "I will, but on one condition: tell me more about the three skulls in the Talpiot tomb as soon as you can, and I will get into what I've been thinking about. The gospels were revised to marginalize the family of Jesus because the Church decided to mold Jesus into a celibate kingpin for their global religion. But, his mother, the *virgin*, was the mother of at least seven children! You get mad about the cover-up on the ossuaries, well the cover-up on Mary and her children is what makes me angry. Imagine what it was like to bear all those children during such chaotic times! The Syrian refugee mothers with so many children make me remember Mary's true story. James Tabor wrote a very good book about the Jesus family—*The Jesus Dynasty*—and he thinks Jesus had to support them all because Joseph was so old when he married her. Regardless of all that, the person to focus on is James, the younger brother of Jesus, who led the early Christians and was murdered by the Romans. James led the Nazarenes, or Ebionites, the group that followed Jesus *and* John the Baptist. This is why the discovery of the James ossuary is so important."

"The *what?*" Simon broke in. "Ebionites? What are *they?*" He got up to stir the fire with an intense expression on his face.

"The followers of James were called Ebionites—Jewish Christians who were also sometimes called Nazarene or Nasoreans. Paul *hijacked* the early church from these early Jewish Christians. Roman Catholicism is *Pauline* Christianity; it has little to do with Jesus, James, or John the Baptist. Catholicism is not the religion of Jesus; it is St. Paul's Christ, a limpid, Greek divinized apostle."

"Sarah," he broke in after he came back to sit down. "Now I remember where I heard that term. Alan Butler and John Ritchie say in *Rosslyn Revealed* that the *Templars* were Ebionites, so you've just connected the dots for me. In other words, maybe the Templars were a secret organization that intended to carry on the James church to protect what Jesus taught, they actually have! I think the gospels were altered to make it look like Jesus didn't have brothers and sisters to erase the memory of James, and *that's* why the authorities are trying to discredit his ossuary!"

"It *is* sick," Sarah growled. "Tabor believes Jesus supported a family of seven children and his mother. If this is true, the Church buried the human aspects of his life as a hardworking man and a compassionate spiritual teacher; they even lied about the woman he loved. But this story will not go away! When I viewed the James ossuary in Toronto, tears ran down people's faces. We are salvaging the true story of a real man who has so radically impacted our beliefs. We can see *how* the historical winners altered every aspect of his life because we understand their motive—to create a new religion of power. But, Jesus was a responsible son, husband, and father who became a great spiritual teacher. I can't wait to talk to my parents once they've read my novel."

"Yeah, I'd love to hear what William says. What does the recovery of the life of John the Baptist mean to you? He sounds like a wild man to me."

"Yes, he was. Except for baptizing Jesus by the river Jordan, he was mostly written out of the Bible. Yet, now the discovery of his ritual cave is bringing *him* back to life. He appears in history with a large following just a few years before Jesus shows up. Considering how long it takes for a teacher to gather followers, especially during Herod's reign, he must have been teaching some years before Jesus came on the scene. Since he didn't have to care for a huge family, he began teaching early. These ideas feel right to me, so that's how I portrayed John and Jesus in my novel.

"Regarding the Ebionites, after age fifty, Paul focused on the bigger population, Gentiles, the ideal power base for the new religion. Paul attracted pagan and magical Greco-Romans, but he denied the spirituality of sex, the value of women, and the importance of family. He transformed Jesus into a spiritual king who gives access to the divine through the Eucharist—eating the body and blood of Christ—but this was and is absolute anathema to Judaism! Paul subverted Jewish Christianity by marginalizing the Ebionites, and then Jerusalem fell into chaos when the Romans destroyed the Temple and the Ebionites had to go into hiding. Then along came St. Jerome who said Mary was a virgin and James and the brothers were the *cousins* of Jesus. Since few people could read Aramaic in the fifth century, Jerome had free rein to edit and rewrite scripture according to his beliefs when he translated the Bible into Latin. If the Nag Hammadi scrolls and other early sources had not been found, we would have no way to uncover the real early church, but now we are. The Ebionites are the closest to what Jesus and John taught." She stopped to catch her breath.

Simon was smiling. "I get it now, the Templars did guard the Ebionites, in a way the Templars are Ebionites. Regardless, once the

Church sanitized the scriptures and hammered out their dogma, they forgot the real history themselves and madly pursued heretics. But no matter how hard they tried to suppress people—murdering the Cathars, attacking the Jews, murdering the Templars—the protectors of the secrets never forgot, truly amazing. As the truth comes out about what the murderous Inquisitors were really doing, the Church is in for a huge backlash, since celibacy unleashed priestly sexual abuse. But, I wonder, how do the Ebionites relate to your earlier studies about Marcion?"

"That's an issue I worked out in my novel. Marcion was born right around the time James and Paul were martyred. Sometimes," she went on after sipping warm tea, "I think Marcion is the big missing piece in the early second century, an essential key to what happened to devout Jews who'd adopted Jesus after Pauline Christianity took over. But his teachings as a bishop were buried because the Roman Church was taken over by an ascetic fanatic who adroitly identified the needs of the new Piscean Age. Paul got the power because he persuaded people to throw out the old stuff that was in their way."

"C'mon, go for it, more, babe! You've never been afraid of being a heretic!" he said while poking the dwindling coals and twirling his spare hand at her.

"Okay. Paul claimed he got his knowledge from Jesus on the road to Damascus. He didn't seem to care about what James believed, and he seemed to think he could trash anything in Judaism that was in the way of converting the Gentiles. Paul's strong tendency to throw away the old and bring in the new utterly fascinates me because Judaism is a religion of the Age of Aries, while Christianity and Islam are religions of the Age of Pisces. Now that Piscean beliefs are being thrown out for Aquarian ideals in our times, what went on during the times of Jesus helps us reflect on the changes we're experiencing now.

"Back to Paul. Outrageously for a Jew of his time, Paul advised dumping circumcision and dietary proscriptions to convert Gentiles as if he was the thirteenth apostle! The times were so chaotic that James couldn't influence Paul, and he distrusted him. *This* is where Marcion

comes in! I think Paul's cleansing of old Jewish practices got Marcion's ✗
attention, since he wanted to let go of Yahweh. But Paul was entrenched,
Marcion got dumped, and Yahweh got even more powerful.

"Then, to better understand how the Great Ages change, we have
to add the Gnostics to the brew. The Gnostics retained an amalgam of
magical and theological beliefs that went back as far as seven or eight
thousand years, the wisdom of the three or four Great Ages before the
Age of Aries. They were teaching about the transitions of the Great
Ages, for example in the Alexandrian Library, the repository of the
wisdom of ancient times. This enabled them to identify positive new
trends and encourage people to terminate negative ones, such as the
mass warfare that gripped the Middle East and Europe during the
Age of Aries.

"The Gnostics were horrified by the rise of dogmatic, exclusiv-
ist Christianity based on the violent Arian war god, Yahweh! They
believed Arian monotheism would inspire religious wars throughout
the whole Age of Pisces, and it did—my god is better than yours. At
this key moment, Paul played the game exactly right. The Gnostics
went into hiding to save what was left of their records after their
great library was torched a few times. Yet, some of their records have
been found, and now we can see they thought Yahweh was merely
a demiurge—a minor creator god that limited human potential—*not*
the divine creator. The Gnostics feared Yahweh would become even
more powerful due to the Christians retaining him, and he did.

"The Gnostics knew Pisces was slated to be the season of love
and compassion to temper Arian violence and obsession with power.
Marcion, as a major Gnostic Christian, was pivotal. He wanted to cut
the ties to Judaism so that Christianity could be a new religion based
on love, and in that sense, he was in sync with Paul. However, Paul was
a very wounded and disturbed person, a psychopath who was struggling
to let go of his old God; love is not there in his theology. Once Paul
got Gentile Christianity rolling, he told the people to pray to Jesus as
Lord—that is pray to Jesus *as* Yahweh—just exactly what Marcion and

the Gnostics feared the most, since Jews were forbidden to pray to any god but Yahweh."

"Sarah, why do theologians like Tertullian say Marcion hated the body?"

"The Church Fathers wanted to get rid of Marcion no matter what because he was a major link to the Jesus family, so they falsified his message. Marcion was a leading bishop with a huge following, and the followers of Yahweh wanted him out of the way. They excommunicated him and made him into a lame duck, but that generated huge East/West tension because Marcion was a great leader for Eastern Christianity. Marcion's belief that the new Christianity should not retain Yahweh horrified Tertullian, so he ragged on him. Paul won the game by using his Judaism to talk to the Jews and Christianity to talk to the Christians. Ironically, Paul spawned anti-Semitism."

"Damn, what a head scrambler you are! No wonder you are so quiet sometimes. You think about this all the time, don't you?"

"Yes, except when I'm cooking or playing with Teresa, the reason I love having a family."

"Jesus would probably agree, so bully for you, Sarah. Let's go to bed."

Jennifer asked Claudia to join her for a walk after lunch to deepen their friendship before they viewed Armando's painting. The invitation made Claudia nervous, and Jennifer knew it, but she was ready because she'd come up to speed intellectually.

"Claudia, I've asked you to spend a few minutes with me alone because I want to clear the air with you, so thank you for coming. I know I've made you feel uncomfortable at times, but it will never happen again because of the wonderful work I'm doing with Lorenzo, he's incredible."

"I agree. My only problem is, *I* don't get to go to him! You are very thoughtful to reach out, so why do you think you've made me feel uncomfortable?"

"I was jealous of you, Claudia. You not only were Armando's lover when he was young, you are brilliant and also gorgeous. It must be hard being so beautiful?"

"*You* are very beautiful, Jennifer. The only difference between us is I'm a fashion queen, my job. I had to do it when I was young to be independent since I didn't marry, and after a while it was fun. Now, it is my style, and I think I entertain people, don't you?"

"Yes, actually that was what I was thinking when we were sitting around talking last night with you in your hot black sexy jumpsuit. You *are* very entertaining, you encourage women to express themselves, and I'd love to photograph you! I really want us to be friends. I don't have very many friends here, you know, since being in Tuscany most of the time means Armando and I don't socialize much. I enjoy Matilda and Pietro's guests, but they are older and they come and go. I want you to know that I wasn't really jealous of you. I seethed when you were around because of what I'd done myself. I had an affair with a married man and almost destroyed a family even though I knew better from my upbringing. So, you pushed my buttons because I was afraid you'd do it to me. But now I know myself better and I know you better. It is something you'd never do and I was not respecting you."

Claudia was listening carefully because she liked women who told the truth about themselves. "I would not under any circumstances sleep with a married man. But, I do not judge you or anybody else who does it. Maybe I'm an arrogant bitch who can't stand the idea of sharing a man! Thank you. I am touched you've shared this with me, very touched." Claudia raised a long arm and slung it over Jennifer's wide shoulders. "You *are* beautiful, you know, and I could enhance your beauty even more. It would be fun for me!"

"That's a great idea! As soon as I'm back in Rome, I'll come to your boutique and have you dress me. Maybe we can look for a few things for Matilda, presents for Sarah. I'd love it, and then I can take you out to lunch. Thank you for being kind about this. It's funny, isn't it? We can be so afraid of something, and yet it is nothing if we can just air it out and let it go."

"Guilt is a totally dysfunctional emotion; the sooner we get rid of it, the better. Guilt is what needs to go out with the Age of Pisces, the Age of Christian Guilt! If one has done something emotionally difficult and complex, it's hard to let it go, yet that's how we evolve, *individuate* as Lorenzo puts it. When I think of the stuff Lorenzo gets laid on him every day, sometimes I think guilt will knock him over like the leaning tower of Pisa!"

They laughed and continued walking down the path, Claudia feeling grateful to Armando for being her inspiration to individuate long ago.

28

Celestial Swan

The group of friends arrived well before the chapel opened its doors. A guard was expecting them and let them in. To avoid attention, Armando and his parents didn't go. The security was intense with guards set up to confiscate all cameras. The four of them wore nondescript dark clothes and made their way through the museum to the wide stone stairs. Once inside the chapel, they stopped in the back and held their breath.

Chapel of Princes

Intense spotlights beamed focused light down from the high dome. Tiny silver molecular fragments, like minnows swimming in illuminated darkness, flashed and sparkled in the thick rays of light, the four beams aimed down to Armando's painting. Bizarre Medici tombs, heraldry, and pompous statues were on all sides, but Jesus and Mary Magdalene were the focus. Simon and Sarah took chairs in the back to avoid scrutiny from people when they came in. Claudia, who was having difficulty breathing, sat close to the front on the right side near Jesus. She relaxed into her chair and contemplated his body rising while Mary reached for him. She detected a low hum in her sphenoid and cochlear bones. *Do I hear bees buzzing?* She opened her eyes to his face, which looked even sweeter than before. As the heavenly face opened her heart, a geometrical crystalline lattice formed all around her body. She glanced over at Jennifer at the other end of the front row.

Jennifer focused on Mary's hands reaching for Jesus. A guard watching her knew she was the painter's wife. As her hands came together in front of her heart involuntarily with long fingertips delicately touching, her face was shining. Something pulled her forward, so she steadied her feet on the stone floor. Pachelbel's Canon played softly way up in the dome. *Am I hearing things? No, they are playing the Canon, a lovely idea.*

Hushed expectant people filed in. The intense light coming down from on high directed their eyes right to the painting—low gasps were audible. Jesus and Mary's flesh in vibrant and touchable clothing was alive in the full color spectrum. Her luscious and sensual red hair was shocking as if the goddess had descended on Florence. People were seeing something they'd always been waiting for. Soon all the seats were taken, they would have twenty minutes; the music ending would be the cue. The denizens of Florence saw the painting, not Jesus on the cross above the altar. *Yes, it is true, just like the rumors. It is Jesus and Mary Magdalene showing their love! He rises as she reaches for him to hold him. His face is so beautiful and feminine that I can only cry and wonder how a man can look like that. He is in heaven while still on Earth simply because she is with him. She grasps for him, but how can anybody grasp the Divine? It is like reaching blindly for the one you love during marriage when you know they will eventually die.*

Claudia felt the people's energy fields weaving into oneness, the Canon braiding their souls into cords of light. *No mistaking it. The morning breeze vibrating the old glass in the windows up in the dome pulsed in tune with Pachelbel—sound waves responding to temperature differentials.* Her body expanded with the music beating with her ecstatic heart. Sweet joy penetrated her body while the people touched their hands, their shoulders, and stroked their thighs to circulate the extreme kinesthesia. They closed their eyes feeling their skin absorb the heavenly sight. Involuntarily they swayed in unison responding to the sensual sacredness. *Without knowing Lorenzo, I would not understand.*

What is that? Claudia could see and hear high intensity light particles slicing the air—infinitesimal star photons escaping the reliquaries. *Are old bones sending memory particles into the brains of the people as they stare at the painting? Weird. I feel their brains expanding and pressing against their skulls.* Some had their hands on their faces making sure their bodies were still in their chairs. Then a strange thing happened . . . simultaneously their minds emptied when the wholeness and oneness of Jesus and Mary opened the cosmic lens to their souls: they sighed in unison when Pachelbel's Canon ended. One by one they got up and filed out of the room while the four remained. The people left quickly, shuffling down the staircase without uttering a word. Then the next group filed in as the music began anew. This would go on day after day with light penetrating people as they absorbed the real story of a great man and a great woman.

Later, they went to lunch in a trattoria below street level near the Arno, making their way to a private booth. They ate lightly and quietly. When the plates were cleared away, Sarah looked at Simon and said, "How did you respond to the painting?"

"For me, it stopped time. Sarah, can you tune in to your ruby crystal and give us some kind of read on what we've just seen? I swear those people were transported and didn't care if anybody could see it happening. I thought some of them were going to levitate!"

"It was exquisite, and they certainly have it displayed beautifully, a Medici miracle, yet Armando *created* the miracle. But, it wouldn't work its magic without the great presentation in that awesome space." Her breathing slowed as she closed her eyes and put her right hand over the ring and began speaking in a very low voice.

"I see a lodestone, an omphalos laced with a lattice covered with bees. The light around it is strange, perfectly split between the dark and light like the yin and yang. White light presses the darkness, a substance functioning in another dimension that imprints what's going on in the Chapel of Princes. Light shining on Armando's painting transmutes the Medici darkness in the dome; it cuts through the primordial zone between the dark and the light."

"Sarah," Simon said in a very low voice. "Can you tell me more about how the light affects darkness?"

"Hmmm," Sarah continued in a total trance, "I'm not sure. The light makes the edges of the darkness organic, magnetized, like when a cell detects cancer cells and alerts its surface. Darkness is more fecund when light pressures it. Seeing the light in Armando's painting transforms dark things in the world, makes them transparent. Ugliness seethes out of a nest of writhing snakes turning to slime. I'm afraid of what's going to happen when the real story of Jesus is known by enough people."

"Why are you afraid, Sarah?" Claudia broke in. "Exactly *what* are you afraid of?"

"Wait a moment; I'm gathering images . . . This omphalos is the world surrounded by darkness struggling to control things. Bombs go off and people scream as Yahweh hovers over the omphalos, laughing obscenely."

"Sarah," Simon said quietly. "What does Armando's painting have to do with this struggle?"

"I see flecks or balls of light all over the Chapel of Princes . . . No . . . bees! They fly all around the painting and the room, looping

and diving behind it, then flying into the reliquary rooms. Bee buzzing vibrates the bones to open the painting's codes in the minds of the
observers. With time going faster, everything in the world is increasing
exponentially as the light exposes the truth. Nothing can hold this back.
The pressure makes people psychotic, but curiosity stronger than fatalism
keeps them from losing hope on the edge of the dark and the light."

"Sarah, come back to us," Simon said softly. "This is too much for
you now. We hear what you are saying, and we feel it too. We'll be
watching to see how this works out. Thank you, my love."

She took her hand off her ring and sucked in a deep breath. When
she opened her eyes, she had no idea what she'd just said.

During fall 2015, the world went further out of control. The European
Union tottered, Greece bled financially, and young Europeans in Spain,
Italy, and France suffered widespread joblessness. England considered
leaving the Union, and the Ukrainian crisis upset Europe's balance with
Russia. Syrian refugees streamed through Lesbos as frantic migrants just
ahead of them pushed through Hungary, Serbia, and Croatia to make it
up to Germany and Scandinavia. Eight months prior, the attack in Paris
against the satirical magazine, Charlie Hebdo, had made Europeans feel
very unsafe. Then, like gasoline thrown on the fire, October 13 came
with a second Paris attack. Heavily armed radical Islamists butchered
130 innocent young people out enjoying an evening. French society was
breaking down as Islamic extremism grew among the children of the
mostly North African immigrants confined to ghettos rebelling against
a society that offered them little opportunity. France heightened its
security and tightened its borders. Europeans realized they had to find
ways to work with Russia and Turkey to solve the Syrian crisis.

Pietro reflected on the European crisis while he waited for Armando.
A few days ago Pietro put on a gray turtleneck and black pants, donned
a beret that slightly hid his face, and went to the Chapel of Princes. He
sat in the back corner to watch people streaming in and out for hours;
something remarkable was happening.

"Hello," Armando said as he walked in and closed the door. "You can't imagine how much I've looked forward to some time with you."

"It is the same for me, son, and thank you for coming. The other day I visited the chapel to observe people's responses. They are finding truth in your painting, balance between men and women, our only hope for peace in the world."

"Something is going on in the chapel because I've been feeling electrified ever since the viewing started. My fears about the unveiling are gone. Almost every day I feel hot energy in my body, you know, kundalini. I didn't expect that!"

"There's more to this than we realize. I've not shared the main family secrets with you because of their complexity. It is easy to imagine Jesus being married, though millions have died over it. Our family records are difficult because they are cosmological, that is, maps that show us how to enter the universe, star mythology—understanding the constellations by means of the human view of the stars. Our family, based in Siena for at least 5,000 years, is the family of Leo because Pierleoni means locating the lion, Leo."

"May I ask questions?"

"Yes, of course, and we can stay up all night."

"I thought our family only goes back 1,000 years, except for the fact we certainly have Etruscan blood, but more than 5,000 years?"

"Yes, because we carry Etruscan blood. Contrary to archaeology, the Etruscans probably came here around five thousand years ago. Remember, this is partly legendary, yet also deeply informed by archaeology. Archaeologists investigate the physical world, yet legends and stories access many dimensions by means of symbols passed down through generations. Our family has retained the secrets of the swan, teachings that go back 17,000 years, that is way before the Ages of Cancer and Leo. Last July you had a visceral response when I told you about the cataclysms. Do you recall me saying we've retained knowledge going back 17,000 years marked by the swan taking flight?" Armando nodded and looked up at the family crest.

"Swans have magnetic crystals in their brains that enable them to fly on yearly flight paths, navigating by the stars. Around 17,000 years ago, when we entered the Age of Libra by precession, the polestar was Deneb, the brightest star in the Northern Cross. Deneb becomes the polestar every 26,000 years. You do understand precession and the Great Year?"

"Only because of Claudia. Everyone in our discussion group has learned about the Great Ages because Claudia and Lorenzo insist it is one of the most informative orientations. They say we lose cultural intelligence by not tracking the influence of the ages. It's fascinating that we actually *can* go that far back. Certainly, symbols such as the ram for Aries and the bull for Taurus verify this idea."

"Your friends have really gotten you up to speed! The Age of Libra is important because it was when humans attained a high point of intelligence, a time when anthropologists say humans mysteriously advanced very rapidly. Our family records say this occurred because of the orientation to Deneb by precession. Armando, listen carefully: *we cannot know what we are capable of without comprehending this Libran peak.* We can't make the transition into Aquarius—slated to be an enlightened era—without knowing what our species discovered then. Look at the state of the world today; our species is going to fail without this knowledge. We always learn a lot during any age, but sometimes the negative aspects of a previous age retard us. For example, if we'd retained the real teachings of Jesus, war would have ended by now.

"When Deneb is the polestar, Earth is directly oriented to the place of entry and exit to the sky world—direct access to cosmic consciousness. It would have been an incredible sight when the Milky Way was turning around Deneb, which formed a great star tree in the northern sky for a thousand years, the source of the extremely ancient Tree of Life legends around the world. Shamans use these legends to travel into the lower and upper worlds for healing. My point is, during the Age of Libra, our souls easily traveled out to the cosmic realms when our bodies died; we were not constrained by death."

"Well, I've heard the Age of Aquarius is supposed to be a free age,

so maybe this is the information we need to remember, *how* to be free—
no fear of death?"

"Yes, *exactly* Armando. As long as we are in bodies, freedom is *sha-manic*. Ancient Egyptians and Native Americans retained the knowl-edge of how to travel out to Orion, then out to the Great Rift in the Milky Way through Cygnus, the Northern Cross. Andrew Collins and Gregory Little call this the Path of Souls. In our case, the swan has always been the symbol for the soul's path, the secret to star traveling. Once there was a temple that is now deep below Siena where people accessed the Path of Souls 17,000 years ago; it's right there under the piazza. That is why the energy is so heavy and dense in Siena, a somber place of encapsulated force. We run the Palio every year to release it.

"Except for remnants of shamanic practices, the world has lost cosmic freedom. Recently Andrew Collins decoded many symbolic systems that portray the Great Ages and orientations to Cygnus. For example, the symbols on the Göbekli Tepe pillars portray the constel-lations with the orientation to the Northern Cross, particularly Deneb. Eventually he wondered whether there was something unusual about Deneb besides its orientation, and there is! The sudden leap forward in human evolution—a nearly instantaneous change in our physical and neurological makeup 17,000 years ago—was caused by a huge increase in cosmic rays that reached Earth from a binary star system that is close to the crossing point of the Northern Cross near Deneb. This star system—Cygnus X-3—is one of the brightest sources of high-energy gamma rays in our galaxy. Since 1980, scientists have been detecting periodic cosmic rays coming from Cygnus X-3 that they call cygnets—little swans.

"This research is highly controversial: Some astronomers propose Cygnus X-3 is our galaxy's first discovered microblazer, a star close to a black hole encircled with ionized gas that feeds the star. When it eats too much, the star burps and emits plasma jets perpendicular to the star's rotational axis. Mysteriously, these jets sometimes aim at Earth sending high-energy cosmic particles our way. This may sound outland-ish, but Carl Sagan proposed that cosmic rays trigger human evolution.

Mysteriously, Cygnus X-3 has been active for around 700,000 years, the time frame for the evolution of mammals."

"Very interesting. I can't say I understand you, but it fits with what's coming up in my conversations with my friends. We believe we are in the middle of a fast wake-up right now, which sadly is in tandem with rising violence in the world. In that regard, I worry that my work disturbs people, but I can't stop creating. Maybe we *are* unusually affected by cosmic rays these days; maybe I am."

Pietro considered Armando's thoughtful face. "I agree with you, and the rising violence also makes me very unhappy. But, when science starts discovering the cosmic factors that accelerate human evolution, nothing will stop the process. Ignorance is the problem. I believe people *will* overcome the centuries of lies that keep them stupid and crazy. Nothing can stop this quest for the truth.

"The Celestial Swan is our symbol, and now you have a sense of what that may mean. As we speak, science *is* confirming our ancient wisdom. For thousands of years, people have used shamanic techniques to lead the soul out into the universe at death and to guide new infants into our world, the fundamental orientation of our world to the sky, our way to be free. The religions of the Age of Pisces almost eliminated our cosmic access, but it is coming back with Aquarius by means of scientific and alternative research. In other words, Armando, we are freeing ourselves amid dire times. I am proud of you, my son. Your painting helps people; you have improved life on our planet. As we reweave our link to the sky world, over the years you will share your Pierleoni knowledge as the leading lion and then hopefully pass it to your child."

"Well then," Armando said, his face blazing with a happy smile, "you might as well know it now; you are about to have another grandchild. Jen is pregnant!"

Pietro blinked. "Are you sure? I can't wait to give Jennifer a big hug tomorrow. Matilda will be ecstatic. What a blessing!"

"Too much is happening all at once, but it's all so great. I look forward to more time with you. Let's call it a night."

29

Christmas 2015

The Appels and the Adamsons came to Rome to be with their children during Christmas 2015. The Adamsons stayed with Simon and Sarah, and the Appels enjoyed the Pierleoni villa. It was Rose's first visit with the Pierleonis in Rome, and she was utterly delighted with the rambling Renaissance home. She spent hours in the library perusing architectural and house design books. Matilda came in when she was lounging in a comfortable chair near the fire. "Hello, Rose. It certainly looks like you are having a lovely morning."

"Oh, yes. Please come join me. I love old buildings as you can see by the pile of books I've been going through. Come sit with me to talk about your lovely home. It must be wonderful to live in such a venerable old building."

"Well, we have our creaks and groans, but over the years, every board and stone has molded into place as if the house is a person. We tend the roof, gutters, and drains and keep the rats away. I love how our home feels because it shelters us against adversity, which is so comforting. If this villa could last this long, there's hope for a better future. Jennifer loves it here and enjoys the way we all live together. When any one of us feels like it, we can have a week or two alone in this house while others go up to Tuscany, sometimes to Majorca. I think she's very happy, and we're all so excited about the baby."

"I've never seen her this happy, not in her entire life," Rose remarked thoughtfully as she closed the book in her lap and put it aside. "She was a complex little girl, yet now she is relaxed and joyful. Some women might not like being alone so much, but she seems to thrive on having her time. It is wonderful for me to see how she actually lives."

"I'm so happy you came to visit. As one mother to another, I've always wondered whether anyone could ever live with Armando, a classic tortured artist. Yet she balances him and he relaxes with her because she is so nonchalant. Armando will love having a little one, and I think he will be a natural father like Pietro was."

"Oh, Pietro is so charming. He's so wise and thoughtful, so cultured and curious, and David just adores him. I wish I could steal him again tonight, but he's asked David to come to the genealogy room. What do you think they talk about up there?"

Matilda giggled and replied, "Everything."

"Great to have time with you, David. I've missed you and have thought of you often. I am so pleased Simon is back in Rome, a blessing for us all. You've seen how people are responding to Armando's painting and the viewing ends this week. Hopefully it will have a significant impact. Presenting this painting was unprecedented for the Medici; they did it by fiat as if it is still the Renaissance. Soon things will get back to normal for the Medici and our family."

"That's what I want to discuss with you, Pietro. While I was in the chapel, I detected strange energy in the reliquary rooms, some sort of a ghostly feeling that reminded me of my experience with Gaudí. His faith was profound and unlike anything I've ever felt, and surely he would have venerated reliquaries. My contact with him has expanded my understanding of myself, and now Armando's painting is dissolving my boundaries. If enough people realize Jesus was a sensual man and married, the differences between Jews, Muslims, and Christians could diminish."

"I think you are right," Pietro broke in. "Considering it from your perspective if I may, as you resonate with the idea of Jesus as a man, then have you ever wondered whether he was the long-awaited Messiah? This may be a sensitive topic, so please allow me to explore it as a Templar. I'm sure you've read about the Crusades and the Templar knights finding treasure in the Holy Land and then guarding it ever since?"

"Of course. I even think the Templars and the treasure came to America way before Columbus. But, please excuse my interruption."

"I was about to say that the divisions between the religions of Abraham really could break down if the people of faith realized the Templars were safeguarding the *Jewish* heritage of Jesus. Going back two thousand years, Christians didn't exist yet when the Jews were waiting for the Messiah. David, what I'm getting at is the Templars protected the true story of Jesus so that he could be the revered teacher for the major religions of the West, not merely an ascetic Christian hero. We need to reclaim this archetype, the divine human, for all religions."

"Interesting, but hard to imagine it ever happening. I want to talk about the *other* side of the Atlantic. The Mayan group I belong to is deeply connected to Native American wisdom, since they are from the same source. Are the Templars aware of this?"

Pietro felt like deflecting him by shifting in his chair. "I may or may not be able to answer that, but I will try. Tell me more about your sources."

"Yes, of course, happily. I'm alluding to the astonishing revelations offered by a modern Canadian Templar who is also Algonquin by blood and initiation, a remarkable combination. His name is William F. Mann. Have you read him?"

"I read a very informative book by him about the Templar meridians and the travels of Henry Sinclair to America." Pietro stood up and went over to the window where a full moon was turning the night into day. "Just imagine Henry Sinclair sailing from the Orkneys to Nova Scotia in 1398. I don't understand why more Americans haven't heard this story since it is exciting, so fascinating."

"Just think how different U.S. relations with Europe might be if everybody knew about these early contacts between Europe and North America," David muttered. "Do European Templars read Mann?"

"Yes we do. We think Mann had a lot of courage initially, nobody threw a pie in his face, and now he can say anything he wants! I hear he has a new book coming out that goes much further; I can't wait!"

"So, most Europeans realize people have been sailing all over the world for at least a thousand years, and now the Americans and Canadians are catching up fast. This new paradigm could change the nature of global politics by dissolving many divisions."

"I expect so. As we all know, the elite sequestered ancient maritime secrets to make money, but they also blocked access to the past, the magnificent story of the ancient days. With the truth coming out, who will control the sea passages above Canada and Alaska when the North Pole melts, the cycle the elite knows all about, labeled "Global Warming." It is time to stop the cover-ups, for example, here in Florence people need the real story of Jesus regardless of what happens to the foppish Catholic hierarchy. Circling back, how did your experience with Armando's painting remind you of exploring your lifetime as Gaudí?"

David twisted his signet ring. "Gaudí came into my body and used my senses to evaluate the accuracy of the completion of his cathedral. He was pleased with what was going on, so he shot up to a very high dimension, which spun all the cells in my body as if I was transfiguring. I feel so much lighter with his shadow gone. His energy was dense as if he was struggling with demons when he was alive; I think I freed him. This may be how people feel when they view Armando's painting."

"Very intriguing, and I've never heard of anything quite like it. I thought you were looking better because Simon is back, but maybe it's because of these breakthroughs?"

"Yes, I am happier now, especially to be with a dear friend like you. We've reached across the Atlantic to touch, and now it is time for millions to reach across the seas. We've been deluded into thinking we are divided, but we never were!"

"A very evocative idea isn't it, that we once enjoyed a global civilization, Atlantis? Perhaps breaking down the modern sense of division will move us toward being peaceful and global again?"

Christmas Eve dinner in Rome was memorable, a table with three families of three generations. Teresa, in a cranberry red velvet Christmas dress that had once been Sarah's, was very excited. After dinner, the ladies took her into the hall of tapestries to enjoy the Christmas tree and cookies. As soon as William went to bed, Pietro winked at David and Armando and said, "Let's take Simon to the library to pick his brain."

The four men were relieved to escape all the food and Christmas joy, yet a cheery fire was burning brightly and a plate of Christmas cookies was on the table. Simon eyed the cookies and said, "I don't know about all of you, but the intensity of this past year makes the holidays seem strange. Anybody interesting in shifting the mood with a discussion about tombs and old bones?"

Pietro replied, "Well, yes, I am."

Simon looked around the group and realized the two elders probably knew much more than he did, and he was just beginning to realize Armando was privy to a lot of secret information. He was surprised when he heard that David and Pietro occasionally had private talks. Armando observed Simon with amusement. *I bet Simon has no idea what my father knows.*

They chatted about what each had been thinking about to get up to speed. Then the topic they'd been eagerly waiting for came up when Simon spoke up again. "So, here we are in your house, Pietro, the count in an unusually long and enduring lineage. Have you heard about the three skulls that were found on the floor of the Talpiot tomb in triangular formation?"

Their faces showed they didn't know much about it, so Simon went on. "When archaeologists first excavated the tomb, they were very surprised to find three human skulls in an isosceles triangular formation sunk in a thick layer of ancient silt that had settled into the ossuary around the skulls for at least a thousand years. It was eerie, and one archaeologist thought it looked like some kind of ceremony had occurred. Any Templar would know that these three skulls indicated some kind of veneration. The bone boxes from the messianic period were very small, which necessitated crossing the femur bones over the other bones and then putting in the skull. The main Templar symbol for this practice is a skull above crossed femur bones, which mysteriously shows up on tombstones in Europe at the time of the Crusades. I think the Templars adopted this symbol to make sure the day would come when people would realize the importance of the ossuaries; that is now!

"Judging by the number of Jesus family inscriptions on the ossuaries from the Talpiot tomb, it would have been intensely venerated. The carriers of the secret tradition in southern France, the British Isles, and the Templars would have carefully guarded the location of this tomb. Well, I propose the Templars captured Jerusalem to find that tomb as well as to search under the Temple Mount, a topic for later. As the centuries went by and the remnants protecting the bloodline miraculously survived, what would have been more valuable than the bones and skulls of the Jesus family?" Simon stopped to look into all their faces to make sure he had the full attention of the room. He continued.

"I think the Templars revisited the tomb during a later Crusade to collect some of the bones, and at that time they conducted a ceremony with three skulls they'd brought with them, possibly the skulls of Templars who died after the First Crusade. They sold the relics at high prices to elite families for reliquaries, families such as yours, Pietro. I think *that* is what's in the reliquaries behind Armando's painting—relics of the Jesus family hidden in plain sight labeled as common saints." He stopped and looked at Pietro . . . Everybody looked at Pietro.

Pietro cleared his throat and sat back. "As you all know, modern researchers are figuring out things the Templars protected for many years. Simon, you are making suppositions that may never be proven, but your summary does match the Maltese Templar." Pietro got up and walked over to a nearby bookcase as they all watched him wondering what he was going to do. He pulled out a few books, reached in, a lever clicked, and the bookcase turned to expose a cavernous space behind. He reached in with both hands and brought out an object covered with a royal blue velvet cloth embroidered with gold thread borders. He put it on a table and removed the cloth to display a twelve-inch-tall Templar sword embedded in a small crystal skull resting on an ornate solid gold base. At the crossing point of the sword's hilt was a glass-covered receptacle with a small bone inside that Pietro pointed at. "This bone is Mary Magdalene's. This reliquary has been in our family since the Renaissance, the next thing I was going to share with you, Armando."

The three men were utterly shocked, yet the feeling emanating from the reliquary strangely calmed them. Dante crouched behind Armando, preparing to jump up on the table, but Pietro shooed him away.

"Father, I'm stunned. All these years it was hidden here?"

They examined the exquisite sculpture. Simon said in an incredulous voice, "All the clues fit together: At Rosslyn Castle in Scotland a small tombstone marker for William Sinclair is exactly the same size as a typical ossuary lid. Experts on Rosslyn puzzle over why his 'headstone' is so small, since William Sinclair was a prominent laird. Rosslyn Chapel itself looks like a giant reliquary. The Talpiot tomb has a very strange symbol above its entrance—an inverted triangle without a base that has a circle in the center—like the all-seeing eye of the Masons on the U.S. dollar bill. Maybe they used this symbol on the money to encode Templar veneration of the Talpiot tomb! In other words, these symbols permeate everything and have guided the evolution of society for two thousand years!"

"Yes," David said. "The truth is coming out now that the Mayan Calendar has ended. And, by the way, this reliquary's crystal skull must be ancient because a thousand years ago there were no modern tools to carve something like this. This must be one of the original skulls."

Simon continued, "Have you considered DNA analysis of this bone, Pietro? The authors of *The Jesus Family Tomb* ordered DNA analysis

The reliquary

of the mineral concretions in the ossuaries and rare bone fragments that were found in the bottoms. One of the researchers verified that all the people in the Talpiot tomb were related maternally *except* Mary Magdalene. To be buried in a family tomb, people had to be related by blood or marriage; therefore Mary had to have been the wife of Jesus. *And,* now we have the DNA sequences of the Jesus family! Pietro, what if *this* bone could be tested?"

Pietro was staring at the reliquary with an inscrutable expression. "Let me put it this way to you, Simon, the inveterate reporter who just won't quit. In time, much more will be possible with these relics, things way beyond DNA analysis. When the human race is ready, it will be discovered that the relics have cosmic DNA—changes and mutations from deep in the universe, in the stars. That's why we value them and protect them. The authentication of the Talpiot tomb and the James ossuary could inspire a wondrous accord between Christians, Jews, and Muslims. Next the world will attain new thought about its scripture, the lost writings. By knowing their story, we will feel them palpably, since truth is the first step to healing."

Pietro put the cloth back over the reliquary, picked it up, and carried it back to its hiding place behind the bookcase. When they said good night, they knew it would be hard to sleep.

30

Avatar of the Piscean Age

The Shi'ite and Sunni schism in the Middle East intensified in early January when Saudi Arabia executed forty-seven Shi'ite dissidents including the highly esteemed cleric, Muqtada al-Sadr. The Saudis beheaded all but four of the Shi'ite dissidents, a hideous reenactment of ISIS beheadings. Enraged Iranian protesters attacked and sacked the Saudi embassy in Tehran, and the Saudis severed diplomatic and commercial ties with Iran. U.S. officials had warned their Saudi ally not to kill Muqtada al-Sadr, but this warning was pointedly ignored. This weakened the Obama administration's influence in the Middle East, and next the Russians intensified their bombing of Syrian rebel positions, which further eroded U.S. policy.

Since the November attack in Paris, Belgium authorities had been combing Brussels to search out well-known extremists, a stepped-up campaign to root out jihadists. But during the spring equinox of 2016, ISIS bombed the Brussels airport and subway, killing at least thirty-five people. Deep helplessness crept into the Euro capitol because the citizens felt horribly vulnerable. Some people thought security should intensify, but feared it would reduce their civil liberties. Were terrorist attacks the future in an open European society?

After the winter of escalating tensions, Simon was on his computer in Claudia's library in the middle of the night seeking news about Brussels after the attacks. "The big question is," Simon muttered to himself, "why doesn't the West just get out of the Middle East?"

He heard shuffling in the hall, looked through the doorway, and there stood Teresa in pajamas with Sarah. She came to him still dripping with sleep and crawled up on his lap. "Hey, little one. What are you doing getting up in the middle of the night?"

"It's not the middle of the night anymore. It's after six. Have you been down here all night?"

"I came down around four because I couldn't sleep thinking about yesterday's bombings. Brussels is a huge and incompetent bureaucracy set up to run the European Union, but have they created a monster? For God's sake, they can't even protect their transportation systems! The elite use Brussels as a source for prestigious and highly paid jobs for their privileged sons and daughters, a modern leech bankrupting the economies of Euro members. I know that sounds simplistic, but their expensive chess game costs a lot while normal European life and security is deteriorating."

"I agree. Sometimes I wonder whether my attempts to uncover the real story of the three main religions mean anything at all; I'm discouraged. The Arab Spring gave people hope for freedom in 2011, but now the countries that participated are more oppressed than ever. The latest bombings break my heart. Teresa and I could be on the street in Rome when there is a terrorist attack; I can't bear it."

Teresa sucked her thumb and nestled deeper into Simon. "Will Europe end its dream of no borders? It's been great fun for Germans and Scandinavians to drive down to Spain, Italy, or Greece on new freeways with no stops. We're told people are making more money with easier trade, but I see little improvement in the lives of the average young European. The elite are the winners as usual, not the people. The police in Brussels don't know who is in the country with all the migrants flowing in bankrupting the government. Border controls to deal with undocumented migrants will have to be reinstituted. Almost every country is throwing up the barriers again, which they say is temporary, but I don't think so. Safety must be first in our troubled world, so I think we are going back to where we were before 1999, but how?"

When Simon needed guidance he thought of his father. As if the universe was on his side, his father called the next day. "You're where? You're kidding!"

"I'm not kidding, Simon. I have a session with Lorenzo today, so I came to Rome last night and landed on Pietro and Matilda. Pietro and I had a great talk last night, and we'd like to see you tonight. We'd like you to join us. Can you come? I hope Sarah won't mind if we steal you away?"

"Of course not, and I'm thrilled you're here. I'm so upset about Brussels that I couldn't sleep last night. Reality is shredding; the psychological pressure is unbelievable. Sometimes I feel like my head is exploding."

"I feel the same way. You've probably noticed that Pietro and I have become close friends, and he'd like to share more of what he knows with both of us. So, see you tonight around eight o'clock?"

"Hello, David. It's great to see you again," Lorenzo said as they settled down in the alcove. "World events certainly do stir up the psyche, don't they? Yet, we are becoming less complacent; there's more potential for change and transformation." Lorenzo put his hand on the table between them, which drew David's eye to a crystal obelisk.

"I do agree, and it is very good to see you. I'm sure you get a lot of strange requests, so I've got one for you. But, first, we're both Jewish, we've never talked about it, and I think we should."

"Being Jewish is a convoluted issue. Yes, my mother was Jewish, as was my wife, but we didn't take our children to temple. Judaism is based on way too many lies—like blaming the Egyptians for the Exodus." Lorenzo paused to see if he was going to get a bad reaction.

"Don't worry, Lorenzo. You're free to say anything you want, since everything in the scriptures about the Egyptians needs reexamination. The Jews doctored up the Hebrew Bible to badmouth the Egyptians, and the Christians doctored up their scriptures to play down the Jewish heritage of Jesus. I don't want to dig into that, since I'm here for a session. I'm bringing this up to get a sense of your comfort with alternative perspectives before I investigate some controversial ideas with you. Same for Rose and me, we didn't push our Jewish heritage on our kids."

"Good, so may I close the topic by saying that I'm totally open to questioning all aspects of Judaism with you, since I do it all the time. Jews need to reconsider their beliefs now that modern theological and historical research has exposed so many blatant falsifications; all religions should constantly examine the basis of their beliefs."

"Great. I thought that was how you'd feel, but how could I know without asking? My question is, can we tune in to *anyone* in the past? That is, if I go back into a life in the past, does it have to be *my* lifetime? Can I time travel freely into the minds of other people in the past with you?"

"That's a very complex karmic question. Sometimes you can travel into the mind of someone in the past, sometimes not. Yet, you can always travel into one of your own past lives, such as Gaudí or Ramòn Llull. In other words, your past lives are *your* records, and usually the answers you are seeking are right there in your own past. I'm amazed more people don't look into their past lives. If you give me an idea of what you want to explore, I might be able to say more."

"Okay. I want to travel back to the time when animosity first developed between the Jews and the Egyptians, which I think was around 1500 BC, around the time of the so-called Exodus. I believe the Exodus was the *expulsion* of the Jews out of Egypt because they were too much trouble for the pharaoh. I think what happened then and its distortion is a major source of modern East/West tension. I want to know some things because I want to share my feelings about being Jewish with Simon. I think the pharaoh Akhenaton left Egypt and then transformed into Moses; maybe he was driven out? Can we travel back into his mind to see if that is true?"

Lorenzo's mind scanned the question. "Excuse me, David. I need to get something." He got up, went to his desk, and brought back a large turquoise scarab.

"That's a beautiful scarab. Is it ancient?"

"Yes, from the tomb of Rekhmire, the vizier of Amenhotep II and Thutmosis III. Please allow me to hold it for a moment to see what I get." Lorenzo cradled the scarab in his right hand holding his left hand over the back and closed his eyes as David watched him intently. Lorenzo jerked as if something hit his body. "Okay, I've got the spirit of the scarab: nothing is more sealed than the royal Egyptian karmic records, so this is not the best way to ask the question." Lorenzo placed the scarab at the base of the crystal obelisk, which David recalled seeing previously when he'd explored his lifetime as Ramòn Llull.

Lorenzo peered into the dancing planes in the obelisk breathing very softly and closed his eyes. "Ahh, I get it, and you could've figured this out. We must go back to Ramòn Llull. He invented his wheels based on the ideas common to all three monotheistic religions so that he could convert Jews and Muslims to the Christian faith. He believed peace would come with a common ground, but suffered a horrible demise. Looks like we need to dissolve another past-life block, don't you think?"

"Lorenzo, at this point, I'm putty in your hands. I'm probably *still* driven by Llull's desire to resolve the conflicts between the three religions, possibly the reason I criticize Judaism."

"You may be right, so let's see if we can bring Ramòn Llull back."

David lay down on the couch and spaced out listening to Lorenzo's hypnotic voice. "Now, David, I have a burning question," Lorenzo said in a sensual and alluring voice. "Tell me, what is it about those wheels? What are they for?" Lorenzo asked because he was watching concentrically arranged circles filled with odd symbols and letters rotating above David's body like a complex astral clock mechanism.

"My wheels express the truths of God—eternity, goodness, wisdom, will, fair judgment, faith, and truth—Christian beliefs in common with Judaism and Islam. They are logical and I am logical, so when I use the wheels with people, they convert to Christianity when they realize *it* is God's religion."

"Why do you *want* to convert them?" Lorenzo probed.

"Look, doctor, consider this. If I don't convert them, their lives will be horrible. I live in Palma, Majorca, where the Catholics recently conquered the Muslims. Most of them left, and we made the ones who stayed into our slaves. Since we have the same God, they should convert to Christianity."

"If you all have the same God, then why does it matter?"

"It is the only way to stop all the fighting. If they convert to Catholicism, that will be the end of the argument, what the pope wants."

"Uh, huh, I see. So you conquered them and enslaved them, and they are supposed to believe in your God? Ramòn Llull, something is missing here . . . What?"

"The Jews don't look at God the way we do because something divided our religions. I don't know what, but maybe someday, somebody will. Until that happens, I'm bringing them back to God whether they like it or not."

"Why?"

"Because Catholicism is the true religion. Remember, I am a holy martyr exalted in death!"

Lorenzo considered guiding Llull through his stoning again, but decided not to. Instead, he brought David back into current time, and they went right to the alcove.

"David, what do you think of Ramòn Llull?" A moment later he looked up from his notes because David was stifling a guffaw.

"I think he was a bull-headed, stubborn fool like the people I run into these days who believe in religion, especially Christian fundamentalists. At this point, religion is such a pile of horseshit that you have to be mindless to stay with it. This session was good for me because I didn't really understand how people like that think and feel, but now I do: they have the truth, so the more people that join up with them, the better off they will be. If they feel threatened, they force people to adopt their beliefs. My rotating rational circles turned me into a zombie in that lifetime, Lorenzo. Since Llull is thought to be the inventor of computational theory, the basis of modern computers, are computers turning us into idiots?"

That evening Simon, David, and Pietro gathered in the library, and David began the think session. "Pietro, thanks for this get-together. Simon, after thirty years of deep thought, I've decided to offer you my real thoughts about Judaism. Pietro is with us because I want to know whether the story I've put together is in the Templar records. My thoughts are based on the work of Ahmed Osman and Sigmund Freud, the thinkers who first made me realize there is something odd about Moses and Akhenaton. Maybe I could hear Freud because he's Jewish, and I also learned a lot from Osman, a Muslim scholar who headed down the same path. The roles played by Akhenaton and Moses and their beliefs *are* too much alike, as if they were the same person, but with an Egyptian and Jewish identity. Once I looked at it that way, I found myself critiquing the Jewish hatred of the Egyptians and I couldn't stand Passover anymore. This hatred *never* made sense to me because the Egyptians were very advanced, much more than the ragtag Semitic tribe in the desert that became the Jews. I'd like to simply tell this as a story rather than explain the sources of it, all the arguments, if that's okay with you."

They nodded. David took time to sip on his red wine before starting in on a mini lecture. Simon yawned.

"Here we go, the original story of the Egyptians and the Jews! Abraham took his beautiful wife, Sarah, to Egypt saying she was his sister. The pharaoh heard about her beauty and wanted her, so Abraham sold Sarah to Thutmosis III. The marriage would have been quickly consummated. Later in Palestine, Sarah gave birth to Isaac, the son of

Thutmosis III. He didn't look like Abraham at all; everybody could see it. Abraham was Isaac's *stepfather,* possibly the reason he almost sacrificed him. Seems to me, Abraham would have fried his stepson on the pyre if Yahweh had *not* intervened!" Simon was embarrassed. *What in hell is going to come out of his mouth next? Is this what he talks about with Pietro? Dad sounds like he's nuts!*

"The Egyptians were the real players. Isaac's son, Jacob, fathered Joseph, who was sold by his brothers into Egypt. The Egyptians would have known he was the *grandson* of Thutmosis III, since they kept very meticulous records of all the royal wives, so Joseph was beloved. He remained in Egypt and married Aseneth, an Egyptian priestess with royal blood. In a few generations, Akhenaton became the pharaoh, but he was driven out of Egypt because he imposed monotheism on the polytheistic Egyptians. If Akhenaton did transform into Moses after the Exodus, there goes Jewish hatred of the Egyptians! Whatever happened, Egyptian religion heavily influenced both Judaism and Christianity.

"It's time to skip ahead in time and go to Jesus, who was a Nazarite—a Jewish group from the *Jewish-Egyptian* lineage. The patrimony of Jesus was Egyptian magic and sacred marriage. Pietro, how does this story fit with the Templar records?"

"Wait a minute, gentlemen," Simon interrupted. "Dad, do you believe this? Sarah and I have looked into this stuff, but I never thought I'd hear it from you. You seem to think that Jewish negativity toward the Egyptians comes from the Jews being part Egyptian and trying to cover it up. Do you *believe* that?"

"These are the questions that plague modern historical analysis, but the faithful never hear about this stuff because it contradicts religious dogma. However, when you view the biblical period through Egyptian eyes, the events in Palestine clarify and sort out because the Egyptians kept solid historical records that they rarely revised. On top of this, the Egyptian *Muslim* scholar, Ahmed Osman, has explored the Koran for a new perspective on Egypt and the Hebrews because he could see that Muhammad had put a new spin on it that reveals some things.

Who cares? Well, the religions derived from Abraham are the cause of the total meltdown in the Middle East and the world. If more people knew the real story, maybe fratricidal divisions could end. Really, is the human race going to destroy the world because of petty sectarian arguments about God?"

"David," Pietro broke in, "I'd like to address your question about Templar beliefs. Your basic story is in our records, and I commend you for being able to examine your own background with such a broad mind. Yet, regardless of all that, the change of the ages gives us much better information about what was probably going on: the Egyptians developed during the grounded and peaceful Age of Taurus over 6,000 years ago; the religions of Abraham developed during the martial Age of Aries; then Jesus brought compassion and love during the divinely inspired Age of Pisces.

"Jesus and John the Baptist *were* Nazarites. As you say, David, the Nazarites were *Egyptian* Jews who believed in the wisdom of Egypt—peace and order—and wanted it to continue in the world. Jesus lived in Egypt when he was young and trained as a magician and healer, a great magus of high Egyptian wisdom. Simon, surely you know that your father is a great magus in this tradition? He has recovered his real origin, which of course can be yours. Jesus wanted to retain the polytheistic and goddess-worshipping wisdom of the Age of Taurus because without it, Arian monotheism would foster violence and the abuse of women, exactly what happened. Jesus brought love and compassion, Piscean ideals, to transmute Arian violence. Jesus was slated to be the avatar of the Age of Pisces, a loving human who was also divine. Significantly, his teachings are not yet complete; they are coming to a head now."

Simon was on the edge of his seat. "Hey, you two sages! You are both chewing on the central distortion that has poisoned the world with overwhelming violence—monotheism. It makes people judgmental, violent, and misogynist by trying to force them into believing in one God, everything black or white. Armando, Claudia, Sarah, and I have been exploring a Jesus who loved Mary, a priestess of some sort, probably Isis. As for me, I need time to think about Egyptian influences on Judaism, particularly Ahmed Osman's Muslim perspective. But it's time to call it a night. Dad, you never cease to surprise me. I thought I knew what a Jew was, but now I don't."

"I know what you mean, Simon. These distortions have spawned ferocious anger and division between Sunni and Shi'ite, between the Hassidim and liberal Jews, and between Christian fundamentalists and liberals. Extreme radicals fight for God, have babies for God, and spit on one another while they wait for the end of our beautiful world. True stories about Moses, Jesus, and Mary could capture the hearts of the masses and inspire people to reach out to each other. Simon, as my son, *you* must know the real story, your friends must know. We are all connected worldwide, and the real truth about our past is exciting, sensual, evocative, and humanly revealing. As the next generation, you and your friends will tell these stories when the liberating forces of Aquarius flow in the hearts of the people helping everyone remember how to share and connect!"

31

The Ruby Crystal

In May 2016, Donald Trump became the Republican Party nominee for the presidential election in the U.S. What goes on in U.S. politics is rarely very noteworthy overseas, but similar rabble-rousing, xenophobic politicians were infiltrating European politics. The U.S. election process confused the world, and the incessant slaughter of young American black people by the police made Europeans wonder whether the great empire was crumbling. They feared U.S. instability and civil violence after living through two world wars. They reasoned that terrorist attacks in the U.S. were next.

In mid-June, Omar Mateen mowed down more than fifty people in a gay nightclub in Orlando, Florida, with assault weapons. The FBI was supposedly watching him as a potential terrorist. The killer, who claimed to be aligned with ISIS, had his day of fame in the media while he left hundreds of families to mourn. As for Mateen's easy procurement of assault rifles, a *New York Times* editorial had reported in 2011 that an ISIS recruitment video said America was fertile ground for ISIS attacks because it was loaded with easily obtainable firearms. The bloody Orlando massacre spotlighted several critical problems in America—radicalized homophobia, the National Rifle Association's assistance to terrorists and madmen by their consistent blockage of effective gun control, and the sad human helplessness in the face of mass shooters—the perfect issues to inflame the public. The incident in Orlando was small in comparison to the suffering going on every day in Iraq and Syria or in any other war-torn country, but its public impact was huge: Americans could see that violence was coming home.

As the world closed in during the summer, the group gathered at Claudia's old apartment. Strolling down her old hallway, Claudia was pleased to see everything was just as she'd left it since moving last summer, except for a small rag doll with red-yarn hair slung over the cabriole legs of a gilded French provincial hall table. Sarah waited for her at the back end of the hall. "It's so good to have you come home, Claudia. Teresa is not allowed to play in the parlor with your best antiques and upholstery where we will meet tonight. She plays in the dining room and only comes into the parlor to sit with us. We've done this to protect your lovely things, yet we've discovered this was also the easiest way to teach her how to behave in anyone's house."

Sarah was very relaxed. They strolled into the parlor arm in arm, basking in the sheer joy of feminine touch.

Simon looked up as they came in and smiled. "Ladies, you are smashing, the three most beautiful women in Rome."

Jennifer was sitting back on a plush chair upholstered in canary yellow and silver stripes. Her short, dark, spandex skirt hugged her hips as she flashed a long thigh when she crossed her leg. She laughed. "Now that Claudia's my designer, I take chances with how I dress."

Claudia appraised Jennifer. "Oh, darling, I wondered how that skirt would look with that chemise top, absolutely divine."

Armando relaxed on one end of the cranberry-and-gold-striped loveseat. He motioned for Sarah to come sit with him at the other end. "Sarah, how have you been?"

Jennifer listened, while watching Armando and Sarah discreetly. *Sometimes I wonder whether I missed the one to be jealous of. Imagine how much he must have adored her. She's saintly, uncanny. I wonder whether she loved him?* Jennifer was seven months pregnant and beginning to show. She bloomed with happiness and expectation.

"Jen," Sarah said, interrupting her reverie. "You look wonderful! You're going to have such a strong healthy baby; Teresa can't wait! Today, she played Momma Jennifer singing to her baby doll!"

The bantering went on for a few more minutes. Simon stood by the alcove window observing them, and then he opened the discussion when they'd all settled easily into place. "World events are going out of control, and it's harder to make sense of anything going on in the Middle East. The suffering in Fallujah is heartbreaking and the carnage of young blacks in America is ugly; it suggests the police can kill anybody and get away with it. Sometimes I wonder whether any of my writing will make any difference at all. Now that I've come up to speed on the Great Ages, I've realized my own father was using this paradigm to decode current events. Chaos and pain take over when we move into a new age, who wants to live during these wrenching transitions?" He looked around the group who were giving him their full attention, so he went on.

"As the Aquarian influence permeates reality, explosive secrets are coming out eroding false beliefs and dysfunctional patterns. Sarah and I have just read the newly released *Templar Sanctuaries in North America* by William Mann, and we want to talk about it. Mann says he's releasing the knowledge that's been passed down to him and found during his research because it is time. I did my best with his book, but I had trouble following it, so let's do the best we can, Sarah?"

"His book fascinated me. The idea of the Grail community making it all the way to the Four Corners region of the American Southwest is astonishing, but I can't describe it clearly yet because it is so dense with new information."

"Lorenzo read it," Claudia broke in. "He thinks Mann is really on to something. He has always thought the search for the Grail as mere treasure-seeking was an elaborate disinformation campaign that led people away from the *real* Grail—the journey of the people of the bloodline. Anyway, what *did* you think, Simon?"

"Based on his meridian analysis of two paintings—as well as secret

Templar information, Algonquin initiation, and his own research—Mann says once the French king drove the Templars into the underground in the early 1300s, some of them ended up sailing from the Orkney Islands to Nova Scotia led by Henry Sinclair and the famous mapmaker, Zeno. They founded a community near the Bay of Fundy but soon had to travel inland because European powers and the Inquisition followed them. I was fascinated by the parallel legends he discusses, for example that the Algonquin hero *Glooscap* actually was Henry Sinclair and that Algonquin initiations are similar to Templar initiations. Amazing!

"Apparently, the indigenous people of America welcomed and supported these desperate refugees seven hundred years ago, who intermarried with Algonquin and other indigenous people and settled in places like northern Vermont and upstate New York. Based on reports about the Inquisition in France, both parties were intensely secretive, the reason this story has been hidden until now. To survive, the fleeing carriers of the sacred bloodline mixed their blood with Algonquin genes, since genocide was aimed at all of them. This story could inspire new respect for indigenous people if people realized how ferociously they were attacked, like the Cathars in Languedoc.

"Soon thereafter, immigrants began arriving in America, which pushed the Grail community farther west through the Great Lakes and into the Midwest. News about the Inquisition from Europe was horrifying, so they desperately pushed farther west leaving markers and traces that have been found, such as the Kensington Stone. Eventually they mixed with Western tribes, for example with the Hohokam and the Chaco Canyon people of the Four Corners region, and the Blackfoot, who were an Eastern Algonquin tribe that was driven west. In other words, *the holy blood of Jesus and Mary Magdalene thrives in the indigenous people of America as well as in European lineages!* This is an outrageous story, yet the more you hear it, the more it makes sense. Now that Mann has delineated the trail of these people, other confusing things make sense.

"Mann thinks the Mormon religion is based on the story of the Grail wanderings, a living religion in the U.S. that is continuing this story today. Notice how secretive the Mormons have always been, and perpetuating a sacred bloodline sure explains polygamy! It's hard to comprehend the full implications of what Mann says because it is all so fantastic; our brains can't register it. Maybe the buzzing reliquaries in the Chapel of Princes are activating the sacred blood that flows in my brain! I think Mann's discoveries are a great example of the new ideas that come forth when a new age arrives, so I can't wait until you've read it too. But, it's a difficult book because it is based on decoding the famous esoteric painting, *The Shepherds of Arcadia* by Nicolas Poussin, the one that Grail seekers have been studying for years. Mann analyzes a map of the trails of the Grail people in the eastern U.S. under the painting!

"He analyzes another painting, *St. Anthony and St. Paul Fed by Ravens,* by David Teniers that reveals an underlying map of the Four Corners region of the American Southwest. In it, the folds in the robes of St. Anthony and St. Paul exactly mirror the flows of the six main southwestern rivers! Actually, once I studied that part of his book, I really got it, and the hair on my back stood on end. His analysis of these geographical layers is airtight and remarkable; Tenier's painting will never look the same to me again. Select initiates must have passed these maps disguised as paintings down through the generations, just as we pass secret knowledge in our family. The big joke is these paintings hang in museums freely viewed by anyone, not to mention all the other encoded art, the treasure trove."

"Both painters *had* to have known these maps depicted Grail community wanderings, which means they were Templars themselves."

Sarah joined in because Simon ran out of breath. "They hid this information in art so that certain people could know where they went. Eventually, somebody like Mann would figure it out and he actually did, astonishing! This has been right in our faces for hundreds of years, another great revelation at the end of the Age of Pisces."

"And at the end of the Mayan Calendar," Claudia mused. "But what could this possibly *mean?* I can think of only one person in this room who might be able to answer that, you Sarah. We need you to use the ruby crystal to discover what this incredible idea means to the world today. Otherwise it is nothing more than one more arcane mystery. After all, people have been chasing after the Holy Grail *ad nauseum.* Can you enlighten us?"

Sarah put her right hand over the ruby crystal, put her hands below her chin, and closed her eyes. They all watched with anticipation. Her voice was silvery.

"I see a crystal icosahedron, the beautiful Platonic solid with twenty triangular faces—five triangles on the bottom and five on top with a band of ten interlocking triangles between. The twelve points of the icosahedron are touching the inner surface of a beautiful luminous transparent golden sphere. The only occlusions in the icosahedron are in the bottom five triangles where information flows in from lower dimensions. With the information radiating through me, I see the phases of human evolution over 100,000 years—people in small clans painting in caves, making music, loving children, and men and women loving each other. These five triangles are a goddess basket, the great mother who creates and holds the five triangles that first birthed our consciousness in the archaic hunter-gathers. She gave her mind to them as a gift—our intelligence. In the beginning the simple basket began as a point that formed five equilateral triangles, the pentagram of the goddess, Venus." Sarah's voice was musical like soft chimes in water.

"Around 10,000 years ago, magic—the ability to shape reality with our minds—arrived as five more triangles grew on the top edges of the basket pentagram. These arriving five triangles fused their edges with the pentagonal rim of the basket with their tips rising, like the triangles in the hat of a dancing jester—magic in suspended animation. In the new triangles, I see people casting spells, making images of what they will hunt, and reaching across long distances and time for their goal." Sarah's hands twisted and writhed as she described the images she was seeing, her eyes moving fast under her eyelids.

"Around 5,000 years ago the people told stories about the magical places and times passed down through each generation. While weaving myths and stories, five new mythic triangles came and slotted in between the five magical triangles, which then became a band of ten triangles filled with magical acts and mythical stories that connect all the people over 100,000 years. The full story of time and human magic lives in the ten triangles of the middle band supported by the bottom pentagram of five triangles." Sarah was breathing deeply and rapid eye movement fluttered her eyelids. Simon had never seen her in such a deep trance.

"So, here we are with a taller basket with the five sides of the middle band of the triangles at the top, and now five new triangles arrive that lock into the five top sides and pull the form together into a peak. As they all fuse, the top five triangles radiate incredible force—the agglomeration of all twenty triangles—and a golden sphere materializes that touches all twelve points. This transparent icosahedron within a luminous golden sphere holds 100,000 years of archaic creation from which magic and myth emerged through the people 10,000 years ago. Myths and stories wove together the whole middle band, and now this intelligence is coming forth in all the people. We are all connected through this linked triangular force of twenty faces."

Simon watched Sarah carefully because she was losing color while she visualized the complex form in her mind. The four of them were perplexed by what she was seeing, yet they understood it in some other dimension where they could see glimpses of the shapes as she described them. Claudia couldn't wait to study her own crystal icosahedron at home. They couldn't hold it all together, so Simon said very softly, "Sarah, perhaps you can make this easier for yourself by describing exactly how *we* connect through these triangular faces?"

Sarah's mind splashed with thousands of computer screens—energy flowing from one computer to another, information flowing back into central connectors and back out again all pulsing like the human circulatory system. As she saw the computer matrixes that were in the top five triangles, the images of archaic clans, magical creations, and mythical stories streamed into the top five triangles. All of this creativity was held in form by the icosahedron within the sphere in emergent layers—mythical emerging out of the magical, the magical out of the archaic, and all culminating in the computer matrix. She spoke again, her voice incredulous.

"This crystal icosahedral sphere is what God is, filled with so much beauty that I can barely speak of it. It is eternity, a diaphanous world that always beckons, never leaves us out, and makes everything transparent. The sacred bloodline is icosahedral DNA, Christ's blood opening new space in our world. Everything is transparent in this form because everything is emerging from what came before. We do not have to fear what is happening right now because it is from ever-present origin, the luminous golden sphere that surrounds the icosahedron with pure divine golden light. Like the geometrical perfection of this icosahedron, what finally emerges in Aquarius will be clear and comprehensible. As we build the top five pyramids to complete this form, the faces of the pyramids at the top will alchemically clarify creation over 100,000 years."

She stopped and almost fell forward as Simon went to her, but Armando was closer. He gently held her shoulders while she opened her eyes. She leaned back on the loveseat and looked at all of them, diamond light in her eyes that Simon had never before seen. She blinked and said, "I have seen the form of God, the living geometrical perfection that underlies nature."

"Do you remember anything you said?" Claudia inquired gently.

"I remember no words, but I see the beautiful crystal icosahedron nested in a golden sphere, the Golden World. It is God, Claudia—higher dimensional spherical geometry. There is nothing to worry about, nothing."

Close to midnight, Claudia crept in through the front door. She closed it carefully so as to not disturb Lorenzo, but he startled her as he headed out of the study smelling like a cigar. "Lorenzo, it's so late; I'm surprised you're still up."

"I just can't stop thinking about it, I mean the story about the Grail escapees in America. The efforts of the Church to suppress heresy have always seemed so bizarre to me, such as the viciousness of the Inquisition and the murderous Conquistadors. Now it turns out they even tried to wipe out the indigenous people of America over the bloodline. I've thought it over; I think Mann is on to something, but it all makes me feel like I'm upside down in my own home!"

"I understand, Lorenzo. I feel the same way when I try to comprehend the implications of *The Lost Gospel*. Yet, the synchronicities are too much. Secrets that people have given their lives for are exploding all over the place just when Syria is being pulverized. It's as if that country contains a hot, mystical core that all sides are trying to rip open with bombs. We are in a time-released nuclear holocaust, the decimation of beliefs that most people thought were rock solid."

"I can barely handle so much so quickly, yet that's what it takes to turn the corner. We must welcome radically different ways of life all around us. We have to listen to others and support new perspectives. Meanwhile, we have each other and our love is deep and beautiful. Come, my lady, bedtime."

32

Chaos Point

During July 2016 as if someone had pulled a cosmic switch, the world devolved into unnerving chaos. Financial turmoil from Brexit—the late-June vote in England to leave the European Union—spilled over into July. Many wondered whether this was a signal for the end for the EU, since cutting back on immigration was the reason most people voted to exit the EU. Just before the end of Ramadan in early July, ISIS bombed three sites in Saudi Arabia, one a disturbing attack in Medina near Muhammad's burial site. Muslims around the world were aghast; nothing was sacred to ISIS! Much of the world was sucked into the maelstrom with coordinated ISIS mass killings in Turkey, Bangladesh, and Iraq. These latest waves of violence linked the migrant crisis with terrorism in people's minds.

Refugees just kept walking and piling into crowded and unsafe boats. Poland and Hungary kept the migrants out, while more than a million refugees from Syria, Iraq, and other war-torn Muslim countries streamed into Central and Eastern Europe. Turkey harbored great numbers, stressing its fragile democracy. Thousands of migrants from African countries made their way to North Africa and then sailed to Italy, while others drowned in the Mediterranean. It was a summer marred by little children washing up on beaches with seagulls and dead fish.

Like throwing dynamite into the fire, a third major attack in seventeen months assaulted France: a weird loner influenced by ISIS rampaged a large truck down a crowded boulevard by the sea in Nice slaughtering eighty-five people who were out walking on a warm summer evening. These mindless murders moved many European countries further to the right. On July 26, two ISIS murderers slit the throat of an elderly priest while he was saying Mass in a Norman church near Rouen. Pope Francis announced the West and the East were in a protracted war.

Simon closed his computer and sat back in the plush chair to go into a deep state of meditation, something he had not done in a long time. He knew one more ugly story would steal his power. *And I contribute to it all.* He'd just sent in an article on priestly sexual abuse to the *Times* that concluded Pope Francis wasn't really doing much to end the abuse. The story was about a lawyer, Jeff Anderson, who represented 350 suspected victims of sexual abuse in the Minneapolis–St. Paul Archdiocese. Anderson showed how all roads in the abuse scandal lead right to Rome; the Rome now led by Pope Francis with Ratzinger skulking around in the background. *What a ridiculous shadow game!*

Simon fell into reverie easily, tapping into his rich inner world. *Yes, my inner world is all there is, but let's be practical. What can the five of us do that will make any difference?* Next he was quite amazed to see his favorite Platonic solid precipitate in his inner mind—a dodecahedral sphere made of twelve equal-sized pentagrams, like a soccer ball. *I didn't know that was still in my inner eye! Okay. What can the five of us do?*

It is very simple, Simon . . .

A clear voice vibrated in the room, as if it were coming out of Claudia's books.

Invite Lorenzo Giannini to your group and you will get your answers.

A few hours later after checking with the others, Simon was on the phone with Lorenzo. "We need you, Lorenzo, I don't know why. A voice came to me in Claudia's parlor that said we should invite you to the next meeting of our group, tomorrow night. Together we have been bringing in many amazing revelations about the transition out of Pisces into Aquarius. I think you probably know what we've been doing, since I assume Claudia has been sharing our discussions with you?"

"Yes she has, and I think you are doing very good and significant work. Ultimately, *thought* is what changes the world. There's not a single thing you have ever seen that did not first come from somebody's idea. We must draw together as these great revelations flood in, because otherwise we could be overwhelmed and lose hope. Also, like birds in flight or schools of fish in a stream, when we attain the maximum change point, everybody shifts in unison. Since you've checked with everybody, yes, I can come and I'll enjoy it very much. I haven't seen the Pierleoni home in Rome, so I appreciate this opportunity very much."

"Be prepared for quite an experience. I will never forget the first time I was in that library meeting with Armando when he asked me to forgive him. See you tomorrow!"

Lorenzo and Claudia parked their car and walked around to the front of the looming villa hidden from the street by a high wall. Lorenzo gazed up at the bizarre gargoyles by the sides of the family crest. "They always have these weird guardians, and look at this house! The stone walls and columns are so worn they look like cliffs drying out after Noah's Flood." A wizened old man in black opened the heavy door and led them in. They strolled slowly through the hallway hung with exquisite seventeenth-century tapestries. "What a treat for me, Claudia. These could have been made in my house!"

"Could be, Lorenzo, and now we come to the library."

The group was already assembled when Claudia and Lorenzo came in. Armando watched his dear old therapist whose eyes were flashing everywhere with delight as he surveyed the room. Armando approached, his hand out. "Lorenzo, having you here is a great joy to me. I've always honored your need for privacy, but I'm grateful you've finally come here. As you can see, there's plenty to read."

"Armando, this is all my pleasure. I've heard so much about this house; everybody has in Rome. It's even more wonderful than I imagined. I'm feasting my eyes on the two stories of bookshelves with high ladders, delightfully medieval. Thank you for inviting me."

All six sat around a large round coffee table. Simon began since he'd invited Lorenzo. "We've asked you to come because between the five of us, we've tapped into some amazing data and reached the point where there is too much to absorb. You could say we are stuffed with too many big issues—*The Lost Gospel,* the Talpiot tomb, the James ossuary, Grail families traveling in America, even John the Baptist and St. Paul. Unless we can grasp the *relationships between* these ideas—especially having the world realize that the blood of Jesus and Mary flows in the veins of millions, perhaps a billion people—the remarkable truths that are coming to light now will be lost and fade into the mists of time without making connections. Since we know that many millions have died to keep these secrets alive until now, we feel like our group must get to that next level, that is, grasp the matrix. Nobody is better at weaving connections than you, Lorenzo."

They waited for him to begin. "All right, I want all five of you to become a magnificent pentagram of light." This startled Simon because of the pentagrams he'd been seeing himself. "I'm going to close my eyes and go deep within my inner mind as you breathe with me, please. I will know when you have become pentagrams, and then I will question each one of you . . . "

His voice softened and became more deliberate. "You have each experienced this way of seeking at Eleusis in Greece because all five of you were there together during the last time the Golden World manifested on Earth around 550 BC. Each one of you has a wisdom teaching that you will remember now, so let us call them out. I begin with you, Jennifer, because I am having a vision of you walking forward carrying a quartz crystal cup filled with spring water." He asked in a sensual and alluring voice, "*What* is this water?"

Jennifer closed her eyes to remember. "I carry the water of Aquarius. I am above the ecliptic seeing all the water in the universe pouring through my crystal cup, my rhyton. I bring this cup from Knossos on Crete where I've held it suspended in the other world, that is until now." When she said that, Simon saw a vision of the Earth riddled like Swiss cheese with great aquifers deep under the surface that were filling up with pure, crystalline water. Sarah closed her eyes because she was seeing the library filling up with pure water, water that was etheric not liquid.

"Jennifer," Lorenzo said in a soft voice, "where are you going with your rhyton?"

"I go . . . I go to the altar of the wind here at Eleusis. As I bring my water to the wind, I pull the switch that releases the waters of Aquarius."

"Thank you, Jennifer. Excellent. Next, I speak to *you,* Armando, because I see you are painting." Lorenzo said in a commanding, slightly loud voice, "Why are you painting on a surface in the air that is not really anywhere? *How* do you paint in the air, Armando?"

"I do it all the time, Lorenzo," he said with eyes shut and a hand drawing in the air as if he held a brush. "Every time I hold a brush, I paint the murals that I once created here—in Eleusis. I think I've been in a box my whole life painting the interior walls of this exquisite turtle temple, but now my box, my lovely cube, is superimposed on the temple, Eleusis—a giant cosmic cube."

"Yes, Armando," Lorenzo said in sweet voice. "Yes, you *are* in the cube there; I see you. Yet, *what* are you painting? Tell me." Lorenzo was enthralled by the sight of a beautiful diaphanous cube that was turning and turning within Eleusis shining refracted starlight onto columns and stone floors.

Armando put his palms out and began raising them as if he was praying. Simon was watching with amazement because he could actually see a quartz cube enclosing Armando. Simon closed his eyes to avoid having his retinas burned as the cube expanded to contain all of Eleusis and the surrounding forests and hills as Armando moved his hand back and back. "Now, Armando," Lorenzo demanded, "I want you to tell me what happens with the *undersurface* of the painting by Teniers of St. Anthony and St. Paul. Tell me, Armando—now!"

"I, ah . . . it is where it is. I mean there is a spot, a place where keys are buried deep in the ground here. The keys tell the story of what's going to happen when enough people—a critical number—realize that the divine mind of Jesus is deeply imbedded in the fields of the planet in our blood. As Jennifer pours the water out of her crystal bowl, millions *feel* overwhelming love, love that is so powerful that people can't cheat, attack, use others, or abuse anymore. The Eleusinian cube holds the *form* of the Aquarian breakthrough."

"Simon," Lorenzo said in a delicate, determined voice. "*You* know some things, don't you? You always do. So, are you going to tell us now?"

Simon, who had never had a session with Lorenzo, felt intense air pressure pushing on him from all sides, like being in a decompression chamber after deep diving. Sarah watched her husband with fascination because his body was moving in a snakelike sinuous standing wave. He said, "As we became more complex—from archaic humans to magical beings to great storytellers, and then so acutely rational that we could not see anymore—we bred with each other according to the logic of our evolutionary origin. The more we've been in control, the more we've controlled our mating, and now we've hit a wall. There *is* a secret lineage, the lineage of the snake, and in this lineage, all breeding is for supporting the reemergence of the goddess. She is the one who holds us in her womb in balance. She is the one who knows what Earth requires. As we embrace ourselves within her, we transfigure."

Lorenzo rose up slowly startled by Pietro walking into the library. He seemed to be in a trance and looked like he was going right into the group! He wasn't invited, so Lorenzo reset his boundaries to hold the new charged etheric field, since the people in the group were already on an amazing edge. As Pietro came closer and Lorenzo scrutinized him, it was clear he was not in his physical body—he was a crystalline essence of himself while somewhere else in the house, probably asleep. Lorenzo shifted his inner eye to register a closer reality when he realized that what he thought was Pietro was actually a golden cat! "Sarah," Lorenzo said in a sweet and imploring voice. "You are layered on nine levels, and your ninth level sees Pietro. Would *you* like to speak to him?"

Sarah, who had been very present and watching everything, suddenly felt intense air pressure pushing into her body from all sides as the icosahedron formed around her. When it totally surrounded her, her feet rose a few feet off the floor where she found herself with Pietro also above the floor. "Pietro, you have come. Why are you here? What would you like to know?"

Pietro faced Sarah and raised his hands, which emanated strong rays of light. As he raised his hands, Sarah's feet lowered to the floor where she followed Dante over to a nearby bookcase and pulled a lever that made it swing around and roll open. Simon couldn't take his eyes off her because he realized she was going right for the reliquary, yet he was sure she had no idea it was there. Lorenzo was watching very carefully monitoring her spine to make sure she was okay, since the level of energy coming in to her body could harm her adrenals; she was fine. She reached in with both hands inside the back of the bookcase and brought out an object covered with a blue velvet cloth embroidered with golden edges. She put it on the table and sat down as Armando stared at it in total disbelief and then closed his eyes. Lorenzo watched Pietro rise up high above the group and fly directly over the reliquary as the golden cat rolled around under the table. *What in hell is going on here? This scene looks like a painting by Salvador Dalí!*

Simon felt the air on all sides push in on him again making him gasp for air. Since Sarah was sitting down and seemed to be fine, he said, "I was here when Pietro brought this out before, and you were too

Armando. Since you are his son, will *you* please remove the cloth?"

Armando's eyes had closed, yet he removed the cloth. Lorenzo's eyes locked on the silver and bronze Templar sword embedded in the top of a small crystal skull that rested on an exquisite pure gold carved base. "Armando. What is this?"

Armando's eyes were still closed, yet he knew what was on the table. Claudia opened her eyes to see the sightless Armando gazing at an exquisite reliquary, a crystal skull set in the top of a golden bee's nest. Armando said in a low, masculine voice, "I see it, I see it now. When this sacred reliquary came to us, we changed. I see my own family changing radically over the last five hundred years preparing for this time just like the Medici. I changed myself, in spite of my own hideous pain. I changed myself because of her, Mary the goddess. Her patience overwhelms me as I see how long she waited for me. She endured genocide and horrible abuse, just like we have endured the Church abusing innocent children. I see . . . "

"Yes, *what* do you see, Armando?" Lorenzo said in a loving voice.

"I see that if I could transcend myself, then we all will transcend. We will crawl out of our old snakeskins. I have to say something to you, Simon. Do you realize what it meant to me three years ago in this room when you came to me and forgave me? Do you know what your friendship and love mean to me? You are kind, Simon. You are a truly kind and good man."

"Armando," Lorenzo broke in. "*What* is inside this beautiful reliquary? I see something glowing in the little glass box. What is it?"

"That, Lorenzo, is a bone from the body of Mary Magdalene, the great goddess who was born to be with Jesus. She united with him long ago, and now her power flows in our bones and blood. She has been with our family for five hundred years. Her bones and the bones of Jesus are all over the planet in sacred places waiting for Earth's transcendence— the Age of Aquarius. Everyone is prepared and waiting. We will all experience her emergence by forgiving ourselves for anything we have done, since we never stopped waiting for her to return, the real Messiah.

We all have divine blood in our veins creating new paths from every-thing that has come before."

"Yes, Armando," Lorenzo said softly. "Now, Claudia, tell me what you know."

"I am archaic woman encoded with planetary intelligence traveling out into the stars to gather my knowledge of the universe. I return from cosmic realms in the morning and weave the stories of all time in my mind. All these levels are in my body, and I feel these levels in everyone I touch. I am the goddess holding the hearts of the suffering people. I am joy."

They sat with the beautiful reliquary for a long time. Lorenzo felt delicate yet whole as Claudia gazed at him, a soft, lovely, and wise man. It was time to say good night. They knew they would gather together many more times to greet the Aquarian dawn.

Acknowledgments

I have been a nonfiction writer since 1976 but always secretly wanted to write fiction. When I attained the grand old age of seventy, I knew it was time to do what I always wanted to do. All the characters for the Revelations Trilogy came to me in May 2011, so it was time. *Revelations of the Ruby Crystal* has been in print since 2015, and now I have completed this book, *Revelations of the Aquarian Age*.

Writing this trilogy has been a huge learning curve for me, and I never could have done it without my editorial team at Bear & Company, Meghan MacLean, my main editor; Trish Lewis, my developmental editor; and Elizabeth Wilson, my copyeditor. You deserve a Bronx cheer! They have been supportive, patient, and brilliant all the way through.

Thank you, Jon Graham, for encouraging me in taking this risky path, and thank you, Ehud Sperling, for your support for so many years and your bravery publishing fiction. I am deeply grateful for all the work of the sales and marketing team, especially my wonderful publicist, Manzanita Carpenter Sanz.

BARBARA HAND CLOW

Books of Related Interest

Revelations of the Ruby Crystal
by Barbara Hand Clow

Astrology and the Rising of Kundalini
The Transformative Power of Saturn, Chiron, and Uranus
by Barbara Hand Clow

The Pleiadian Agenda
A New Cosmology for the Age of Light
by Barbara Hand Clow

Awakening the Planetary Mind
Beyond the Trauma of the Past to a New Era of Creativity
by Barbara Hand Clow

The Mayan Code
Time Acceleration and Awakening the World Mind
by Barbara Hand Clow
Foreword by Carl Johan Calleman, Ph.D.

The Mind Chronicles
A Visionary Guide into Past Lives
by Barbara Hand Clow

Eye of the Centaur
A Visionary Guide Into Past Lives
by Barbara Hand Clow

The Pleiadian House of Initiation
A Journey through the Rooms of the Wisdomkeepers
by Mary T. Beben
Foreword by Barbara Hand Clow

INNER TRADITIONS • BEAR & COMPANY
P.O. Box 388, Rochester, VT 05767
1-800-246-8648
www.InnerTraditions.com

Or contact your local bookseller